MAR 1 0 2014

THE
SEEKER

THE
SEEKER

R. B. CHESTERTON

PEGASUS CRIME
NEW YORK LONDON

THE SEEKER

Pegasus Books LLC
80 Broad Street, 5th Floor
New York, NY 10004

First Pegasus Books cloth edition 2014

Interior design by Maria Fernandez

ISBN: 978-1-60598-500-8

10 9 8 7 6 5 4 3 2 1

Printed in the United States of America
Distributed by W. W. Norton & Company, Inc.

For my sister Susan Haines, HH, and all the readers who love a good scare.
And for Kristine, who gave me the key to unlock this story.

"Let nothing come between you and the light."

Henry David Thoreau,
Letters to a Spiritual Seeker

THE
SEEKER

Prologue

My grandmother was born with a port wine stain on the left side of her face. The exact shape of Narragansett Bay, the birthmark ran down from her eye to touch the corner of her mouth. In moments of anger, it pulsed with a purplish cast but otherwise was a dark red. Siobhan Cahill was her name. Though she never married, she gave birth to a son, my father, Caleb.

To know who a person is, you must know his history, Granny Siobhan told me. Our family's history has a nasty habit of repeating itself.

⚶

Shortly after the turn of the 18th century, my ancestor Jonah Cahill abandoned the old, superstitious ways of his tribe of Irish travelers and bought land on the western coast of the Emerald Isle. He was a pious man with a strong personal attachment to his god. He established a grand farm in Galway, Ireland and in the span of ten years built an empire of cultivated fields that stretched across the rolling hills as far as the eye could see. Jonah meant to grow things, from potatoes to children. And he did. He produced seven stout boys, two beautiful girls, and neat productive fields bordered by stone walls.

For two decades the sun shone on Jonah and nature blessed each thing he turned his hand to. The Great Frost put an end to his ambitions. In December 1739, Ireland and most of Europe froze. The bitter cold iced potatoes in the ground, eliminating the major food source and destroying seeds for the next year's crops. Coal shipments from Wales, the primary means of warmth, jammed the frozen rivers. Desperate, the Irish stripped the land of burnable trees and shrubs. With no fuel to keep warm and no food to eat, Jonah's family began the process of slow starvation.

They endured for two years, managing to keep oatmeal on the table, but the farm was a ruin. The crops were destroyed, the animals dead. With no relief in sight, Jonah took his sons and emigrated to the New World in 1742.

Though many of the *Kathlene's* passengers and half the crew died on the tempestuous, brutal voyage, Jonah Cahill, named for a minor prophet of the Old Testament, was as solid as an oak. He and the boys made the passage alive. They landed in Boston Harbor and moved inland to soil that had never seen a plow. His intention was to make enough money in the New World to buy passage for his wife and two daughters.

Jonah worked against the clock, knowing that with each passing week Margaret and the girls struggled to survive. He and his sons sold turnips, firewood, wild berries, honey, and poteen they brewed in small pots behind their makeshift shed of a home, each penny hoarded. Jonah was tormented by dreams of the frigid cabin in Ireland. Thrashing and sweating each night, he saw Margaret weakening with the harsh task of survival, the girls with no man to help them, searching for firewood and enough oatmeal or scraps to keep body and soul together.

Jonah bargained with god. He tithed and continued deeds of charity. And the Cahill males worked without rest until the money for passage was secured. Two winters passed with no word from Ireland. He left the boys to mind the family ventures and went to collect the rest of his family.

He found the Galway farm demolished, the house and fences burned for fuel. His wife and daughters gone.

He learned from neighbors that starvation had taken them only two months after he left. His work—and his bargains with god—had all been in vain. Margaret buried both daughters. She'd died in the field attempting to dig frozen potatoes from the icy ground. No one had thought to mark their graves, and because there was no money to buy a blessing from the church or proper burial, they'd been left in unsanctified ground.

For two weeks Jonah dug up the fields, searching for the bodies. He never found them. Before he left Ireland, he cursed the God he'd served so diligently and pledged his future to a darker entity.

Granny Siobhan said this was the beginning of the black luck and blacker deeds that grew to define the Cahills.

Jonah returned to Massachusetts, sold the farm, and moved his sons to Rhode Island. They cast their lot with the sea—the land had betrayed them, and Jonah Cahill swore that he'd rely no more on sod for survival. Turned out the Cahills had a knack for sailing. And butchery. Jonah and his boys vented their fury on the whales that populated the northern Atlantic Ocean. They came to be known as the most brutal slayers of the sperm whale, taking high numbers a year for the fat and ambergris, which was rendered into lamp oil and perfume.

The Cahill reputation for savagery spread to their competitors. Rumors of scuttling and burning ships drifted back to shore even as the ships and sailors did not. At least twice Jonah was arrested, but there was no proof against him. He grew meaner and more dangerous. One by one, the boys found wives, but peculiar maladies struck the family. And it only made Jonah more defiant.

For better than a century, the Cahills took their living from the sea, but changing times demanded a new approach.

With civil war looming, the Cahills left Rhode Island and settled in the Kentucky mountains "before the law could pull tight the noose around their necks," as Granny told it. In 1860, they took their pirating and scuttling practice into the employ of the Confederacy and turned their skills on the Yankees and anyone else who crossed their paths. The bloody saga continued with a new focus.

After the end of the Civil War, the family discovered that while they had no talent for growing corn, they could distill it into some of the finest whiskey in Kentucky. From moonshine the Cahills progressed to the family's current cash crop, OxyContin. Hillbilly heroin.

⚶

The curse came down hard on this current generation. It was seen mainly in accidents but also in mental instability, violent acts, and, in my case, a penchant for dark imaginings, vivid daydreams, fantasies of an only child. Granny Siobhan saw promise in me and was determined that I wouldn't fall prey to my family's heritage. She knew that only distance and education could knock such nonsense out of me and save me from the Cahill Curse. To that end, she helped me apply to Amberton Boarding School in Massachusetts. I wrote an essay on *Moby Dick*, blending Melville's cruel tale with the legends of my own family. It won me a full scholarship.

At fourteen, I left Kentucky on a Greyhound bus. With Granny's help and an education, I would defy DNA. I would lead a happy, normal life. I, Aine Cahill, would be the exception to the Cahill Curse.

1

The clean scent of the woods pressed me to momentary stillness and I stopped on top of the ridge, inhaling like a woman long imprisoned and finally freed. All around me fallen leaves of red, gold, and orange scuffed my ankles. A few dark evergreens in the distance provided a shaded contrast. Nearby, but hidden from view, was Walden Pond.

How I loved this place. The Massachusetts woods surrounding the gem-like pond had been populated by the great thinkers and writers of the Transcendentalist movement. Ralph Waldo Emerson, Bronson Alcott, and Henry David Thoreau had been my constant companions through graduate school, and now, with more than half of the work for a Ph.D. behind me, I'd come to write my doctoral dissertation in the quiet solitude of Thoreau's beloved Walden.

The intimacy of the one-room cabin he'd built and lived in for two years, two months, and two days played a vital role in my research and graduate work at Brandeis University. Now I hiked the very ground that had inspired him.

In my imagination, I'd navigated the nearly two miles around the deep blue pond in spring, summer, and fall. Now, while winter bore down and I wrote my doctoral dissertation, I could walk here for real, experiencing the same magic that had held Thoreau. I understood the link between land and writer, the sense of place, the way the seasons dictate thought and development. Thoreau was bound to this land, and by living in his footsteps I too had rooted myself at Walden Pond.

My face was cold as I followed the ridge for half a mile, feet crackling through the leaves. Below me Walden Pond winked blue in a bold shaft of sunlight that brightened the landscape for a fleeting moment, then was consumed by clouds. Late October. A time to celebrate homecoming, and that was exactly what I intended to do. Though I was far from my self-destructive family I felt as if I'd come home. I was all alone, but not lonely.

The upcoming holiday season stretched before me with endless possibilities. Time to read, to research, to write. These activities had become my comfort and close relationships.

"Miss?"

The voice startled me. My feet tangled in the leaves of a dead branch. Before I stumbled, a strong hand grasped my arm.

"Are you lost?"

Before answering, I assessed the man who held my arm. He was tall and lean, dressed in a thick jacket, a hat, gloves, and a holster complete with a weapon. His eyes held easy curiosity. "Who are you?" I sounded rude and suspicious, and I was both. He'd taken me by surprise, and it unsettled me.

He released my arm. "Joe Sinclair. I'm the ranger. Didn't mean to startle you." If he had a badge or identification, he didn't offer to show it.

"The park isn't closed." I had a right to wander the woods. I'd come too far, sacrificed too much, to be banned from the place where Thoreau's essence lingered.

"No, ma'am. The park is open. It's just we don't get many visitors this time of year. I wanted to be sure you weren't stranded or lost."

"I came because of the isolation."

"The Thoreau influence."

"Why, yes." He'd caught me by surprise yet again. "I'm studying his work."

"That would explain a lot."

I couldn't tell if he was making fun of me or not. "How so?"

"Not many campers or hikers when the cold settles in. I didn't see a vehicle in the lot, either." His tone implied a question, though his words did not.

"I walked from the inn. It's actually the isolation I was seeking," I repeated.

"And exercise is a noble endeavor. Thoreau would greatly approve." Humor notched up the corners of his mouth. "The inn's a nice place to stay, and you'll have plenty of isolation if you hang on through the winter. Just watch the weather. Don't stray from the main path if a heavy snow is coming. I walk around the lake several times a day, but if it's really cold, you could freeze before I found you." As if he could read my mind, he added, "Cell phone reception is iffy. Actually dismal. Spotty in a lot of areas."

"Thank you. I'll use common sense. I'm here to work and I certainly don't need an injury." I almost went on to explain my quest at Walden Pond—to justify myself—but I managed to stop. Climbing the ladder of higher education had taught me to seek validation from others. It was a nasty habit I was determined to break.

He pulled a card from his pocket. "This has my cell phone number, and the number for the ranger's quarters. If you run into anything you need help with, give a call, Miss . . . ."

"Cahill. Aine Cahill." I tucked his card in my pocket, unsure of his intentions. "Thanks." I turned away and retraced my steps. My mood was shattered. I might as well go back to the inn and work.

"Do be careful, Miss Cahill. Winter can be a deadly season here. I understand your desire for solitude, but be smart about it."

Something in his voice touched me. My carefully constructed wall of caution cracked. When I swung around, the sun had peeped from the clouds and was falling upon his shoulders, almost as if he were spotlighted. Almost as if he were a gift. "Thank you, Ranger Sinclair."

"If you have questions or need anything, call me. You have my numbers."

"I do. And I will." Feet crackling through the leaves, I left him beside the water.

⚬

I'd taken the cottage behind a mid-sized bed-and-breakfast that called itself an inn. The location was perfect. I was near enough to Concord and Walden to run my errands and research on foot, but I had the solitude I so craved. The Colonial Inn wasn't far from Orchard, the home of Louisa May Alcott. She'd paid for the home and supported her family with her writing. Odd that Louisa May achieved financial and popular success, but was still somehow less than Thoreau and Emerson in the canon of literary studies.

Of the three writers, my reading preference was Alcott. Her story of the March sisters had once made me long for siblings. But it was Thoreau I'd chosen for my research. I had my reasons.

Thoreau was my ace up the sleeve; the magic trick an English doctoral student needed to gain a secure job in a collapsing economy. A philosopher, naturalist, and anti-development environmentalist, Thoreau had written about the duties of man—to himself, his community, and his god. Yet he'd hidden a large portion of his true self from his readers. Generations of literature students had been taught to view him as a solitary aesthete and intellectual, a man given to isolation and thought. One who'd surrendered the joys of companionship and relationship to serve the interests of his mind. There is no doubt he was a deep thinker, but he was also a man of great passions. Obsessive passions.

His time at Walden Pond had not been spent alone—I had proof of that. His depiction as a solitary thinker and writer had been perpetrated with all the care of a modern-day spin doctor. His romantic life had been thoroughly eradicated from his accepted biography, but I had a bombshell.

Whether his solitary image was deliberate or not, I knew the truth and intended to reveal him for what he was. A man who loved totally and deeply, who shared his innermost thoughts with a woman. His passion for Bonnie Cahill, my great-great-great-great aunt, would rival any movie or romance. While some would think this was merely family lore, I had proof.

Thoreau had shared his walks around Walden Pond with her. He'd planned and executed surprises and small jokes for her. They'd shared a magical time, the two of them, in the tiny cabin hardly big enough for one. My aunt described herself as a seeker, and in Thoreau she'd found her soul mate. The truth of their life together had been meticulously recorded in my aunt Bonnie's hand in a leather-bound journal. Bonnie was his equal, his partner, in every aspect of his life.

The journal was more than a dear diary, much more. It was a collection of Bonnie's thoughts and musings, her hopes and fears. Included among the pages were pressed flowers and herbs, poems, and what appeared to be incantations, folk wisdom, and lore to ward off illness and ill fortune. In her flowing script, Bonnie documented the day-to-day of life with Thoreau. While I knew beyond a doubt that the journal held the truth, I had to find third-party documentation. My quest at Walden was twofold: to write my dissertation and to find records of my aunt's existence.

Bonnie's love for Thoreau, a man ill-equipped to defy his family and marry her, had moved even me, a woman immune to flutterings of the heart. My only adventure in opening myself to another had ended in tragedy. But Thoreau and Bonnie had shared passion and love. They'd united against the norms of society. And when it ended, Bonnie disappeared and Thoreau's health broke.

This would be the basis for my dissertation. I would change the worldview of Henry David Thoreau. While I lived in Middlesex County and traced the paths the two lovers once traveled, I would write my future and find proof of Bonnie's past.

After years and years of being the scholarship student, the student who worked for room and board, the poor relation with no social skills, I would be sought after. I would be Dr. Cahill. Victory would taste sweeter than honey.

≈≈≈

The three-mile trek to the inn in the brisk air left my ears feeling as if they might shatter and fall off, though I'd taken care to cover them with a scarf. The Middlesex County damp cold was more bitter than the misty mountain cold in Harlan County, Kentucky, where I grew up.

I pushed away those early years. Memories always rode double with pain and remorse. My stomach grumbled, and it was good to anticipate the tempting food awaiting me. Dinner would be served at the inn within the hour.

I stopped by the front desk, which retained the old-fashioned pigeonholes for room keys and messages. Dressed in a long gown and white apron with a mob cap, Dorothea Benton, the inn manager, shook her head. There were never any letters for me. Since Granny died, I'd cut all ties with my family. They had no clue where I was, nor had anyone looked for me. I had no friends who might write me. I'd failed to make the lasting friendships that most girls do in college.

Truth be told, I didn't miss it. Any of it.

"Evening, Aine," Dorothea said. "No post today."

"Thank you, Dorothea."

"How's your supply of clean towels?"

"Everything in the cabin is fine." I'd refused maid service, and the curiosity was eating Dorothea alive. There was little likelihood the cleaning crew would recognize the significance of Aunt Bonnie's journal, but I was taking no chances. Besides, my papers were scattered about the cabin's floor in what I viewed as organized chaos. To another's gaze, it would seem to be piles of junk. To me, it was a filing system.

"Will you be having your dinner here tonight?" Dorothea asked.

"I will." The inn was a cross between a full-service hotel and a bed-and-breakfast. The kitchen prepared a meal each evening, and Dorothea did her best to get a head count on who would and wouldn't be eating. Waste not, want not.

"Hettie's making chowder." She pushed her mob cap off her forehead. "A good dish for a cold night. Shall I have some extra blankets brought around?"

"I'll pick up a couple after dinner."

"Would you like Patrick to lay a fire for you?"

I considered. "Yes. That would be nice." I often wrote and read into the wee hours, and a blaze would be cheerful company. The fire would help chase away the morbid thoughts that sometimes dogged me. I couldn't afford to waste time to the inertia of depression. Besides, the trip to the woodshed on a dark night made me uncomfortable. I'd escaped the Cahill Curse, but my imagination was my own worst enemy. Sometimes it caught me by surprise.

While dinner was being prepared, I started out for the cabin. It was older than the inn, which was saying something. Caulked with mud in the old style, it was snug and perfect for me. A fair distance from the inn and roadway, the log structure sat back in woods that crowded close to the narrow lane. On sunny days, I enjoyed the multitude of hues in the trunks of the quaking aspen, yellow birch, maples, and a scattering of oaks, red and black. The trees were slender but numerous and, even without leaves, created a place of shadow, especially on an overcast, leaden day. The path took a turn and the inn disappeared behind me. I faced a wall of woods, silvery trunks blending into black. So different from the green of Kentucky, where even in winter something alive could be found. I kept walking, uneasy due to my foolish fancy that the woods closed in behind me. An active imagination was a bane, and mine was more active than most. Growing up, I'd imagined all sorts of impossible things.

As I used my key to open the door, the first snowflake drifted onto my mittened hand. Large and fluffy, it was a tiny speck of perfection. The gray sky's promised snow had arrived. I paused at the door to watch the flakes thicken in the air. I loved the way snow wrapped around a place and snuggled it into silence. It would be a good night.

Stepping into the cabin, I caught movement at the edge of my vision. Something larger than a fox or dog. I stopped. I wasn't afraid, but I was wary. The forest surrounded the cabin on three sides, and the path that led to the inn had been empty when I traveled it.

"Who's there?" I spoke firmly.

The wind was my only answer, rattling a few dying leaves in the branches of the trees.

Could it be Patrick, the inn's bellhop/errand boy? Though he was younger than me by a handful of years, he'd flirted when he'd carried my bags to the cabin. He was a handsome young man who no doubt saw plenty of action—as long as Dorothea didn't catch him. She'd pinch his ear off, repressed schoolteacher type that she was.

"Patrick? If you're up to a prank, this isn't funny."

I shifted my body toward the open cabin door and heard what could have been a smothered sob, or maybe a small creature frightened by a predator.

"Stop clowning around, and step forward." The warm air from the fireplace coursed out around me into the cold night.

Enough foolishness. Pivoting on my heel, I caught sight of a child-like form rushing into the woods on the west side of the cabin.

"Hey!" I stepped out onto the porch. A kid shouldn't be out in the cold and the dark. "Wait up!" I jogged to the edge of the woods and stopped. It was futile to chase the child. Maybe it was a guest of the inn, or a grade-schooler from a nearby street. There were plenty of neighborhoods filled with Boston commuter families just a few miles from the inn.

Whatever the circumstances, I would do no good flailing about in the woods. When I went back to the inn, I'd mention it to Dorothea. Chances were high she'd be able to name the child and family. One phone call and she'd sort it all out.

I returned to the cabin and closed the door, sorry so much warmth had fled into the night. I'd postpone my shower until after dinner, when the cabin had had time to reheat.

I walked to the window and looked out upon the snow, now coming down thick. A light dusting already covered the ground. Soon the snow would insulate my world. It was perfect weather for writing.

At my desk, I jotted down a few notes and observations from my venture around the pond. My daily notations honored Thoreau— observations of nature and the weather, but hunger fractured my concentration. With little accomplished, I made the trip back to the dining hall, my mouth watering at the scent of bubbling soup and home-baked bread that drifted on a breeze.

The ring of an axe diverted my attention to the large woodpile behind the inn. Patrick worked with quick efficiency as he split firewood.

He caught sight of me and grinned, resting a moment on his axe. "I'll take care of your fire while you're eating. I'll bring in enough wood to keep you warm all night."

"Thank you." I watched him return to chopping, his lithe body making short work of the chore. The complaints of my stomach drove me in to the feast Dorothea set in front of me, and for half an hour I lost myself in the simple pleasures of a fine meal.

2

I have begun a new journal, a new page, because I have begun a new life. From banishment to a welcome homecoming. From rejection to acceptance. From solitary to united. How quickly my life has changed, and all because of him. Yes, I am impetuous. He has changed me from a cautious woman to a wanton. He has taught me that risk is the measure of a living heart. And I have taught him that solitude does not preclude companionship. In the short time we have known each other, we have taught each other so much.

But let me start at the beginning. I am Bonnie Cahill, nineteen years old this past April. I have left my home in Narragansett Bay, Rhode Island, and moved inland to Concord, Massachusetts, to save my body and soul from the misdeeds of my family. We are a clan cursed by previous generations of bloodlust. The Bible predicts my fate if I do not escape my family. Exodus is clear. The iniquity of the fathers will be visited on the children and on the grandchildren to the third and fourth generations.

And so I have fled. In doing so, I have found a man who touches me to the bone. I once disdained the lovesick musings of the poets, and now, joyfully, I *have been proven wrong. My heart has been awakened from an icy pit, and I am alive in a way I never believed possible.*

I met Henry David Thoreau strolling along the streets of Concord with his friend the philosopher and intellectual, Mr. Ralph Waldo Emerson. I had heard Mr. Emerson speak at the McGill home where I had taken a job as a governess. His talk was not necessarily religious, but it offered me a freedom I had never dared to dream of. He ignited a spark in my soul, a need to step out from under a God always angry, always looking for a reason to punish. I am tired of retribution and suffering, especially as I have done no wrong. In Mr. Emerson's estimation, each person is responsible for his own actions—and for no one else's.

My admiration for Mr. Emerson knows no boundaries.

I stopped to speak to him on Post Road, and he made the introduction of Mr. Thoreau. I am only a governess, but Mr. Emerson does not make such distinctions. We chatted for a moment and I was terribly distracted by Mr. Thoreau's presence. He, too, was agitated. We never looked at each other directly, only those silly glancing looks I'd chastised my fourteen-year-old charge, Rachel McGill, for practicing. Ears burning and cheeks flushed, I bade the gentlemen farewell and we went our separate ways. But I had learned Mr. Emerson and Mr. Thoreau would be at the McGill home that very evening for a discussion group. I was invited to attend. Not as a governess, but as a member of the audience.

All day I thought of the slender gentleman with the burning eyes and bashful glances. There was something about him. That night, he did not speak to me, nor I to him, but our awareness of each other was acute. Mr. Thoreau's presence, and the dangerous ideas put forth by Mr. Emerson regarding individual thought and responsibility, fired my desire to live a full and complete life. I recognized the truth of Mr. Emerson's lecture. We are all bound to nature, to each other, to a moral responsibility to uphold right and good. He is considered dangerous by some, especially those who want to lull the population into complacent sleep. I have been awakened, both in spirit and in my heart.

I knew that night—my destiny was linked with Mr. Thoreau.

I put the leather-bound journal aside. That was Bonnie's first entry. And from there, she recounted the time she spent with Thoreau on Walden Pond. Their love was no secret. Emerson knew of it and, if Bonnie's journal entries could be trusted, approved of the liaison. The romance that blossomed between Thoreau and Bonnie was apparently championed by all of the Transcendentalists. The Alcott family invited Bonnie to their gatherings, and she documented conversations with Louisa May and her father, Bronson Alcott, another great thinker of the era. Surely I would find the evidence of these meetings I desperately needed.

My forefinger traced the gold-embossed lettering on the journal, an expensive thing in the mid-1800s. Thoreau gave it to Bonnie, and it in turn came into my possession. What I held in my hand was more than just a remarkable account of a romance and life; it was my destiny. Bonnie had found hers beside Walden Pond, and I would do the same.

Turning on my computer, I continued the work of condensing and outlining my dissertation. It would follow the natural flow of Bonnie's journal, bringing into sharp focus Thoreau's habits, thoughts, and writing. I had been gifted with a unique lens through which to explore Thoreau—the magnifying glass of love.

At half past nine, I put my writing away and found my coat and mittens to go back to the inn for a book on local history I'd seen in the inn's front parlor. Dorothea had offered the use of any of the books in her specialized library. I hoped by now all of the dinner guests would be gone. I didn't dislike the residents of the area, but they distracted me. They claimed Thoreau as if he were their own flesh and blood, even those who hadn't a clue to his philosophy. They told their tired old stories as if they were truth.

I found it annoying and a bit tedious. Most of the anecdotes were hogwash, because none included the mysterious woman who shared his life. Bonnie had been totally excised from his biography. It was as if Thoreau's family had accomplished exactly what they'd set out to do. Not even in memory were they allowed to be together.

My doctoral thesis, and the ensuing publicity I expected, would change that forever. Bonnie Cahill would get her due.

Before I left, I tossed more logs on the fire. Patrick had left me well supplied. He was taken with me and made no secret of it, though it would come to nothing. To the dismay of the giggling teenage girls who took tea at the inn hoping to catch his eye, he ignored them but would sit for a moment and chat with me. I admit that I liked his bravado and his brash attempts to flirt. I was pleased that he tried. I was nothing more than a challenge, but it made me feel young and desirable.

Stepping out onto my small porch, I paused. Snow blanketed everything, at least an inch thick in the short time I'd been writing. But it wasn't the snow that stopped me, it was the set of little footprints, child-sized, that ended right at the porch. As if a child had come out of the woods and stood on the top step, watching me through the window while I worked.

3

"No, dear, no children in the inn this week." Dorothea dusted a tiger oak sideboard as she talked to me. Never one to waste a moment, she always did two or three things at once. It was a truly annoying habit. "Footprints? No right-minded mother would let her brood out in this weather. It's a blue nor'easter headed right at us, if you can believe what Patrick has been spouting. He watches the weather channel back in the pantry. He says that bald-headed weatherman is headed our way because they're predicting a record snowfall and a drop in the temperatures. Black ice. That's what the highways are going to be. Good thing you're tucked in for the holidays."

"The shoe prints were small." I was concerned. "Maybe a young child. Nine or thereabouts."

She paused and the queerest expression shifted across her face. "Really." It was a flat statement, not a question. "What's wrong?" I asked.

She stood up, wadding the dust cloth into a ball. "You wouldn't recall, but a decade back there was another bad snowstorm and a local youngster, a little girl, went missing."

A chill climbed my spine. "Was she found?"

Dorethea gazed into the distance, and I was aware of the clatter of plates and flatware, a bit of laughter from the bar where old Cooley Butler played some 1940s love songs on the piano.

Dorothea spoke at last. "No. She was never found. The not knowing drove her mother insane. It broke Helen. Just broke her in two like a rotted stick. Can't say it wouldn't have done the same for me."

I leaned closer to the desk where Dorothea's electric heater churned at full blast. "How old was the child?"

"Third grade. A lovely child. A bonnie lass, as my dad would say."

"You knew her well." It was written clearly on her face, the loss and the sadness.

"Dig around at Henry David, but leave this alone. Bad memories. That child went into the woods and never came out."

The creepy sensation crawled along my back again. I didn't care for it. "People don't just disappear."

Dorothea's lips thinned and straightened. "You're welcome to use any of the books in the parlor. Just return them when you're done. You might want to wait here for a bit. I'll put in a call to the police chief. He should get over here before the snow covers everything. If there's a child about, the authorities need to know."

"Do you think it's really a matter for the police?" I was a bit taken aback. I didn't want to be involved in even the most benign investigation. I had work to do. Grinding work that required my total concentration.

"Chief McKinney will want to know. He'll check it out. No bother to him or you."

The color rising along her throat revealed her thoughts. "Those prints don't belong to your missing child from ten years back. She'd be grown by now."

"I know." She pushed away from the desk. "Help yourself to the books." She hurried to the office where she could talk privately on the phone.

⚜

Will McKinney was a stout man with a walrus moustache and heavy jowls reddened by the cold. He found me at the inn, arms loaded with books. He'd already been to my cabin.

"No footprints," he said without preamble. "Snow's coming down like a mother. Covered everything by the time I got there. Even *your* prints."

"I saw them." The instinct to defend myself made my voice more strident than I intended. This wasn't a case of my overactive imagination.

"Don't doubt it, but they're gone now. Damned snow. Morons who shouldn't be driving will be wrecking everywhere. This is no weather for grown-ups to be out, much less a kid. Folks today don't mind their children."

"I saw someone in the woods earlier, and I thought it might be a child. It was just a flash of a figure moving through the trees."

"You seen any young'uns hanging around your cabin?"

The question felt loaded. "No, should I have?"

"Last year, when the cabin was empty, Dorothea discovered a group of middle-school kids hanging out there. They'd busted the lock. Smoking cigarettes, likely dope. They drank the liquor she'd stored there." He pursed his lips and his moustache jumped like a caterpillar. "Might be they were hoping to use the cabin again."

"How old were these kids?" A ten-year-old was a different matter from an eighteen-year-old. I could handle the younger ones. The nearly grown ones could be treacherous.

"Twelve and thirteen." He sighed. "Kids today get into stuff that wasn't around when I was growing up. Both parents work, they're left to their own devices. Too often that means drugs or alcohol, or both."

"Did Dorothea press charges?"

"No need. The two ringleaders went off to military or boarding school. A hard decision for the parents, but it was the right one. They were headed for trouble, and if Mom or Pop can't watch over them, paying a school to do it is the next best option."

In theory I agreed with him, but I knew first-hand the brutality of boarding schools. Rich kids with money and no moral compass tortured the weaker, more sensitive kids. Some grew out of it, others grew into it.

"I'll keep an eye out. Chief, Dorothea mentioned a young girl who went missing years back."

The smile faded from his face. "Doesn't take much to bring back that bad memory."

"Dorothea said she disappeared."

He rolled his shoulders and stood straighter. "That little girl vanished. We searched high and low for weeks. Dogs, helicopters, volunteer searchers. It didn't make sense then and it doesn't now. She was just gone." His bleak expression told me how much the past troubled him.

"Do you think a predator picked her up?"

"I don't want to think that, but she sure didn't hitch-hike out of town. Someone had to take her."

"That must have been horrible for her parents."

"For all of us," he said. "For every single person in town." He inhaled. "Give me a call if you see or hear anything that troubles you." He gave me a card. "Winters here are usually calm. The weather causes problems, but none we haven't handled for years. Dorothea tells me you're a writer."

I shook my head. "I'm a doctoral student at Brandeis. I'm writing my dissertation."

The first genuine grin crossed his face. "And here I was hoping you'd be the next Stephen King. I like a good ghost yarn on a cold winter night."

"I could recommend a few. 'The Turn of the Screw' is one of the scariest stories I've ever read."

His eyebrows shifted up. "I read a bit of Henry James when I was younger. I once thought I might be a scribbler myself. Have to say I like the new breed of writer. They get to the point and don't use a lot of ten-dollar words."

Everyone was a critic, but I was pleasantly surprised. McKinney's honesty was refreshing.

"If I see any children, I'll let you know." It was late, but I had more writing to do.

"I'd appreciate it. Young'uns don't always understand the capricious nature of the weather and how deadly it can be."

"I hear you."

"Joe told me you're hiking the pond trails. You take care, too. When the snow covers the ground, it's easy to step in a hole or trip over a vine or limb. Grownups freeze just as readily as a child. You want me to drive you back to the cabin?"

"No, thanks. I need the exercise. I grew up in the mountains. I'll take care."

He put his smoky hat back on and left. I followed him, ready to get back to work.

I entered a warm, comfortable cabin and set immediately to work. By midnight, my neck was cramped and stiff and my shoulders aching. Putting aside my writing, I turned off the computer, swallowed a mild sleeping pill, and took Bonnie's journal and a glass of wine to bed.

Sipping the wine, I read from the middle of the journal. I'd perused it front to back numerous times, and now I liked to let the pages open on their own. The section dealt with Bonnie's abilities—and Thoreau's interest in the supernatural.

Strange dreams have always attended me. Some forecast the future, others seem untethered to any time or place. My most recent dreams involve the child, Louisa May. She is a precocious young lady with an active mind, and a will of her own. She is not a spirit who will be forced into the constraints of a corset and a marriage.

In my dreams, I see her surrounded by numerous children. Vivacious girls. There is laughter and tears, as there would be in any household. And Louisa is writing at a desk beside an open window that gives a view of the orchard.

These are not her children. Perhaps she is a teacher, like her father, and these are her future pupils. She loves them greatly, each for their individuality. They will bring her happiness.

With the clarity of hindsight, I knew Bonnie was describing the March family, the literary children who would sustain the entire Alcott family. Jo, Meg, Beth, Amy, Laurie—I recognized them. Bonnie would never have, though, because Louisa May Alcott was still a child. She hadn't written the first word of *Little Women*.

But there was another passage I sought. The police chief's visit brought to mind a mention my aunt had made of finding tracks near the cabin at Walden. It had been only a brief mention, more of a curiosity than anything else. I had come to believe that my aunt longed for a child.

As I found the place and began to read, dread caught me. This was not the way I remembered it. I had read the journal repeatedly, and though I knew of Bonnie's and Thoreau's attempts to speak with departed spirits, I didn't remember this dark account. I held my breath and read, more and more concerned that I had no recollection of my aunt's words.

I'm reluctant to put these words on the page. This morning, before he went to attend his surveying chores, Henry asked that we attempt a communication. He sorely misses his brother, John. Though I was reluctant to do this, I yielded to Henry's impassioned pleas.

I should have heeded my instincts. The session was a disaster. I haven't honed my abilities to bring forth the dead, and what I brought into our cabin was not his brother. The creature, for I am sure it had never been human, was racked with horrid spasms. It gasped for air and thrashed about. Though it tried to speak, it could not. Something gagged it. And before I could banish the entity, Henry leapt up from the table and fled into the woods crying his brother's name.

I remain shaken to my core. Whatever good I'd intended to do has been overshadowed by a terrible harm. Henry is beside himself with a grief I am helpless to console. And we are being watched. I'm certain of it. Someone comes up to the cabin while we sleep. I've found footprints. Small ones, as if a child were spying on us. But there are no children loose in the Walden woods at night. I've told no one of this. Henry is too distraught, and others would

19

think me mad. Perhaps it is just a fancy turned into a shade. Before I speak
of it to others, I need to discover more.

How had I missed this? Had my aunt really called up someone,
or something, dead? I didn't doubt that generations of past Cahills
had such talents. It was in our blood. It was the curse I'd escaped,
thanks to my grandmother. But how had I missed the terror of
that passage?

I pushed the journal aside, poured another glass of wine, and took
another sleeping pill. The pills were mild, harmless, and my nerves
were too on edge to sleep without assistance. Tomorrow, I would
re-read the journal. Sunshine would destroy the dark images, and I
would laugh at myself and my foolishness.

The wine and sleeping pill kicked in, and I snapped off the bedside
lamp. The fire flickered merrily, casting moving shadows about the
cabin. Snug beneath a pile of quilts, I drifted into sleep.

⚜

Granny Siobhan rocked gently in a chair before the fire. Her body was
too thin, almost skeletal. The hands that clutched her shawl reminded
me of a dead person. I burrowed deep beneath the covers, but she
knew I was awake. She came to the bed and sat beside me. Her sunken
eyes were unreadable; for the first time, I was afraid of her.

"You'll soon need your gift," she said. "You did not come to
Walden Pond by accident. Your destiny brought you here. Use care,
my child. Use care."

I woke up struggling against the heavy quilts. I knew I'd been
dreaming, but the images were so vivid, so real. I glanced toward
the fireplace expecting to see the old rocker my grandmother loved.
There was nothing there. No chair, no Granny. Just the fire and the
soft pop of a few pearls of moisture.

I wanted some water and the bathroom, but I was reluctant to put
my feet on the floor. A childhood fear—the bogeyman under the

bed—kept me rigid beneath the covers. I checked my watch. It was three-thirty-three. At least three hours until daybreak.

Had Granny really visited me, drifting across the divide of the dead? Or had Bonnie's journal ignited my overactive imagination? Either answer was plausible.

As a child I'd seen vapors in the shape of people, but Granny gave them no credence. She had a logical explanation for each incident. She told me reason was the key to happiness, and urged me to focus on my studies and not phantoms. I willingly heeded her cautions. The idea of the dead traipsing around scared me, as it would any sane person. I didn't wish to have them following me, tapping bony fingers against the glass windowpanes of my bedroom late at night. Their time was done, and I wanted no part of them.

4

The sun on the snow blinded me. The predicted nor'easter had passed to the north of us, running into Vermont and Maine with downed power lines and impassable roads. I stood at the edge of the woods beside Walden Pond. I'd been drawn there to see the snowfall. My reward was a purity and brilliance that almost knocked the breath from me. Walden Pond seemed caught between the powdery blue of the sky and the snow-coated evergreens. The edges of the water had begun to freeze, a process that would continue until the surface of the lake was solid.

I caught sight of a spot of color at the edge of the water, so I tramped down to see what it was. Lying atop the snow was a Barbie doll. She wore a ball gown like Cinderella. It took me a moment to realize there were no tracks leading to her. It was as if she'd been dropped from the sky.

Barbie in a ballgown. I glanced around to see if someone might be playing a prank. The doll, sitting atop the snow, couldn't have been out there for long. She was pristine.

Had I once had a doll like that? I tried to remember, but dredging the past brought other things up from the muck of memory. I'd successfully buried so much of my childhood. Selective memory. That was how I'd managed to deal with my family. Too many bad memories like the death of black-haired, blue-eyed Uncle Mike, my father's youngest brother, blasted almost in half by a rival oxy dealer with a sawed-off 12-gauge on the side of a backwoods road.

Once the past began to uncoil, I couldn't stop it. I tried not to remember the still ticking of the hallway clock as my mother died. My father's sobs and pleadings with her to stay, not to leave. The red splotch of blood that soaked his white shirt and left a permanent stain in the heart-of-pine floor around the chair where she sat.

I'd played with dolls. I was sure of it, though I couldn't pin down an exact memory. Maybe a blond-haired Barbie like the one that lay in the snow. Easing down the lip of the bank, I moved cautiously toward the doll. The snow covered a multitude of hazards—holes, branches, undergrowth. A wrong move could mean a sprained ankle or worse.

At last I reached the Barbie and picked her up. Her dress was barely damp from the snow. She wore a blue gown with a white net overlay that glittered. Snow Queen Barbie. On her perpetually pointed feet were silver sandals, and over her arm was a white fur wrap. Elegant. A fantasy figure for a young girl.

But there was no girl. And no footprints. Just Barbie. I laid her back in the snow and turned to leave. My bootprints were deep and irregular. Impulsively, I picked up the doll again and tucked her into my pocket. It seemed wrong to leave her in the freezing snow.

Back at the cabin, I picked up my well-worn copy of Thoreau's *Walden* and read from it again. *"I went to the woods because I wished to live deliberately, to front only the essential facts of life, and see if I could not learn what it had to teach, and not, when I came to die, discover that I had not lived. I did not wish to live what was not life, living is so dear; nor did I wish to practise resignation, unless it was quite necessary. I wanted to live deep and suck out all the marrow of life, to live so sturdily and Spartan-like as to put to rout all that was not life, to cut a broad swath and shave close, to drive life into a corner, and reduce it to its lowest terms, and, if it proved to be mean, why then to get the whole and genuine meanness of it, and publish its meanness to the world; or if it were sublime, to know it by experience, and be able to give a true account of it in my next excursion."*

~•~

There was no doubt Thoreau's intention was a solitary pursuit of life's meaning. But fate handed him something else entirely. A time of intimacy and shared love. It ended much too soon. And in ending, it had stolen Bonnie's life.

What is the cost of love? Is it worth the price that must be paid?

A sharp knock at the door made me drop my pen. I got up to discover Patrick standing on my doorstep, his handsome face flushed with cold. "Dorothea told me to ask if you'll be at dinner tonight."

I recognized a lie when I heard it, but I motioned him inside. The thought of tackling Thoreau's great work of solitude and turning it inside out loomed too large on such a cold day. Patrick would be a smashing distraction.

"Would you like a cup of cocoa?" I had fresh milk and sugar and chocolate. The tiny kitchenette held a two-burner stove where I could heat things.

"With some rum?" he moved an old rocker from the corner and plopped down in front of the banked fire. "You need another log. It's about to go out." He threw wood on the fire and stirred it into blazing light. Men were never content with hot embers. It was always the blaze for them.

"Why are you really here? You didn't come for a cup of cocoa." I took the straight-backed chair at my desk and set it beside him.

"You're right. I don't want cocoa. I saw you go out early this morning. I thought you might need someone to warm you up after frisking about in the snow."

"And that someone would be you?"

"You could go a long way and do a lot worse."

He was impertinent and I couldn't stop the smile. "Are you on the clock for Dorothea?"

He looked surprised. "Yeah. But I figure keeping her tenant happy is a good service for her. A beautiful woman like you, alone. That's not a happy picture."

"And this is all for Dorothea's good?"

"You bet." He leaned forward and put his hand on my knee.

Whether it was the suddenness of his touch or my own reluctance to partake of intimacy, I moved away from him. "I'm not one of the girls who follow you like puppies, Patrick. I'm here to work."

He chewed his bottom lip. "I like you, Aine. I flirt with the others, the girls, but I don't take it any further than that. They like the attention. You're different. You're . . . serious."

"And that wouldn't be a good thing for either of us."

He pushed out of the chair. "I warn you, I don't give up. Maybe if we just climbed in the sack and tested it out, I could let you go."

"Not going to happen." The desire of a younger man is a flattering thing, but wisdom prevailed. Patrick might become a vice that would be hard to break. I wasn't immune to my physical needs, but I'd sworn off emotional engagement. I suspected Patrick would be fun, and I was smart enough to know I couldn't miss what I'd never had. With so much riding on the work I accomplished while at Concord, time was too precious to expend on romantic endeavors.

I went to the kitchen and filled a glass with water. "I'm serious, Patrick. You need to leave." I drank deeply, waiting for him to comply.

At last he accepted my decision and sauntered out the door, and I returned to my desk. Thoreau's book slipped off the desk and fell to the floor. Beneath it was Bonnie's journal, opened to a page near the middle.

While I thrive in the Walden solitude with Henry, I also yearn for more. He tells me that each moment is precious, and life is wasted by wishing for the future, yet I can't stop myself. This morning I came across a young girl in the woods, a beautiful child with golden ringlets and blue eyes framed with thick dark lashes. She stepped out from behind a sycamore holding her dolly. Too timid to come forward, she simply watched me with her deep blue eyes. Then she was gone. The pain of her departure forced me to realize how much I want my own child. Henry is opposed. He immerses himself in his studies and the solitude of nature. I love those things, too, but my arms crave the solid weight of a baby.

This passage I remembered. I'd read it a dozen times, but it had taken on new meaning after my Barbie encounter. The parallels between the past and present were unsettling, to say the least.

I flipped the journal closed. I understood Bonnie's desire too well. I'd once felt the longing for a child. A great weariness settled over me.

Now wasn't the time for depression and the morbid glumness that robbed me of ambition. Research on the Internet was all well and good, but nothing could take the place of a library. I needed the older records stored in the Concord library. Tomorrow, I would find time to explore the town's records. I would establish Bonnie's presence in Concord and anchor my dissertation in solid, proven fact.

5

My library research took me down a rabbit trail of men's hairstyles in the mid-1800s. The information was useless for my dissertation, but it amused me. I'd awakened with a maddening depression, and I'd learned to pace myself when the blues settled on my shoulders. Sometimes a bit of laughter was better than the bottle of pills my therapist had prescribed. Swallowing medication is hard for me. A mild sleeping pill now and again I can manage, but no more. Dr. O'Gorman tells me it's psychological. An aversion to the family industry of peddling oxy has affected my gag reflex when it comes to pills. No worries that I'd ever kill myself with drugs.

Walking home, I paused at a coffee shop and bakery. My mouth watered at the scent of cinnamon and hot bread wafting from the Honey Bea. I'd worked up an appetite and hadn't eaten lunch. A latte and sweet bun would remedy the situation and hold me until Dorothea served dinner.

I'd pushed the door open and stepped inside before I saw Joe. He sat at a back table, coffee steaming in front of him in a large white mug. He watched me with undisguised interest. My first inclination was to back out the door, but I held my ground. My reaction was unreasonable. I behaved as if I were guilty of something, and I knew what I suffered from. I'd felt it at Walden Pond, and now I couldn't pretend I wasn't attracted to him. He was a good-looking man with a defined jaw and dark hair that fell across his forehead. Ruggedly handsome. My body reacted to him even if my brain denied my interest.

After placing my order, I took a seat and pulled a book from my satchel. Joe could stare, but I would ignore him. I buried myself in a critical analysis of Thoreau's socialist leanings. I read the same paragraph over and over again.

"Miss Cahill." Joe stood over me, coffee in hand. "Mind if I join you?"

I wanted to say yes, that I minded greatly, but it would have been a lie. Nodding to the chair across from me, I marked my place in the book and closed it.

"How's your stay at the inn going?"

Warmth crept up my neck and into my cheeks. "It's very nice." What was wrong with me? The question was harmless enough and not even personal.

"Dorothea's a talker, but she has a huge heart. She'll take care of you as if you were her own."

"Yes." I felt like a callow schoolgirl instead of a grown woman.

"She said you were working on your dissertation."

"Yes. On Thoreau." My hands hugged my elbows, although the room was toasty warm and my face was hot.

"So that's your interest in Walden Pond." Joe seemed genuinely curious. "He was always one of my favorites. He understood serenity and the value of being alone." He rubbed the dark shadow of a beard. "My mother always said a man needs to live alone for a couple of years to appreciate the company of a woman. Thoreau would've been just about ready, based on Mother's standards."

Surprise must have scurried across my face, because he laughed. "Is your reading of Thoreau different?"

"I'm sorry. I've been in town a week and no one I've met has even read Thoreau. He's a historical figure, a tourist attraction, maybe even an icon, but no one in Concord knows his work. They know he's famous but they don't know why."

"There are some folks hereabouts who study his work. They understand the significance of the way he combined human life and the natural world. He was the first nature writer." His fine, dark hair hung over his left eye, giving him a youthful look. He was in his early thirties, but when he smiled he looked younger. "A few of us rogue Bay Staters still read him. Crusty single men with no prospects."

The man had a sense of humor in his flirtations. "I don't think I've run across any of those."

"You might just have one in your sights." That grin again. The one that said "don't take me seriously but at least laugh."

"My lucky day." My humor was rusty from disuse, but Joe was the most interesting person I'd met in Concord. A park ranger who read Thoreau. "Why do you read Thoreau?"

"I didn't study literature, but I loved it. Thoreau was a significant influence in my decision to become a ranger. He was a conservationist before anyone even knew what the word meant." Leather, probably his gun belt, creaked as he put his elbows on the table and leaned into the conversation. "He wrote about and demonstrated the importance of individuals in challenging the system. He understood the hardships and appeal of walking a different path."

He had me and I didn't want to resist. "He was far ahead of his time. He was a visionary and a conflicted man." I caught myself and gave a self-deprecating laugh. "Oh, crack the door of my favorite topic and I'll lambaste you with talk."

"A dissertation is too much hard work to write about a topic that fails to ignite your passion."

Finding someone to discuss my thesis topic was like stumbling on a hundred-dollar bill on the street. "What drew you to Thoreau, other than the obvious location, location, location?"

He chuckled at my imitation of a realtor. "I greatly admire Thoreau's independence. His willingness to live alone and deny himself the comforts of a relationship so that he could fully experience nature."

Perfect! This was exactly the rendering of Thoreau that had been taught in high schools and colleges for over a hundred years. "And what if he wasn't alone?"

A crease touched the place between his eyes. I liked the way his black brows winged up to a peak and then tapered. Expressive.

"What do you mean he wasn't alone? Folks accept that he visited with his family and his friends. But his journals—"

"It's just a question. What if he wasn't alone? Would you discount his experiences if you found he'd had a companion at Walden? A girlfriend or something like that?"

His finger absently traced the handle of his mug. "I'd have to think about that. It would make him a fraud, wouldn't it? To pretend to be alone to experience the solitude and self-exploration? It's like he's selling one thing and living another."

"A fraud? That's pretty judgmental." His assessment made my gut clench. I didn't want to discredit Thoreau or his work. Would that be the reaction to my revelation?

"It would change everything."

I nodded agreement, but waited for him to continue.

"Why would he lie about such a thing?" he asked.

"Perhaps his family objected to the relationship. Or if he was living in sin, the weight of community disapproval would have far offset any value of his writing. Or maybe he was protecting his companion from public censure."

He sat up tall. "I don't believe there was anyone at Walden but Thoreau. That kind of secret couldn't have been kept for nearly two centuries."

"A conspiracy of silence." Despite the anxiety that his words provoked, I grabbed a pen from my purse and wrote that down. It was the perfect title for my dissertation.

"Do you have evidence that Thoreau had a companion?"

Before I made any public confessions, I needed solid verification. I took a good long look at him. Aside from his obvious handsomeness, he had a sense of humor and a lively intellect. I didn't want to answer his question, so I asked another. "If your love is literature, how did you become a ranger?"

For the first time, he looked a bit uncomfortable. The skin around his eyes tautened, and he looked down. "It's a long story."

"I'm a good listener."

"Another time. You're the stranger in town. Let's hear about you."

"Egghead doctoral student. Poor childhood, dysfunctional family, scholarships, and here I am." The waitress brought my sticky bun and coffee and I inhaled the delicious aroma of roasted coffee and cinnamon.

"Dig in." His hand indicated my fattening treat. "Chief McKinney told me about your strange intruder. Mind if I ask a question or two?"

"Intruder is an exaggeration." I swallowed a bite of bun and licked my lips. "A child stood on the top step of my porch. There was no attempt to enter the cabin, so I don't think you could call it an intruder."

"Did you get a look? Male, female, elementary age, older?"

I pictured the figure I'd seen darting among the trees. "Not high school. Younger, a child. I couldn't guess the gender. Whoever it was could move quickly in the woods, but that was before it snowed." I started to describe the tracks and how they stopped at the top step, as if the child had flown away, but I realized he would think I was either lying or crazy. Neither impression was the one I wanted to leave.

"Most of the kids around here are good kids. Only a few bad apples, but keep your eyes open."

I was learning fast that what Joe left unspoken was more important than what he said. The demographics of Concord didn't lead to images of inner-city turmoil. "Are you warning me of something? Gangs of white, upper-class children hiding in snowbanks and waylaying head-in-the-clouds dissertation students?"

"No." Again the charming smile, but he held my gaze. "No Dickensian waifs waiting to steal your mittens. But every community has

31

problems these days. Drugs are rampant, even for middle-class kids. I like for things to run smoothly. If you lock the cabin and stay alert, you can avert trouble. That would be the best for all of us."

"Thanks for the tip. If I see any kids breaking the law, I'll know it's my fault." I meant to be flip, but it fell flat.

He didn't react. "That's not what I meant. Just be aware. It's the same thing I tell everyone. A lot of tragedy can be avoided if you keep your eyes open."

What kind of tragedy did he refer to? Somehow, I thought it might be personal. "I'll do that." I reached down for my book satchel and my hand brushed the doll I'd picked up in the snow. I pushed it across the table to him. "I found this near the edge of the pond early this morning. There seem to be a lot of children running wild around the community."

He leaned forward, frowning. "Where?" His fingers grasped my wrist with unexpected speed.

I tried to shake free, but he held on. The expression on his face frightened me. "At the edge of the pond. In the snow. What's wrong?"

"Tell me how you found it."

The espresso machine whistled and sputtered as the young barista made a coffee for a slope-shouldered mother standing at the counter. No one had observed Joe's fingers on my wrist. "Please, let me go. You're hurting me."

He dropped my arm. "Sorry. Please tell me where you got the doll."

His intensity was out of proportion to a doll left in the snow, but I obliged him with the details. "I was walking by the pond and I saw the doll in the snow. No footprints. She was in a clearing as if she'd dropped from the sky. I retrieved her. End of story."

"What part of the pond?" His tone was more restrained.

I told him, watching his unease build as I spoke.

"Did you see anyone?" he asked.

"No. The doll must have been left during the snowfall. There were no tracks." But the doll had not been buried in the snow, either. Very strange.

"Tomorrow, will you show me where? If there are children wandering around unattended, I need to know. As I told you, the woods can be dangerous in the winter."

My morning routine included a hike around the pond. It wouldn't take long to show him the spot. For all the good it would do. Still, it was obviously important to him, though I couldn't fathom why. Against my better judgment, I agreed. "Meet me at nine. At the Walden Pond cabin."

"I'll be there." Joe stood up, took his coffee cup to the counter, and left the shop. A cold blast of winter air entered the room as he left.

6

Rain swept in, and a brutal wind coated the roadways and sidewalks with slick ice. My rendezvous with Joe was postponed until better weather. The delay chafed at me. Instead of indifference, I felt something akin to disappointment. Did I want to meet the ranger at Walden Pond? He was attractive, yes. But I knew plenty of attractive men. The problem was that I *liked* him. Bitter experience had taught me that men were dangerous. Some lessons were so painful, they didn't bear repeating.

Patrick's flirtations, and the love Bonnie felt for Thoreau, had awakened a longing in me I'd thought my high school experience had bludgeoned to death. Joe's smile, the way his dark hair swept over his eye. Would his kiss be gentle or demanding? My body responded, and while I was afraid, I was also enthralled.

Such thoughts unsettled me, and I pushed them to the back of my mind and spent the hours writing, and reading. Comparing and contrasting Thoreau's written words with Bonnie's journals left me in a fluctuating state about Henry. Why had he failed to acknowledge my ancestor as an important part of his life? Did he even know of her burning desire for a child? What Bonnie revealed in her journal and what she told her partner *could* be two different things. Women weren't always truthful about their needs.

I couldn't judge Thoreau knowing only one side of the story. It was possible he was selfish, that he didn't care what Bonnie wanted or needed. I'd learned that truth when I was sixteen. But I refused to tar Thoreau with the same brush I'd used for Bryson Cappett, former classmate and heir apparent of the New England Cappetts. He'd been a brutal teacher in the expectations of love and lust.

Pushing aside my personal past, I put my focus for the day on recreating the 1850s and the life and rhythms of Concord. I'd read extensively about the time period and the area. If I closed my eyes I could visualize the gathering of the intellectuals and the discussions held in various parlors around town.

Emerson's emphasis on "trust thyself" flew in the face of the church, which demanded that sinners trust God. In the 1850s, self-reliance sounded like heresy to the religious. Self-reliance was something I'd learned early on, and perhaps it was one of the long tentacles that drew me to the Transcendentalists.

There was no God in the Kentucky where I grew up. At least not around my family. They lured the weak-minded and the helpless into their web of dependence, lining out the crushed oxy for a snort until the victim was truly hooked. Then the price went up and enslavement began. I'd seen a lot of people harvested by the Cahill clan. I still had nightmares about some of the events I'd witnessed.

Eventually, my thoughts were so depressing and the rain outside so cold and relentless, I decided to call it a night. I sipped a small glass of merlot and warmed my feet in front of the fire before sliding beneath the quilts and letting the amnesia of sleep take me.

Come morning, the weather had not improved. The relentless storm made my head throb. I worked sporadically for most of the day, but with little to show for my efforts. At last, I took three aspirin and climbed beneath the quilts and hid from the lightning and thunder.

The second night of the long rain I dreamed of my family, the ones still living in the Kentucky hills and hollers, and those long departed. The whalers. The men who took to the ocean in a tiny sailboat and brought back a mammal nearly the size of their ship. In my watery dreams, I heard the clicking of the whales and watched their amazing grace as they spun and circled, unaware that my kin meant to kill them.

And then I was one of the whales, a calf seeking my mother. I saw her, blood streaming from the harpoons, the ropes pulling her away.

I woke up briny. Sweating and crying. The emotion of the dream choked me as surely as the salt water of the ocean would have filled my lungs. It took a long time to calm my breathing and slow my heartbeat.

Vivid dreams had always haunted me, but I didn't need to study Jung to realize this last one was fraught with symbolism and personal pain. Like as not, I would never get over my mother's death and my father's abandonment. He didn't leave, physically, but he couldn't hold fast to me and a bottle. Whiskey won.

The day I'd left for boarding school, he'd stood on Granny Siobhan's front porch, arms crossed, tears streaming silently. "She's too sensitive, Caleb. The curse will destroy her. Amberton will teach her the difference between what's real and what she makes up. It's her only hope, to deaden the darkness with education."

Granny was set on having her way, and so I was sent away. The pain of separation would be worth the price. Distance and education would save me.

And my father had said not a word to stop me from getting into the truck with Cousin Willie for the drive to the bus station and the long ride to a place where I fit like a maggot amongst butterflies. I would never forget that he didn't even try to keep me home. I'd never been out of Kentucky, never had the luxury of high-speed Internet to broaden my horizons. Living in the mountains, nature had been my teacher. I was painfully unprepared for the sophistication of Amberton students.

These wounds festered and ruptured in my dreams. There would be no more sleep for me that night. I turned on the bedside lamp and reached for a book.

And then I saw the doll.

Someone had taken it from my coat pocket and set it on the foot of my bed, legs splayed wide. Propped against the footboard, Barbie stared at me with blank, lash-fringed eyes. Her red, red lips formed a pout. For a terrifying second I thought she would rise and stand on her own. She would walk toward me on legs with no knee joints, pointed chin and breasts aimed at my heart.

A terrified yell caught in my throat and I kicked the covers, sending Barbie flying across the room. I threw back the quilt and ran to pick her up off the floor. In an instant she was in the fireplace. Her hair caught first, and then her features began to melt. An awful stench came from the burning, blackened mass of fabric and molded vinyl.

Her long, tapered legs were the last to burn.

7

"Aine, darling, are you ill?" Dorothea came from behind the desk and pressed a cool hand to my forehead. "You've caught a fever, I think."

I'd awakened in full light to discover the cabin stinking with the smell of burned plastic. I remembered throwing the Barbie on the fire, but I couldn't remember why. Something to do with whales and harpoons. All I knew was that the images were borne in a fever. My throat felt like I'd swallowed glass, and something resembling a cement block had lodged in my sinuses.

"You don't have a doctor here, but I can recommend Dr. Frederika Wells. Excellent general practitioner. She'll fix you right up."

"I don't go to doctors." It was true. Dr. O'Gorman didn't count. He was a friend. Nine years had passed since my last appointment with a regular doctor. My health was excellent and I had no need of intrusive medical practices. Besides, I didn't trust the modern medicine men—or women. The profession had lost touch with the combination of mind, body, spirit that I believed kept things in balance. My only concession was an occasional visit to Dr. O'Gorman for my tension-related migraines. I'd started seeing him after the Cappett incident.

"You've got a temperature of at least a hundred and one. Maybe higher. You're congested, coughing, and only going to get worse. Best take a positive step and seek medical help before you get pneumonia. Think about it this way. Spend an afternoon waiting on the doctor now or three weeks recovering from a lung infection."

Dorothea had a way of putting things. "Can you call her?"

"I can." She beamed, having won the argument. "I'll call a cab to take you. I'd do it myself but I can't leave the desk. It's a good thing the sky is clear. A bit of sunshine, some antibiotics, a steroid shot, and you'll be right again in two days."

With that cheerful prediction, I climbed in the cab and rode to the doctor's office, which was, thankfully, only a few miles away.

Petite and animated, Dr. Wells seemed more suited to a perpetual cheerleader than a doctor. Ten minutes into her exam, I realized she was nobody's fool. She had read and memorized my chart.

After a steroid shot, prescriptions, and an admonition to get in bed and stay there, she freed me. Her intense scrutiny left me feeling vulnerable. Back in Kentucky, the doctor was called only hours before the undertaker. I suppose a healthy fear of medical practitioners was a good thing for a population that couldn't afford to pay for treatment.

I returned to my cabin and piled up in bed with my cough medicine, orange juice, and books. Iron bands locked my chest, restricting breathing. The cement block in my sinuses refused to budge, and a rattling cough made me fear I'd suffocate. Another dose of cough medicine eased me into sleep.

I found myself on Walden Pond, wandering the woods on a lush spring morning. It could have been 1850 or 2050, I couldn't tell by the soft hush of the forest and the beauty of the pond. Whatever the time period, the area was untouched by man, and the magnificence of nature was mine alone.

My hands traced the peeling bark of a plane tree, the smooth skin unlike any other. Energy hummed, emanating from the core of the tree. Behind me, someone coughed. I turned to find a bearded man dressed in trousers, braces, and a long-sleeved shirt.

"You should be in bed," he said. "A cough can be dangerous."

He proved his point with a wet hack that left blood on the palm of his hand when he tried to stifle it. He examined the lung hemorrhage with curiosity, then wiped his hand on his dark pants.

"Let me take you to the cabin." He caught my arm, and I realized for the first time that I wore tight-fitting sleeves that went with a long black dress. My feet were bare, a fact he disapproved of.

"You must care for yourself," he instructed. "I fear for you, Bonnie. You can't let them lure you out here. Impulsiveness can be the same as carelessness."

I didn't need to answer. He didn't expect me to speak.

"You can't risk your health." He led me through the trees to a clearing with a small wooden cabin. He assisted me inside and ushered me to a chair beside a stove. The weight of my belly was exhausting. Large and tight as the skin of a drum. Running my hand over it, I felt the thrum of new life.

Outdoors in the sun, I'd been warm enough. Now I was cold. He noticed and wrapped a blanket around me. His hands lingered on my shoulders, the warmth of his palms comforting and yet disquieting.

"I can't do this alone," I told him.

"We need nothing but each other." He kissed my cheek and pulled the blanket tighter around me. "Two against the world."

His words were both comforting and disquieting.

Knuckles rapping the door of the cabin pulled me up from the depths of sleep. I came to the surface of the dream sobbing. Obeying my first impulse, I clutched my flat stomach, greatly relieved that it wasn't swollen with child. The intensity of the nightmare was such that I had felt the pull of the unborn child's weight, the oceanic turning of the fetus in the womb so similar to the sensation of my other dream, that of a whale calf somersaulting in the Atlantic.

"Aine!" Patrick's voice called sharply. He must have been battering the door for some time.

"Coming." I pulled the sheet around me and went to the door. Patrick balanced a tray on one hand, the other aloft to knock again.

"Dorothea sent you hot soup, but it's likely cold now, since I've been pounding on your door for fifteen minutes." His tone was annoyed, but his gaze roved over my bare shoulders and down to my hand clutching the sheet. "Busy?" He looked past me into the room, no doubt expecting to find my lover.

"Put it on the table." I stepped back to allow him to enter and closed the door against the icy blast of wind. A spasm of coughing took hold of me and I doubled over.

"Hey!" Patrick had relieved himself of the tray and caught my shoulders in both hands, reigniting the memory of the dream. "Get yourself back in that bed!" He half-pushed, half-carried me. He pulled the covers high on my chest. "Woman, you don't have a tot of sense."

The coughing fit had passed, and I found myself amused at Patrick's concern. Whether feigned or real, he made me believe he was worried. "Thank you. I'll wear the cough out soon enough."

"Not if you stand half-naked in open doorways."

"Don't pretend you didn't enjoy it." I realized how flirtatious the words were as soon as I spoke, but there was no getting them back. Such behavior was wildly inappropriate, and shame heightened the heat in my face. "Thank you for bringing the soup."

"I'll get more wood." He struck a ridiculous pose and flexed a muscle. "I have the brawn to tend to the needs of a beautiful sick woman."

I laughed. I couldn't help it. The foolish exuberance of youth and good health amused me. His unrelenting attempts to seduce me were a delicious serving of flattery, but he knew, as I did, that it would come to nothing. "I'm not really sick. It's just a bad cold."

"It gives me pleasure to help you, so pretend to be a damsel in distress."

There was wisdom in his flippant sentence, and a truth I'd never faced head-on. "Stoke the fire." I waved a feeble hand. "And maybe you could feed me, too. I'm so weak I may expire." I slumped into a classic swoon.

"That's more like it." He brought the tray to the bed and lifted a spoonful of broth to my lips.

The intimacy silenced my tongue, but my heart pounded. I'd laid the challenge and he'd called my bluff. As the adult, I had to set the boundaries. He was a young man and Dorothea's surrogate son. She wouldn't be amused. It was up to me to control the situation. I was older, not to mention contagious.

I took the bowl and spoon. "Thank you, Patrick. You're a considerate young man."

"I'm not just a boy." He pushed my hair from my face. "You're beautiful, Aine."

I caught his hand. "Hardly. I'm a doctoral student worn to a frazzle. And I'm sick. I shouldn't flirt with you. It's wrong."

He made no attempt to touch me again, but he didn't leave the bedside. "Why are you so scared of feeling? Who hurt you?"

"I never took you for a sensitive young man."

He laughed at my honesty. "Just because I like girls and they like me back doesn't mean I'm thick as a brick wall. I've watched you. The way you're always alone, even around other people."

I put the soup on the bedside table. "You are observant. Right now, I'm focused on my work. That's the way it has to be. You're a handsome young man. I see the girls who come here to be near you. You can have your pick of all of them."

"I'm interested in you."

"You're wasting your time, Patrick. You only think you're interested because you know it's impossible."

"We'll see about that." He picked up the tray and left without a backward glance.

8

The fever passed and I met Joe at Walden Pond. The sky was blue and the sun was out. The snow had melted, but there was no doubt that winter had set in for good. Barrenness pervaded the scenery. Not unpleasant, but different from the dancing golden foliage I'd encountered when I'd first ventured around Walden.

Standing at the edge of the pond where I'd found the doll, I saw no sign of humanity except for the man beside me. We could have been dropped into a wilderness at any point in time. A songbird, which should have long been south for the winter, trilled a buzzy *sree* and a sharp whistle. Civilization might be a mile away, or a hundred.

Joe's thoughts must have run somewhat parallel to mine, because he said "Makes you wonder how Thoreau stood it, all by himself. He had to walk to town for human company and the weather often kept him barricaded in his cabin. I guess back then folks spent more time alone with their thoughts."

I held my peace. While my general dissertation topic was not privileged information, my groundbreaking revelation was. I had learned that for the area population, Thoreau was sacrosanct. Messing with his reputation could be like stirring a hornet's nest with a short stick. "You must be alone a good bit as a state ranger."

His deep laugh was confident. "Lots of time to read. I've always loved books. The more popular types. Writers with a story to tell."

"Most of our greatest writers were popular. Dickens, Shakespeare, Faulkner, Fitzgerald, Collins, Poe. They were storytellers first and foremost."

"Why are you studying Thoreau if you speak so fondly of the plotters? Thoreau wasn't much for story. Philosophy and thought."

Strangely enough, I wanted to share with him. "I have a family connection to Thoreau."

"Cryptic."

I couldn't help it, the laughter bubbled out. He'd hammered me with one word. "Okay, a family member knew Thoreau. I have some journals that give a unique perspective on him and his work."

"Care to give a few more details?" he asked.

"Absolutely not."

He considered that and wisely changed topics. "Are you over your cold?"

"I am, thank you." Our coats brushed against each other, sounding a little *zing*. I pointed. "This is the place." Focusing on the chore at hand seemed like the smartest action. My awareness of Joe was acute, so I turned my profile to him.

"What are you thinking, Aine?" he asked.

"Nothing of importance." I pulled my lips into a smile. Women who didn't smile weren't trustworthy, I'd learned.

"Oh, I doubt you have unimportant thoughts," he teased.

"I miss the snow." It was the first thing that popped into my head. I briskly rubbed my arms, though I wasn't cold. His scrutiny made me want to move, to run, to suck in big lungfuls of the cold crisp air and yell with the joy of being alive and able to feel. It was as if I'd stepped off solid ground into magic.

"You say there were no footprints where you found the doll?" Joe continued, unaware of my emotional turmoil.

"Are you implying that I'm a liar?" My response was out of left field. I had to get a grip on myself. "I'm sorry, I just don't like to be called a liar."

"That wasn't what I meant." His tone was patient. "It's a time issue. The Barbie was on top of the snow, you said. Yet the footprints had been covered by snow. It's a way to judge what time the doll was left. Speaking of which, did you bring it?"

"I burned it."

Disbelief pinched his face. "Why?"

How to explain that the doll had moved by itself onto my bed? If Joe thought the lack of footprints was hard to believe, the doll escaping my coat pocket and climbing onto the bed would prove I was nuts. "It unnerved me. Barbies objectify women. I offered her to you at the coffee shop. You should have taken her then if you wanted her." He'd been uninterested at the coffee shop, so why now?

What seemed to be relief swept across his features. "No, I didn't want the doll. I should have examined it, though. My fault, not yours."

"I overreacted. I'm sorry." I could help with a few details. "She wore the blue, white, and silver ball gown and shoes of the snow queen from *Swan Lake*. I don't think that's an official Barbie outfit, but it was exquisitely made."

"Official outfit?"

"Only one company makes official Barbies and her various outfits. When I was a kid, there was Shopping Barbie and Tango Barbie and Nurse Barbie. As far as I know, there wasn't a Snow Queen model. Not made by Mattel." I wasn't a Barbie expert. Dolls had never been my thing. I was more of a tomboy, but I'd done some research. "I think someone made the ball gown. Hand-stitched. Someone with a lot of skill."

He turned away and stared into the distance. "And you saw no one near here?"

"I've never seen anyone here. Except you."

He cupped a hand on my elbow. "Let's get you back to a warm place. You might be over the worst of the cold, but freezing won't do you any good."

I'd hoped for a hike around the pond, but my strength flagged even as we headed back to the little cabin that was a replica of the one where Thoreau and Bonnie lived. A docent was there to unlock it and welcome the tourists—an unlikely occurrence in the cold. Joe steered me to his car.

"Could we get a coffee?" I asked.

"Sure." His reaction was unreadable.

He drove to the Honey Bea and we hurried out of the cold and into the aroma of freshly ground coffee beans. Joe ordered two coffees and two sticky buns. "Very presumptuous," I said, but I took away the sting with a smile.

"You look like you lost twenty pounds while you were sick. And I'm starving. If you don't want yours, I'll eat both."

"You'll have to fight me."

We settled at a table and fell on the hot, sweet rolls as soon as they were served.

Our conversation centered on Thoreau and his writing. I let Joe talk, offering a few insights. We finished the food and coffee, and he rose to take me home.

At the cabin, he stopped me before I got out of his truck. "Have dinner with me tonight."

His invitation caught me unprepared. I had no ready excuse, and didn't want to turn him down. Conflicting emotions assailed me. It was a mistake to accept the date, but I was lonely. I'd been by myself for a long time. And I liked Joe. Maybe too much. "Okay."

"I'll pick you up at six and we'll drive into Boston. Have a few drinks at Bayside Bill's, then dinner at Filbert's. How does that sound?"

"Perfect." My dating experience with men was limited, but I liked that he knew how to arrange an evening. He made the choices and asked if I wanted to go along. None of the waffling of modern men. "Casual?" I wasn't familiar with either establishment, but Joe didn't strike me as a tie-and-tails kind of man.

"You named it." He opened his door but before he could exit the truck, I popped out. "See you at six."

9

In Bayside Bill's, the Bay State accents were as ubiquitous as the beers sliding down the bar. It was a rambunctious place filled with loud laughter and cheers for a televised football game. Celtic music floated in the background—tin whistle, drum, and fiddle. Among the raucous crowd, Joe was known and well-liked. Men came to our table to slap him on the back and check me out. New blood. It wasn't a bad feeling.

A pretty redhead at the bar felt otherwise. If looks could kill, I would be skewered to the wall with a spear in my heart. Joe had a sweetheart, whether he liked it or not.

"Who is she?" I asked, staring at her. She refused to back down, even when I'd caught her glaring.

"Her name is Karla Steele." A flush touched his cheeks. I couldn't tell if it was embarrassment or anger.

Karla Steele had pretty eyes, nice hair, a good figure. "What went wrong?"

Joe touched my hand, the first intimacy of the evening. "I wouldn't have come here if I'd known she was here. Please just ignore her. She's not . . . stable."

"In that she might come over here and pull my hair for dating her beau?" I meant to be flip, but my attempt at humor failed.

"She's liable to do more than pull your hair, Aine. She's an unhappy person and she has to blame someone. Right now, I'm her target."

"What's the quote? 'Hell had no fury. . . .' Did you spurn her?"

"When I realized she was mentally unbalanced, I stopped dating her. She didn't take it well."

"She still wants you." Her desire was palpable. It rose off her in waves. I looked away, disconcerted. She wasn't someone to mess with. Unstable people were extremely dangerous. They'd as likely chop off a hand or sever an Achilles tendon as spit in someone's soup. It all depended on what mood they were in.

"She seeks reasons to be angry. Then the anger justifies her bad behavior. I'm topping her list right now. I didn't do anything wrong or dishonorable," he added defensively.

She clearly didn't see it that way. I was unreasonably sensitive to her rage and frustration, and that troubled me. "Maybe we should go."

And so we did. Filbert's was quieter, but by no means stuffy. White linen covered our table, where we ate the traditional fare of haddock and trimmings. Joe ordered a good bottle of crisp white wine, and we savored the meal and made small talk.

When we were almost finished, I asked, "How did you and Karla meet?"

"At a basketball game. I haven't seen her around for months. I thought she'd left town." Joe frowned. "I haven't been to Boston in a while. I've had a lot to do at Walden."

"Dorothea said you'd returned to the area after an absence. Did you leave because of Karla?"

He hesitated, looking down at his plate. "I came back to the Concord area because my mother was very ill. I'm an only child, and she needed care. There was an opening for a ranger at Walden, so I took it. Last spring, Mother died. Karla came along when I was adjusting to my mother's death. We dated for several months before I ended it."

"I'm sorry about your mother, Joe. You must have been close."

"She never let me down. She believed in me. That's an invaluable thing, Aine."

"Yes." Granny Siobhan had always believed in me. "Was she sick for a long time?"

"Cancer. She died by degrees."

My hand found his, a touch of sympathy. "That's a hard thing. I'm sure you were a comfort and help. She was lucky to have you."

He withdrew his hand and looked out the window at the lights of the city. "On good days, I can pretend that was true."

"What do you mean?"

He stood. "Excuse me a moment. I'll be back." He dodged through the tables toward the men's room. There was some darkness in his past, and pain. Maybe one day he'd tell me.

When he returned, he'd found his composure and a rueful smile. "So you came to Walden to finish your dissertation. And with your Ph.D., you'll apply to teach? Around here?"

"Getting the doctorate is the first step. I'll worry about a job when I have the degree. I'm footloose and fancy-free. I can move anywhere there's a good job."

"What about your family?"

"Mostly dead. At least the ones I cared about. No one back in Kentucky is thinking I'll come home."

"We're on the loose, the two of us." He offered his wine glass for a toast.

After the clink, I asked "Why'd you break up with Karla?" It was a nosy question, but a fair one. Karla was furious. Maybe she had cause.

"I really liked her. We had fun together." He spun the golden wine in his glass. "One night I got a text from an old friend. A female. Karla must have been checking my cell phone. She just lost it. Went completely crazy, saying I was cheating on her. It was like she turned into someone I didn't know. Someone frighteningly irrational and out of control. That's when I realized she was abusing drugs. I confronted her and she said she'd stop. Later, she attacked me while I was asleep. Slugged me. Hard. That's why you should steer clear of her."

I'd seen that kind of crazy behavior from people hopped up on meth or spice or any number of drug combinations. Once the addiction was set, they'd try any substance to relieve the need. "Do you really believe she'd come after me?"

He reached for my hand and held it. His thumb moved across my knuckles, soothing, exciting my skin. "No. I don't. But Karla isn't a bear you want to bait. Stay away from her, and if you see her, go the other direction. Why risk a confrontation?"

"Thanks." The lightest anger simmered at the fact Joe had dragged Karla into even the fringes of my world. "I need a Karla in my life. Things are just too calm." My sarcasm was clear.

His grip on my hand tightened. "I'm sorry. Honestly, I haven't seen her in months. I broke it off with her that night. I haven't responded to her phone calls, e-mails, or texts. I've done everything I know to make it clear I have no interest in seeing her."

Great, Karla was an obsessive, psycho witch. Then I realized I was being unfair. Hell, my entire family was as irrational and crazy as Karla. That was the pot calling the kettle black. "Don't worry about it. I can handle myself."

"Let's hope Karla stays in my past where she belongs." He turned my hand over, studying the palm. "I was sweet on her. I admit it. Makes you wonder if you ever really know another person. I mean behind the mask, beneath the public skin that everyone wears. Every single one of us is capable of things we never suspect until the moment is upon us."

10

I heard nothing from Joe for a week. Thoughts of him interrupted my work. The weather held, crisp and beautiful. Instead of my morning walk around Walden Pond to connect with my muse—I didn't want to appear to chase after Joe—I stayed in the cabin or wandered the inn's grounds.

The date had concluded satisfactorily. He brought me home and walked me to the door. He'd kissed my cheek, his lips lingering before they brushed over my lips. And he'd left.

Had I done something wrong? Had I said something to push Joe away? The foolish questions of my insecure inner child niggled in my brain.

Dorothea didn't help. She asked me every morning at breakfast if Joe and I had plans for the evening.

"He's smitten with you, that much is clear to see," she said on the sixth morning as she poured coffee into my cup. "I just wonder why he's not knocking on your door. That boy has always been a little on the strange side."

"I have more important things to worry about than my dating life."
I sounded as priggish and stupid as a dime-novel heroine.

"Yeah, I see that." Dorothea winked at me. "You're wandering
around like a moonstruck teenager. I don't miss much. And I see how
Patrick sniffs after you. He's a good kid, but he likes to fancy himself
a real Don Juan. Don't hurt him. He's got it bad for you."

"He's a kid."

"And a fanciful one at that. He thinks playing the great lover
would make him a man. He'll get his heart broken if he isn't careful.
Just be aware he's built up a fantasy around you. He's pretty naïve.
He'll swagger and talk big about his conquests, but the reality is he's
inexperienced. And he is sweet on you. First love is always painful."

"I'll keep that in mind. Thanks for letting me know the score."

"Now Joe, he's perfect for you. Women today go on and on about
career," she said. "But when push comes to shove, we all want a man
we can rely on. The yin to our yang, the fish to our chips, if you get
my drift. We desire the *other*, the essential completion of ourselves
into a whole. I look at Joe, and I see the things you lack." She winked
again and went on her way.

After I finished my breakfast, I struck out for town on foot. I
needed copy paper, a new ink cartridge for my printer, and a few
simple office supplies. My solitary wanderings had begun to yield
results. The thesis was taking shape. Once it was outlined, I would
turn to finding sources to prove Bonnie's existence.

The day was brisk and sunny with white clouds scuppering across
a deep blue sky. I yearned for Walden Pond, but I had chores to do,
and I didn't want Joe to think I was stalking him. Perhaps I'd end up
in a story he told his next date about an avid academician who simply
couldn't bear to let him go.

His comments about Karla were not unkind, but his demeanor had
been clear—he didn't want her and she refused to accept it. Pathetic
was a worse label than prude. Karla was pathetic.

All the same, once I invoked Karla's name, I couldn't shake the idea
he'd spent time with her recently. He said she was unstable, which was

often code for sexually exciting. Unstable people lacked the inhibitions and restraints of normal people.

The cuticle of my ring finger beaded with bright red blood. Fretting, I'd picked it to the quick. I had to switch my mind off Joe and Karla. Determined to regain control of my mental energy, I entered an office supply store. Ten minutes later, an ink cartridge, highlighting pens in several colors, gel-tip black pens, clips, and Post-it notes were snuggled in a recyclable shopping bag. Not a huge haul, but enough of a financial setback to make me hesitate over an expensive coffee and sticky bun at the Honey Bea. The sacrifices I made for my education!

While I was in town, I ambled over to Cassidy's Vintage Resale. I loved vintage clothing, and New England had the best shops I'd ever seen. Most mountain people in Kentucky were poor. Dresses were utilitarian by design and worn out by the number of hand-me-downs. A Sunday dress might last three generations in the same family.

Photos of my female relatives showed women with clear gray eyes, glossy dark hair, high cheekbones, long-fingered hands, and severe dresses, none with the slightest frill. "Pretty for the sake of pretty" seemed to be considered sinful. The Cahill clan nurtured some far-fetched ideas about sin and redemption. In between the two, the Cahill Curse waited to spring upon the unsuspecting.

The dress shop smelled of lavender soap and vanilla. I migrated to a sale rack, where a beautiful sage-green silk dress caught my eye. The ruched bodice was tucked with tiny pearls, and the hem floated free and swingy above the ankle. Holding it against my chest, I consulted a mirror.

"It's the perfect color for your eyes," the saleswoman said with a well-aimed strike at my weakness. The dress brought out the dark green streaks in my irises, my one vanity.

"Thanks." I checked the tag and put it back on the rack. Right size, wrong price.

"If you lived in Salem two hundred years ago, you'd find yourself hanging at the end of a rope." The clerk laughed nervously. "It's your eyes. During the witch trials, people were hanged for a lot less than unusual eye color." She went behind the counter and brought out a book on Salem's infamous witch trials and hangings. "Sorry, it's been slow today and I've been reading too much."

She was my age or maybe younger, a pert woman with dimples and smooth, pink skin. Her make-up was elegant and understated. The ring on her finger told me she had both a career and a private life. "Innocent men and women were murdered, all in the name of stopping Satan." She opened the book and read: "To spot a witch you must look for the mark of Satan upon her body. A mole or mark, a crooked finger, the unusual coloration of the eyes." She put the book down. "Beautiful could get you in a lot of trouble, I guess."

I cast a glance in the mirror. The dress seemed to focus the light directly into my eyes. Maybe a spell had been cast on it. "And I thought green eyes weren't unusual."

She shrugged. "Any reason was good enough to accuse someone of consorting with demons and the devil. Green eyes like yours, marbled with light and dark. Pretty extraordinary."

"Good to know. I'll steer clear of Salem."

She laughed, a bubbly sound of fun. "The witch trials were a long time ago. 1700s, I think."

"Actually, the witch trials were held from 1688 through 1692, and in many cases they were about property." I'd researched this topic in gender studies classes. "The women who died were mostly land-owning widows. The cheapest route to land acquisition was to accuse them of witchcraft and steal their property for a pittance when they were dead."

The sales clerk frowned. "That's not in the history books. Not this one, anyway."

"History is written by the victors. The dead women didn't have a chance to tell their side of the story. At any rate, allowing hysterical children to testify against helpless widows eventually backfired. When the children began accusing the rich, the trials were shut down."

She studied me openly. "You're not from here, but you sure know a lot. Are you a teacher?"

I shook my head. "Not yet."

"You have a funny accent."

I'd tried to eradicate backwoods Kentucky from my diction, but not as successfully as I'd hoped. My "hick" accent had made me a target in boarding school and even into my undergraduate years. Reading aloud in class was comparable to taking a beating.

Now, I didn't care. My accent, though diluted by years of Massachusetts, was a point of pride. Perhaps I'd go back to a good school in the South. Emerson or Duke or Tulane in the City that Care Forgot. Anywhere but Kentucky.

"I'm from Harlan County, Kentucky," I said with a rural twang.

"But you're smart." She covered her mouth with her hand. "Sorry, that came out wrong."

"No need to apologize for falling victim to a stereotype." I'd become immune to people's accidental cruelty.

"Try the dress on." She'd wisely moved to a new topic.

I slipped it from the rack, held it up to my chest, and stared at my image in the tri-fold mirror. If I put it on, I'd have to own it. The dress was that gorgeous. Better to walk away now. I had no occasion for such elegance.

"You won't know if you don't try it on. I might see my way clear to marking it down another twenty percent."

The dressing room was large, with a chair and three mirrors. My fingers slowly worked the pearl buttons, and soon the dress floated down over my head. I stepped out to see how I moved in it.

"It's perfect." Awe inflected the clerk's tone. "As if it were made for you."

The mirror agreed. Nothing I'd ever worn had shown my hair, skin, eyes, and figure to better advantage. "I'll take it."

How I would pay my credit card bill at the end of the month was another matter, but when I left the shop, the dress was in a box under my arm.

I window-shopped at the hardware store and the pharmacy, where Christmas ornaments had already nudged Thanksgiving aside.

"Hey! Hey, you! Bitch!"

I turned to see Karla striding toward me. She wore black tights, high-heeled boots, and a purple coat with fake purple fur around the hood. I assumed she wore a skirt of some kind, but I couldn't swear to it. Micro-mini?

I ignored her and moved down to a florist's window, all a-dazzle with glittery red, green, and white sparkling bows and red and white poinsettias.

"Bitch, don't walk away when I'm calling you."

I didn't want to, but I faced her. She was alone, and I couldn't think of a single thing to say.

"So you're the one Joe has taken up with."

"You should speak to him." I did an about-face and started walking.

She caught up to me and gripped my upper arm with enough strength to bite through my thick jacket. "If I wanted to talk to Joe, I'd be in his face. I'm speaking to you. It's a pretty simple message. Stay away from him."

"Or what?" I wrenched loose and put my packages down at my feet. Anger simmered, a silvery liquid coursing through my body. I hadn't grown up with brothers, but I'd had cousins, and I'd learned to protect myself. Fighting was a survival tool.

"I'll kick your ass back to whatever redneck place you came from." Karla clenched her fists.

"Give it your best shot." I spoke softly, a deceptive tactic my cousin Wally taught me in grade school. Lure them closer, then cut loose.

"You daring me?" Karla was smart enough to be wary. She'd expected me to run.

"Yeah. I am. You want to start shit with me, bring it on. Right now." I hadn't been in a fight since my first year at boarding school. The girl who'd jumped me went home and never came back. She had to be fitted for a bridge.

Karla edged sideways instead of forward, as if to corner me. "Stay away from Joe. That's what I want to tell you."

All bluff and no action. I bent down for my packages. The blow to the back of my neck was unexpected, and painful. Only the thickness of my coat collar saved me from serious injury.

I forced myself upright and punched her hard in the face. There was a crack and blood blossomed on her face. Her squawk sounded like a mortally wounded seagull. I stood and watched as she sank to the sidewalk. Someone started screaming, and people ran out of shops and then stopped, unsure what to do.

"Press charges," I told Karla, "and I'll make it a point to find you." I picked up my packages and headed back toward the inn.

"You think you know Joe." Her voice was blubbery from blood, snot, and tears. "Ask him about Mischa. Just ask him."

11

By the time I reached the inn, I'd stopped shaking. I'd exploded in violence—like one of my hopped-up relatives. I'd crawled away from the oxy trade, the guns, the beatings, but I hadn't left it behind me. It was part of my DNA. Aggression and addiction, a few birth defects and mental instability, these were the hallmarks of the Cahill clan. There wasn't a substance invented that a Cahill couldn't grow dependent on, except maybe money. No matter how much of it a Cahill earned, it never stayed around.

Through the long years of my education, I'd worked in fast food, clerked in hardware stores, and nannied for families who could afford the luxury. I'd sold myself cheap to survive. I'd changed my hair, my clothes, my diction. I'd beaten back the dark superstitions, the fantastical visions that had plagued me as a child. Granny Siobhan told me that educated people knew such things weren't real and that if I ignored them, they would go away. Midnight fancies were buried along with my past.

I'd worked hard to reinvent myself, but scratch the surface and the Cahill violence leaked out. My thoughts were black, and my self-loathing grew as I bypassed the inn and went down the path through the woods to my cabin. I saw the note pinned to the door before I got there.

We need to talk. Joe.

Simple as that. I hadn't heard from him in a week and now he wanted to talk. Another wave of anxiety and anger passed through my limbs, but I contained it. It had taken years to gain the composure necessary to navigate the pettiness of academia without physically assaulting someone. A temper could be a fatal flaw in that environment. And now I'd had a brawl on a public street. Because of Joe.

Maybe not because of him. It wasn't fair to attribute Karla's crazy behavior to Joe. It also wasn't fair that she had accosted and ambushed me. Still, I knew I'd likely have plenty of time to rue my hasty action.

But not as much time as I thought. The knock on my door a few minutes later was official and demanding. When I looked out the window, I saw a uniformed officer with Dorothea at his heels. Curiosity was clearly killing her.

"Miss Cahill?" the officer asked when I opened the door.

"Yes."

"Please come with me. You're wanted for questioning in an assault charge."

This development wasn't unexpected, but I still felt as if I'd been gut-kicked by a mule. "Let me get my purse."

I put on my coat and preceded the officer onto the porch.

"What's this all about?" Dorothea asked.

The officer ignored her, so I answered. "I was in an argument with Joe's ex-girlfriend. Could you call him?"

"You bet." She hurried back to the inn, and I followed the officer to his car.

Just as I ducked my head to get into the patrol car's back seat, a slender figure appeared in the shadow of the trees not fifty yards away. She wore a puffy red coat with a hood and black pants. Her size, the slenderness of her legs, told me it was a female.

"Who is that?" I asked.

"Where?" The officer turned toward the trees, but the figure had vanished.

"It was a child. Over by that big fir."

"Probably someone from the inn." He closed the door and slid behind the steering wheel.

A second later we were gliding away from the inn. I twisted in the back seat and tried to examine the woods. A streak of red shifted between the dark tree trunks. She was still there. She didn't want to be seen by anyone but me.

⚓

The bare green walls in the holding room were marked with brown stains that could have been dried blood or other bodily effluvium. Every corner was crusted with filth and dust. The place hadn't been thoroughly cleaned in at least a decade. Justice in Concord was neither swift nor sanitary.

A particular wall blotch put me in mind of Granny Siobhan's birthmark. Another spray of reddish brown reminded me of a pod of whales. No matter where I found myself, I was never far from my heritage.

I'd been alone for the better part of an hour, waiting to be questioned. Waiting to be charged. Waiting for the words that could end my academic career. I doubted I could get a job teaching with a conviction for assault and battery on my record. What would I do with myself if no school would hire me? The answer was a black void.

"Look, Ms. Cahill was defending herself." Joe's voice funneled down the police department's main corridor. Dorothea had been as good as her word.

"I have witnesses," Joe said. "Cassidy Holmes saw the whole thing. Karla Steele accosted Ms. Cahill and struck her in the back of the neck. Aine was only defending herself. If anyone should press charges, it should be Aine."

The mumble of the officer wasn't clear.

"She cannot have this on her record," Joe said. "A conviction for assault could jeopardize her future career."

More mumbling.

"Charge her, and you open the city to a lawsuit. Karla Steele isn't rational, and you know it. Look up *her* record before you make a big mistake."

The hubbub died down and I was left to walk the width of the small green room with minimalist furnishings—a table and two chairs. I wondered if there were cameras or audio devices so they could hear and watch me. I didn't care. Pacing wasn't a criminal act.

After an eternity, the door opened and Joe came in. "I'm sorry," he said. "This is my fault." An officer stood at the door, looking in. Joe closed it.

My temper had cooled enough that I didn't respond with mayhem. Practicality was my new mode. "I need a lawyer."

He shook his head. "No. Karla dropped the assault charge. I just talked with her."

My heart thudded against my ribs, and the inexplicable pressure of tears built. I was suddenly furious once again. Tears were ridiculous. "She got what she wanted, didn't she? Your attention."

"Not in the way she wanted, I assure you." Anger pulsed in a jaw muscle. "I'll make this right for you, Aine."

Watching the pain shift across his features, I didn't doubt his apology. I couldn't hold him responsible for Karla's actions even though I wanted to. "Who's Mischa?"

Had I slapped him, he could not have jerked back more sharply. "Who told you?"

"Told me what?"

"Who told you to ask about her?"

"Karla. Who is Mischa? Another girlfriend?"

"God no." His hands splayed on the desk. "We'll talk about this when we get out of here."

"Why not now?"

"Because it's private, and this is a police interrogation room. Can we leave it until I get you home?"

I considered. His reaction made me want to pursue the matter, but pushing him into a corner wouldn't yield results. "Okay."

"Let's go." He tapped on the door and it opened. When he stood aside, I walked out. The police department hummed with activity, but several officers looked up.

"Golden Gloves contender," an officer said as I passed.

I didn't bother to respond. I only wanted to step into the sunshine and go home.

"I'll take you to the cabin," Joe volunteered.

I didn't own a car, and walking in the cold from the police station was out of the question. I got into his truck and stared out the window as the town passed. Joe drove straight back to the cabin.

"None of this will be on your record," he said. "It was clearly self-defense. Cassidy from the vintage store gave a statement. So did Mr. Black in the pharmacy. They saw it all."

"Maybe I'll press charges against her." It was a tempting thought.

"Let it go, Aine. Just let it go. Karla is leaving for Nebraska to spend some time with her sister. She's using again, and she's out of control. Maybe, with some help, she can get a grip on herself."

I reached for the door handle, but I didn't open it. I needed closure on this, but I didn't know what would give me the measure of satisfaction I required. "You put me in a situation where I could have been hurt."

"I promise you, I had no idea Karla was in the area. I took her to Bayside Bill's one time. I haven't been there in months. It never crossed my mind she'd lurk there."

He was almost bleeding sincerity. He'd asked me on a date. He wasn't psychic. He couldn't have known Karla the Psycho would stake out that particular bar.

"Okay. I need to let it go."

His hand touched my shoulder. "I am sorry, Aine."

"Me, too." Sorry for my actions. "Will she be okay?" I couldn't bring myself to say her name.

"Yes."

"No details?"

He swiveled in the truck seat. "Her nose wasn't broken, but you did a number on it. She'll think twice before she jumps anyone again." His grin was unexpected. "She'll probably look like a raccoon for a few weeks."

"With any luck at all." I softened the statement with a roll of my eyes.

"Aine, she's unstable. And she has a drug problem. Once I realized how bad it was, I stopped seeing her."

"She hasn't given up on you."

He put both hands on the wheel and forced himself to relax. "Can I come inside and talk with you?"

Sitting in the cold truck was silly. Smoke rose from the cabin chimney—Patrick must have laid a fire for me. "Okay." My body didn't move exactly the way I anticipated, and I stumbled getting out. Joe was at my side in a flash. He held my elbow as he guided me to the steps.

It took me a minute to see the package leaning against the door. Patrick must have left me a surprise. My run-in with the cops probably garnered his sympathy and made me even more attractive to him—young men loved a rebel. The brown-paper-wrapped box was light. I shook it and something inside rustled.

"A secret admirer?" Joe asked.

"I don't know." After the day I'd had, a gift would be a pleasure. I unwrapped the box, while Joe put another log on the fire and stoked it up.

The paper fell away in the flickering light of the fire. When I opened the box, I heard my breath rush out. My fingers lost control, and the box dropped to the cabin floor. A beautiful red ball gown, perfect for a Valentine Barbie, splashed against the cream rug.

"Who sent it?" Joe snatched the box and wrapping from the floor and examined them. There was no name, note, or mark. I'd already checked.

"Who did this?" He strode to the door and looked out, but I knew the gift-giver was long gone. I'd seen her in the woods as I was being taken to the police department. The child had come back and left me a present. To go with the doll she'd placed in the snow for me.

The idea of it made my heart pound with an emotion I couldn't identify.

"Holy shit!" Joe dropped the box and wrapping like they'd burned him.

"What?" I bent down to retrieve them, but Joe's grip stopped me. "What is it?"

"Don't touch it." He didn't ask, he told.

In no mood to follow orders, I reached again. He clenched my wrist firmly. "There's something dead in the box." He eased me onto the sofa. "I'll take care of it."

"Take care of *what*?"

"A bird," he said. "A little canary." He took the box and wrapper outside. When he came back in, his hands were empty.

"Why would she do that?" I didn't understand. The doll and the ball gown were gifts. Things a child would value and share. But a dead bird? A pet? Why would she leave that for me?

"She? Who did this?" Joe asked. "If you know, please tell me."

I had no answer. "I've only caught a glimpse of her here and there. A child . . . she watches me. I don't know why she runs wild in the woods. She should be in school."

"Describe her."

"I've never seen her up close. Today, she had on a red snow coat. She was barely visible in the trees. When the police car carried me off, she ran through the woods after me. She was so fast."

Joe sat beside me. "Could it have been . . . Karla?"

His words changed everything. Karla was petite. Perhaps it had never been a child. Perhaps it was Joe's ex-lover spying on me, leaving me things to upset me. Not gifts, but wicked talismans.

Joe's arm attempted to pull me against him. "I'll handle this. I promise."

I resisted, then yielded. His body was solid and warm, and I realized again how much I enjoyed a man's touch.

"Can I make you some tea?" he asked.

"Wine."

If surprised by my early cocktail hour, he didn't show it. He took two glasses from the cupboard and poured from the open bottle of red on the counter. Settling again on the couch, he eased me into the crook of his arm.

"I'll make this up to you, Aine."

"How long do you think Karla has been spying on me? And why would she leave a doll?" I didn't even want to consider she'd been inside the cabin—the night the doll moved from the desk onto my bed. It was such a violation, I couldn't say it aloud.

"She's messed up. I don't know." Frustration laced his voice.

No point asking if she'd hurt me. I already had the answer to that. "How can I stop her?"

"My hope is she'll board the bus to Nebraska. I bought the ticket and gave it to her." He stroked my hair gently. "We could get a restraining order."

"Those are worthless when a psycho is involved. No." I was done with police stations.

"Let's go to the inn and have some supper," Joe suggested.

The idea held no appeal. The knots in my stomach had killed my appetite, and I didn't want to answer Dorothea's thousand questions about the experience of being hauled to the P.D., even if I hadn't been arrested. "I'm not hungry, but I'd like another glass of wine."

Joe obliged, and refilled his glass while he was up.

"Let's stay by the fire." The wine relaxed me, and I let my head rest against his shoulder. Watching the flames leap and crackle, I pushed all thoughts away. The crisp wine, the heat from the fire, Joe's scent—a woodsy, smoky odor that reminded me of long-ago nights when bonfires were part of my coming-of-age. Those nights had held magic, and it was lucky that I wasn't married to some upper-level participant of my family's drug empire. Nothing like danger, daring, and rebellion to a fourteen-year-old child.

"The wine was a good idea." Joe's lips were close to my ear. So close, his breath tickled and sent a chill down my neck.

My brain signaled a warning, but I shut it off. It had been a rotten day, and the one thing I didn't want to be was alone. Or to think. I wanted to feel. I'd been so careful. I'd denied myself so much. Now, I wanted to feel the touch of a man. It had taken me some time to get over Bryson Cappett—for a long time I didn't trust the physical needs of my body. Still, those compulsions were hard to resist, and I'd had lovers in undergraduate and graduate school. Fellow students involved in the intensity and competitiveness of academics. Young men who shared the bond of literature and language. But I'd kept my heart safe. Joe made me want to risk again.

I twisted at the waist and kissed him with demanding hunger, and he responded in kind. I pushed him against the arm of the couch and let my hands mold his body. He was solid, a grown man. And he also liked control. He shifted me into his arms and lifted me. In a moment we were in the bed.

Though I tried to hurry him, he took his time undressing me. Where I would have rushed, he forced me to wait, tantalizing me with a whisper of a touch, a deliberate kiss. Whatever else Joe might be, he knew how to drive me to madness.

I tore at his clothes, but he pinned me down and continued his torment. At last we moved together in the age-old rhythm, and I came again and again. He turned me inside out.

When at last we were spent, he refilled our wine glasses and returned to my bed. "This wasn't the way I expected the evening to end," he said.

I thought I heard amusement in his voice, but I couldn't see his face. The fire had burned too low to cast light. Darkness had descended over us. "Are you disappointed?" I asked.

His answer was a soft chuckle. "Are you kidding? I've never experienced such passion. Aine, you're a sorceress."

"Hardly that. You shouldn't stoke a fire unless you're prepared for the heat."

He laughed and leaned over to kiss me. "I should go home, but I'm not certain my legs will ever work again."

"Don't leave me, Joe." I wasn't afraid, exactly. But I balked at spending the night alone. If Karla was watching my cabin, I didn't want another encounter with her. As long as Joe was beside me, she couldn't hurt me.

"You know Dorothea will make it her business to check and see if my truck stays."

"And what will she do with that information?"

"Gossip, perhaps."

"I don't live in Concord. You do. Does it make a difference to you? Maybe you can convince her you were guarding me against your ex-girlfriend."

"And that wouldn't be much of a stretch." He sank back against the pillow. His arm slipped behind me and he snuggled me against his side. My fingers idly traced the contour of his stomach. He worked out. A perfect physical specimen.

I drained my wine glass and kissed his jaw. His thumb brushed across my nipple. Just like that, we were ready for round two.

12

A loud knock at the door dragged me from the soundest sleep I'd had in years. Curled against Joe, I felt anchored, solid, safe. Sleeping alone had always seemed dangerous, as if my physical body might not be held by gravity, might float away.

Joe was real and weighty. I pushed my head into him and pulled the covers over my ears. Dorothea could see Joe's truck parked outside. She had to know I wasn't alone. Maybe when she realized I wasn't going to satisfy her curiosity, she'd take the hint and leave.

The knock came again, this time more forceful.

"Shit, shit, shit." I rolled away from Joe. He was awake too, but it wasn't his place to answer my door.

I pulled the top quilt off the bed and wrapped it around myself. I yanked open the door and was struck speechless. Patrick stood outside bearing a huge tray of food and an amused look. "Dorothea thought you two might have worked up an appetite. When you didn't show for breakfast, she asked the cook to prepare this. We have waffles,

Vermont maple syrup, bacon, coffee, and cranberry mimosas." He pushed the tray at me.

If I grasped it, I'd have to release the quilt. My dilemma widened his grin. "I can bring it in," he offered.

"No." Though everyone obviously knew what had transpired between me and Joe, they hadn't seen any real evidence. They were left with only prurient interest and speculation. Joe, in my bed, was physical fact.

Patrick put the tray down and scooted it across the threshold. "Enjoy." He backed across the porch, started down the steps, then stopped. A worried look replaced his grin. "Someone cut your screen."

"What?"

He walked to the window that gave a clear view of the bedroom. "The screen has been sliced and looks like someone tried to jimmy your window."

"Let me get some clothes on." Behind me, I heard Joe's feet hit the floor and the jangle of his belt as he slid into his pants.

I set the breakfast tray on the cabin table and dressed in yesterday's clothes. They were the easiest thing to find, scattered across the floor. Joe went outside first. As I tied my shoes, I heard the low murmur of male voices. When I joined them, Joe was ashen.

"Karla won't give this up. She's worse than I thought."

"You've got yourself a jealousy problem," Patrick said. His smirk made me want to slap him. "Karla's buzzing with a bee in her bonnet."

"How can I stop her?" I asked Joe.

"You should press charges for the assault yesterday." The tension in his lips betrayed how worried he was. "A restraining order won't do much good. She can only be arrested if she violates it, and she might hurt you before anyone could come to your assistance."

"You think she'll try to hurt me?" I leaned against a porch post, dizzy at the prospect of a mentally ill woman plotting to cause me suffering.

"I'm afraid she will. Karla wasn't like this when we dated. Not at first. She's into something. Maybe meth. Maybe something worse. We have to take whatever actions are necessary to protect you."

I didn't need this. Not at all. "Are you certain Karla cut the screen?"

He pointed to markings where a tool, like a screwdriver, had been inserted under the window. "Somebody was trying to get in, Aine. Who would have an interest in what you were doing, other than Karla?"

"No one." The words were little more than a whisper. I was scared. Awake, I could defend myself. But if I was asleep and Karla got inside, she could hurt me before my defenses were up. And she'd gotten in once before, because I hadn't been careful about locking the door.

"Was that crazy bitch watching you while—" Patrick laughed. "Man, that's kinky."

"Shut up." Karla watching while Joe and I made love was disgusting. And sick.

"This isn't funny," Joe snapped. "I'll speak with the police chief. This will be taken care of, Aine. Don't worry."

But I couldn't stop worrying. I'd been the target of mean girls in boarding school. They'd been relentless in their teasing and pranks, all of which the administration viewed as girlish high spirits. I knew better. Scrawling filthy words on my clothes in red lipstick, stealing my underwear and leaving them around campus, laughing whenever I walked by. Those acts were designed to drive me from school, to make me feel the brunt of being an outsider, unwanted. This was the same. Karla wanted me banished from Walden Pond, away from Joe. And she'd already demonstrated her willingness to use physical force.

"I want her gone." I said it clearly.

"I'll see to it," Joe said. His arms pulled me tight. "This will end. Right now," he whispered into my ear. "The police will come and take fingerprints. In a way, this is the best thing that could have happened. Karla's lost touch with rational thought. This will prove it and they can pick her up. Maybe she'll accept help."

Help for her wasn't my priority. Loading her on a fast bus to Nebraska was more what I had in mind. If not that, then behind bars.

"Better eat your breakfast," Patrick reminded us. "You'll need something hot in your belly to deal with this."

Joe grasped my elbow and assisted me back into the house. He closed the door in Patrick's face.

13

Joe went into town to talk with the chief, and I tried to focus on my work. Crime-scene technicians arrived to take prints, but there were none. She'd worn gloves. She might be crazy, but she wasn't stupid. The techs deduced that the tool used on the window was a cat's paw, a type of crowbar small enough to fit in a large coat pocket or purse.

Patrols searched for Karla, but she'd obviously squirreled herself away in a hidey-hole.

At three o'clock, I could stand it no longer and walked to Walden Pond. The brisk air and a bit of exercise did more to clear my head than anything else. Images from the night flashed in front of me, blocking out the passing cars, the road to the pond. With each pulse of my heart, I witnessed the firelight playing on Joe's muscled back as his shoulder blades drew together and expanded. My omniscient vantage point allowed me to watch his face and mine tighten and relax in pleasure. My hands rippled over his ribs, my fingernails lightly digging into his biceps as the slight scruff of his beard rasped my cheek and breast and stomach. The intensity held me in a trance, and my heart pounded with fear. This wasn't a casual romp. Joe had unshackled my heart, and I couldn't find my equilibrium. Sex for sex, I could handle. But not this wild, hungry emotion. Intellectually, I knew my feelings were far out of proportion to events. Logical thought didn't count for much, though. In my head I could hear Granny lecturing me about the necessity of mental discipline over emotion, reality over daydreams. Both feet planted firmly on the ground. Stay in the sunshine, avoid the shadows.

Joe had upended all of that, and the worst part was that I couldn't say how he'd done it. His touch, his humor, his gentleness. Not one single thing, but the whole of it. I doubted that he was aware of his impact.

Breathless and weak-kneed, I found myself at the pond. An old stump beside a stand of bare maple trees offered a seat. I dropped onto it, seeking calm by watching the wind ripple the water and send fragments of light to pierce the surrounding forest.

The woods were alive in the winter sun. Brown birds darted and chirped. Small creatures rustled through the fallen leaves. These familiar sounds of childhood settled over me and my heartbeat slowed. Joe wasn't part of my future. I had to keep that foremost in my mind. Long ago I'd learned that sexual intimacy did not forge a lasting bond. Pleasure was fine, pain was not acceptable. If I couldn't control my emotional reaction, I would have to walk away. I inhaled slowly and deeply and willed the tension from my shoulders. I would master this.

Enclosed by such beauty and stillness, I shifted my thoughts to Thoreau's attachment to solitude. Had he, too, been a victim of past pain? Had he come to Walden to avoid the tentacles of emotional attachment that so often ended in amputation? He and his brother had courted the same girl, who'd rejected him. And then Bonnie had found him. She'd loved him, and by all readings of her journal, he'd loved her back. Had she undone him?

Part of my reason for choosing Walden Pond as the place I'd write my dissertation was to allow me access to public records, unavailable online, where I hoped to find evidence of Bonnie's life before

Thoreau. While I knew the journal to be authentic, I had to have solid, physical proof of Bonnie's existence in this place. I wasn't naïve enough to believe that my revisionist view of Thoreau's time at Walden Pond wouldn't meet resistance. Proof was critical.

Thoreau's time at Walden and the area was well documented—if inaccurate, since Bonnie was never mentioned. At least there was a sense of history about the man. My only knowledge of Bonnie came from her journal, which encompassed the months, often not clearly defined, she'd spent with Henry. Before that and after, there was no record of her existence. From the journal, I knew she was a flesh-and-blood woman who'd worked as a governess in Concord. That was a good starting point. Surely I could find a record that proved this. I had to.

After the time at Walden, Thoreau was collected by his family and carted home, only to eventually die, at age 44, of the tuberculosis he'd initially contracted ten years before Walden at age 18. And Bonnie? Did she contract the disease from her lover and die in a New England boarding house? Perhaps she married, but I doubted it. If she had children, none reconnected to the Cahill roots. Or if they had, I hadn't yet discovered it.

A jay flitted among the gray tree branches, a flash of blue neoned by a shaft of sunlight. It would be night before long. I'd been woolgathering for nearly an hour. Closing my eyes, I sought a deeper understanding of Thoreau's pursuit of the delicate relationship between man and nature.

While he must have loved my aunt, he was, at heart, a man most comfortable with his own thoughts. He understood the darkness in the center of man's soul. Man destroyed the natural world at a pace that outstripped any other living organism. Thoreau glimpsed the future, perhaps with Bonnie's help.

Based on a section of the journal I'd recently read, Bonnie believed she had the power of second sight, a talent I had yet to fully grasp. Granny said second sight did not lead to happiness, that it was a dance with the devil. Had Bonnie seen the future? Did she know her fate, the way her relationship with Thoreau would end? If so, how did she have the courage to go forward and love? That was a battle I'd yet to win. When life taught a person that the worst pain imaginable came from loving, why risk it?

For a brief time, Thoreau explored love and my ancestor helped him. To the world, he was the most famous virgin of his time. To Bonnie, he was the tender lover, the seducer, the seeker who broke her heart.

Behind me a stick crackled, and my chest contracted. Not because I was afraid, but because I realized I was waiting for Joe. I anticipated he'd find me gone from the inn and come here.

I didn't turn around. The total silence of the woods told me he was near. What did it mean that he'd come? Was it obligation or chivalry or true concern? My pulse rushed at the thought it might be desire. I pretended to be unaware.

He was skilled at moving silently and swiftly. Faint noises from my left made me wonder if he was moving away. Sound in the stillness of a woods can be deceiving.

My eyes were not tricked, though. I opened them and saw red streaking through the trees just beyond the edge of the pond. Cold dread drained away any thought of romance. It wasn't Joe who'd come to keep me company. It was the figure I'd seen near the inn.

I hit the trail back to the main road where passing cars would give me some safety. As I darted through the trees, dead limbs tangling about my ankles, the red-coated person followed. She kept pace with me. Not coming closer, not falling back. She stalked me. If it was Karla, she would strike before I gained the road.

To my surprise, she suddenly stepped out of the woods into a slant of sunlight some fifty yards away. I stopped. It wasn't Karla, it was a child. Blond curls escaped the hood of her red snow jacket. She wore black pants and boots.

She watched me with the patience of someone much older. She wasn't hiding—she was out in the open. But at such a distance, I couldn't distinguish her features. She was slender, and could have been any age from seven to fifteen. I guessed nine or ten.

I waved, but she didn't respond. Who was this child that roamed the woods with total freedom? I'd glimpsed her near the inn several times when she should have been in school. Why wasn't she? And where were her parents?

I decided to skirt the pond to ask those questions. By the time I arrived, she'd vanished. I couldn't tell if she'd stepped back into the trees or taken a trail to Thoreau's cabin. The sun sat on the treetops, soon to ease below the horizon. I'd never been afraid of the woods at night—streetlights didn't exist in the part of Kentucky where I grew up. But Karla's attack had unnerved me. I didn't want to be out in an isolated spot in the dark.

I took the trail to Thoreau's cabin. The docent who gave lectures would be gone by now, but it was the shortest route to the main road. When I reached the parking lot, the peaches and mauves of sunset were giving way to cobalt blue. The eastern sky led night's march, and I made a wish on the first star. I refused to waste it on Karla, so I wished for support from my dissertation committee. If I could focus on my work, I'd leave the Concord area before March.

There wasn't a sign of life around the replica of Henry David Thoreau's cabin. The child had obviously gone home. It was time for me to do the same. I'd tarried too long at Walden.

A giggle caught me off-guard. I spun in all directions. Was it the little girl? It wasn't Karla. The sound had been too young, too filled with mischief.

"Will you play with me?"

The question stopped me cold. I pivoted to find the child standing by the corner of the cabin.

"Who are you?" I asked.

"Who are you?" she repeated.

"Aine Cahill." My name was no secret.

"You can call me . . . Mary or Martha or Mattie or Mabus."

I knew the odd name but couldn't place it. "What are you doing in the woods alone?"

"Playing. I like to play here in the quiet. It's where the best things are. Secrets."

She stood at the edge of the trees. The lack of light blurred her features. Blond hair, carefully brushed and curled, cascaded down her chest. She was no older than ten. "Where do you live?" I asked.

"It's a secret." She giggled as if she'd told a joke.

"Come over where I can see you."

"Do you like dolls?" she asked.

"I did, when I was your age." It was a lie. I'd never cared for dolls. "Did you leave the doll for me?"

"Someone did. Someone watches you. Someone not nice."

The total creepiness of this conversation made me anxious. "Did you see who left the doll?" The child was peculiar. More than peculiar, but I couldn't put my finger on exactly what or how.

"Someone left a doll for you. Someone did," she answered in a sing-song voice.

"I need to head home. Will you come with me?" I couldn't just leave her alone in the woods with night dropping over us by the second.

"You live in the cabin at the inn."

This child knew all about me, yet I couldn't even clearly see her. The hood shaded her face. "That's true. Come with me."

"No."

"You can't stay here. Night is falling."

She shrugged. "I'm not afraid of the dark."

"I'll take you home. Where do you live?"

"You're silly." With that she ran behind the cabin.

By the time I jogged there, I found only emptiness. I circled the cabin. Nothing. It was time to go back to the inn. At least now I had another puzzle to chew on, something to keep my mind off the fact that Joe had never even come to check on me.

14

I awoke the next morning with renewed determination to pursue my work. I headed into town, enjoying the fall day.

Concord prides itself on being the first inland community settled in Massachusetts *and* the location where "the shot heard 'round the world"—the beginning of the Revolutionary War—was fired. Each street I traveled echoed with the footfalls of war heroes, learned men, Native Americans, and women far ahead of their time, such as my aunt Bonnie and Louisa May Alcott.

I meant to employ my research skills to find a link between Aunt Bonnie and the novelist who penned *Little Women*. At the time Bonnie lived with Thoreau, Louisa May would have been thirteen or so. While she was schooled by her father, her world views differed from the Transcendentalists. An activist in women's rights, she chose to be a nurse in a Washington, D.C. hospital during the Civil War, confronting the battleground horrors in the most brutal way.

Her beloved novels brought the duties and joys of family life to millions of young readers. Fiction and free-thinking sustained Louisa May. If I could prove that Bonnie Cahill, flouter of social conventions and seeker of love, had known the novelist, possibly even influenced her, I would conquer another academic peak.

On a more realistic level, if I could find a mention of Bonnie in Louisa May's work, I'd score a huge victory in proving that Bonnie Cahill really existed.

In the daylight hours, I could convince myself that I'd overreacted about the encounter with the child in the woods. I'd been upset, my abandonment issues regarding Joe had kicked in. I knew all the proper psychological terms. I'd exaggerated the creepiness of the little girl. In an effort to regain control of myself and my future, I needed to focus on work and nothing else.

I loved the history of Concord, and the past was recorded in architecture and monuments—the old North Bridge where Revolutionary War re-enactment battles were staged each year, the statue of the Minuteman rendered by the same sculptor who created Abraham Lincoln in his chair at the memorial in Washington, D.C. Exquisite detail gave both subjects life and hinted at their humanity.

It was to the Concord historical records that I ambled. Tight budget or not, I stopped at the Honey Bea for a stuffed bagel and coffee. I didn't breakfast at the inn, couldn't bear Dorothea's suggestive comments and pointed questions about my night with Joe. I had no good answers. I hadn't heard from Joe. Not a text or call or whisper. Not a hint that the night had meant anything of the smallest significance to him. The silence triggered insecurities I'd fought hard to overcome.

Under other circumstances, I might have enjoyed Dorothea's good-natured teasing and veiled hints at the pleasures Joe provided. Had I been secure in the knowledge that he wanted to see me again, I could take pleasure in the night before last. I didn't expect flowers and poems, but a phone call would have done wonders for my sagging confidence.

Granny had warned me that a man's interest fades the moment he achieves his conquest. My boarding-school romance with Bryson Cappett had left scars both physically and emotionally. Perhaps spiritually. I hated the thought that I might have been a fool—again. It was a hard lesson to learn twice, but such was the Cahill way. I'd escaped the curse, but my past followed me like a shadow as I entered the library.

Data prior to 1850 were collected in the Concord Registry of Vital Records. I dug up a host of interesting things, but none related to Bryoni Cahill, which was Bonnie's legal name. I'd hoped, against all odds, that Henry had done right by my aunt and made her an honest woman. Then again, if Bonnie ran true to Cahill form, the conventions of society wouldn't have meant a lot to her. Not surprisingly, my search showed no record of a marriage.

And no record of her birth, or that of any Cahill in Middlesex County. I fought back disappointment and a growing anxiety that I might not be able to prove that Bonnie's journal was valid. I couldn't allow even the whisper of such a thought. It would take more time and effort, but I would prevail. I didn't have a choice.

From all I'd been able to deduce, Bonnie's branch of the family descended from Daniel Cahill, eldest son of Elikah. That whole branch had returned to their traveler ways and were lost in the miasma of history. No permanent home, no connection to a place, they moved constantly. Babies were born in the wagons they called home. The dead were buried at campsites along the way in unmarked graves. They were ghosts in many ways.

Granny Siobhan had been reluctant to talk about this Cahill branch of travelers, but she'd told me they survived by hiring out to complete chores that often took more manpower than one farmer could muster. Barn raisings, well digging, pasture clearing—these were Cahill skills. And the womenfolk would laugh and read cards or gaze into a crystal ball to foresee the future of the farmer and his family. The next morning, when the farmer went out, the travelers would be gone with only a cold campfire to show they'd ever been there.

When I was younger, I'd fancied I saw them. On a chill fall morning, they appeared out of the Appalachian mountain mist. Wagons creaking, horses plodding, they showed up in a flat patch of pasture and camped for the night.

I told Granny I'd seen them, shadows in the fog, and she'd told me to keep my imagination in check and would hear no more of it.

Granny loved a good ghost story, and she told me plenty, but none explained the things I saw. I learned quickly, though, that it was best to keep my visions to myself.

Poring over land records, I hoped to find some trace of Bonnie Cahill's existence. The journal included dates and specific events I hoped to match up with items in the local paper, but that wasn't the primary evidence I would need to defend my thesis.

Knowing the academic world as I did, I expected resistance. My dissertation took aim at a beloved figure of literature, a man whose writing had supported a generation of sit-ins as peaceful protests. Civil disobedience—the hippies took it to heart and changed a nation. While tactics of peaceful protest go far back in history, Thoreau was the father of peaceful protest in modern America. The view of him, alone, wandering the woods of Walden, bordered on sacred. My work would appear to some to be an attack on an icon. The virginal hermit of Walden Pond had consorted with a woman.

I wanted all the corroborating documentation I could find.

I searched every record available and could find no mention of a Cahill. The long-ago issues of the local newspaper were on microfilm, and I went through those. There were public notices of Emerson's lectures, of the school built by Bronson Alcott, of the stimulating school of philosophy brewing in Concord. The dates mentioned in Bonnie's journal bore fruit, but nowhere was Bonnie's name included. Though this substantiated the journal to some degree, I needed much more.

To my surprise, I realized that the Concord of the 1840s was not a small town in the middle of a forest. Most of the forest had been cut down for fuel, with the exception of Walden Pond.

Thoreau had settled in the one area where his comings and goings weren't visible to his neighbors. He wanted privacy. Because of Bonnie?

My imagination conjured them, walking along the rim of the pond. The bright green of new spring leaves unfurled in pale yellow sunlight. I heard Bonnie's laugh and watched as she grasped Thoreau's hand, swinging around to face him. His dour, bearded face broke into an expression of delight.

This was fancy, but I hoped Bonnie had such golden moments with her lover, for ultimately that romance was fated to die a brutal death. One of the latter entries in her journal spoke of the intervention of Thoreau's family.

The bitter scene unfolded in Bonnie's words. Her handwriting, normally elegant and controlled, belied her sorrow and frustration. Henry's father appeared at Walden Pond and demanded that his son return to the family. Curses and damnation rained down on Bonnie as she refused to step aside. She held her lover's hand and stood firm against the derision. Thoreau broke, possibly to spare her further humiliation. He acquiesced to his father's demands that he leave Walden Pond, leave her.

An entry in Bonnie's journal followed shortly after that confrontation and Henry's abandonment of her.

I hold no grudge or judgment against Henry. He wanted only solitude when he came to Walden Pond. My presence shocked his system, as well as offered the comforts of companionship and the love of an open heart. Together we explored the natural world and the wonders of this small woodland. He taught me of the simple joys of a scented breeze or the bloom of a flower. My gift to him was a way to face the future with courage. I do not believe he now will fear his own mortality. He is a gentle and kind man, and while the balm of love and the nurturing elements of nature have kept deterioration at bay, he

*is not a healthy man. He would have left me eventually, but oh, the pain of
such an abrupt ending.*

*I never told him of my condition. He nor his family will ever know. I will
leave Walden Pond without a trace I ever existed. No search will lead them to
me, for I will not be found. There is nothing here for me now.*

My memory of Bonnie's journal was accurate down to the word.
I didn't carry it around with me. The value was too great, but I knew
passages by heart.

After Thoreau's family reclaimed him, Bonnie disappeared. I suspected suicide, but I had no proof. Thoreau and the solitude of Walden
Pond had stabilized her. With Thoreau, she'd been a woman with
unique talents, and they'd explored her abilities together. Thoreau's
abandonment could have pushed her to end her life. I understood
how it could happen. As I knew from personal experience, a human
heart could take only so much suffering. The quiet of the grave could
be appealing.

The only thing of Bonnie's that made its way home was the
journal. It had arrived at Brandeis the semester I earned my master's
degree. My goal had always been a doctorate in literature, but the
journal, wrapped in plain brown paper and addressed to me, offered a
stunning opportunity. Few doctoral students broke new ground. If I
could validate the journal, I would be the exception. With this strange
gift, which bore no return address, the horizon suddenly opened. My
life had been a series of challenges brought on by my bloodline. If the
journal paid off, it would be a blood connection that launched my
success. The irony wasn't lost on me.

At first I'd thought the sender had been Granny, but she denied
it. She asked to skim through it, but I resisted putting it in the mail.
The journal was too precious to risk again in the post or a delivery
service. From the moment I touched the beautiful leather cover, I
knew it was mine. It came to me by right.

For some reason, the idea of the journal sent Granny into a
panic, even after I explained what a valuable tool it would be for my

dissertation. Granny's mind had started to slip by then. She urged me to destroy it. I promised her I would, because she was so agitated. Instead, I began preparations to enter the Ph.D. program. The journal was a compelling cautionary tale of the wounding power of love and loss. It was also a personal glimpse into the life of an iconic American writer, and I would share it with the world.

Lost in my research and thoughts, I jumped when the librarian tapped my shoulder, indicating it was time to close the library. Snow covered the ground, and darkness crowded the sun from the sky. I packed my notebooks and left, walking home in a wintry wind that smelled of pungent fir and the thick curtain of flakes.

The snow depressed me. Rolling my aching shoulders, I continued to the inn, the snow obliterating any trace of my passage.

15

Snowflakes dusted my shoulders and teased my lips and eyelashes as I walked back to the inn. The large white flakes had been falling for a while. A six-inch-deep accumulation covered open areas. Deeper drifts piled against buildings and curbs. The world had changed radically while I was inside the library, and I hadn't noticed. The encroaching night and layer of snow made everything different, purer. The air smelled cleaner. Most of the shops had closed, and the street was empty except for an occasional car.

My stomach's loud complaints reminded me I'd worked through lunch, immersed in the lives of two dead people. Only writers and readers could understand the way a story captured me and pulled me into another reality. Some would say I *escaped* into the lives of others. They would be right. This ability to give up reality and allow the story to absorb me had saved me many times in Harlan County. For the space of a book or story, I could flee Kentucky and live in another place, another life.

I left the town behind and the forest was swallowed in white as I trudged along the empty road. In snowfall, there is a unique silence. The cold precipitation muffled the man-made sounds of cars, leaving a magical stillness. I turned down the winding road to the inn. Almost there, I stopped to admire the lighted windows that radiated a sense of safety and welcome.

The distant noises of people gathered to eat and socialize reminded me that others found happiness in community rather than solitude. Instead of stopping by the dining room, I continued on my path. The scent of freshly baked bread tormented me as I passed the inn to leave my computer and books in the cabin.

Navigating the narrow path, I stopped, startled. With its brown unpainted exterior, the cabin was a square box against the last light in the sky. It should have been a dark building. Someone must have gone inside and lit a fire, because smoke curled out of the chimney and my desk lamp shown bright in the gathering dusk. Dorothea must have sent Patrick.

There were no footsteps in the snow that dusted the steps and front porch. How long ago had Patrick been there? I hoped the fire was fresh. At night I banked the glowing embers, but right now I needed dancing flames, the snap of a hot, fresh fire to cheer me up.

My hand reached to put the key in the lock when I stopped. I slipped to the window with the cut screen and peeped inside.

The fire burned bright, hot tongues of flame licking around the freshly laid logs. In the glow of the lamp I could see the entire cabin. A rise in the covers of my bed told me someone was there.

Joe! The jolt of happiness came and went in a split second. Where was his truck if he was inside, in my bed? I knew instinctively it wasn't Joe.

Caution stayed my hand at the door. The intruder could have come before the snow drifted down, but the fire was freshly made. Disquiet prickled my skin, and I spun around to make sure *I* was leaving footprints. My panic warned me to abandon the cabin. I could go to the inn and ask Dorothea to come back with me to check out who snuggled in my bed. Or I could call the police.

That wasn't really an option. What if it *was* Joe, waiting beneath the quilts? He might have left his truck parked somewhere and hoofed it to the cabin. For privacy, to avoid others poking their nose into our business. If I brought Dorothea or the police, all manner of unwarranted attention would follow, and I wanted no more interaction with the law.

I turned the key and stepped in. The lump in the bed remained completely still, like a dead thing. My heart thudded so hard I placed a steadying hand against the doorframe. I slammed the door sharply.

The figure in the bed sat up, throwing back covers. Blond tousled hair poked up on the head of Patrick Leahy. Not Joe, but Patrick. His grin was slow and lazy. I didn't move or say a word as he pushed back the covers and stood, completely naked.

His body was a work of art. Lean cut muscles defined his chest and stomach, and the indentation beneath his hip bones made me inhale sharply. At nineteen, he was physical perfection, and he knew it.

"I've been waiting for you," he said in soft invitation. "You know I've wanted you since you moved into the cabin. My god, Aine, you're so beautiful and you don't even know it."

My common sense urged me to run, to open the door and flee. To safety. To a place where I couldn't make another bad choice. But another, wilder voice argued differently. Patrick was here, and Joe wasn't. Joe hadn't called or in any way hinted that the night we'd spent together held special significance. For all I knew, I might never hear from him again. Patrick adored me and wasn't shy about confessing it. Granny had urged me to choose the real, the solid, and Patrick was very, very solid. Still, I hesitated.

Patrick reached out for me. "When you come down the lane beside the inn, I stop work just to watch you, Aine. You're incredible. I've never wanted anyone as much as you."

It would be wrong to sleep with Patrick, but my feet didn't budge. My gaze moved over him, lingering on those hip bones and the ripples of his torso, leaving no doubt that he affected me.

He stepped closer, allowing the firelight to play over the contours of his body. "We've wasted a lot of time. I want to make you feel as beautiful as you are. I want to make love to you."

It crossed my mind to order him out, but I didn't. Instead, I walked toward him and the bed. I kissed him hard, and he tilted me into sheets still warm and smelling of his aftershave. Clean with a hint of the ocean.

16

The fire burned low, a bed of red embers. Patrick slept beside me, his leg thrown over my thighs, his hand tangled in my hair. He slept without anxiety or trouble. I, on the other hand, lay wide awake with the reality I'd let impulse and wounded pride rule the last two hours of my life. Regret kept me motionless beneath his weight.

A log burned through, snapped, and a shower of sparks jumped up the chimney. The sound woke him and he gave me a sleepy grin. "Man, you are something else," he whispered against my temple. "You're beautiful, Aine." His hand circled my breast.

I eased to the other side of the bed. When he glanced out the window, he sat up abruptly. "Holy shit, what time is it?"

"Just after eight." My stomach growled. Another hour and I would miss dinner at the inn. I could order pizza, but I would have to walk to the main road to fetch it, and my meals at the inn came with the cost of renting the cabin.

"Dorothea is going to kill me!" He jumped out of bed and into his jeans. He pulled on his socks and boots as he walked to the door.

Remembering his shirt, he stooped low and swept it off the floor. His arms slid into the sleeves in a fluid movement. Patrick wasn't innocent. I was willing to bet he'd had plenty of practice dressing rapidly.

I wasn't as quick as he was, but I wasn't far behind. We left the cabin and walked through the snow to the inn, side by side, but not touching. The ground was pristine, a crisp white wonderland.

"We shouldn't tell Dorothea about this," he said. "She'd be upset with me. She wants you for Joe."

"It's in my best interest to keep this to myself." I was strangely detached from the situation, but in the dead of night, anxiety and remorse would likely choke me. The cost of a few hours of pleasure would be many days of regret. Patrick was a teenager. I was twenty-eight. No matter that he'd made every advance and lain in wait in my very bed.

"That was, like, the most important thing that's ever happened to me," Patrick said. "I'm a different person."

"No. It was just sex. Nothing more. Don't get all romantic and mushy, because it won't happen again." A little late in setting ground rules.

"Didn't you like it?" He grabbed my coat sleeve and tugged me to a halt. His eyes glittered in the moonlight. "Was I bad? I mean, I'll get better. You know, with practice."

"There won't be practice." My harsh words caused him to inhale sharply. "I don't mean to be cruel, but this shouldn't have happened and it can never happen again, Patrick. I'm too old. You're too young." The familiar tang of bad choices filled my nostrils. Remorse had its own peculiar odor.

"Joe's more experienced. He's a better lover, isn't he?" He loosed my coat sleeve and stalked away.

I ran to catch up with him. "No. You're a terrific lover, Patrick. But I'm nearly a decade older than you. I feel like I've taken advantage. It makes me dislike myself. It's like I'm some kind of sad old predator sniffing around a young man." I shuddered at the thought.

"That's not it. Not at all. The truth is, Joe wouldn't like it, would he?" Patrick chuckled softly. "Maybe I should be worried."

90

"Don't be a fool. Joe couldn't care less."

"Then there's no reason we have to stop. You were wild, Aine. You enjoyed it."

This had to be settled for once and for all. "I intend to be a teacher, Patrick. If word gets out that I sleep with young men, it could ruin my chances at a good job. Can't you see that?"

He resumed his pace toward the inn. "That's hogwash. It's Joe. You don't want him to know. He'll be angry. Doesn't matter that he's ignored you for days. He thinks he has a claim on you."

Patrick was like a lot of men I'd known—figuring that every other dog wanted the bone he chewed. Male delusion. "Joe doesn't pretend he's staking out a claim. He isn't interested. What makes you think he is?"

"He's had a tough time getting a date since Mischa disappeared. Never made any sense to me why he came back here."

I put a hand on his arm and stopped him in the cold, still night. "Who is Mischa?" Karla had hurled the name at me as if it were a disease. I'd asked Joe, but in freeing me from the police station, he'd never answered my question.

Concern drew his eyebrows together. "Shit. I thought you knew." He shifted from foot to foot. "He didn't tell you?"

I tightened my grip on his arm because I knew he was about to bolt. "Who is Mischa?" I repeated, squeezing a little on his wrist.

"Ask Dorothea." He tugged free of me.

"Patrick, please." My words held him. "Please. Just tell me." I'd known something wasn't right.

The snow had almost ceased, but a few flakes dusted Patrick's blond hair. We stood outside the inn, haloed in light coming from the dining room windows.

"Joe was an elementary teacher, before he became a ranger. About ten years ago one of his students disappeared, a young girl about nine or ten. Mischa Lobrano. She was a really pretty kid, and she lived in the same neighborhood as Joe. She often ended up at Joe's house after school, and he played kickball and stuff with the neighborhood brats.

One day, Mischa was gone. She made it home after school and then went out to do a science project. Her footsteps led into the woods at Walden Pond and then just stopped. She was never seen again. Like the goblins got her."

My gut twisted in a hard knot. I knew exactly where this story would lead. Accusations of a sexual predator. Ruination of a teaching career. A reputation that makes a man a neighborhood pariah.

"Was anyone ever arrested?"

He shook his head. "They searched for weeks. With tracking dogs and helicopters and volunteer groups. It was October, and the weather was good. Folks held out hope for over a month that she might be alive."

"What happened to her?"

"No one knows." He spoke on a sigh. "Trouble is, folks suspected Joe. A lot of folks, actually. Said he was too close with the children. Mischa talked about him all the time at home and with her friends. She had a crush on him the way young girls can get with a teacher."

I finished the story for him. "They suspected Joe molested her and then killed her to keep her quiet."

Patrick didn't deny it. "Dorothea never believed it. She said Joe liked children and wasn't it a crying shame that a man who loved his job could be tainted with foolish rumors. There was no proof. None at all. Joe was never charged with anything."

"Yet he gave up teaching."

"He wasn't fired. He quit. He got hired on as a ranger and left here. Only came back last spring when his mother was dying."

I felt exhausted, barely able to stand upright. "Thanks, Patrick." I started toward the inn at a slow shuffle. I needed time to think, to process this new picture of Joe. Pedophile and child murderer didn't fit the Joe I knew, but *he* should have told me. I would have slept with him anyway, but he should have given me the option of saying no. Taint was like a virus. It passed from one to the next.

Then again, I hadn't bothered to tell him about my family, about the oxy selling, the guns and shootings, the brutality for the pleasure of hurting others.

Patrick's hand pressed into the small of my back. "I'm sorry," he said. "I didn't mean to start anything."

"I'm glad you told me. I have a right to know who I slept with."

"I gotta run, Aine. I'm going to slip in the back door to the kitchen and get busy. Maybe Dorothea won't notice I'm hours late."

"Don't count on it." My remark followed his disappearing back as he darkness swallowed him.

Standing alone in the snowy dark, I tried to feel something about Joe and the little girl who'd disappeared. Mischa. Numbness deadened all reaction. I'd slept with a man many believed to be a child abuser, a child killer. And I felt nothing at all.

That wouldn't last long. Fury would arrive quickly enough. Dorothea could have warned me. Joe should have told me. Once again, I'd been played for a patsy.

Inside the inn, Dorothea served coffee to the Wescotts at a window table. They laughed and cut up, unaware that I watched from the darkness. Patrick hustled to bus several empty tables. I almost turned back to the cabin, but I knew I couldn't last the night without food. I had to go in.

Dorothea saw me before I could slip into an empty seat. She grabbed a glass of water and came my way. "Aine, are you okay?"

"Why wouldn't I be?" I asked.

She frowned at my cool tone. "Has something happened?"

"You should have warned me about Joe. About the child."

The smile slid down her face. "I see. I maybe should have told you, but Joe deserves to be judged on his own merits, not by gossip. He was never charged with anything. He didn't harm the child. He wouldn't."

Several tables of diners had stopped eating and were looking our way. I hated being the center of a scene. I'd already had a fight on a public street and been taken to the police station because of Joe. Now I was making a spectacle. "Drop it."

Dorothea lowered her tone. "I did what I thought was right, Aine. I'm sorry if you feel hurt by it. Folks around here are quick to judge and slow to forgive, even if they're wrong. Joe has suffered at the hands of gossips. He likes you and it was a chance for him to date a woman without the wall of lies."

"You should have told me and let me make up my mind. *He* should have told me."

"Perhaps. But how hard would it be to tell a romantic interest you were once accused of a horrible act, one you didn't do?"

I saw her point, but it didn't make me feel less betrayed. "You put his interests above me."

"I'm sorry you see it that way." She edged toward a table where a man held up his hand to get her attention. "I'll bring you some food. We'll talk when the rush is over."

Patrick brought me a glass of dry red wine, chili, crusty bread, and a salad. He served me with a wink and a wicked grin. I ate, focused on my food. When I was finished, I slipped out the door and headed to the cabin. I didn't want another confrontation with Dorothea, and I couldn't look at Patrick without a rush of guilt and shame. He was a young man. Too young.

The snow had only partially covered my and Patrick's footprints. No new ones were evident, yet when I heard the crackle of a stick deep in the trees, I almost panicked and ran back to the inn. Perhaps this was the Cahill Curse for me, an overactive imagination that would push me to foolish conduct.

Reaching the cabin, I climbed the steps to the porch. Before I could put the key in the lock, the door inched open.

I had locked it. I had taken great care to do so. Now it was open, and Patrick had not been here.

But someone had.

Sitting in the middle of the floor was a Victorian doll. She wore a red-and-white-striped dress, and her dark brown curls cascaded onto her shoulders beneath a pert hat. Her red lips curved in a smile. Where there should have been two bright eyes that shut whenever she was laid down, two empty sockets glared at me.

17

In moments of blind panic, the brain can't form a single thought. It's a holdover from prehistoric times. Animals are labeled fight or flight in their response to danger. Humans vacillate between both reactions. Karla attacked, I fought. Now, confronted with a hellish doll that appeared out of nowhere, I fled.

My feet slipped on a thin layer of ice beneath the snow as I sought traction on the porch. My boots scrabbled on the wood, but I couldn't find a purchase. Momentum hurled me down the steps headlong into the night. I stumbled several yards before I fell. When I looked back toward the cabin, in the open doorway I could see the silhouette of the doll. She stared out at me with her eyeless sockets. I cried out and tried to get on my feet.

The blow caught me across the back, sending me sprawling in the snow. "You thought you had me, didn't you, bitch?" Karla's furious question came before another hard blow crashed on my shoulders.

I rolled toward her legs and grabbed her ankle. With all of my strength I bit into her calf. She tried to kick free, but I chomped harder, the iron taste of her blood filling my mouth as I tore through her legging.

"Let go! Let go!" She hopped on one leg, screaming and swinging the hockey stick she'd whacked me with.

I clamped down until she squealed in anguish and fell over. She caught me in the mouth with her boot, bursting my lip. I punched her in the gut as hard as I could, hampered by her heavy coat but connecting next with her jaw. That took the fight out of her and I released her and clambered to my feet. My back and shoulder felt like I'd been hit by a train. Blood gushed from my lip. I couldn't see anything clearly in the darkness, but I heard her sobbing and moaning.

"You're insane," I said, spitting blood into the snow. "I'm calling the cops." I marched toward the inn. I had a cell phone but there was no reception until I got to the main road.

Headlights swung down the driveway and came toward me. I stopped, highlighted in the beams. I waved my arms, signaling the driver to halt. When the vehicle drew closer, I saw it was a truck. Joe's truck. He left the engine running and stepped out.

"Aine, what's wrong? What happened to you? You're bleeding!"

"Karla attacked me. She's back there."

"Are you hurt?" Joe's hands captured my cheeks and turned me into the beam of his headlights. "Holy shit. Your face—"

"I know." I shook, like I had neurological damage. "She's insane and dangerous."

"Go to the inn and call Chief McKinney. I'll see about Karla." He moved past me. In a moment, the darkness absorbed him. I didn't move. Now that Joe had arrived, I had no desire to call the police. They'd force me to go to the station and fill out reports and complaints and explain how I'd managed to bite Karla's calf and hopefully break a few ribs. Even though it was self-defense, it would still paint me as a vicious savage, my second episode of physical assault.

I heard Joe calling Karla's name and I walked toward his voice. In a moment, he stepped back into the light cast by his vehicle's high beams.

"She's gone."

I almost didn't believe him. "Where?"

He shook his head. "I put her on a bus to Nebraska last night. I sat with her and made sure she got on. I watched the bus leave, and I saw her in the window. How the hell did she get back here? And why?"

"She put a doll in my cabin. I was afraid and tried to run to the inn, and she attacked me with a hockey stick." I panted as I talked. "She tried to kill me."

Joe eased me to the passenger side of the truck. In a moment he was turning the vehicle around.

"Where are we going?"

"To the hospital. There's blood all over your face and down your coat. You might be seriously hurt."

"I'm okay. My lip is just busted." It felt huge, and I started to laugh. I tried to smother the giggles, but I couldn't stop.

"Aine, you're hysterical."

"I am." I doubled over with laughter. "I am."

Joe stopped the truck. "Get ahold of yourself."

I tried, but the laughter seemed to bubble from a deep pressure. Tears ran down my cheeks and I couldn't catch my breath. The whole time my body shook with mirth.

Joe pulled me across the seat and into his arms. He cocooned me with his warmth. I laughed until I realized I was crying. While I sobbed against his chest, he stroked my hair.

"It's snowing again," he said once I'd calmed a little.

I lifted my head to look out the window. Fat, fluffy flakes tickled the windshield.

"If it keeps up like this, they'll cancel school tomorrow."

He chattered on about the inconsequential in an attempt to help me regain my equilibrium. My anger about the missing child, Mischa, evaporated. My remorse for sleeping with Patrick was still there but I buried it deep. I let Joe comfort me.

When I was twelve, I'd traveled the half-mile from Granny's house to the little store that serviced our community. My mission was a package of Baker's coconut to make a cake. Granny's birthday was the next day, and coconut was her favorite. I'd saved pennies and nickels to buy the ingredients, and all I lacked was the lacey white coconut, so sweet and moist.

I made my purchase and was headed home when my cousin, Amon Cahill, met me on the road. Amon had red hair and pink-rimmed eyes, and it was common knowledge that his mother had a real fondness for family members. Granny never allowed me to go swimming at the creek with Amon or any of his relatives. She just said they had a different way of living life and it was best for me to stay clear of them.

Amon thought I was stuck-up, and he told me so. I tried to walk past him, and he pushed me down. He snatched my bag of groceries and stomped the coconut into the dirt, laughing as I fought and cried.

After Amon left, I picked the strands of coconut out of the dirt and took it home, wondering if I could wash it somehow. The hopelessness of the situation sent me into a fit of tears, and by the time I got home, I was completely out of control.

Granny washed my face with a cool cloth and held me against her, stroking my hair until I went to sleep. It was the last time I remembered such a touch.

Until now.

"Aine, I'm so sorry." Joe smoothed my hair and rubbed my back the way a mother would put a baby to sleep. "I thought Karla was gone. I had no idea she'd doubled back here to attack you."

I burrowed deeper into the padded nylon of his coat. My body temperature rose, and my breathing stretched and relaxed.

"We have to report this to the police." He put the truck in gear, but my hand stopped him.

I sat up. "No. I'm already the talk of the town."

He turned the interior light on and examined my face. "I don't want to be an alarmist, Aine, but we need to at least go to the hospital to get you checked over."

"I'm not hurt. She hit me a couple of times with a club, but she missed the vital places."

He punched the steering wheel. "You said you bit her. Karla was doing drugs. What if she has an illness? We need to get you checked for Hepatitis C."

I hadn't considered that Karla's blood might be the ultimate revenge. "It's too early to test for Hepatitis C or AIDS."

He leaned his forehead against the steering wheel. "Everything I touch suffers."

He was talking about me, but also the child. "What happened to Mischa?" I asked. Sitting alone in the dark cab of his truck was as good a place as any to have this conversation.

"I was going to tell you about Mischa tonight. I should have told you sooner."

"Yes, you should." I sighed. "I should have had the choice to say yes or no. You should have told me, and so should Dorothea."

"You have every right to be angry." His left hand tightened on the steering wheel. "I wanted you to know me as a person before I told you. I didn't want to scare you off, but I see that wasn't fair to you." His fingers made tiny sounds of protest, he clutched the wheel so hard. "I tried to call you last night, and again today. To tell you. But I knew I should have told you before we made love. And I was ashamed."

I put my palm on his cheek. "There are things I should tell you about me, too." If I confessed about Patrick now, he might forgive me. He might understand that he'd hurt me and I'd sought any comfort I could find. If I told him.

He kissed my palm. "Mischa was a third-grade student at Middlesex Elementary, where I taught. She was a bright child, happy. Well-loved by her parents and family. I foresaw a tremendous future for her. She absorbed knowledge." He paused. "We developed a relationship. Teacher-student, nothing more. I encouraged her to read and learn and ask questions. We played kickball afternoons with the other children in the neighborhood."

The strain of his words cracked his voice and he cleared his throat.

"One October afternoon she left her books at home after school and went back outside. I'd taken several of the kids to Walden Pond the previous Saturday for a nature walk. Mischa had great curiosity about the natural world. Insects fascinated her. She called it a secret world. A couple of the other children asked where she was, but I wasn't concerned about her absence. I assumed she was tramping around the woods." He quit talking.

"But she wasn't, was she?" I prompted.

"No. She went into the Walden woods. Footprints led into the trees for a ways. Then they just stopped. No obvious signs of a struggle. But that was it. No trace was ever found. She was gone. A beautiful, bright intelligence was simply gone."

"Was she a blonde?" I asked.

"Yes, long blond curls. Blue eyes. Like a doll."

My mouth was suddenly dry. "Did she like dolls?"

"It was the only childish thing about her. She had Barbies and some other dolls she'd collected." He rubbed his eyes. "She said she would grow up to design fashion. She liked dressing the dolls in different outfits. Her mother was an exceptional seamstress and made clothes for the dolls."

Fear held me in a vise. "How old would Mischa be now?"

He leaned back in the seat. "I don't know. Eighteen or nineteen. If she's alive."

"But she isn't, is she?"

He grew still. "I don't think she is, Aine. I've never stopped looking for her, but I don't believe she's alive. I think someone took her and killed her."

"Did she live near here?"

"There's a neighborhood not far from Walden Pond. I lived there with my fiancée."

"Karla?" I couldn't believe he'd been engaged to such a trashy person.

"No, Amanda. She broke the engagement a few months after Mischa disappeared. It was too hard. The accusations, the suspicions. I withdrew from her and everyone." He fell silent.

"Why did they think you hurt the child?" I had to ask.

"She liked me. Nature and biology excited her. She told her mother I was taking her for a nature walk. When she didn't come home, her parents assumed she was with me. Very quickly it began to sound dirty and awful."

"What do you think happened to her?"

"I can hardly bear to think about it. I believe she was abducted and taken away. I've come to conclude she's dead."

My mouth tasted of ashes. "Do you believe the dead can visit us?"

A long silence stretched between us. "As in ghosts?"

"Ghosts or spirits or wraiths. Some essence of a person left here that's visible to the human eye."

He twisted my shoulders so he could look at me. "Why do you ask?"

"I've seen a child in the woods. Remember the doll? What if it wasn't Karla? What if is was . . . someone else?" My thoughts were too terrible to pursue.

"No. I don't believe that. Why would Mischa come to you? That's crazy, Aine. You're upset and not thinking clearly."

What I was thinking made more sense than a crazy ex-girlfriend leaving Barbies in the snow. "You reacted when I showed you the Barbie."

"I did. It shocked me."

"Because Mischa had a similar doll."

"She did. The photograph they put in the newspaper when they were trying to find her. She was holding that doll. One like it."

I didn't respond. Joe would have to come to the conclusion on his own. As for me, I'd already begun to put the pieces together. What I had to ask myself was why the spirit of a dead girl came to me. What did she want? Spirits, like regular people, always had an agenda.

My dream of Granny's visit had been prophetic. At last I'd been given the glimpse of what the Cahill Curse would mean to me. I would communicate with the spirits of departed people. I'd seen them as a child, and Granny had warned me not to speak with them. She'd made me believe it was my imagination. She'd conveyed her fear of them to me, so that I stopped seeing them. But this was my gift.

The little girl, Mischa, would be my first true encounter.

18

Joe couldn't stay with me. He left me behind in the truck while he removed the doll. He put her in a plastic trash bag and hauled her out.

"I'm sorry, Aine," he said. "I'll take care of Karla once and for all. I'll find her and make certain she never bothers you again." He was determined that Karla was behind the dolls—felt she'd been stalking us even before we encountered her in Bayside Bill's—and he meant to find her and put an end to her mischief. To be honest, I felt more than a little awkward. The tumbled bed told the wicked story between Patrick and me. Joe didn't linger in the cottage, and I wondered if he knew, if he could tell that intimacy had occurred only hours before.

When he was gone, I checked my shoulders and back. There were bruises below my shoulder blades and across my right shoulder, but no real damage had been done. I could only hope Karla suffered from the wounds I'd inflicted on her.

Unable to settle down to work or read, I paced. At last I got out my computer and did some basic research.

The Concord Journal covered the little girl's disappearance without sensationalism, a fact I could appreciate even if those involved might not. The story was straightforward and on the front page of the Oct. 30 edition. LOCAL CHILD MISSING. The article matched the details Patrick had given me. Mischa Lobrano had disappeared after school. I studied the school picture of the little blond girl. She could be the child I'd seen in the woods, but I couldn't be certain. If it was her, had she come to tell me what had happened to her? To warn me? To exact revenge?

I knew that stray spirits were not always benevolent or merely lost.

Gradually the stories in the paper grew shorter and shorter. Until at last, Mischa dropped from the news. As Joe told me, no trace of the child was ever found. An unnamed "person of interest" had been questioned; no arrests were ever made. Joe's name was never mentioned. But in a community as small as Concord, his career as a teacher had been destroyed. Yet he had come back here to serve as a ranger at Walden Pond when his mother grew ill and needed him. To me, that spoke of his innocence.

I poured a glass of wine. When I checked the time, it was after midnight. I was exhausted, but my brain refused to slow down. I took another sleeping pill and prayed for dreamless slumber. Tomorrow, in the daylight, I would search for answers about the little girl I'd seen at Walden Pond. Now, though, I pulled the quilts over my head and sought the escape of sleep.

My aunt Bonnie had endured dreams foretelling Thoreau's death. In hindsight, they were clearly prophetic. One in particular came to mind as I drifted in that drugged state of paralysis that preceded sleep. She'd happened on handkerchiefs spotted with blood all around Walden Pond. She'd recounted vivid squares of white, the red, red blood staining the cotton fabric, the way they lay so stark against a tree stump or cluster of leaves. She'd found them in all seasons, from the riot of fall colors to the greens of spring. As she'd walked around Walden Pond in the span of the dream, she'd experienced snow and the kiss of summer sun. The only constant had been the bloodstained handkerchiefs. Bonnie couldn't have known it, but Thoreau would die of tuberculosis.

And what of Bonnie? How did she die? I left my questions behind and trod the path at Walden Pond, littered with bloody handkerchiefs, before I stepped into the black void of sleep.

I awoke in the pink light of a cold dawn. At first I couldn't be certain what had pulled me from a deep sleep, and then I heard it. A child singing. The song was plaintive, a familiar old English ballad. Voice high and true, the child sang, "Oh Mother, Mother, make my bed. And make it deep and narrow. Sweet William died for me today, I'll die for him tomorrow."

I knew the story of scorned love resulting in the death of two young people, hard-hearted Barbrie Allen and lovesick William. And I knew without looking that the singer was the child I'd seen at Walden Pond. She'd found me again, and now she waited for me to wake up.

The cabin was freezing, the fire long dead. I slipped from the bed, dragging several quilts after me and wrapping in them as I made my way to the window. It wasn't even six o'clock and sunrise teased the eastern edge. Staring out the window, I saw her.

In the fringes of the trees, her red coat was a splotch of bright color in the monochrome forest. She watched the cabin. Was I meant to help her or suffer at her hands? I couldn't say, but I accepted the futility of trying to hide from her.

I dressed as quickly and warmly as I could. The day lightened as I stepped onto the porch and walked to the place I'd last seen her. It was time to talk with her. No more games. No more hound and hare. Whatever she wanted, I meant to find out and resolve it.

She was gone, of course, and no footprints marred the snow. But she'd left me a present, and this time it wasn't a doll. In the gloom of the woods I picked up the old tintype. It showed a handsome woman with chestnut hair and pale eyes, her jawline as square as any Cahill in the family tree. Her right hand rested on a child's shoulder. Only a bit of lace collar and a rich velvet sleeve remained of the child—the jagged edge of the tintype told me the youngster had been deliberately cut away.

My heart ached, and I realized it was exultation, not fear. I had discovered no information about Bonnie Cahill in the historical record, but perhaps I'd stumbled on a means of connecting with her. My gut said this was her photograph, and it was possible that the excised child might be none other than Louisa May Alcott. If I could prove that, I would prove Aunt Bonnie had been here in Concord and that she did indeed have a connection with the Alcotts. It was one step closer to putting her in the cabin at Walden Pond.

I gripped the evidence of my aunt's existence in my hand. It could be no one but Bonnie. Now I had to prove that it was her.

19

Instead of working, I walked into town and rented a car. Once on the road that skirted Walden woods, I turned off my cell phone. My quest demanded solitude, and the temptation to keep checking for a call from Joe was too distracting. At Wayland I took Route 27 and followed it south to 95. The once-thriving whaling port of Warren, Rhode Island, was my destination. This was where the Cahills had settled in the mid-1700s.

I hoped to find some record of Bonnie Cahill. While her branch of the family roamed in the traveler tradition, their central hub had been the New England states that bordered the ocean. This was as good a place as any to search.

I tried to imagine her in Warren as I walked along the downtown area. I had no success. If Bonnie had traveled the routes I now covered, she left no echoes.

The scent of salt water slowed me. The smell carried life and also death, the undercurrent of rot and decay. The waves entranced me with their rhythm, the tidal pull. Here the water was calm, but on the far horizon where the brackish bay waters mingled with the saltier Atlantic, the ocean showed her power. I was generations removed from the whalers, but the open water still called to me. I understood in a way I hadn't before.

Had Bonnie been born nearby? Had she returned here to die after Thoreau abandoned her? Had the water spoken to her in that seductive whisper?

The stinging salt wind on my cheeks hinted at the harshness of winter in February. The women of the whalers often struggled for three to five years without their men. They boiled water in the yard to scrub clothes with lye soap they made themselves from rendered hogs. They chopped wood for cooking and heat. They baked and cleaned and schooled their children, knowing the boys would sign onto a ship as soon as they were old enough. They lived most of their days without men.

They were a colony of widows, for all practical purposes. In those households the sea was the wife, and the wife was the maid and caregiver. Not much of a life for a woman, but then that was true for almost every life. Jonah had not remarried, but that didn't mean he failed to have a woman who kept his house and warmed his bed for the few months he put into port.

Jonah's sons married and produced children. I imagined these women, all pregnant simultaneously because their husbands had returned from the sea just long enough to fill their wombs with a child. Women carried on the line. They kept the home fires burning while their men spent weeks and months chasing whales they meant to butcher. Such a life was incomprehensible to me. I could find not a single speck of joy in such an existence.

The cry of the seabirds, so much more demanding than the woodland wrens that wintered in Concord, brought up images of my ancestors. I could clearly see Jonah standing on the prow of his whaler, the *Badb*. He was a massive man with shoulders as wide as an axe handle. Standing with him, his sons were as powerful as their father. Granny painted them so—bigger than life. Tough and fit and capable. They, too, were scavengers. And predators. They demanded and took what they wanted.

I turned my back on my long-dead ancestors and headed to the heart of the town. Boat building and whaling had once been the mainstays of the Warren economy. Now the harbor was jammed with fishing vessels, but those after seafood, not whale blubber. It was a sunny day and the town was alive with folks tending to their chores. I enjoyed the sea breeze and the sun on my shoulders as I walked through downtown and several residential areas.

Any trace of the land belonging to the Cahills was long gone. Granny Siobhan had told of weathered houses that faced the stiff breezes lashing off the Atlantic and up the bay. I walked the picturesque streets and imagined a time when the roads were rutted dirt and horse-drawn wagons carried the spoils of the ocean up the incline to the town. It would have been a hard life, for sure.

In the town archives I found the record of the property owned by Jonah Cahill and his sons. I photographed the line of spidery writing that proved my past. Jonah was listed as a shipmaster. He had no wife and only sons. Granny's oral history proved remarkably accurate. Amazing so many facts had passed down through the generations.

Once I'd found what I could on my own, I asked the clerk for help. She sent me to the Whaling Museum in New Bedford, Massachusetts. Bright sunlight warmed the day, and the idea of a drive along the edge of the bay pleased me. Hill people, as my family is described, know creeks and swift rivers. The vast expanse of the ocean is alien. But I had the blood of Jonah Cahill, whaler and pirate, in my veins. The bay winds whispered freedom to me.

As I drove across Fall River, I wondered if I would ever truly know my heritage. Did anyone? Some families were documented in portrait and deed. Some bloodlines inspired permanent records. Little about the early Cahills had been written down. Bonnie's journal was an anomaly.

I found a quiet coffee shop in the New Bedford downtown and pulled out my laptop. I'd been told in Warren to check the American

Offshore Whaling Voyage registry for the Cahill vessels. Granny had spoken of the *Badb*, the first of Jonah's fleet. I'd researched the name and knew it was that of an Irish shape-shifting warrior Goddess. Appropriate for a ship used to lure other whaling vessels to their demise.

Sure enough, the *Badb* was listed as "lost on the Minerva shoal." I knew that to be false. Jonah had re-fitted the ship and used her to run the British blockades under the name *Bridgit*.

All told, the Cahill Clan had run five whaling ships, and I found the registry for each one. Their fates were "lost at sea," "wrecked on shoals," "sold to a foreign land." The entries that interested me were the ones for ships Jonah had likely scuttled. Many were listed as lost at sea or burned. That much was true, but it wasn't the hand of God that sent those men to their watery graves, it was my ancestors.

I didn't have a printer with me, so I saved my research and packed up for the walk to Johnny Cake Hill and the New Bedford Whaling Museum. As I strolled the old downtown, I had the strangest sense someone was watching me. I turned around several times, wondering if Joe had somehow divined my whereabouts. Wishful thinking. No curious eyes met my search.

Above the door of the museum, Moby Dick floated. The great white whale drifted in and out of my life. Some would call him an omen, others a sign. But of what? Change? Death? New opportunity?

Those answers were unsatisfactory, even to me. I stepped into the museum and immersed myself in the days when whaling reigned supreme.

My appreciation for the courage of the whalers grew as I toured the half-scale replica of a whaling vessel, the *Lagoda*. The bones of the blue whale, Kobo, dwarfed me. But it was the videos of the ruthless, savage pulse of the kill that brought fully home to me the bloodstock I descended from. Economic necessity could never justify such cruelty.

Before I left the museum, I calmed myself by viewing the paintings and glasswork. When I happened on a display of scrimshaw, I took a moment to learn that the sailors on whaling vessels, at sea for such long periods, used knives and needles to scratch the scenes into whales' teeth. Umbrellas and corsets were made from the whale's bones.

Most scrimshaw scenes showed ships or sailing themes. The intricate ivory carvings were rubbed with soot or gunpowder to make them stand out. Scrimshaw—a way to pass the time. In our society, people played video games or watched television. What would our culture leave behind?

In the glass case displaying scrimshaw, I caught the reflection of the child. She stood perfectly still, behind me, watching. But when I whirled around, I startled one of the docents but found nothing else.

"Where did the little girl go?" I asked. I'd seen her in her red jacket, long blond hair hanging down the front from beneath a hood.

"What child?" The docent was a middle-aged man with a mutton-chop beard.

"She was there. Just inside the door." I pointed.

He checked the hall in both directions. "No one there," he said.

"Did you see her?" I couldn't drop it, though I knew he was growing uncomfortable.

"I didn't see anyone." He left me to pursue another chore, or perhaps he wanted to escape a seemingly desperate woman with a fat lip that showed some connection to violence.

In the gift shop I bought postcards of whaling vessels and whale sightings, and old drawings of bearded shipmasters who looked as weathered as the unpainted wooden houses that took the full brunt of the sea's winds.

I had not found Bonnie, but I had found Jonah and a strangely visceral link to the past. I could consider it a good day's work. I had no proof or documented statistics, but I had something better, emotional truth. I had begun to know Bonnie. We were becoming friends.

It was a straight shot up 140 to 24 and west on 495 until I reached the feeder roads that took me back to the Concord area. The drive gave me plenty of time to think what life must have been like for the Cahill clan when they first arrived in America. The death by starvation of Jonah's wife and daughters turned him into a man incapable of compassion but fully capable of murder. He took what he wanted, without regard for the cost to others. Had he been shaped by fate, by the disaster of a freezing winter and a lack of money to buy passage to America for his entire family, or was the ruthlessness part of him long before tragedy marked him? Impossible to say. But I saw clearly the talent for bloodletting in my uncles and cousins in Harlan County. They killed because they liked it. They ruined the lives of everyone they touched, because it didn't matter to them.

Images long repressed—desperate men willing to trade their wives or children for a few pills. Women who thought nothing of selling their bodies for a fix. Oxy and meth, the seeds of destruction for the poor and uneducated. Granny Siobhan—I owed her a lot. She'd stood up to my father, forced him to send me to boarding school. She'd never allowed me to return for summers, only a handful of holidays. I'd barely had time to unpack my suitcase, kiss my father's tear-stained cheek, and eat a meal before she had a driver to take me to the bus station and the long ride back to the school.

Yet she'd written me long letters detailing the history of the family, recounting the mishaps and jailings of cousins, the violent acts of revenge, the feud with the Dunagans that claimed a dozen men on each side, and the births of distant cousins, some of them so damaged by the drugs in their mothers' systems they couldn't breathe on their own. She counted it as the interaction of a merciful god when they were taken. She told me these things because she never wanted me to return. Her love was like the sea, blowing me far away from the Kentucky mountains.

I drove through the winter landscape, the bare red and white oak trees a fringe of gray lace on the horizon. My day spent near the ocean had ignited a yearning I'd never known before. From water life rose, and to water we'd return. I'd heard the saying often enough, yet I'd never felt the pull of the tide and wind as I had today.

My first memories were the treetops singing as the Kentucky wind came over a hilltop and down into our valley. The music of waterfalls, where the bright creeks cascaded over boulders and fallen trees, was my childhood companion. I knew the rocks underfoot as I explored, barefoot in the summers, along a pig trail through the woods, far safer than I'd ever been in a city. Isolated yes, but books provided the only entertainment I needed, and they also gave me a chance to escape for real.

I missed those long-ago summer days when the sun beat down on a hot, flat rock where I could lie and tan my arms and legs, longing for the kind of life I read about in magazines where teen girls worried about zits or leg hair or make-up. My childhood centered around lazy searches for honey or berries through small fields and copses of leafy trees that cast a cool shade.

The longing struck me so suddenly that tears filled my eyes. I missed Granny, and I even missed my drunken father who, though ineffective, was often kind. I was distressed to discover I couldn't clearly picture him. It was as if the alcohol, which numbed his wit, had also blurred the edges of his features into a fetal image that might be human or sheep.

Only sheer will beat the tears back as I turned down the drive to the cabin. I was supposed to return the rental car, but I couldn't. My emotions were raw, my longing for home writ so clear in my eyes that I'd pay the extra day for the use of the car and return it tomorrow. I wanted a glass of wine and my bed.

20

The cold and a pounding headache woke me at three A.M. The over-turned wine bottle on the floor told its own story. I'd drunk the whole thing, eaten no supper, and stumbled into bed by eight o'clock. Duty folded beneath drunkenness, and I'd forgotten to bank the fire. In my alcohol haze, I'd also failed to properly close the door. It swung open several inches and then closed on a gusting wind. No wonder I was freezing.

Nausea hit like a hard fist in the gut, but I managed not to vomit as I made my way to the door and closed it. I was too hung over to worry with the fire. Instead, I limped back to bed and buried myself in quilts.

I returned to consciousness at lunchtime, when Patrick appeared with a tray. He came into the cabin and closed the door with a thud.

"Dorothea stopped by this morning to give you a message, but she said you were out to the world." Dimples gave him an angelic countenance. "She sent a bit of the hair o' the dog."

I groaned and burrowed beneath the pillow. "Aspirin." I could barely push out the word.

"Drink this." He eased the tray on my desk and offered a Bloody Mary sporting a straw. "Take it." He pummeled my pillows to sit me up. "It's freaking freezing in here."

I forced myself to sip as he rebuilt the fire. The spicy tomato mix jolted me awake. Soon, a blaze jumped in the fireplace. The cabin warmed quickly. Against all common sense, the vodka did seem to make me feel better. No wonder my father started each day with a mug of whiskey—to chase the whiskey he'd drunk the night before.

Patrick perched on the edge of the bed. He looked me steadily in the eye, and then his hand grazed my cheek. "You look a mess, Aine Cahill."

"Dying couldn't be worse." His laughter made me smile.

"You're a poor excuse for a hard-drinking woman." He picked up the wine bottle. "One measly bottle put you in your bed?" He tsked. "That's sad, woman. You need more practice."

"I need to take the car back to the rental agency." My brain was beginning to function. My budget didn't allow for extravagances like rental cars sitting unused.

"It's just now noon. They don't close until five, and I'll follow you there in my car and bring you back."

"Thank you." I wasn't ready to move. Not yet. The nausea had gone, but my stomach still wasn't steady.

Patrick retrieved the tray and set it across my lap. "Eat the toast and hash browns. Starch is good for a hangover."

"Sounds like the voice of experience." He wasn't old enough to be an authority on hangovers. Or sex. But he'd demonstrated his abilities.

"I've had my share. It's part of the testosterone experience. You know, you have to prove your manliness in high school, which generally means lying about sex and drinking too much." He kissed my palm. "I won't have to lie about sex ever again, since I met you. If I told the whole truth, I'd be voted the luckiest man in the world."

Even though my head throbbed, I had to laugh. "You're full of the very devil, Patrick Leahy. Someone taught you the gift of blarney."

"And you love it, don't you?"

The truth was, I did. Patrick made it so easy. And fun. Not serious and responsible. Nothing permanent could possibly be struck with Patrick, and therefore there were no expectations. "Dorothea will be wondering after you."

"It's my lunch break." He built a fresh fire and lit it as I ate.

He might be lying or he might be telling the truth. I only knew that the drink made my head better, and the food had settled my stomach. Due to excess drinking, I'd lost half a day's work. I had no more time to squander.

"Let me make you feel better," Patrick said. "I know exactly what to do."

I picked up his hand and held it. "I can't. You know why."

"You're back with Joe, even though he's never here when you need him."

"Joe isn't part of this. I have to work, Patrick. And this thing between us has to end. It's improper and will only mean trouble for both of us. Please take the tray back to Dorothea and thank her."

"I won't give up, Aine. I love you." He picked up the tray and hurried out the door, slamming it behind him.

I almost called out to him. Hurting him was painful. But better now than letting it drag on.

⁂

The day was drawing to a close when Patrick let me out of his car at the inn. Despite his anger at me, he'd kept his word and picked me up at the rental agency. His silence on the drive home told me of his hurt.

I got out on the lane to the cabin and he wheeled around to park on the opposite side of the inn. Before he left for the day, he had to finish moving some furniture for Dorothea. She stood in the back doorway making certain he didn't dodge her. If she knew there was something wrong between Patrick and me, she didn't let on.

"Did Patrick give you your message?" she asked.

"No." I hoped she'd think the flush in my cheeks was from the cold. "He must have forgotten."

"The boy has nothing on the brain." She rolled her eyes. "I sent him with the tray *and* the message. Joe tried to call you all day yesterday. He said something was wrong with your cell phone. He'll be by to visit tonight if that's good with you. If not, you can use the phone in the inn to call him."

"No, it's fine." I wasn't certain it was, but I didn't want to discuss Joe with Dorothea.

"I'm glad you're giving him a chance, Aine. He did nothing wrong. He was a good teacher. Possibly a great one. His only sin was caring about his students. He loved watching them learn. It cost him everything to be accused of Mischa's disappearance."

"I understand she was working on some project. Do you have more details?"

"She was after a toad or slug or something she'd talked to Joe about. Biology and the natural world, Joe's big interest. No one thought a thing about the extra time he spent with the students, until Mischa didn't show up for supper. Then it was like a perversion."

"What do you think happened?"

She had come out of the inn with a dishcloth in her hand. She wiped her hands on it, threw it over her shoulder, and stuffed her fists into her apron. Dusk was falling and the cold was settling in. "I think one of those sexual predators grabbed her up. He did things to her, and then he got scared she might talk so he killed her. That's what I think. They shouldn't let those people live near children."

"Were there sexual predators in the neighborhood?"

"Yes, one. But they couldn't find any evidence implicating him. Folks ran him out of town, though. They ran him straight out of town. The deviant was lucky he wasn't strung up on general principle, but it was too late for Mischa. She was gone."

It wasn't hard to see why suspicions fell on Joe, no matter how innocent he might be. He was a grown man, and he spent free time with a young girl. Our world had become a place where such a thing was viewed as questionable, rather than commendable. What I would have given for a grade school teacher—or anyone besides Granny Siobhan—who sensed value in me.

"I saw Mischa's picture in the newspaper, but it wasn't a good photo."

"So, you checked into the story." Dorothea's tone held neither censure nor approval.

"I owe myself the facts."

"You do, though facts are hard to determine. Just because a story is printed in a newspaper doesn't make it a fact."

Dorothea's reaction made me wonder if my search had been thorough enough. "I'll speak with Joe about this."

"Give him a chance. And let me know if Patrick is bothering you. It seems you're his latest obsession. Give him a week or two and his fancy will turn to someone more appropriate. If he annoys you, I'll set him straight."

"Thanks for the message." I stamped from one foot to the next to warm myself, impatient to be on my way.

Dorothea gently caught my forearm. A line gathered between her eyebrows. "Karla is trouble, Aine. Watch your step with that one."

"You don't have to convince me. She's come after me twice." I longed for the warmth of the cabin. Dorothea's warning brought the darkness closer and again I felt the uncanny sense that someone was watching me. It didn't feel like the child. Malice tickled icy fingers over my neck, and it occurred to me that Karla might be waiting to ambush me yet again. I glanced at the surrounding woods but could detect no sign of life.

"She's hopped up on meth and god knows what else."

"Is there a solution?" I wanted a course of action, not a rehashing of old facts.

Dorothea brought her other hand from her apron pocket and held out a black canister. "Take it. Pepper spray. I keep one at the register and I brought my spare to you. It'll stop her dead, but it can also blind you if you aren't careful how you use it."

The small canister fit snugly in my coat pocket. "Thank you."

"Joe felt sorry for Karla. And he was lonely. Only a few weeks after Mischa disappeared, his fiancée Amanda left him. She couldn't take the scorn of the community. That scarred Joe. He left town for several years, changed his life. When he came back to care for his mother, Karla took advantage of him, but she also gave him something no one else would. She didn't care what anyone said about Joe, or about her. She showed him that public talk and innuendoes could only hurt if he let them. We humans are frail in so many ways."

"We are indeed." I inched backward, the gravel of the drive crunching beneath my feet. "I'd better get some work done before Joe comes by."

21

Showered and dressed in jeans and a warm sweater, I straightened the cabin. Dorothea had brought over clean sheets while I was returning the rental car. As I shook them out, something flew from the bed and struck the floor.

Kneeling to look under the bed, I reached for the object. My fingers detected the strange texture and shape before my brain registered what I held. A whale tooth. A scrimshawed one, like those at the museum.

I felt as if the breath had been knocked from my lungs and I slumped on the floor, the tooth clutched in my hand. I didn't have to ask where it had come from. I knew. I'd seen the child at the whaling museum. Only a flash, but it was her. She'd followed and watched. And she'd left a souvenir so I'd know.

How she traveled from Concord to Rhode Island begged an answer I didn't have. I could only presume a ghost child went wherever she chose. Next time I saw her, I would ask. How she'd acquired such a valuable artifact, I didn't want to know.

I rose and turned on the desk lamp. Under the good light I was able to study the image cut into the ivory tooth. It was a ship's figurehead, a young girl in a hooded cape with flowing curls. Above her was an unfurled banner with a Latin inscription I couldn't read. The girl's eyes, as black and glassy as obsidian, held my attention.

Logic presumed she was the ship captain's daughter or a child lost at sea or a beloved family member. But I knew better. My little friend had brought me a scrimshawed likeness of herself. I didn't recall seeing the tooth at the whaling museum, so where had it come from?

I studied the intricate cuts and scratches in the ivory. Like the antique scrimshaw at the museum, this too had been rubbed with gunpowder or soot or ink to bring the image to life. The artist displayed great skill and talent. The child's hooded cloak hung low on her forehead, almost obscuring her eyes—black and oblique. Bored out. The effect was more than a little unsettling.

If this was Mischa Lobrano, who had carved her image in an expensive whale's tooth? Did a Concord artist have such talent? Was Mischa sending me on a quest to resolve what happened to her?

I held the scrimshaw tight for a time, but I could instill no warmth in it. What had once been a part of a living creature and the image of what had once been a living child were incapable of warmth.

Joe's knock brought me to myself. I realized the bed was unmade and the cabin still a mess. There was nothing to do but let him in. Time for him to see the untidy, chaotic side of me.

Joe's face was drawn with worry and stress. He stepped into the room, closed the door, and pulled me against his chest in a tight embrace. He made no effort to kiss me. He merely held me, and I realized I liked the sensation.

"We have to talk," Joe said.

My first concern was that he knew about Patrick. I stepped back, playing for time to think. As he fed more wood onto the fire, I pulled the desk chair closer so that it faced the rocking chair.

Satisfied at last that the fire would burn hot, he sat on the edge of the rocker and took my hands. "It's Karla," he said. "She's claiming you attacked her unprovoked. She says she's going to bring charges against you. She said she came here to speak with you and you went after her."

The revelation stunned me. I'd expected to defend myself for sleeping with Patrick. Never in a million years had I thought Karla would lie after she'd hidden in the woods near my cabin and viciously attacked me.

"That's crazy."

He nodded. "Be that as it may, she intends to make trouble for you. She doesn't want to leave Concord, and she thinks this is a way around it. She said if I continue to press her to leave town, she'll file charges against you."

"I'm not afraid of her."

"It doesn't matter that you're right. She's going to make it bad for you."

"And for you," I said.

He nodded. "If this makes the newspaper, they'll bring up everything about Mischa again. Karla is unstable. She's a drug user. That will all tie back to me."

I wondered what he expected of me. I had bigger problems than Karla Steele's craziness. "She's vindictive and I want her gone or behind bars. That's not going to change."

He turned my hands over so that he could examine the palms. "She promised she'd leave town and then reneged. The best thing for you is to avoid her. I've talked with the Chief, and he's aware of her drug use. She's careless. She'll eventually get arrested for that. I'll continue to urge her to leave Concord. I've spoken with her sister, and she's willing to come to Concord and take her back to Nebraska."

I tried to think through his request. Had I been slower, Karla might have done me serious damage. Even killed me. It could take weeks to catch her buying drugs or committing another crime. Even if her sister begged, there was no guarantee Karla would leave with her.

"Why does she hate me so much?"

Joe rubbed his thumbs lightly over the pulse point in my wrist. "She's jealous of you. She asked questions around town. You're everything she's not and will never be. She knows who you are, that you are working on your doctorate. She's mentally ill, Aine, but I believe she'll get the help she needs in Nebraska with her family. Jail won't help her. Her sister has promised to commit her to a mental health facility."

"All well and good, but it won't prevent her attacks on innocent people." My anger surprised even me. Joe asking for compassion for a crazy woman after she'd tried to kill me was too much. "She should rot in jail."

"Think, Aine. I'll help you do whatever you want, but be sure you think this through."

I calmed the surge of anger that made me seek revenge against a woman who'd targeted me for her misplaced jealousy and rage. I'd given her far more than she'd ever anticipated when it came to physical reprisal, maybe enough to scare her. "Okay," I said. "But I want to know when she leaves for Nebraska. And it had better be soon."

"I'll make certain."

"You said that last time."

"I was deceived. It won't happen again. I promise. Karla's sister will arrive tomorrow. I'm picking her up at the airport. She intends to persuade Karla to fly back to Nebraska and get help."

"Last chance, for both of you."

He brought my left hand up to his lips and kissed my wrist and then the center of my palm. "Thank you."

I had news for him, too, but decided it was best to keep the scrimshaw a secret until I checked out my hunch. If Mischa Lobrano was communicating with me, if she'd chosen me to receive clues to her disappearance, then perhaps it should remain between us. At least until I figured out what happened to her. If she'd wanted Joe to receive the leads in her disappearance, she'd have shown them to him. "Let me get some wine." I stood and went to the kitchen area.

"What have you been up to lately?" Joe settled back in the rocker, his profile warmed by the glow of the fire.

I told him of my adventures in Warren and New Bedford. "I found the original American Cahills." I'd told him I had a family connection to Thoreau, but I'd never shared the journal. I was tempted now, but I still held back.

His strong hands captured my arms and lifted me into his lap. Rocking gently, he kissed me. My body responded, and I wrapped my arms around his neck, my fingers seeking purchase in his thick, dark hair.

"Let's put those sheets on the bed," he suggested. "I think you need warming up."

"And I think you're just the man to do it." I slipped from his lap and led him to the bed. In only a few moments, we had the sheets tucked in and the quilts smoothed. Joe threw another log on the fire as I undressed and slid across the cold sheets. In a moment, his body was beside me and his touch ignited a fire that seared through both of us.

22

Joe brewed coffee and brought in wood for the fire long before dawn. Tucked beneath the quilts, I traced the hand-stitched patterns with a lazy finger and sipped the steaming coffee he served me in bed.

As he slipped into his coat, he said "I'll let you know how it goes with Karla and her sister. Hopefully, she'll be gone very soon."

My emotions were still conflicted, so I nodded.

"Stay home today," he said as he sat on the edge of the bed. "The forecast is for bad weather. Most folks manage the snow, but if there's ice beneath it there will be accidents."

"I have to write today." It was true—I needed to spend hours pounding on my dissertation—but my plan for the morning was already laid out in my mind.

"I'll give you a call later," he said. "Don't take up with any strangers." He kissed my forehead and then my lips, his scruff zinging the tender skin of my face.

He left as the sky lightened from black to gray. Thick clouds obscured the light and warmth. It would be bad weather, as he'd predicted. I showered and dressed to go out. After a breakfast at the inn, I had research to do. Unfortunately, it wasn't on my dissertation but on the scrimshaw I put in my jacket pocket along with the pepper spray Dorothea had given me.

Joe intended for Karla to leave, but that didn't mean she'd cooperate. If she stalked and cornered me again, I'd make certain she never forgot the encounter. My cousins had taught me a few important things about dealing with crazy people and drug addicts. They didn't give up. The only solution was to hurt them so badly they *couldn't* come after me again.

The aroma of bacon hit me as I entered the dining room. Dorothea indicated I should pick my own seat while she checked out two customers. Her smug expression told me she knew Joe had spent the night and approved. I could only hope I'd put my fling with Patrick in the past, where it would never surface.

She served me hot coffee, cranberry juice, flapjacks with maple syrup, and crispy bacon—a breakfast fit for a lumberjack. And I ate every mouthful.

"Worked up an appetite, did you, girl?" she asked.

"I did."

"That Joe, he's a fine catch. You with your fancy degree and teaching in college. Maybe he'll return to what he loves best."

"He loves being a ranger." I couldn't say why the thought of Joe returning to teaching troubled me.

"Teaching was his first love. You know how it is." She swept my plate up in her capable hands and was gone.

I put on my coat, hat, scarf, and gloves and set out for the gift shops in town. Whaling wasn't the focal point of Concord. This area had another bloody tourist trade, the Revolutionary War. Still, there were several art galleries, and local artists tended to know each other.

While my dissertation languished, I pursued the riddle of the girl in the red hooded cloak. Mischa Lobrano. And I had to be careful what I asked.

My first three stops yielded nothing. The fourth business was an artsy shop that featured prints of local artists, some sculpture, and depictions of historic events in ceramic and bronze. Some of the work was quite good, and other pieces were clearly targeted for the tourist market.

The man behind the counter was thin, balding, and in his seventies. Perfect. He might know a few things about events from a decade past.

"May I help you?" he asked.

My finger traced the image of the girl carved into the tooth lying snug in my pocket. "Do you have any scrimshaw?"

His expression shifted from helpful to disinterested. "You'll find a better selection in New Bedford and communities with historic ties to the whaling industry. The older pieces are valuable; ivory is illegal to purchase now. Endangered species."

"I didn't know."

"Are you looking for something in particular?" he asked.

"An expert to tell me about a piece. And about the process of scrimshaw."

He came out from behind the counter and went to a back shelf. After rummaging for a moment, he handed me a pamphlet. "I have this, a history of the art. Through the years, I've had a piece or two of scrimshaw, but not many. A few years back a local young man wanted me to carry some pieces. He'd worked up Revolutionary War scenes on whale teeth."

My frown made him laugh.

"Exactly my reaction. An unhappy marriage of Concord history with the whaling industry. I put a couple of pieces in my cabinet but they never sold."

"What happened to them?"

"He came by and picked them up. Said he was heading back to the sea, leaving Concord behind."

"Was he a local man? Maybe he's still carving."

"Let me see. Let me see." He went behind the counter and brought out a receipt book. "Sailors with nothing to do carved scrimshaw on those lengthy whaling voyages. Pretty much a lost art."

"Some of the work is beautiful."

"I never sold any of his, but I might have logged it into inventory."
Pages fluttered as he perused the book. "Let's see. Here's something."
He pointed.

Leaning over the counter I read the name Roger Brent. "Is that
him?"

"Ayuh. Roger Brent. My memory's coming back. Tall young man.
Thin. Lived at the end of Yerby Lane. Well, the only building on
Yerby. Roger Brent. He was sort of a history and nature enthusiast.
Liked to hike." He nodded as he talked. "A loner type. Said Thoreau
had it all figured out. Man did best on his own, he said. Solitude
brought wisdom and all that crap. Brent was all caught up in the talk
about the new century. Polar fields shifting, Y2K, all of that foolishness. If he was here now, he'd be ranting about solar flares or some
going-up-in-the-rapture foolishness."

"Is the invoice dated?"

He pushed pages back to reveal a blurry date.

"Would you recognize his style of scrimshaw?"

"Nope. Never that interested. Put the pieces in the cabinet to
shut him up. He was a kook. I wondered how he kept body and soul
together, and now that I think about it, he surely didn't eat regular.
Musta been mental, you know." He tapped his temple. "I should have
tried to help him. Back then, though, he was just another person
with a strange twist. We attract a few of them here. Folks who read
Emerson and Thoreau and want to live in the woods. Danger now
is they aren't just recluses but those crazy survivalists. Any dern fool
in the country can own an assault weapon or buy the goods to make
bombs."

"Where did you say he lived?"

"Yerby Lane. Not so far from Walden Pond. Never been paved. The
lane goes back to an old shack." He held out the pamphlet of scrimshaw
history. "Take this. Might be of interest to you. Take it as a gift."

I thanked him and reached into my pocket. "Does this look like
Roger Brent's work?"

He scrutinized the tooth. "The work is good. Whoever did this used a combination of needle and small blade. Depth of cut is used to give the image a three-dimensional quality. This could be quite valuable."

"Does it look like Brent's work?" I asked again.

"Can't say for sure. Where'd you get it?"

I wasn't about to tell him that the ghost of a little girl left it for me. "I bought it at a junk shop in Rhode Island."

"You have quite an eye." He took it to the light from his front door for a better view. "Unusual treatment of the child's eyes. Never seen anything quite like it."

"I noticed that."

"It's the only sign of amateur craftsmanship I can detect." His finger gently tapped the carving. "If you want to sell it, I'll put the word out."

"No, it's not for sale. Can you tell how old it is?"

He shook his head. "I don't have the experience. The substance used in the cuts seems to be gunpowder, which might date it, but you'd need an expert to tell for sure. Maybe someone at a university. The archeology departments should be able to help you." He held it out to me.

"Could the young girl depicted be local?" I asked. "Maybe she modeled for him or was a relative."

That stopped him. "I can't say."

I pointed to the writing on the furled banner. *Praeterita est numquam mortuum.* "What does that mean?"

"It's Latin, I think, but I can't say the meaning. Like I said, your best bet is a university."

I took the tooth and returned it to my pocket. "Is Yerby Lane in walking distance?"

"Ayuh. But there's nothing there. I doubt the shack is still standing."

"Thank you," I said as I headed for the door.

Snow hadn't begun to fall, but the sky was leaden and heavy. The clouds looked ready to really cut loose, but the forecasts promised the weather would hold until tomorrow. I had plenty of time for a hike.

I took the route toward Walden Pond. I wasn't certain where Yerby Lane might be, but I needed to move. Whenever I stopped, images from the past two days caught up with me. Patrick's body in the glow of the fire, Joe asleep in my bed, the thud of fist on flesh in the darkness, and the flash of red through the woods riding on the giggle of a child.

I couldn't really say how far I'd walked or how long it had taken me, but I stood at an intersection. The lane leading west wasn't marked, but it fit the shopkeeper's description of Yerby Lane.

23

The first flakes drifted down as I turned onto the trail. Thick and heavy, they stuck to leaves, limbs, and eyelashes, and accumulated immediately on the ground. The snow fell so dense and fast that visibility was only twenty yards. Looking down the rutted dirt trail, I guessed no one had recently traveled this path. It was isolated, as the shopkeeper said. The wisest move would be to head back to the inn and return another day when the weather was better.

My impatience wouldn't allow retreat, though. I'd be home in an hour. There was plenty of time to finish my exploration. I trudged down the lane wondering how far it was to artist Roger Brent's former cabin. A shack ten years ago, according to the shopkeeper. Would anything of the structure remain?

Instead of lightening the sky, the onslaught of snow seemed to pull the gray clouds lower until it felt as if they rested on the tops of the bare trees. Suffocating. I struggled for oxygen as I pushed on down the path.

The trees pressed closer and closer the deeper I went. The path was not wide enough for a vehicle now, barely accommodating a human. The woods were alive with the sound of small limbs snapping beneath the weight of the snow. Scuffing through it, I realized how wet and heavy it was. Joe was right. If the temperatures fell another few degrees, the terrain would be layered with ice beneath the snow, a dangerous condition.

Perhaps it was my imagination, but it seemed the temperature was dropping. Maybe it was only the damp snow. Still, my fingers, in warm gloves, and my toes, nested in heavy socks and leather boots, had numbed out. Even protected by a scarf, my ears ached from the cold.

Pulling my collar higher, I pushed on. The adversities only made me more determined. Granny Siobhan called it the "bitch in the ditch" syndrome. It was a famous Cahill trait based on some distant relative who'd wrecked three cars trying to get a load of moonshine down the mountain to what turned out to be an under-cover revenuer.

I could still hear Granny's voice. "Providence stepped in three times to prevent Mare from delivering the 'shine. Three times she climbed out of the ditch, shook her fist in Fate's face, borrowed or stole another vehicle, and continued. In the end, she was carted off to jail for her troubles."

Cahills were known for hardheadedness. Chances were, if Captain Ahab could trace his lineage, he would discover he had Cahill blood. No one but a Cahill, fictional or not, would chase a whale around the world just for the pleasure of trying to kill it.

The thought of the Great White made me reach into my pocket for the whale's tooth. My gloved fingers surrounded it, too numb to truly feel, but I knew it when I touched it. The canister of pepper spray was also there. I felt a little less vulnerable when I held it.

At last a shack came into view. It stood, if one could call two timbers holding the whole thing upright standing, like the ghost of a house long dead. A good wind, or a heavy snow on the roof, would send it toppling. Today might be the day.

I scrabbled onto the tiny roofed porch so I could shake the snow out of my hair. Coming here had been a mistake. Admit it now or suffer later.

My cell phone was fully charged, and I decided to use it. Joe would come and get me. Or Patrick. If I called the inn, Dorothea would send Patrick for me.

"Shit." I shook the phone. No reception. The damn thing was useless in Concord. It didn't work at the cabin or in the woods. The first tingle of unease pricked my spine.

The five-by-five-foot porch barely covered my head and shoulders, so I pushed at the front door. It swung open without complaint. A great reluctance tugged at my feet, warning me not to step inside. It wasn't trespassing that worried me—it was something far more frightening, though I couldn't put my finger on what.

Falling snow obscured everything, even the tree line, which was no more than twenty feet away. The cabin might be my only chance at survival. I'd never make it back to the road around Walden, and it was another three miles home from there. I was stuck. Either the cabin or the woods. Not much of a choice.

I crossed the threshold.

The cabin was dark. No windows, but that also meant at least a bit of insulation from the wind. I couldn't see much, and with each step inside, I wondered if my foot would go through the flooring. A gash or twisted ankle could prove fatal under these conditions.

Feeling my way, I groped across the top of a table. As I patted the surface, I found an old oil lamp. Beside it was a book of matches. I stopped. I had the sense I'd stepped into some awful fairy tale where things had been put in place especially for me. As if someone knew I would come here.

Granny Siobhan's stories frequently featured malicious fairies and elves, changelings and gremlins. She'd read to me, and one story that never failed to frighten me was *Vasilisa the Beautiful*, about a young girl sent into the woods to find firewood. She stumbles upon a witch's house and her life changes dramatically, and not for the better.

I struck a match and lit the lamp's wick. At first I didn't see her sitting so quietly in the corner. When I did, I thought my heart might stop.

"I knew you'd come," she said. "I've been watching. And waiting."
She sat perfectly still, and in the dimness I couldn't be certain if her
lips were moving or if she was communicating telepathically. The
urge to run consumed me, but my legs refused to work.

"I'm not going to hurt you," she said. Her lips twitched at the
corners, but her eyes remained wide and black. "I'm just a little girl.
I can't hurt you."

How did one speak to a ghost? "Why are you watching me?"

"Because you'll listen. So few people will. You can see me, and so
many can't. Or won't."

She sat so still that had the lamplight not caught in her eyes I'd have
thought I was conversing with a shadow. "Are you Mischa Lobrano?"
I asked. "You never told me your name. Back at Walden."

"Researcher that you are, I thought you'd dig it up. A joke, if you
will." Her smile was too cynical for such a young girl. "My name
matters not. Call me whatever you wish."

"To me it does matter. What's your name?"

"Mischa will do. Where I live now, names aren't so important.
Understanding is."

"What do you want of me?"

She didn't seem to move, yet she was standing in front of me. "Not
so very much. I promise I'll make it worth your while."

In the lamplight, her eyes were as black and bottomless as those
in the scrimshaw.

24

There wasn't a fire in the tiny cabin, no method of heat, but strangely I began to warm. The walls blocked the wind, and the roof, though tenuous, kept out the snow. When I went to close the door more firmly, I noticed drifts piling high against tree trunks. The skies showed no signs of letting up.

"Worried about the walk home?" the child asked. "It can be dangerous cutting through the woods, but that's the fastest way. In the snow, the roots and holes are covered up and can't be seen. You have to be very careful."

"Did you cut through the woods the day you disappeared?"

She cocked her head to one side like a bird. "Little Miss Nancy Drew. You can't stop gnawing on the mystery. Do you really care what happened to a little girl?"

I did. "Who hurt you?"

"That's the crux of your worry. You suspect one of your lovers did something very, very bad."

She looked like a child, but she spoke like a much older woman. And she meant to tease me by withholding whatever I asked. "What do you know about lovers?"

"I know most people think fucking two men is bad form. Some might call that promiscuous. Or desperate. Or maybe insane."

She shocked me, and also pissed me off. "Who are you to judge, flitting through the woods leaving dead birds and dolls?"

"Just an observation. Social mores come and go. In the place where I live, such things aren't of any significance. We understand that monogamy isn't part of the human condition. In the natural world, animals pick the vibrant, strongest mate. The man who can provide and survive. That's the way of nature. Who can fault a woman for being natural?"

Such sentiments coming from the mouth of a child made me backpedal toward the door. This was very wrong. My fingers found the knob and I turned it slowly, praying it wouldn't rattle or squeak.

"Leaving so soon?" She never moved, but the latch slid home. "I don't want you to go. Let's play a game. I haven't had a playmate in such a long time."

"Who are you?" I no longer felt certain this was the ghost of Mischa Lobrano. She wasn't even a child. There was age-old intelligence in her gaze, a jadedness that scared me.

"Mischa. You like to think of me as her."

"No child talks like you do."

A small hand slid down her face as if she meant to wipe her expression off. "I'm sorry." Her voice remained childlike, but her entire bearing changed. Rounder shoulders, limber spine. "Being dead does strange things to you. Dead means lonely. You're the only person who can see me. Think what it's been like for the past days and nights. I've been here. Stuck, in-between. I've tried to tell people what happened. No one listens. Years have passed. It's true, I've grown testy. I was once the princess. My parents loved me so much. Do you know how hard it is to watch them suffer?"

"So you *are* Mischa." It had been nearly a decade since the kid disappeared. Had she lived, she'd be a smart-mouthed teenager. It fit. She'd matured, but not physically. I thought of Ann Rice's sorrowful creation, Claudia, the child vampire, doomed never to go through puberty or experience a sexual relationship.

"Do you know why you can hear me?" she asked.

"No, but I'd like to." Because I felt sorry for her, I offered friendship. Not to mention my curiosity and the hope this child, who produced dolls and tintypes, might also help me with my primary quest. Aunt Bonnie.

"You're a Cahill. You aren't the first of your blood with the gift of communicating with the dead."

"My aunt Bonnie had a gift. Predicting the future by dreams. Second sight. She hinted at communicating with the dead."

She clapped her hands. "Very good. You're smart, too. I like that."

An awesome possibility presented itself. "Can I speak with Bonnie?"

She shook her head and her blond hair shimmered in the lamplight. "I can't answer, because I don't know. *Maybe* you can. If she'll talk with you. She may not want to."

My head was reeling, and I felt slightly nauseous. I put a hand on the table to steady myself. This was incredible. I was having a conversation with a long-dead child. A wave of heat washed over me, and I feared I might be sick.

"Let me help you." She was at my side. The door opened and a blast of frigid air brushed over me, bringing sweet relief from the nausea. I inhaled and closed my eyes, allowing my stomach and head to calm and settle.

"Better?" she asked.

"Yes." I blinked and stared into the black depths of her eyes. They weren't black, but a deep navy blue. I pushed the hood back from her face. Her blond hair was silky and a pure golden yellow, the color of childhood, of innocence, of summer sun. No bottle could duplicate that shade. "I'll bet your mother's heart broke when you didn't come home."

She glanced down at her feet. "A lot of people hurt. Joe was one of them."

I found I couldn't ask the question I most wanted an answer to. I couldn't ask if Joe had hurt her.

"Don't ask if you can't take the answer." She flipped her hair over her shoulder and went to close the door.

I would forever berate myself as a coward if I didn't try. "Do you know what happened to you?"

"No."

I wondered if she was lying, and to what purpose. "What do you remember?"

"What do I remember?" She spun like a child, arms wide. I grabbed the oil lamp for fear she'd knock it off the table.

"I remember walking in the woods. Mr. Sinclair had taken us on a nature walk the first of the school year. We talked about ladybugs. They're the state insect for Massachusetts, you know. The state called for 'citizen biologists' to help find and photograph all the ladybugs." She spun again, her features gleeful. "Mr. Sinclair said if we could find any nine-spotted ladybugs—they called them C-9—and photograph them, he would give us each ten dollars."

"Did Joe mean for you to go into the woods alone?"

She twirled, halting in front of me. "No. He had no idea I was going into the woods. He'd probably forgotten all about ladybugs and the money." Her voice lowered. "But he didn't tell me the C-9 was thought to be extinct. It's not right to send children on a quest that hard."

My knees weakened. If Joe hadn't tempted her into the woods, he wasn't there waiting to take her. He hadn't asked her to meet him. She'd gone on her own initiative. I might not be able to tackle this issue head on, but I could nibble away at it.

"That makes you feel better, doesn't it?" she asked.

"Yes."

"You like Mr. Sinclair."

"I do." She seemed able to read my mind, so why deny it?

"And the boy, Patrick? Do you like him, too?"

"Not in the same way." I didn't mind her curiosity about my life. She'd been cheated out of hers. Why not share a little? "Patrick is fun. Joe is serious. There are days when I'm lonely, and I just want to laugh and feel good."

"I know how that feels." All life drained from her face. "I'm lonely all the time. Until you came."

I had the strangest urge to comfort her. She might be a ghost with too much knowledge, but she was also a little girl who'd died before her life had even begun. "I tried to befriend you at Walden. You ran away."

"I couldn't be certain what you'd do if you realized what I am. I've tried so many times over the years and failed. People are afraid of me, but you're a special person, Aine."

"I had a lonely childhood, so I can empathize."

"You want a child, don't you?"

She had the uncanny ability to read me. "Maybe once I get my doctorate."

"You want a little girl. Like me. A blonde." Her smile hinted at things she shouldn't know.

"No. A boy." I spoke too quickly.

"No, you don't. You want a girl. To replace the one you killed."

Her words ripped at me. I raised my hands in self-defense. How did she know? She couldn't know. It was impossible. Even if she was a ghost, she'd have no way to know my personal history.

"It's okay, silly," Mischa said. "You were only a kid. You couldn't have a baby. Everyone knows that."

My hand found the latch and I eased it open. Before she could protest, I yanked the door open and ran out into the darkness. Stumbling over a loose board on the porch, I hurtled into the snow. I went down on my knees and scrambled to my feet, lurching forward, gasping for air.

When I turned back to look at the little shack, I could see the glow of the oil lamp through the open door. The day had disappeared, and while I'd been inside the shack with Mischa, night, so perfectly still and silent, had slipped over me. I'd lost hours of time.

Standing alone in the woods I could hear the snow falling. I'd never felt the world so hushed and shut down. Had I been inside the cabin at all? Standing knee-deep in snow, I couldn't be certain. I couldn't even find my footprints. The snow obliterated them.

The light visible through the open door, though, reassured me that I hadn't imagined the encounter. I hadn't. She was in there. A little dead girl's spirit. An angry child who had every right to be furious. Someone had taken her life, stolen her future. She knew things she shouldn't, but perhaps that was a compensation to the dead for all the pleasures of life they'd never know again. I couldn't run away from her. She held the answers about my aunt. Answers I needed.

Even though I didn't want to, I shook off the snow and started back to the porch.

Without warning, the door slammed shut.

25

When I made it to Route 126, the major road skirting the forested land around Walden Pond, I knew I was in serious trouble. Within a few minutes of leaving the cabin, I was lost. Somehow I managed to stumble in the right direction.

I'd thought finding 126 would solve my problems, but that wasn't the case. Once I reached the ribbon of clearing that had to be the road, I got a better picture of what I faced. Everything familiar had vanished under a covering of soundless white. Heavy clouds obscured the starlight and the white cold obliterated my senses. It seemed I'd gone deaf and mute and blind. I was completely alone. Everyone with good sense was indoors. There would be no passing cars, no help from strangers. I was stranded in a world absent of everything except snow.

My years in Kentucky hadn't prepared me for this kind of snow-fall. I'd been a fool to wander so far away from town, and I had no explanation for what had happened to the daylight hours. It had been afternoon and then night. Granny Siobhan had taught me to read the clouds and hear the whisper of the leaves. Mother Earth gave warnings of her intentions for those who listened. I'd witnessed the pregnant sky, swollen and gray, and the jittery warning of the wind in the trees—and hardheadedly pursued my own agenda. No matter that I'd assumed I could call for help—a cab or Joe or Patrick. My cell phone was useless. I'd ignored nature's plentiful signals and continued on, driven by the unsolved murder of a child.

Not an innocent child. She might have been naïve once, but Mischa Lobrano was far from blameless now. Death had taught her many things a young girl shouldn't know. And at least one trick. She possessed a keen ability to read the past. My past. How, I wasn't certain. All I knew was that she could discern my secrets. That was not a comfortable thing for me.

The snow piled up to mid-thigh and I floundered forward, afraid to stand in one place too long. I'd heard it said that people who were caught outside during blizzards often grew too weary to keep moving. They were found curled in a ball in the snow, dead. They gave in to weariness, to the desperate need to stop and sleep.

Would that be such a terrible death? It sounded peaceful enough. The cold was biting, but that wouldn't last long. Numbness would set in. Already the cold pulled at me, promising a rest would refresh me. But I remembered Pauley Cahill, a cousin who got lost hunting in the mountains during a frigid February.

That winter had been an anomaly. The snow had come down fast and thick, like now. Pauley was an experienced woodsman. All of the Cahill boys were taught to hunt and kill before grade school. Pauley knew his way around the forest, but he'd slipped and sprained his ankle. Unable to do anything more than hobble, he'd gone as far as he could and then curled up under an overhanging rock to rest and wait for help.

When they found him, he was almost dead. They should have let him die. They took his feet above the ankles. A week later, they severed his hands just below the elbows. He lost both ears and his nose. What was left of Pauley was barely human, and he burned with a fury more terrifying than his noseless face over what had been taken from him by the cold. He was in charge of making sure the Oxy buyers paid their bills. He showed slackers the same compassion the cold had shown him.

That image got me moving. Pumping my legs as hard as I could, my feet slipped off the edge of the blacktop and I nearly twisted my ankle, which would have been a harsh irony.

The landscape ended ten feet in front of me in a curtain of white. It was impossible to see anything. The inn was a good three miles away, and without landmarks I couldn't be sure I was moving in the right direction. It would take everything I had to get there, but the alternative was to stop and freeze to death. The denim pants I wore were soaked and icy. I pushed myself forward, thinking about the little girl in the cabin.

Mischa Lobrano, if that was who she really was. She'd never answered my question about her name. In fact, she'd told me nothing about herself, and she knew a lot about me that no one should.

My abortion was a secret I'd shared with no one except the father, Bryson Cappett, and he hadn't told anyone. I'd been a kid. Sixteen, away at boarding school without anyone who cared about me. The girls at school hated me. They took every opportunity to show it, too. Bryson was the best-looking and most popular boy at school. When he asked me out, I thought it was a joke. I figured Kimmie, one of the popular girls who made it a point to torment me, had put him up to it to humiliate me. I declined his offers of dinner, skating, hockey games, and parties.

He worked on me relentlessly for three weeks, telling me that he was sorry the other girls were so mean, that he thought I was beautiful, and that he liked my accent and how it made me unique. He was kind and gentle and interested in me, and he made it clear that I was his number one priority.

Three months later he was telling me how much of a stupid hick I was because I hadn't been on the pill. It had never occurred to him that I wouldn't know enough to use protection because I'd never needed it—until him.

Struggling against the snow, my stomach cramped at the memory of the whole sordid mess. I'd been such a rube. I'd swallowed his lies and basked in his compliments. He made me feel so special. And I'd given in to his demands for sex, not because I couldn't control myself, but because I was afraid if I didn't let him, I would lose him.

Who would have thought a privileged young man with cars and boats and money for entertainment would wage such a long and single-focused campaign to have sex with a girl he didn't even like?

In the end, abortion was the only answer. If I'd gone home pregnant, it would have broken Granny's heart, and my unbalanced relatives would have hunted Bryson down and killed him. He wasn't worth that price.

Also, if my pregnancy had become public knowledge, I would have been kicked out of school. So would Bryson, which is why he gave me the money for the abortion and kept his mouth shut about the pregnancy. A week later, he was killed in a skiing accident.

I never told a single soul. Not one. And Bryson wasn't a fool. He'd died with my woeful past untold.

Yet Mischa knew. A child dead for years knew my darkest secret.

The puzzle was so intriguing, I wanted to sit down and reason it through. I couldn't figure it out while I was slogging through the snow. It required too much energy to walk and think. If I could rest for a little while, I would be stronger.

The temptation to take a breather, even for a moment, was great, but I beat it down. I would die in this snowfall and never understand who had killed Mischa or how she knew my secrets. A part of me didn't care, but another rebelled. I couldn't just quit. I had to keep fighting.

Far in the distance I heard a motor. I remembered the racket of the trucks my male cousins drove, glasspack mufflers echoing across the valleys so that it was impossible to tell if they were near or far away. The snow had something of that effect.

Or perhaps it was just an aural mirage, a manifestation of my desperate need to hear help on the way.

My foot slipped and I landed facedown into the snow. My feet were completely numb, my leather boots worse than useless. Needles of pain prickled my feet and lower legs. How much easier it would be to stay down, just for a little while.

The vehicle seemed closer. I forced my body up to my knees and turned around. Headlights approached, and the noise of a big motor reverberated off the snow. Not a car but a snowplow. As it crept forward, the blade scooping, rolling, and parting the snow, the danger struck me. If I didn't stand up and move, I'd be buried by manmade snow mountains. I struggled to my feet.

"Aine!"

I continued to thrash away from the dangerous machine.

"Aine Cahill." A hand gripped my shoulder.

I spun to confront Will McKinney. His mouth, moustache, and nose were covered by a muffler, but I recognized his eyes beneath a heavy winter hat. "What in the hell are you doing out here?" he asked.

"Freezing," I replied.

He hustled me toward the snowplow, but my feet refused to work properly. I couldn't make them move. He picked me up and carried me to the cab. In a moment I was sitting in the passenger seat with hot air blowing over me. Funny, but it was colder in the heated cab than outside.

"You could have died from hypothermia," he said when he was behind the wheel. "Do you realize how lucky you are that I came along? I don't normally run the plow, but the snow came down so hard and fast we didn't have time to get emergency crews in."

I closed my eyes and my head flopped against the seat. I could hear him, but I didn't care what he said. There were no answers to explain what had happened to me at the cabin in the woods. I didn't care. I only wanted to sleep.

26

My recollection of the next few days was limited. Strange dream images tormented me, and I remembered struggling against the heavy covers, pushing them aside from my sweating body, only to take a chill and beg for warmth. I didn't know the people caring for me, and I cried out for Granny Siobhan and even for my father.

Joe was there at times. And Patrick. And women who bathed my forehead with cold cloths and forced medicine into me, even when I fought them. They told me their names, but I couldn't remember.

At times, I sauntered along the green-canopied trails of the Kentucky mountains. Sunlight warmed me, and I could hear the gurgle of a running creek. The beauty of my surroundings saddened me, and I couldn't remember why I'd left.

Other times, I was in the forest at Walden Pond. I saw the blond child. She watched me from the safety of the thick trees. "I know your secrets," she said. "I know all the things you wish to hide." Her dark eyes seemed to absorb the light. "I know things you wish to know."

"Who killed you?" I asked her. "Tell me."

"I know secrets," she said. She taunted me and darted away whenever I tried to talk to her.

I woke up, a swimmer held underwater and struggling for air, with two strong hands holding me down in the bed.

"For god's sakes, let's take her to the hospital."

I recognized Joe's voice. I tried to reach for him, to put my hands on his face, but he grabbed my wrists and held them so tightly that my fingertips went numb. I tried to get up, but I couldn't feel my feet. Had they been amputated? For a moment the dream blizzard howled around me. I saw the blackened lumps that had once been my feet. Frostbite. They had taken them off.

No matter how I screamed and thrashed, I couldn't get away. Exhausted, I drifted into sleep.

Dorothea told me my fever spiked on Thanksgiving Day at 104.5. Afterward, I began to feel better and think more clearly, and was greatly relieved that all of my limbs were intact. I realized the women caring for me were nurses monitoring drips and medicines prescribed by Dr. Wells, who had visited me several times each day. Instead of sending me to the hospital, Dorothea had taken it upon herself to make sure I had the best medical care. She and Joe and Patrick and her friends.

"You were like a woman possessed," Dorothea said as she fed me chicken soup after she'd helped me into clean pajamas. "We had to hold you in the bed. You were all upside down about some girl in the woods. You kept talking to her, asking who killed her. You were convinced she knew secrets and you had to ask her questions."

I watched her expression and saw no sign that I'd blurted out my past. "It was a dream," I said. "What else did I say?"

"Most of it was gibberish. You cried for your grandmother. And your dad. And you talked about Kentucky. I think you're a little homesick, Aine. Do you want me to call anyone for you?"

"No. There's no one to call. Granny is dead, and my dad too. He had a strong fondness for the whiskey. Took out his liver. The males in my family tend to die young, either from drink or dangerous miscalculations."

Dorothea closed her eyes and her lips moved.

"Are you okay?" I asked, concerned by her strange conduct.

"Just saying a prayer of thanks for you, girl. You scared me. I was afraid you might not come back, but you sound like your old wicked self." Dorothea put the backs of her fingers against my cheek. Her cool hand felt wonderful. "I should call Joe. He sat with you during the nights. He'll be relieved to hear you're coherent."

"How long have I been sick?" Looking out the window, I saw snow on the ground and bright sun.

"Two days." She smoothed the covers. "You missed Thanksgiving, but I saved turkey and dressing for you."

I tried to sit up. "It's Friday?" I'd gone to Yerby Lane on Tuesday. I'd lost two complete days.

"It is indeed. You've missed nothing except acres of snow, so don't try to jump out of bed. You need to get your strength back."

Panic flooded over me at the thought of all the things I hadn't done. For all practical purposes, I'd lost a week of work on my dissertation. "Would you hand me my computer?"

"Aine, you need to rest." She offered the soup to me so I could feed myself. "What were you doing so far from the inn? Chief McKinney said he had no idea where you'd come from."

Though I wasn't hungry, I focused on the soup while I tried to compose an answer. She wouldn't be the only person asking that question. Had any of the events really occurred, or was I already sick, my imagination fevered, before I found the shack and the child?

"I was looking for a building where an artist used to live."

"Out off Yerby Lane?" Dorothea's expression said it all.

"Roger Brent. Have you ever heard of him?" Dorothea knew the merchants of the town, she might know the artists.

She took the soup that had grown cold and placed the tray on my desk. Her back was to me when she answered. "I never heard of a Roger Brent, and I can tell you there's been no one living on Yerby Lane for the past fifty years. How did you come upon his name?"

I told her about the shopkeeper. I almost showed her the scrim-shaw tooth, but the tooth was between Mischa and me. Perhaps it was nothing more than a lure to get me to Yerby Lane. But it might also be a clue.

"So that's what you were doing way out there. Why didn't you call me or Patrick to come after you?" She sat in a chair someone had placed beside my bed.

"No cell phone reception. And the snow started coming like someone had unzipped the clouds. It got bad before I realized it. By then, there wasn't anything to do except start walking."

Dorothea picked up my hand and held it between her own. "What did you hope to find, Aine?"

"Evidence of what happened to Mischa Lobrano."

Dorothea reeled back in shock. "What kind of evidence?"

"Of who might have harmed her."

"You think this artist, this Roger Brent, is responsible for Mischa's disappearance?" Hope lit her features. "No one even brought up his name in the investigation. What makes you suspect him?"

Caution ruled my answer. The tooth was impossible for me to explain. What if Mischa had stolen it from the museum? I would look like the guilty party. No one would believe a dead girl had committed theft and I somehow ended up with the stolen object.

"The shopkeeper said Roger Brent sometimes used young girls as models. He lived out by Walden Pond." I pushed back the covers and sat up. "I went looking for him."

"Did you find anything?"

"No one has lived there for a long time." The interior of the ram-shackle cabin came back to me. "Roger Brent lived alone out there. I wonder where he went."

"Maybe Chief McKinney can track him."

"I doubt your chief has a lot of respect for me right now." I could only imagine what he thought of a woman in leather boots and a wool coat out in a blizzard. It certainly wasn't a reflection of "good Yankee sense."

Dorothea offered a steadying arm to help me to the bathroom. My weakness troubled me. I was like an old woman tottering along.

"You aren't from these parts, Aine. You probably haven't witnessed the violent turn the weather can take in the blink of an eye during the winter."

"I won't be that careless again."

"That's all that matters," she said as we walked slowly across the cabin to the bathroom. "You'll get stronger and before you know it, you'll be back at work on your dissertation. Just give yourself a few days to heal."

I didn't have the time to waste, but I kept this to myself. As soon as she was out of the room, I'd begin a search for Roger Brent online. If he was still alive, the chances were good he was somewhere on the Internet.

After fussing around the cabin tidying up the bed with fresh linens and insisting that I let her wash my clothes, Dorothea left. Ten seconds after the door shut, I got my laptop and searched for a Concord artist named Roger Brent.

Not a single result popped up. I expanded the search. Nothing. If Roger Brent had lived and worked in Concord, he'd failed to use the most basic tool of promoting his art—the Internet. Often if an artist or writer didn't create a page on the Web, a fan would. Not in the case of Roger Brent.

I was still sitting in bed with my laptop when a knock came at my door. To my surprise, Chief McKinney entered.

"How are you, Aine?" he asked.

"Better. Thank you for bringing me here. I might have died had you not come along."

"I'm glad you realize that." There was no lecture in his words. "The weather here can turn in an instant."

"So I understand. I won't make that mistake again."

"Good." His eyebrows drew together and he stood uncomfortably by the door.

"Is something wrong?"

He stepped closer to the bed. "There's no gentle way to say this, Aine. Karla Steele is dead."

I heard what he said, but I couldn't take in the meaning. "What do you mean? How did you find out? She's in Nebraska with her sister. Joe said they had plane tickets . . ."

"I wish that were true. We found her body this morning."

This couldn't be happening. "Where?"

"Hikers found her in the woods at Walden Pond."

"Walden Pond . . . this isn't possible." I pushed the laptop aside and slid out of bed. "She left days ago for Nebraska. Joe said her sister came to take her back." For the second time. "What happened to her?"

His face told me the answer was gruesome before he spoke. "She was beaten to death, Aine. The coroner says some of her bruises date back to before she was killed. As in several days before. Do you know anything about that?"

I didn't know how to answer. If I said the wrong thing, I could be facing serious trouble, murder charges. Lying, though, never led to anything but hard times.

"Several days ago Karla attacked me here, on the path from the inn to the cabin. She came out of the dark and tried to kill me. I fought back. That's how Joe got her to agree to leave town. I said I wouldn't go to the authorities if she would leave. Joe said she'd get help in Nebraska, that her sister had made arrangements for voluntary commitment, some psychiatric help."

"And the last time you saw her?"

The days blurred together. "I can't remember exactly. It was that night. Monday night? I've lost track of time and I couldn't say for certain what today's date is."

McKinney visibly relaxed. It seemed I'd passed the test of truth-telling in his book. "Joe said you were pretty beat up in that encounter too."

So Joe had already told the chief. Probably for the best. "She ambushed me and clubbed me with a hockey stick. If I'd gone down, I don't doubt she would have killed me."

"Karla had a violent streak." He took off his gloves and unzipped his heavy coat. "Couldn't say if it was natural or if it was drug-induced. Doesn't matter now."

"Who killed her?" Images of her body, blood red against the white snow, infiltrated my brain and the urge to vomit caught me by surprise. I managed to suppress it.

"We're working on it." McKinney's face furrowed. "This doesn't look good for Joe."

"What do you mean?" I stood up, bare feet freezing on the floor. But at least I had feet and not the blackened stumps of my fantasies.

"She was found in Joe's territory, a place he's charged with patrolling. It's also a place where he would have free rein, should he happen to want to beat someone to death. No one goes to Walden Pond in this kind of weather, and no one would know that better than Joe."

McKinney didn't sugarcoat his thoughts. "You know Joe couldn't do that. Tell me you don't suspect Joe of hurting her. He tried to *help* her."

"He's just lived down the disappearance of Mischa Lobrano. This won't raise public confidence in him."

"But he had nothing to do with this!"

McKinney ignored my passionate statement. "Tomorrow, when you're stronger, I want you to come down to the station and make a statement about the assault. You should have called me when it happened."

It was more what he didn't say that upset me. "I *told* Joe we should call you. I wanted to report the assault, but Joe persuaded me not to. Now look! It's a thousand times worse because it looks like I hurt her and then she died."

He didn't deny it. "I'm afraid that's exactly how it will look to some people. Joe's been tarred by the brush of tragedy in the past. Folks will dredge that up and see that now his ex-girlfriend is dead. First his student, then his girlfriend. Some people will see more than coincidence in that. You can see how that looks bad for him."

I couldn't hold back the tears. The unfairness frustrated me so badly that I wanted to cry or break something. But I knew losing it and smashing a plate or glass against the wall wouldn't help my case. "Joe had plane tickets for her and her sister to go back to Nebraska. He didn't know she was in town, and neither did I."

"Have you talked to Joe?"

"Dorothea said he's been here at night watching over me. I was really sick. She said he would be here in half an hour."

"Please ask him to call me. I don't like this any better than you do, Aine. Concord used to be a sleepy place where the biggest excitement was a reenactment of a battle from two hundred years before. We don't have a lot of murders here, which is why Mischa Lobrano's disappearance caught in the public's imagination.

"Mischa *disappeared*. It was never proven that anything bad happened to her." Even though I knew better, I wasn't about to admit I'd conversed with her ghost.

McKinney shook his head slowly. "She was nine when she didn't come home. And it's been nearly a decade. Imagine, all that time with not a sign of her."

"Are her parents still in the area?"

"They are, and you'd better leave them alone. They've been dragged through hell backwards. Don't stir this up with them." He was warning me, but he was also issuing an edict. The Lobranos were hands-off. No outsider would be allowed to stir that fire to a hotter burn.

"Do you have any photographs of Mischa?"

He looked down at the gloves in his hand. "Why would you want a photograph?"

I couldn't tell him the truth. "I don't know. I want to see what she looks like. Now she's a part of my life too."

"Stop by the office and I'll pull the file. We might have given the pictures back to the parents, but if we have copies you can look at them." His fingers tightened into a fist around his gloves. "There wasn't anything else we could give them. No peace. No closure. That girl disappeared without a trace. If you'd asked me before if such a thing was possible, I would have said no."

"Were there tracks? Snow?"

He pointed to the chair beside the bed and I waved him into it. "I don't want to tire you. Dorothea gave me my orders before I came in here."

"Please. This will help me."

He puffed out his cheeks. "She was a pretty child. Nine, as I said. Fourth grade. Just at that age where they begin to develop real personality and interests. Mrs. Cooper, the principal, said Mischa had fallen in love with biology. She had an impressive leaf collection and she'd started drawing the insects native to this area."

"She sounds like a very smart child," I said. "She was blond, right?"

"She was. Long blond hair that curled naturally. Blue eyes. She looked more like her father than her mom. DeWitt Lobrano had that all-American look. Mischa was like him."

"No child is perfect, but she sure sounds close."

"She had a temper, her mother said. And she was competitive with a streak of daredevil, but from all accounts she was a sweet-natured child." He leaned back in the chair. "It doesn't seem possible that she won't come back."

If the little girl I'd met at Roger Brent's shack was Mischa, Chief McKinney might revise his opinion. Whatever had happened to her, she wasn't the child he described.

"Were there other children in the family?"

"None."

"What do you think happened to her?"

He didn't hesitate. Chief McKinney had spent many hours going over what had happened to Mischa Lobrano. "It was late October, and the first snow fell that day. The leaves at Walden Pond, still red and yellow, were caught by surprise, like the rest of us. The tourist traffic was slacking, but there were still visitors. I think that afternoon, some stranger with a penchant for little girls was at the pond. Mischa went there, looking for a bug. I think she was snatched and was out of the state before the sun went down."

"Do you think she's still alive?"

This time the answer was slower. "There are days I hope she isn't. I know too much about what happens to children who get pulled into that life. They're traded like furniture. One man gets tired or wants a younger child, and he trades up. Each week a child gets older, less appealing. Until in the end, it's simpler to kill them than it is to provide for them."

His words stunned me. "You really think a little girl from Concord, Massachusetts, could have ended up in the flesh trade?"

"That's exactly what I think happened. She was walking through the woods of Walden Pond. She went in right about the place I found you. She was seen by two of her mother's friends as she headed down that path. And that was the last anyone ever saw of her."

"Thank you for telling me."

"Joe doesn't like to talk about it, but you should know." He stood up. "When you see Joe, tell him to give me a call."

27

Joe showed up at the cabin, Chinese takeout in hand. The relief on his face when he saw me dressed and sitting at my desk made me smile.

"I'm too tough to let a bit of snow take me out."

"I was worried." He put the food on the kitchen counter. "You were really sick, Aine. The doctor was flummoxed. You didn't have pneumonia, but you had such a high fever and were so disoriented."

I stood up and went to him. I'd developed my own theory about my illness: it had come compliments of Mischa. She'd held me in the cabin for hours, filling my mind with lies and probing for my secrets. She'd infected me like some kind of virus. But I couldn't tell Joe. I couldn't tell anyone. "Whatever it was, I'm fine now. When I was a child, I would sometimes get sick, like a wave encompassed me. Then it would pass. Like now." I kissed his neck. "I assure you, I'm healed."

Joe held me, his hand stroking my hair. "Chief McKinney told you about Karla."

"He did." I spoke with my cheek pressed to his chest. "I'm so sorry, Joe. McKinney wants you to call him."

"I stopped by before I came here." He eased away from me.
"What happened?"

"They're still investigating. She was at Walden. You know the place where the two big black oaks make a natural place to sit?"

I knew it well, because I often sat there daydreaming about Bonnie and Thoreau. While Joe unbagged the takeout, I arranged the chairs so we could sit together. "She shouldn't have come back."

"No, she shouldn't have. From the brutality of the murder, the chief thinks it was drug-related. Karla always thought she could lie and cheat and never face the consequences. McKinney figures she was trying to make a buy from someone she already owed money to."

"I told him she'd attacked me, but he already knew. He was a little upset we didn't call and report the incident, but I think I explained everything—how it would drag you back into the limelight, reopen old wounds. I told him she'd promised to leave town if I didn't press charges."

Joe put his elbows on his knees and lowered his head into his hands. "You were right. We should have reported it when it happened. If she'd been locked up, she'd be alive today."

I stood and massaged the tight muscles of his shoulders. "If she'd gone to Nebraska, she'd be alive." My anger boiled to the surface. "She's put you in a terrible place, and me too. Now we're both involved in a murder investigation for a freaking meth head!"

Joe eased out from under my hands. "I'm sorry, Aine. I am." Pain touched his features. "When Mischa disappeared, it was such a blow. I was fond of her, as a teacher is often connected to a student who shows curiosity and a love of learning. She was a special child. Gifted. And the way she disappeared, going into the woods. I felt responsible. I'd encouraged her interest in biology."

I pressed him back to the chair and knelt in front of him. "But that's what teachers do."

He captured my hands and held them. "I was certain we'd find her, maybe lost. But safe. But she was gone. Fool that I am, it never occurred to me I'd be accused. When the investigation zeroed in on me, and the parents of children I'd worked with and been friends with all turned against me—"

I wanted to comfort him, but there was nothing I could do or say to change the past. Time doesn't heal all wounds. How well I knew that lesson. The best I could offer was to hear him talk. When he continued, I held myself still.

"My mother's health broke. She was a vibrant part of the Concord community, active in little theater and her church. She became a recluse who wouldn't even open the door to the grocery boy who delivered her order. The media was up in her face, asking questions about my childhood, my sexual proclivities, checking into innocent games of kickball or nature walks with students. Every single thing I did as a good teacher came back to haunt me."

"I would have given a lot for a teacher who cared like you did."

My words earned a smile, but it was fleeting. "My fiancée, Amanda, was dogged everywhere she went. She was a teacher too, and the implications that she might have assisted me in some kind of sick, sexual predator activity ruined her. She couldn't take it. She tried. She tried hard. But I was suspended from teaching and every day at work was hellish for her. She broke the engagement and moved. I don't blame her, but it only made me look more guilty."

"I'm so sorry, Joe." I was glad he wasn't married, but I wouldn't have wished a breakup for such horrid reasons. "Now I understand why you didn't want to tell me about Mischa."

"I intended to tell you. But I wanted you to know me. To know who I am, before you had to judge the past accusations."

I filled our wine glasses and pressed one into his hand. "I believe you."

His palm grazed my cheek. "You don't have a disloyal bone in you."

Now was the time to tell him about Patrick. To confess that my own wound and fear of abandonment had pushed me into an action I wished to eradicate. But I couldn't. Not now. Not when the scab had been ripped off the past. "You were never charged with anything. Surely that was enough."

"Not by a long shot." He sipped the wine and put it down. "For a teacher, an accusation of sexual predation is a death sentence. Top that off with the possibility of child-murdering and there's no overcoming the perception."

"It's just unfair."

"What's unfair is that a smart, curious young girl disappeared and was never found. My career was damaged. My mother's life was ruined. But Mischa is gone, and god knows what she suffered or is suffering still."

"And this Karla business will resurrect this."

He nodded. "And this time, you'll be tarred with the same brush. It can and will impact your future plans."

Heat coursed through me. "Screw them all. You didn't hurt Mischa and you didn't kill Karla. Let them think what they will."

"You're so brave, Aine, but you have no idea what's in store for yourself. Or me."

I could have told him of the Cahill Curse and the lengths my grandmother had taken to remove me from a family tainted by violence and bad choices. I understood how the past could drag behind a person like a ball and chain. The only solution was to find the guilty party. "The issue before us is Karla. If they find the real killer, this will blow over."

He nodded, but without much conviction.

"Does McKinney have any leads?"

He rose from the chair. "I'm shut out of the investigation. For obvious reasons."

But I wasn't. I could discover things. "Sit down and relax. You're too tense."

"I can't. I brought the food for you. There's some hot and sour soup and Buddhist Delight. Eat while it's still hot." He picked up the jacket he'd draped on the back of the chair.

"You're leaving?" He couldn't leave. He'd only just arrived.

"I'm upset and you're still recovering. I think it's best if I go. I'll be by tomorrow."

I grasped his hand. "Don't go. Please."

His gaze met mine and then slid away. "I bring trouble to people. Look at Karla."

"She's dead because she was a drug addict. I grew up around them, which is why I don't have much sympathy. Their whole world becomes finding the next fix. They don't care who they use or hurt or destroy, and they view those who care about them as marks and victims."

For an answer, he drew me into his arms and held me tight. For the longest time, we stood there in silence.

⚜

By Saturday at noon, the snow was melting and the sun warmed the day to a cozy forty-two. I bundled up and went into town. My first purchase was a pair of waterproof boots. My second was another rental car. In five minutes I was coasting out of town toward Walden.

The park was closed. Crime-scene tape blocked the entrance, a deterrent to the curious. And to me. Karla and I had exchanged blows. She'd managed to taint the very core of my thesis, Walden Pond. Now I couldn't afford to be seen poking around the murder site. I slowly turned around.

Joe had gleaned some details of the murder investigation, and I learned that Karla had been struck in the head with a blunt instrument, probably a hammer. She'd lain in the snow until Thanksgiving Day, when she'd been discovered by a hiker walking his dog. They estimated the time of death was Tuesday.

Though I wanted to, I didn't duck under the tape and examine the scene. McKinney hadn't asked me any more questions about Karla, and Joe wasn't forthcoming with a lot of detail. Patrick, though, was a wonderful source. Dorothea was hooked into the gossip vine in Concord, and Patrick knew what she knew.

The police hadn't found the murder weapon, which made the law officers view the killing as premeditated. Who went to a nature retreat with a hammer? Not likely to be an erstwhile carpenter. If the murderer took the weapon into the woods with him, then he meant to hit someone. There was a tool shed behind the replica of Thoreau's cabin, and the hammer could have come from there, but Joe didn't know, and he looked uncomfortable when I asked, so I dropped it.

The police hadn't ascertained why Karla was in the woods. That was a question demanding an answer. Judging from appearances, Karla wasn't the kind of girl who enjoyed a woodland romp or went looking for bugs or birds. She was scoring drugs if she was doing anything. I could only hope McKinney would turn his investigation toward her supplier and the criminals in her life.

Catching up to the speed of traffic, I merged onto 126 and drove toward Yerby Lane. This time I wouldn't be caught on foot. This time I would be smarter. I didn't expect Mischa to be there waiting on me. The very idea made my stomach flutter and my mouth go dry. If she was, at least I could make a getaway in the car. But she wouldn't be there, and I could examine the old shack. Strange, but I couldn't remember anything about the décor or what was in it. Not a single detail except the lamp on the table, the way it had glowed so brightly just before the door slammed and locked me out in the freezing weather.

I couldn't drive all the way to the shack, so when the path narrowed too much, I left the car and set off walking in my new heavy-duty boots. The snowmelt had made the ground slippery, and I took my time. In truth, I was apprehensive. What if she was still there? An underlying malevolence made me fear her. Perhaps she was merely a little girl angry that her life had been cut short. I'd read and heard stories of unhappy ghosts who lingered for revenge or to guard something they cherished, and some poor confused souls who simply died so abruptly they hadn't been able to adjust to their own deaths. Mischa was angry. And she could crawl inside my head and my past. Those were dangerous talents. The possibility that she was something more than a disgruntled spirit couldn't be ignored.

Mud sucked at the soles of my boots as the path became little more than a deer trail through the trees. That I'd found my way out of there in the snow was a miracle. Slogging forward, at last I came to the small clearing. I stood for a long time, unable to comprehend what I saw.

The small cabin, or what had once been a cabin, was completely destroyed. The roof had fallen in and the tiny front porch I remembered was wrecked. When I forced my way onto the porch, I used extreme caution. On the third step, the boards gave way and I almost fell. The front door was askew, and I lunged into it, pushed it inward, and peeked through the crack.

Dirt and water covered everything. Leaves had blown in through the roof and littered the small table that centered the room. A filthy lamp sat upon the table. Beside the fireplace where sunlight pierced through chinks in the bricks was a worn rocker. Teetering on the rotted boards that had once been a floor, I looked around in disbelief. This wasn't the cabin I had been in. I remembered the way the lamplight reflected on the soft shine of the wooden walls. These walls were planks of unfinished lumber. Rough, rotted in places.

Relief that I'd told no one about being inside the cabin was my first reaction. If Chief McKinney or Joe had come here to search, they would have thought me a complete liar. Whatever else the child was, she had the ability to create a cocoon of her own making around her. And she'd pulled me in, letting me see what she'd wanted me to see.

My fingers sought the scrimshaw tooth in the pocket of my jacket. The temptation to hurl it was strong. Best to be rid of the evidence. Either I was losing my mind or this strange child had bewitched me.

Fear struck hard, squeezing my heart until I thought it might rupture. When I calmed enough to breathe, I leaped from the porch and ran back toward the car. I wouldn't be tricked again by the child or Karla or anyone else.

28

The temperature rose, and the drip, drip of melting ice accompanied my diligent reading and writing. The books were a sensory delight—the feel and smell, the typography, the binding. One day, if I found the documentation necessary to prove my aunt existed, my dissertation would be bound, a physical reality.

I reread all of Thoreau's essays and his daily account of life at Walden Pond. I linked the influence of Emerson and Bronson Alcott to Thoreau's meditations. The economy of the mid-1800s impacted Thoreau tremendously. What had once been deep woods was now open fields and clear-cut abandoned lands. The forest had fallen to the axe as the town of Concord grew. This ravishment of the natural world was like a wound for Thoreau. I understood. I'd seen the same things with coal mining in the Appalachians, the destruction of forests and creeks, the pollution that washed down streams, sickening everything it touched.

I made a timeline of the two years, two months, and two days Thoreau lived at Walden Pond, and I penciled in what I knew of

Bonnie's life lived in Thoreau's company. The more points between the two I could match, the better for my thesis.

While Bonnie often wrote passionately about Thoreau and his daily activities, his writing was impersonal. She gave the tiny domestic details that enriched my picture of their life. He lived only in his head. I wondered if he truly cared for her. No matter how I searched, there was no mention of my relative, or of any relationship. But he also failed to mention how he often ate lunch with his parents in town—an accepted biographical fact and an oversight that spoke of his nature and his unwillingness to share any personal revelations in his writing.

From what I could deduce, Thoreau and Bonnie lived separate lives, except for the nights they spent together, the walks and discussions Bonnie documented, and the meals they shared in the evenings. I was more than familiar with Bonnie's essays about soups and bread baked during the cold winter, about her worry over Thoreau's cough or the long hours he spent tramping around Walden in bad weather.

During this pass at the material, I avoided Bonnie's journal. I'd read and reread it numerous times, but I needed to hammer in the pegs of Thoreau's literary output to see if I could track Bonnie's presence. So far, I had found no physical evidence to prove her existence at Walden Pond—or even in Massachusetts, a fact that gave me terrible anxiety. Because of that, it was up to me to show her influence on Thoreau's life in his own words.

None of this would matter, though, if I didn't get down to work. Completing my dissertation and securing a job for the coming school year was *the* priority. My near-death experience and the high fever had set me back. Like the snow, weeks had melted and slipped away. I had to complete my research and first draft to meet with my thesis committee in January, only a month away. So I gritted down and worked from the moment I rose until I fell into bed exhausted.

It wasn't just work that kept me sequestered. Fear held me captive in the cabin. I left for only one reason—to seek meals at the inn. But never in the dark. In the daylight I could keep my worst anxiety at bay. With my gaze on the ground I could traverse the lane from the cabin to the inn and back. I didn't look toward the woods.

At night, though, I knew the child watched me from the edge of the trees. I felt her draw closer. She wanted something from me, but I wasn't certain what. If I ventured out, she might approach me, so I stayed within the bolted door and got Dorothea to give me curtains for the windows so I could close them. My last encounter with the child, when she'd been willing to let me die in the blizzard, had made me wary of her motives. I'd been more than ready to try to solve her murder, but that hadn't pleased her. Had angered her, it seemed. Now I only wanted to avoid contact with her.

Patrick and Dorothea were kind enough to bring supper to me because I pleaded exhaustive work. I'd failed to cool Patrick's ardor, and he was hurt that I rebuffed his advances. I'd wrongly assumed that once he'd slept with me, he'd tire of "an older woman" and date a girl his own age. Instead, he'd developed a crush that was becoming difficult.

Joe, too, was busy with his job. Karla's death troubled him. Though he never spoke of the details, I think he blamed himself. He was also busy hunting for her killer. Several leads on drug dealers hadn't panned out, but he hadn't given up and consulted with Chief McKinney whenever he had a new idea.

On occasion Joe brought takeout, and we shared a bottle of wine and made love with the light of the fireplace dancing on our skins. Those nights I slept soundly. He knew I was afraid of something in the dark night, and while he niggled at the edges of it, he didn't press too hard. The solidness of his body in my bed, the scent of woods and man he left on the sheets gave me the only moments of peace I could count on.

The impulse was strong, but I couldn't tell him about Mischa. It wasn't fair to burden him with the guilt that might come if he believed the child's spirit was roaming the area, looking for justice. But at the heart of it, I didn't trust how he'd take my confession that the ghost of a child long-murdered had dark designs on me, and now I believed that Mischa wanted something from me. She'd singled me out, sought me in the woods at Walden Pond. To what purpose? I couldn't say, but I had my suspicions.

I rued the Cahill Curse. I hadn't grasped the full impact of it, and I was aggravated that Granny Siobhan hadn't prepared me, choosing instead to pretend that my imagination gave me vivid visions. Bonnie had suffered from it. Now, generations later, I, too, was a seer, a medium, a person who could probe beyond the veil of death. Bonnie's journals and her life spoke to me because I shared so much with my long-departed relative. My gift, though I didn't view it as such, had come to me whether I wanted it or not.

And no one had taught me how to use it properly.

Granny, doing what she thought best for me, had taught me to repress this ability. But I'd sensed entities in the shadows of Granny Siobhan's house. Even now, I could recall the woman in a severe dress who wavered in the corner of the parlor beside the old phonograph. I'd described her, from the chestnut bun at the nape of her neck to her black dress and piercing gray eyes. Granny had assured me it was only my imagination, a trick of poor lighting in an old house.

Roaming the woods, I'd imagined a presence slipping silently between the aspens and poplars. At times, I'd been certain I'd caught sight of a real Indian. Once I'd found a clay bowl crafted with strange symbols in the bottom. It had been left sitting beside a stream where I often played. When I'd suggested that the Indian left it for me, Granny had insisted the water had washed it up from the bed of the stream. She refused to consider any other possibility, and the bowl disappeared.

When I was nine, I walked home from the store with a tall, bearded man who spoke with a funny accent. Later I saw his photo and learned he was a great-uncle, dead in a shootout with revenuers during a whiskey run.

"An active imagination" was what Granny said when I'd relate one of my adventures. She'd been worried, though. She kept no pictures of dead relatives out in the open, and she warned my aunts not to encourage me "in such mental foolishness." She'd wanted to spare me this "second sight," as some called it. She'd ignored it, hoping that time and boarding school would kill it.

The result was that I had no clue how to control it. There was only one place where I might find help. Bonnie's journal. In recent readings, I'd found several passages where she'd hinted at darker spirits. Those troubled me, because I had no recollection of reading them in the past. Had I forgotten them because my dissertation committee would find them irrational? Bonnie's credibility was vital to my plan. Or was it merely my encounters with Mischa that had opened my eyes to the darker level on which Bonnie wrote?

I put more wood on the fire and picked up the journal and a thick quilt. I shifted my chair closer to the licking flames. The temperature was rising, but the cabin was cold. Snuggling in the folds of the quilt, I found the passage I sought.

Late October, evening. Henry has gone into town to dine with his family. He finished surveying Mr. Emerson's property today, and he carried the maps into Concord to register them. He was proud of his work, happy to have completed the task for his benefactor.

I am here alone, but not quiet. There are others here. Those who would like to speak but have no voice. I avoid looking to the west when darkness has settled over this small cabin. If I am alone, they gather at the window, looking in, wanting . . . what? They tap with their cold, dead fingers, and I pretend it is the beaks of birds. At times, I think they merely want my help, to send a message or attend to business left incomplete. There are some, though, who want more. They demand what I cannot give them.

My mother called them the Sluagh, the spirits of the dead trapped between this world and the next. She said they flew together as a flock of birds. She said to beware if someone was dying and to close all the windows and doors, because they would capture the soul and steal it away.

At times, when Henry has one of his coughing fits, I've heard the tapping of a beak at the west window. When I pulled the curtains back, nothing was

there. Still, I am wary. I've seen them flitting among the shadowy trees. The
child troubles me most. She knows things.

The journal slipped from my hand and fell to the floor. I remembered the passage about the birds, but the last line hadn't been there.
I'd memorized most of the journal, and those words were new. They
hadn't been there a month before.

I picked up the book and bent over it, turning it so the light from
the fire illuminated the page. I expected to find the ink fresher, the
handwriting different. But it was the same fluid script of my aunt,
the ink fading slightly with age.

But the last two sentences hadn't been there before. I would
swear it.

The fire popped and crackled, and I sat, unmoving. Afraid to
even think, because the thoughts that tried to force themselves into
my head terrified me.

At last I closed the journal in my lap. What was this child to my
Aunt Bonnie? What was she to me? I wasn't certain I wanted an
answer to those questions. A little girl who spanned the decades,
who assumed the identify of a missing child, who watched from the
shadow of the woods, who left me alone in the snow to freeze. What
did she want?

My fears spun wildly until dizziness made me grasp the chair and
close my eyes. At last the spinning stopped, and I let the fire flush
my cheeks with warmth. Exhaustion was playing tricks on me. I was
seeing things in the journal that didn't exist. It was my imagination,
putting my fears on the page as if my Aunt Bonnie had written them.

I let the journal slide to the floor as weariness held me in its grip. I
slumped in the chair. The warmth from the fire was seductive, pulling
me toward sleep. What could an hour's nap hurt? I'd been up since
dawn. I was safe in front of the fire, and I allowed myself to yield to
unconsciousness.

In the dream, for I knew I was dreaming, I strolled along a path.
Leaves of red and gold filtered down on me, soft and gentle and silent.

My feet scuffed through them, making a delicious shushing sound. I could smell a wood fire on the crisp air and it made me hurry. I was headed home toward a table laden with my favorite food.

As I walked I saw my boots, topped with a fleece collar. Shiny and black. They were expensive. I wore thick tights. My red jacket was snuggly buttoned. From behind a grove of aspen, a young girl stepped out. She, too, wore a plaid skirt and red jacket. She came toward me. "Want to play?" she asked.

"I'm going home. I'm hungry."

"You should play with me."

"My mother is waiting." I was afraid, though I didn't know why. No one else was near. I was alone in the woods with this other girl. She stepped toward me.

"You should play with me."

I backed away. She stepped forward. The hood of her jacket concealed her eyes, but not her blond hair, which fell nearly to her waist. "What's your name?" I asked.

"Names don't mean anything."

The red and gold leaves shook free of the trees and fell to the ground, revealing bare branches reaching into a sky that changed from blue to gray. Heavy clouds massed, and snow began to fall.

"I have to go home." I was suddenly freezing.

"You have no home to go to." The girl came toward me. Her hood slipped back and revealed eyes of solid black.

I turned to run, but I couldn't move. The snow, so thick, trapped me, rising in a high wave to crest over me and wrap me in cold white.

29

For two weeks I wrote like a madwoman. My project involved mapping the months Bonnie spent at Walden. Her journal hadn't been written to document her life. It was more intimate, her thoughts and emotions as much as factual information. Her focus was the life she shared with Thoreau. I used mentions of holidays and blooming plants to pinpoint dates as best I could. These I overlaid on the dates associated with Thoreau's writing. It was slow and tedious work that left my shoulders aching and temples throbbing. Still, I was far from producing the documentation that would be necessary for my dissertation.

And then there was the journal itself. I'd read it numerous times and even committed much of it to memory, but I had difficulty finding passages I clearly remembered. I simply couldn't locate them. In numerous passages, the words had shifted from what I recalled. Was my memory that faulty, or did my new perspective of Bonnie give some references meaning I'd never seen before? In addition to the passage on the Sluagh, there were half a dozen mentions of Bonnie's attempts to connect with departed spirits that I would have sworn were new.

When I'd first read the journal, I'd been caught up in the romance between the two. My current examination revealed other, darker things. As I learned more about Bonnie and her association with the little girl in the woods, her written words took on a new interpretation.

Thoreau's interest in my aunt's abilities left me wondering about his motives in regard to her. Did he love her, or was he more interested in her talents than a romantic liaison? There were indications that he didn't approve of her attempts to call up the dead, but then she would write of his desire to communicate with his brother, or with a dead poet or writer. The results of these sessions were aggravatingly vague. But much worse than that, they prompted me to doubt myself and my reading of the journal.

The process frustrated me.

Dorothea, and even Patrick, respected my desperation and left me in my solitude to write. Joe called each day after he got off work. We spent the nights drinking wine and making love. My passion for him was quick and dangerous, consuming me when he walked into the cabin. We made love like people drowning, clinging and gasping. Though I knew the dangers of being swallowed by need, I couldn't stop myself, and neither, it seemed, could he.

When he was gone, my thoughts returned to my work. Rigid control kept me from seeking Mischa. I couldn't afford to follow her down the rabbit hole she offered, and I doubted her truthfulness. At times I wondered if she was a creation I'd conjured simply to keep me away from my work. Fear of failure posing as a murdered child. Such would fit my family heritage. We were masters of self-sabotage.

Joe and I seldom talked—about anything. Our relationship was not about chitchat, yet I gleaned some information. Little progress had been made in Karla's murder. While Joe might be a suspect in Karla's death, he wasn't the only one. Joe told me that a young man named Anton Dressler was the prime suspect. He sold meth and crack on the outskirts of Boston, and was rumored to be Karla's dealer.

He'd been seen in Concord the day she died, and he was known to have a violent temper. Those who dealt with him did so in fear. His ruthlessness impressed even an addict.

So far Chief McKinney hadn't broken Dressler's alibi—four of his associates testified Dressler was at Trader Mike's bar in a back-room high-stakes poker game that didn't end until three Wednesday morning. The medical examiner put Karla's time of death at Tuesday evening. The weather made it impossible to get an accurate time.

Neither the chief nor Joe believed Dressler. His alibi witnesses were thugs, pimps, and dealers, but they never changed their story during intense interrogation, and there was no real physical evidence to tie Dressler to the murder. In fact, the murder scene was remarkably clean. McKinney's hands were tied.

Joe blamed himself for Karla's death, though that was ridiculous. He tried to hide his guilt, but without success. It crept over his face in the quiet moments of exhaustion before he fell asleep. I did what I could, but I knew from my own family that outside intervention wouldn't work. If Joe wanted to punish himself, he would, no matter what I said.

Ten days before Christmas, I woke unable to face the computer. Sun streaked through the windows of my cabin illuminating the quilt pattern with vivid colors. The snow was gone, and I felt as if I'd been in a deep sleep for weeks, in a world that was monochromatic, agonizingly slow, and composed of computer screens and books. I had to get out, to walk in the shadowed trees. Walden Pond called to me. I hadn't been to the pond since before Karla's death. The pond and surrounding woods were my muse. A visit might spark the creative flint that would ignite my writing again.

The day was glorious, and I hiked along, buoyed by the blue, blue sky and the sunshine. It was a day that alluded to the future hope of spring, though the browns and grays of trees and lawns let me know winter still gripped Concord. While it might be December, I could still dream of April.

For the first time in weeks, I was warm. Since my adventure in the deep snow, I'd been cold. My own skin felt corpselike, though Joe never complained. I realized these fancies stemmed from my imagination. My flesh was no colder than anyone else's. Winter had slipped into my bones, and it came from Mischa, not the weather.

I deliberately turned my thoughts from the macabre and focused on life. I passed the dress shop I loved and continued on. Dorothea was planning a lavish Christmas Eve dinner at the inn. A troupe of players performed an annual comedic Christmas play involving literary icons: Charles Dickens, Nathaniel Hawthorne, Edgar Allan Poe, Thoreau, and Emerson, as well as Emily Brontë, Charlotte Mary Yonge, and Harriet Beecher Stowe. It was literary theater I was eager to sample. The event was a fundraiser for local charities, and everyone who was anyone in town showed up.

Dorothea had been babbling about the dinner for days, and I'd finally consented to attend. I had the beautiful green dress I'd bought the day I fought with Karla. An extravagance far out of my normal expenditures, the dress begged to be worn. This was the perfect occasion. In truth, I wanted Joe to see me in something other than jeans and sweats. There was enough girlishness left in me to long for admiration in his eyes.

I'd even agreed to help Dorothea bake desserts. Granny Siobhan, a fabulous cook, churned out breads and cakes and cookies, and she'd taught me to make many of her specialties. Dorothea had been so kind to me, helping me through my illness and generally caring for me, the least I could do was spend a day or two helping her prepare for the party. Besides, I was sick of my own company and my contrary writing that moved forward by minuscule fits and starts. No matter how much thought and elbow grease I applied, my prose remained lifeless and boring.

I'd found it harder than I'd imagined to link Thoreau's writing to Bonnie's journal. The man was infernally distant. He wrote down every tiny thought he had, but not a single emotion. Nothing at all about a woman who loved him and cared for him. Nothing about a helpmate who made hot soups on blustery February days, or who chopped and brought in wood to keep the tiny cabin warm.

I'd begun to resent Thoreau for his cavalier treatment of my aunt. He presented himself as this solitary virgin, a man who loved the quiet and sought it so he could relate to nature. To my horror, I couldn't help but now view him as something of a charlatan. The man who craved solitude had kept a mistress. He'd excised Bonnie from any record of his life, and I knew why. His reputation was more important to him than accuracy, and that I found dishonest. He should have married her if he was ashamed to "live in sin" with her.

Deep in thought, I passed Chief McKinney without seeing him. He called my name and I met him with a smile.

"Glad to see you're all recovered, though you are a mite pale," he said.

"I've been working too much."

"So Joe tells me. He says you're a woman possessed." He fell into step beside me as we continued down the street. I'd journeyed into town to buy binder clips and more Post-it notes before I took a jaunt around the pond. My intended purchases were just an excuse to get out in public, though. I was happy to stroll along with the Chief and chat.

"Any progress on Karla's murder?" I asked.

He tucked his chin and kept walking. I didn't press. McKinney now had two unsolved cases. Mischa Lobrano and Karla Steele. A disappearance and a brutal murder. The ten-year span between the two meant nothing to him. For all the cases he closed, these two would devil him.

At last he sighed. "I don't understand why Karla was in the woods near Walden Pond. It doesn't make sense as a place for a drug deal. The area is patrolled regularly. There are other places where privacy would be easier to come by."

"Karla knows Joe patrols the state park land. She might have thought it would be safe." I spoke without thinking but realized my mistake almost instantly.

The chief cast a sharp look at me. "Are you saying Joe wouldn't arrest Karla because he knew her?"

"Not at all." My words had exited my mouth in a crooked fashion. "Only that Karla's *perception* might be skewed. She was a druggie. Logic isn't their forte. I've had a bit of experience with addicts in Kentucky."

"That's true." The frown remained on his face. "But there's only one way in and one way out of the parking lot. No dealer in his right mind would agree to a transaction there. I don't think her murder involved a drug deal."

I could come up with no response. We continued in silence.

A youngster on a bicycle whizzed past, and McKinney called out, "Be careful, Brendan. You don't want to be barreling into pedestrians."

The boy rode on without looking back, but he waved a hand to signal he'd heard.

"He's a good boy. A little thoughtless, but a good kid."

"Shouldn't he be in school?" I asked.

"I'll speak to his parents." Pause. "I'd rather be overly cautious than. . . ."

"Have a repeat of what happened to Mischa?"

His breath whistled harshly and he unfastened the top button of his coat. "She was precocious. And she loved Joe. She thought he hung the moon. If he said slugs were fascinating, Mischa thought they were the second coming. His interest in the woods and nature became her own. She was a bright child, and Joe said she had fallen in love with biology and science. He said someday she'd get a scholarship to one of the Ivy League schools if she wanted. She was that special, and I couldn't uncover a single damn lead that went anywhere."

"And it was her profound interest in science that put her in danger." I said it because he wouldn't.

"Yes, but it could have been field hockey, piano, or riding her bicycle. Anything could have put her in harm's way."

"What was she doing alone in the woods?" I almost blurted out "if she was so smart," but I managed to bite it back in time. How smart was Mischa, though? The blonde in the hooded coat was cunning; had manipulated me in ways I still couldn't explain. But cunning and smart were two different gifts.

"It was a miscommunication. She told her mother she was meeting members of her class. Helen never questioned it. Mischa was a reliable kid. Helen believed she was meeting her classmates."

"Yet she was in the woods alone." I wasn't criticizing. Granny and my dad had allowed me to roam all over the hills and hollows near my home.

"She was a spirited girl who felt safe. Concord's a town where folks look after the children. No one could have thought she'd be harmed after school. In broad daylight. In a place that's a refuge. I would have let my own daughter lark about those woods. Her disappearance changed the town."

"Which makes me think an outsider took her." I'd followed his logic and found my own conclusion.

"Took her or killed her. We don't know." He smoothed his moustache. "Mischa and Karla share things in common. I can't see anyone here taking Mischa or killing Karla. I'm not naïve about my town. There are plenty here who'd steal. And there are drugs and whores and all the things that come to play in modern society. But the brutality of the beating." He opened his jacket another button. "She was struck in both eyes with the claw end of a hammer. The bones in her face were shattered."

I turned slightly away to hide my discomfort. "How awful."

"The strange thing is, the medical examiner said some of the blows were struck from below. As if Karla had been standing over her attacker."

The image that came to mind stopped me dead. McKinney continued before he realized I'd halted. "What is it?"

I couldn't say it. I simply couldn't utter the words. "You're positive the blows were struck from below?"

He nodded. "The coroner is positive. It doesn't compute, you know. She should have run, or at least tried to get away. She must have been caught completely by surprise. Someone tricked her, I think. She never suspected."

"I have to go back to the inn." I spun.

"Wait, Aine. I'll give you a ride. You aren't strong enough."

"I'm okay to walk." I kept marching. I had to get to Walden Pond. I had to find Mischa. She'd done a terrible, terrible thing, and I had to know why.

30

The quiet settled around me like a blessing, but I had no time to enjoy it. My heart crashed against my ribs, and when a flock of small wrens startled from the tall grass and flew into the sky, I feared the Sluagh. My first impulse was to run as fast as I could back to the safety of the inn.

But that would accomplish nothing. The confrontation I didn't want could no longer be avoided.

I knew exactly where to find Mischa. I passed the replica of Thoreau's cabin and continued down the trail. The day had grown warmer, a balmy fifty-two according to the outdoor thermometer nailed to a tree beside the gift shop. I removed my jacket and tied it around my waist as I moved deeper into the woods.

When I spied the two oaks, I listened. The chirping and rustle of birds and small creatures had ceased, leaving a vacuum of complete silence. No wind stirred a limb. No tweet or scolding squirrel spoke of habitation by any species. Mischa had sucked the life from a place that had once been filled with busy creatures. She'd also managed to get her hooks into my existence. Who was she? What was she that she could slam a claw-foot hammer into a young woman's eyes?

Her actions unreeled in my imagination like a disgusting movie. She curled, so innocent and helpless, right here beside the oaks. She must have looked like a broken doll to Karla. And Karla had gone to her, to offer assistance, as anyone would, to an injured child. And Mischa had struck with the speed and surety of a cobra.

"You wanted her dead." She'd made no sound as she crept up.

"You don't have a clue what I want."

"Oh, but I do. You wanted her gone. Dead and gone. Once she came back to Concord, your biggest concern was getting rid of her. Permanently."

She was going to frame me for what she'd done, and I'd played into her hands by coming here. Oh, she was clever indeed. "That isn't true. I needed her in Nebraska. Not dead."

She shrugged a shoulder. "Whatever you say, Aine." Her tone made it clear she was humoring me, like I was the child.

"How did you get her alone here in the woods? "

"People see and hear exactly what they wish to see and hear. You know that, Aine. Look at your aunt Bonnie, in love with a man who failed to acknowledge her in any way. Yet she stayed with him. She cared for him. She taught him her secrets. The truth was staring her right in the face. He never meant to admit their relationship. His family would never approve of the likes of Bonnie Cahill, kin to an empire of cutthroats and thieves. But Bonnie wouldn't see it."

"Great lecture. How did you get Karla down here alone?"

"How did I get you to Yerby Road?"

"A trail of breadcrumbs." Oh, yes, she was smart. "The shopkeeper. He told me exactly what you wanted me to know."

"Was there ever a shopkeeper?" She giggled and the hair on my arms rose to attention.

"What are you?"

Her smile was slow, a fox staring at a crippled hen. With great deliberation she pushed back the hood of her jacket. Blond hair tumbled about her shoulders. In the curve of her cheek was the innocence of childhood. Her dark lashes kissed her soft skin until she opened her eyes. They were black and shiny, hard obsidians where blue should have been. "Does it matter so much what I am? Isn't it what I can *do* that really intrigues you?"

I didn't want to know any more of what she could do. What she *had* done. "Why me? No one else sees you. Why me?"

She turned toward the location where Karla had been bludgeoned to death. The area had been raked clean, and a tatter of yellow crime-scene tape hung limp from a tree branch. A dark stain splashed across a root. Blood.

"You called me, Aine. You summoned me."

"No, no, I did not." I longed to grab her and shake her, but I was too afraid.

"Yes, you did. All your life, you've known you could communicate with the dead. You tried to deny it, but deep down you knew. Coming here to Walden Pond, working on this topic for your dissertation. You wanted to know about your great-great-great aunt. You wanted to dance with the devil. It's in your blood, after all. You read Bonnie's journal and couldn't wait to come here and find me."

"Her journal is about Thoreau, not . . . this!" I waved a hand at her.

"You've always had a flair for fitting the truth to your needs. I wonder if your dissertation committee will see that and be generous. You had to know it would never be accepted without corroboration. A journal from the woman who shared Walden Pond with Thoreau? Who would believe it without physical evidence?" She laughed, and I had the sense she was empty. Sound echoed inside her. "That was never your goal. You came here to learn about your aunt's talents. About me."

I challenged her. "You sought *me* out. You left the dolls for me. You spied on me. You—"

"Lured Joe to your bed?" She laughed again. "He's like a drug, isn't he? Sad to say, but you and Karla aren't so far apart. You both have your addictions. For you, it's belonging, having a man to hold during the lonely hours of the night. And like Bonnie, you're willing to take extreme action and great risk to have that. You're a liar, Aine. You've deceived him about who you are."

Her black eyes held me transfixed. "There's always a price, Aine. You should have learned a decade ago—the hardest things must always be done alone. No man can save you."

"Leave me be. If I called you, I can send you away. Go!"

She started down the path and hope flushed through me like a fever. She was obeying. I'd sent her back. All I'd had to do was tell her to go and I was rid of her.

But then she turned, her countenance serene, childlike. "It isn't so simple, Aine. I'll be back. We have business together, you and I."

I couldn't have that. "You stay away from me! Don't come back. Ever."

She sprinted down the trail and vanished in less than five seconds. Birdsong again trilled from the trees.

31

The green dress caressed my body as I twirled in front of the small mirror in my cabin. Joe would arrive soon to escort me to the inn for the gala dinner. Even though Dorothea tried to comp me a ticket because of the baked goods, Joe had bought one for each of us. Community public relations, if such a thing mattered. He'd taken a serious beating in public opinion over Karla's murder. As Dorothea and Chief McKinney predicted, the rumors and gossip about Mischa resurrected and shambled after Joe like zombies.

Stepping out with him in public showed my belief in him. The money on my dress would be well spent. From erstwhile student of literature, I had transformed myself.

Thoughts of Cinderella made me smile. I was no stepdaughter, but I had been working very hard, and the dinner was as exciting as a royal ball. While toiling in the kitchen, I'd heard a little of the play when the actors rehearsed. I'd read Poe, Hawthorne, Stowe, and all the other authors, but it was interesting to see them brought to life. Theater drew me. Had I possessed a whit of talent, I would have gone on the stage.

I checked my makeup one final time and sat down in the rocker to wait. In most regards, Joe was punctual. A good trait, since I hated to wait on anyone. Tonight, anticipation had driven me to get ready too early, and now I had nothing to do but sit and watch for Joe's arrival.

For the past several days, the weather had remained in the fifties, but a cold front had moved over us from the Midwest, dropping temperatures and clearing skies. I went out on the porch to stargaze for a moment. The night sky calmed me.

In Kentucky, I'd often slipped from Granny's house and wandered the meadow behind the old barn. We hadn't had cows or horses that I could remember, but the barn was still referred to as the "cow barn." As if there were another.

For a time, my uncles hung marijuana in the barn to dry, but that had been before I went to live with Granny. My arrival had prompted a crackdown on any illegal behavior on property held in Granny's name. No criminal conduct would taint me. As a result, the barn was empty and unused. The tang of decayed manure was still there, and halters and ropes, rotted leather, an old saddle chewed by mice. When the summer nights cooled the day's heat, the creaky old barn drew me to investigate and daydream about my own golden steed.

The hay in the loft was old and moldy, but I could lie back in it and stare up through the cracks to view the stars and occasionally the moon. Granny told me stories about the face on the moon. One of my favorites involved a time far in the past and a beautiful Kentucky girl, who, of course, looked a lot like me. The young girl braved the dark woods and hollows of the mountains to travel the miles necessary to care for her grandmother. She was, of course, a loyal and loving girl who left her young husband alone on many a night so she could be certain the old woman was safe and had plenty of food and wood to burn.

One night as she walked along the edge of a steep bluff, her foot slipped and she fell to her death. Her husband was heartbroken. He couldn't overcome his grief, and day by day he faded. The gods, seeing his distress, revived his beautiful bride, but there were conditions.

Because she couldn't take human form, they hurled her into the sky, and she became the moon.

Her husband could still gaze upon her beauty, though he could never touch her, and he was forced each month to watch her mature and then die. But for many nights in the cycle, she was able to look after her husband, and her light guided the footsteps of other young women who were forced to travel alone in the dangerous hills.

It was a story Granny invented to entertain me, and I was still charmed by it. Gazing at the moon from the little porch of the cabin, I thought for a moment I saw the features of a lovely young woman. Her name had been Monde. Or that's what Granny had called her.

"Homesick?" Patrick asked.

I almost yelped. I hadn't heard him approach. "No, I'm not homesick, and yes, you startled me." I couldn't completely hide my aggravation. He'd scared at least ten years off my life. I'd avoided being alone with him since I'd recovered from my illness. He found it difficult to take no for an answer. He had a bit of the dog-in-the-manger attitude. I didn't flatter myself to think he'd fallen for me, but he resented the idea that Joe would have me. Because I didn't chase after him, he pursued me.

"You're so beautiful." With one long stride Patrick mounted the porch to stand beside me. His fingers slid over the fabric of my dress. "I've never seen you in a dress."

"I'm going to the Christmas dinner at the inn. I thought it would be nice to look presentable for a change." I rubbed my arms against the cold. I hadn't intended to stay outside and I'd neglected to grab a coat. In truth, I'd lost my heaviest winter coat. I'd searched everywhere for it to no avail. My assumption was that one of the women caring for me while I was sick had borrowed it and forgotten to bring it back.

"You're Joe's date, aren't you?"

"Yes." I sounded defensive, which teased my temper.

"You like him better than me."

Dear god, why had I ever slept with a teenager. Patrick had zip for emotional maturity. "My relationship with Joe is different, Patrick.

We've been over this, more than once. I admit I was wrong to sleep with you. You're a wonderful young man, but you need to find someone more age-appropriate to date. You're young and—"

"That was a plus. You said youth was in my favor. You said I had stamina."

Who'd have thought he'd take my silly banter to heart. "Patrick, I'm almost a decade older than you."

"Age doesn't matter. I fell for you. You let me. You encouraged me. You were wild for me. I know it. Joe has made you turn your back on me."

Those accusations could only make trouble if he said them around town. "I was wrong to say those things. I was wrong to sleep with you. I forgot you're only nineteen."

"Let's go inside." He took my arm and angled me toward the door. I balked. "That's not a good idea. Joe will be here any minute."

"He doesn't know we're lovers, does he?"

I was at a loss. I needed to defuse this situation, and I hadn't a clue how. "We aren't lovers. We had a good time. Once. You have young girls stopping by the inn for lunch or dinner just to see you. You're a charming young man. They adore you. What we had was a fun fling. Let it go."

"It wasn't a fling and it isn't over."

"It's over because I say so." Firmness was called for. If I let him bulldoze me now, I'd never be able to control him. "It was fun; it's over."

"No, it isn't." He opened the cabin door and pushed me inside.

In the uncustomary heels, I stumbled and almost fell, but I caught myself on a table. By the time I regained my balance, he was behind me. He slammed the door and shot the lock home.

"What does he do that I don't?" His voice was loud, demanding.

I'd known Patrick for the four months I'd lived at the inn. He was a happy, carefree kid who loved life and a good roll in the sack. The young man standing in front of me wasn't the boy I'd laughed with, tickled, and made love to. Even the planes of his face were different. His eyes were more deep-set, his mouth sullen.

"He doesn't *do* anything. It isn't about sex. Joe and I have a relationship—"

"Liar! You don't have a relationship with him." His voice clotted with emotion. "You fuck like rabbits. I see you. He comes in the door, throws back a glass of wine and you fuck each other silly. You don't do things together. You don't talk. You don't love each other."

"Calm down." His anger was completely out of proportion.

"Fuck calming down. You fucked me and then you threw me over for him. I want to know why."

This wasn't happening, couldn't be happening. But I knew differently. This was a looming disaster of my own making. There would be a terrible price to pay unless I took it in hand. "I thought we both understood we were having fun, with no strings attached. Nothing more. Just sex, because it felt good."

"Well, it doesn't feel so good now. Not to me. I care about you, but you act like you don't even remember my name."

"Patrick, you have to leave. This instant." I brushed past him and went to the door. Undoing the lock, I threw it open. "Leave."

"Or what?" he asked. His head tilted in a strange manner and his gaze was leveled on the floor.

"Or I'll tell Dorothea."

"She won't do anything. You're the one in the wrong."

I had the creepiest sense Patrick was no longer speaking. Someone else was there. Someone who took pleasure in the pain he felt. "I didn't break any laws. You're of age. Push me and I'll call the police."

His head snapped up and for a flash I saw black obsidian eyes. "Go ahead, Aine. I'd love to tell the police chief the things you like me to do when we fuck."

"Patrick!" I stepped back from him and the door. If he'd struck me I wouldn't have felt more assaulted. The charming young man I knew was gone. Someone—or some*thing*—else stood in his shoes.

"Don't act so shocked. You wanted to know how I got Karla to Walden Pond."

I grasped the back of the small sofa for support. She'd revealed herself to me in all her power. I'd asked to see, and she'd shown me. But I didn't know what to do about it. About her.

"You're here, aren't you?" I forced calm into my voice.

"It took you a while to figure it out." His lips tried for a smile but failed. For one brief second I thought I saw Patrick, terrified and struggling to escape.

"Let him go, Mischa. Do it." It was more request than command. "Please, let him go. He's just a kid."

"You hurt people all the time, Aine. You do it and never think twice. Anger is better than pain." Patrick's voice came to me, but the words were Mischa's.

Headlights illuminated the interior of the cabin. Joe had arrived, but I didn't know whether to be relieved or upset. No telling what Patrick would say in front of him.

Patrick grinned at me as he waited for Joe to get out of the truck and come to the door. "Exciting, isn't it?" Patrick asked. "What will I do? What will he do?"

Joe tapped lightly and stepped inside the cabin. He paused just past the threshold and looked at Patrick, then me. "Is something wrong?" he asked.

"Not at all," Patrick said. "I came to see if Aine needed any help taking the cookies she baked over to the inn. She's already carried everything over." He brushed past Joe and clattered down the stairs. "See you at dinner," he called over his shoulder.

Frowning, Joe closed the door. "Am I missing something here?" he asked. "What was Patrick really doing in the cabin?"

"He was acting strange," I said. "I'm so glad you're here. I was getting worried. Maybe he got into Dorothea's punch. He knew I'd delivered the cookies early this morning." I forced a laugh. "Teenagers. Who knows what goes on in their heads?"

"He was so intense."

I put a hand on Joe's cheek. "Patrick's a kid. Let's go before Dorothea sends someone to check on us."

32

Red, white, and green candles glowed at every table, and garlands of holly and cedar draped the doorways and mantel top above a roaring fire. A miniature crèche centered an enormous mirror in a gilt frame. The most delicious smells wafted from the kitchen each time the swinging door opened and closed.

As Joe and I snaked our way toward the bar at the back of the largest dining room, I was well aware of the glances that followed us. I hoped part of it was my beautiful dress, but I knew people disapproved of Joe. And therefore of me. The taint of Mischa's disappearance had been resurrected. A couple of people actually turned their backs to us when we went past.

Joe's grip on my hand tightened. "You shouldn't have to put up with this," he said. "I'll leave and you can enjoy the party."

"Of course not," I said, my shoulders back and my chin high. "They can't run us off. You didn't do anything and you won't act like a guilty man." Joe's concern over the guests allowed me to search the area for Patrick. My worry for him was genuine, if also self-centered. Mischa had begun to truly frighten me. She was powerful. There was

186

no doubt in my mind that she'd taken control of Patrick. What could she force him to do? I didn't want to think about it.

"So you're the doctoral student living in the cabin?" A tall thin woman held out her hand. "Eleanor West." She wore a huge diamond ring and a jewel-crusted Rolex. Her clothes fit her trim body perfectly. She could have been the mother of any of the girls at the boarding school I'd attended a decade ago. My dislike of her, based on my past suffering, was instant.

"I'm Aine Cahill," I said, "and this is Joe Sinclair."

"Yes, the school teacher turned park ranger." Eleanor didn't offer her hand to Joe. "Dorothea says you're writing your paper on one of our local icons, Henry David Thoreau. Actually, David Henry is his birth name. He never changed it legally."

"I am." I was surprised she wanted to talk to me. About anything.

"What prompted you to select Thoreau for your dissertation, Miss Cahill?" she asked.

"He believed each man had the right and the responsibility to stand up for his beliefs. I admire that, don't you?"

"Actually, I find him outdated." She smiled only with her lips. "But I think Kenneth Jenkins does an excellent job portraying Thoreau in the play. He's reprised that role for the past ten years. I'll be curious to get your take on his performance."

"I'm eager to view the show. Do you have a favorite work of Thoreau?"

"He was a bit of a kook, don't you agree?" She watched me with the eagerness of a crow zeroed in on a shiny object.

"He was different." I tiptoed through a minefield.

"So what angle are you using to approach his work?"

I was unprepared to make small talk about my dissertation and I was bored with her rudeness to Joe. "Most people aren't interested in literature dissertations. I suspect you really aren't either. What do you want from me?"

She didn't even blink at my direct assault. "David Henry is a distant relative. I want to be sure you're treating him fairly." Her smile barely concealed her animosity.

"I assure you, I'm a fan of his writing. Would you mind if I asked a few questions?" This was a tremendous opportunity and even though I found Mrs. West haughty and rude, I couldn't pass up the chance to see if she had special insights.

"While you chat I'll grab some drinks," Joe said, excusing himself.

"Thank you, Joe. This won't take long." I turned back to Eleanor. "Thoreau was such a loner. Do you have family history about that aspect of his life?"

"The consensus of family opinion was that he was appallingly unattractive. Physically. Unlike today, there wasn't an abundance of eligible women in his time. He did ask Ellen Sewall to marry him, but she declined. She was eighteen and he was sickly, which would be a burden no sane woman would take on. Had he lived, I suppose he would have married. The family would have arranged some type of union."

"No family stories about a girl, other than Ellen Sewall?" I tried to hide my disappointment.

"None." She almost sneered. "He was an odd duck, and I personally find his writing dry and boring. Tell me, do you really think it interesting enough to deserve years of study?"

"I do."

"Takes all kinds." Her laughter tinkled in practiced ripples. "And Joe Sinclair? Do you find him interesting?"

"Joe's been kind to me. As has Dorothea."

"She does take to the strays and waifs. She has a good heart." Her gaze sought Joe out, and her lips thinned when she found him. "Looks like your date is running for cover. He's headed out the door."

"Probably for some air that isn't tinged with suspicion. You don't like Joe," I said. "Why not?"

"I'm close with Helen and DeWitt Lobrano. They'll never recover from the loss of Mischa. Too much evidence pointed at him."

"There was no evidence. None. She disappeared."

"Sinclair should never have come back here. His mother is dead. He needs to leave." She leaned closer. "It's salt in the wound."

Eleanor's connection to the Lobranos might be a lode of information to me, but I had to defend Joe. "He returned to Concord to take care of his sick mother, a deed that would be exemplary in anyone else. Not a lick of evidence connected him to what happened to the Lobrano child."

"And nothing to exonerate him, either. Now his ex-girlfriend is beaten to death in the park he patrols." She dared me to look away. "Either you're very brave or very stupid."

"Neither, actually. I don't believe Joe harmed the child. He couldn't have. And he didn't hurt Karla Steele. Her drug-infested lifestyle caused her death."

"How many woman have expressed similar sentiments after the man in their life did something horrid? It's almost a cliché."

"You shouldn't malign a man without proof." She had gotten under my skin.

"Have you ever lost someone you loved, someone more important to you than life itself?" Her expression softened.

"I've lost a lot, Mrs. West. Plenty. But I don't accuse innocent people of taking the things I've lost."

"You're young. You have no clue how people can deceive you."

I wondered if she was talking about the Lobranos or herself. "Tell me about Mischa," I said. "From all accounts, she was a perfect child."

"Ask Joe Sinclair. He was the last one to see her alive."

"That's not true. Besides, there's nothing to indicate she's dead."

"And nothing to show she's alive." She tilted her head, as if reforming her opinion of me. "You're not quite the bookworm Dorothea paints you. I predict you're going to surprise all of us. Yes, I believe you'll make us all sit up and take notice." She saw someone over my shoulder. "Excuse me, Miss Cahill."

She brushed past me and met another couple with a hearty laugh and a scathing glance over her shoulder.

"Bitch," I said loudly enough for several people to turn and stare at me.

Joe had fled the party, and I went outside to find him. He couldn't allow fools to run him away. The night was chilly, and I walked through the parking lot to search for his truck. It sat where he'd parked it, but there was no sign of Joe. Cold and concern hit me at the same time. Where had he gone? More importantly, was he alone? Had Mischa used the guise of a child to lure him deeper into the woods?

Laughter and music floated out of the inn, but I heard only the thud of my heart. I had to find Joe. Hoping against hope, I went to the highway to see if he'd walked that way. Because I didn't want to think he'd gone to the cabin. Not there, where he was bait for Mischa.

When he wasn't at the main road, I accepted my fate. I would have to go to the cabin and search for him. But first I would get my jacket and make excuses to Dorothea.

Happy partygoers jammed the inn, and I slid between them, searching for Dorothea's round face. She found me and tapped my shoulder. "Have you seen Patrick?"

The possibilities almost made me stagger. "No. I'm looking for Joe."

"Behind you. At the bar. If you see Patrick, tell him to find me in the kitchen. I need him. That boy can disappear on a dime."

"I'll do it."

Dorothea was swept away in a surge of the crowd that also brought Joe to me. He held two glasses of red wine. "Sorry for the delay. I had to step outside and pretend to smoke a cigarette. That woman would have gladly put a stake through my heart."

"Mrs. West is a snot. Don't worry about her."

"She's a neighbor of the Lobranos. I should have warned you. I'm sure she was only too eager to tell you what a bastard I am and how you'll wake up with your throat slit or some such."

"She's a privileged bitch." There was no point repeating her hurtful words. "I suspect she doesn't really like anyone except those with a similar bank account."

Joe leaned over and kissed my cheek. "You always say the right thing, Aine. Thank you."

I clinked my glass against his. "Drink up. The evening is young."

As I lifted my glass, I saw Patrick. He stood in the kitchen doorway searching the room. When he saw me, he started forward, then stopped as if he were in pain. Fear of what he might have in mind made me move toward him. I didn't want a confrontation between Joe and my former lover in the middle of Dorothea's Christmas bash.

"Are you okay?" Joe asked.

"No. Excuse me for a moment."

I went to Patrick. When I was only a couple of feet away, he stared at me as if he'd never seen me. "What's wrong?" I asked him.

He trembled as large drops of sweat traced down his cheek and dripped onto his dress shirt. "I don't feel well." His jaw tightened and he could barely speak. "I'm sick."

"I'll get Dorothea." I rushed past him and into the kitchen. Several helpers labored over the hot ovens, but there was no sign of Dorothea. I went along the back hallway to the suite of offices. She often did her books at night after the inn closed. I tapped on the door but no one answered.

I turned to leave and smacked into Patrick. He'd followed me and stood like a hulk in the hall. "You need to go home," I said. "You're sick."

"Dorothea needs me tonight. This is a big event for her."

A gong sounded. The entertainment was about to begin. I had to get to my seat or risk disrupting the play. "Patrick, you need to lie down and rest. You're muscles are jerking." His breathing came shallow and fast.

"Can I go to your cabin and wait for you?"

I closed my eyes and sighed. "No. Joe can take you home."

"I took care of you when you were sick."

"Yes, you did. But it isn't appropriate for me to nurse a nineteen-year-old boy in my cabin when he has a mother and a home."

He staggered. When I caught him, he was hot and clammy. "You're very sick, Patrick." How had he gone from a healthy young man to someone who looked as if he might keel over in such a short time? "What happened to you?"

"I fell in love with you."

Before I could respond, he slumped to the floor.

33

After clearing the guests out of the inn, I joined Dorothea and Joe in the small back bedroom where Patrick thrashed and moaned while we waited for paramedics and an ambulance. Joe had carried him into the spare room and stretched him out on the narrow single bed.

Joe and Dorothea worked frantically to loosen his clothes and check for any bites or wounds while I fetched cold water and towels in an effort to give him some relief. His eyes rolled wildly as he fought. Every few minutes, he would bolt upward and try to free himself of Joe's grip as he cried out in pain. He complained of backaches and an inability to breathe, and at times his jaw seemed to lock in place.

He rambled, but most of what he said was incomprehensible. To Joe's repeated questions of what happened, Patrick's answers had no meaning. At least not to me.

At one point, he stilled. His eyes opened and he looked directly at Dorothea as if he recognized her. "Don't let me die," Patrick said weakly. "I'm afraid. She gave me something. She poisoned me."

"Who did?" Dorothea asked.

"She did. She wants me dead."

Muscle spasms set in. "Oh, god! Oh, god. I'm dying. The pain—" He contorted as if his limbs were rigid. I stepped away, terrified at what I witnessed.

Patrick's beautiful body bent backwards until his head drew close to his feet. He screamed in agony. I cowered in a corner, my hands over my ears, unable to successfully block the sounds of his anguish or do anything to help him.

"What happened to him?" Joe demanded. "What could he have gotten into? Poison? Pesticides? Can you think of anything?"

"No," Dorothea said. "I don't know. He was fine an hour ago. He disappeared for a little while, but he came right back. I thought he was talking with a guest."

"She did it." Patrick gasped the words. "I saw her. In the woods."

I pushed forward. "Who did you see?" I tried to take his hand but his arm was inflexible. "Who did you see, Patrick?"

His eyes rolled up in his head, his body spasmed, and then he fell back, unconscious. The only sound in the room was Joe's ragged breathing and Dorothea's soft whimpers.

The paramedics arrived and started fluids and oxygen. An ambulance waited to transport him to Boston General, but the EMTs wanted to stabilize him. They feared he would convulse in the ambulance and they wanted fluids and monitors in place.

Joe, Dorothea, and I were shuffled into the hallway. "Aine, would you call Patrick's parents?" Dorothea asked.

"Me?" I didn't want to. How did one tell parents their child might die?

"Please. I can't do it. I can't. Patrick has worked for me for over five years. He'd come after school even before he could drive. I love him like my own child."

Joe put a reassuring hand on my back. "Just tell them to get here as quickly as they can. But hurry, Aine. They may not have much time."

At first Mr. and Mrs. Leahy couldn't accept the seriousness of their son's condition. He'd been fine when he'd left home for work only five hours before. Nothing too awful could happen in such a short time. They said they were on the way, and when I urged them to hurry, they finally understood.

I returned to stand vigil outside the room with my friends. Through the open door, I could see the two paramedics hovering over Patrick's too-still body. Their expressions made me want to cry.

"What could have happened to him?" Dorothea used the cuff of her holiday blouse to wipe her tears. "He was teasing me this afternoon. He was in good spirits and though he was a little preoccupied, he wasn't sick."

"I don't know," I answered automatically. He said that *she'd* given him something. What had he meant? Was he delusional, or had someone made Patrick ill? My thoughts were like cockroaches, scurrying for dark corners. In the back of my mind, the suspicion that Mischa was the source of his illness took root and blossomed. She'd entered him—possessed him. She'd taken control of his body and his mind. Was this horror the result? What had she done to him?

A commotion in the room riveted my attention.

"We're losing him!" a paramedic said.

Dorothea gripped my hand, squeezing the bones so harshly I almost cried out. We stood unmoving, holding our breath, as the medics got out the cardiac paddles and tried to shock his heart into beating.

After three attempts, they grew still.

"No!" Dorothea hurled herself into the room and put her hands on Patrick's face. "No! Bring him back! Do something!"

The paramedics mumbled and turned away. Joe went to Dorothea and pulled her back from the body. "Come on," he said gently. "This won't help him. He's gone."

"No!" Dorothea turned to me, her face a mask of anguish. "Make him—" she broke off and sobbed.

I'd never felt so useless. I stood, clenching and unclenching my hands, unable to find a rational action to take. It was impossible. A young man who'd been vital and alive was dead. It was too much to process.

Patrick's parents arrived in a rush of questions that turned to wails. I moved back, giving them room.

Dorothea and Joe spoke with them and tried to calm them. The inn had become a place I wanted to escape, but there was no going back to my cabin. Things needed to be done. My past was littered with the work of the dead. Food preparation, cleaning, putting away reminders—the soft work of women to ease the loss of a beloved.

When Granny Siobhan had died, I returned to Kentucky. I entered the house I'd grown up in to find a clutch of crows had taken over the kitchen and downstairs. Everywhere I looked, old women dressed in black stood sentinel, their faces drawn in long lines of sorrow. As they cleaned the kitchen, prepared the front room for the wake, and washed the body, they rustled in their black. It was a sound I'd always associate with death.

The thing I remembered most was that they never spoke. The ritual of death was well known. Each woman played her part, whether it was cooking or dusting or braiding Granny's long, gray hair. There was no discussion what she'd wear in her coffin. Her best black dress. The pattern would not vary as long as that generation of Cahills lived.

I slowly inched away from the bedroom and went to the inn's kitchen. I didn't know the role I was meant to play. The hired help stood motionless, unsure of the next move. They looked to me as if I might have answers. Mountains of food ready to be served covered the cook tops and counters.

"Put it all away," I said, finding something I could do for Dorothea, and for Patrick. "Refrigerate what you can. Take the rest to the homeless shelters. No one will be eating here tonight."

My command freed them from the spell of dread that held them immobilized. Eager for action, they took up the chores.

In the dining rooms I blew out the candles, aware yet again of the still beauty of the night outside the windows of the inn. The silvered woods and the starry night held a different reality than the one inside.

Cries of despair rang out from the back room, and I worked to ignore them. Joe was better equipped to comfort Dorothea and

Patrick's family than I. My value culminated in tending to the details no one else remembered. Food put away, candles blown out, fire banked and ashes swept up, china and crystal returned to shelves, Christmas decorations pulled down and taken outside. I would leave no memory of this night for Dorothea to wake to.

Shock anesthetized my brain, but random questions floated to the surface. What had happened to Patrick? How had Mischa done this to him? In taking control of him, had she stripped his ability to function? Or was it something else she'd used? Food, drugs, allergic reaction—what was the source of his death?

The possibilities deviled me, but focusing on the medical mystery forestalled grief. Patrick dead wasn't a reality I could accept. At times, I deceived myself. The doctors would fix him. Somehow. Any minute I would hear relief from the back room. Dorothea, still crying, would come out to tell me he'd been revived. He was too young. Surely there was something to be done.

As time passed and only silence came from the back, I knew my fantasies had no substance. So I set the inn to order. When the caterers had everything packed, I made a list of the food sent to the homeless and helped them stack it in a van.

I'd forgotten how cold it was outside, but the arctic chill broke the malaise holding me emotionless. When the caterers drove away, I yielded. Standing in the bitter cold, I cried for Patrick, for Dorothea, and for myself.

The wind cut under the skirt of my dress, freezing my legs in the thin stockings and dress shoes. My wrap was inside the inn, but I didn't care. I wanted to go to my cabin. I couldn't go back inside the inn. I couldn't make myself do it. I didn't trust myself to maintain control of my emotions.

Before I really thought it out, I started running. At first I ran to get away from the inn, to defy the cold, to gain the solitude of my little cabin. I needed a place where I could cry without fear of being overheard. Icy tears ran down my cheeks, but I brushed them away and picked up my pace. Running was hard in the little leather heels.

The path, though illuminated by the clear sky, was uneven and difficult. Several times I almost twisted an ankle.

The sense that someone was watching me grew with each passing minute. At first I tried to convince myself it was only wild imagination. I knew better, though. Deny it all I wanted, I had the Cahill gift. I could sense the spirits of dead people.

Then I heard her. She was in the woods.

"Aine!" a childish voice called to me.

A small, quick creature darted through the trees to my right.

My heart rate tripled. I was more terrified than I'd ever been and only halfway to the cabin. I'd been a fool. She'd waited until I was between both places of safety. Now I was alone.

"Aine, come and play with me. I know, let's play a game." She wheedled like a child, but I knew better.

"Leave me alone." My voice was weak. I sounded old and feeble. "Go away!" I shouted.

"Aine, what about Hide and Seek?"

I didn't answer. I slowed to a walk. Each step took me closer to the cabin. The locked door was no barrier to her if she really wanted in. But it was all I had, and if I could get there, I'd figure a way to fight her. Bonnie's journals would tell me.

"How's Patrick?" The question came from the darkness to my right. She kept pace with me, yet she never made a sound. She slipped through the dense woods without a single limb cracking. "Poor boy. He was a little green around the gills the last time I saw him. Did you break his heart? Did you kill him?"

The words drifted to me on the wind. It struck me that I'd never seen her walk. For some reason that terrified me more than anything. In all the times I'd communicated with her, she'd just appeared. I'd turn around and she'd be there.

I followed the thin ribbon of the winding trail, swallowing my fear and trying to force my legs to take measured, even steps. The night was clear, and the stars were bright in the swath of sky between the trees. I rounded a corner and saw a light.

The cabin was closer than I thought! The rush of hope was almost debilitating. I lumbered into a run. My shoes rubbed blisters on my feet, but I pushed myself to move faster. To run for the light and the cabin. Maybe she would let me go.

"Aine, I'm still with you."

A tree root snared my foot and I fell. When I hit the dirt I bit my tongue and busted my lip. My beautiful dress tore apart. Pain bloomed, but I gained my knees and crawled. I would not lie in the dirt and wait for her to hurt me.

I didn't hear her, but when I looked up, she stood inches away. Her red jacket was zipped snug around her. Blond hair hung down her chest. In the moonlight, the hair looked silver. Her eyes were shaded by the folds of the hood.

"What did you do to Patrick?" I pushed myself up on my knees and spat blood. The red glob landed by her foot. My dress gaped open from breast to crotch. I tried to gather it up to cover myself, but my hands shook from the cold.

"What did *you* do to Patrick?" she asked.

"Not a damn thing!" Outrage at her accusation made me struggle to one knee. If I could gain my feet, I meant to charge her. She might not be human, but she wasn't smoke or fog. She appeared to have substance, and if I could I would harm her.

"Oh, you hurt him, Aine. Don't play coy. You rebuffed him. You threw him over for Joe. You sent him into such a depression that . . . he died." She spun on one heel as if she meant to leave, but she only laughed and turned back to face me. "You were instrumental in his death, Aine."

"That's a lie." My voice shook.

"No, it's the truth, though you'll try to deny it. Especially to yourself. You set him up for me. You hurt him, and so he drank. You're at the root of his death, and this time they'll trace it back to you." She closed her eyes, held out her arms, and spun, a child playing Blind Man's Buff.

"That's insane. There's nothing to trace back to me."

"Don't be so sure. Remember the epidemic of rabid raccoons the last time you were home? What did you buy at the feed store?"

"What are you talking about?" At Granny Siobhan's funeral, I'd been sent to the store to get something to poison the raccoons. I'd handed the strychnine to my cousins.

"You signed for the poison. There's a record."

"You're sick and dangerous." Even as I said it, I knew she wasn't crazy. She was evil. She'd plotted two murders, and each time she'd put me in a place to be the prime suspect. "Why Patrick? What did he ever do to you?"

"*You* wanted him dead. I merely obliged."

"How dare you?" My fingers clawed the dirt patch for rocks. With every bit of my strength I hurled them at her.

"Ouch," she said. "That wasn't very nice."

"I didn't want Karla dead and I certainly didn't want you to kill Patrick. He was just a kid."

"He was in the way. He meant to create trouble for you."

"I'm going to find a way to kill you. My aunt knew things. I'll figure out how to do it."

"Yes, Aunt Bonnie, by all means." She faded to a red stain against the shadowed woods. "You've been afraid to do it until now. Grit up, Aine. Do it. Consult Bonnie's journal. You can really read it now. There are secrets there you're finally ready to understand. But remember, things didn't go so well for Bonnie, did they?"

I clutched another handful of rocks but when I drew back to hurl them, she was gone. The path before me was empty of everything except moonlight.

34

Panting in terror, I reached the cabin, wrenched the unlocked door open and slammed it shut behind me, sliding the thumb bolt home. The rough wood rasped through the thin material of my ruined dress. When my fears calmed, I pushed away from the door and stumbled into the chilly room.

The fire was almost out, and I added logs and stirred the embers with a poker until a bright flame jumped toward the chimney. As I stood, I caught my reflection in the dresser mirror. My hair, disheveled and tangled around my head and shoulders, was filled with twigs and leaves as if I'd run pell-mell through the woods.

My face was scratched, bruised, and bloodied. The beautiful dress I'd wanted so badly hung in tatters from my shoulders. Blood from my busted lip splotched the front of it. Runs laddered my stockings, revealing the purplish skin of my naked legs. Based on my coloring, I could pass for a corpse. At last I looked at my ruined shoes and bleeding feet.

Self-pity rose in me, and tears stung my eyes—until I noticed something else. Two wine glasses sat on the kitchen counter. One bore a trace of lipstick, and contained half an inch of wine. The other glass was empty and rested beside the uncorked red wine I preferred.

I had no memory of drinking wine with Joe or anyone else. I didn't remember opening the bottle.

Someone had been in my cabin.

I walked slowly to the counter and picked up the dark green bottle. The foil sleeve was torn, not cut. I always used a knife, rather than leaving it jagged. Long ago, vintners used lead foil to keep rodents away from the cork. Knowing that, I always removed the entire sleeve.

The truth slammed into me. Patrick had come back to my cabin. He'd opened the wine. He'd drunk from the empty glass, a glass which would test positive for poison. Patrick's fingerprints would be on the glass.

I'd been set up.

I didn't know how she'd done it, but Mischa had lured Patrick here and coerced him into drinking my wine. And she'd poisoned him. She'd concocted the perfect trap and she'd herded me and Patrick straight into it.

I put the two glasses in a paper bag. I poured the wine down the sink and added the empty bottle. I had to get rid of them right away, before Joe followed me to the cabin.

Sacking the clinking glass in a kitchen trash bag, I pulled it from the can and tied it off. I didn't have a car, so I'd have to hide it in the woods until I could bury it or figure a way to dispose of it. But Mischa was in the woods. Terror and indecision held me captive.

A gentle tapping came at the front door. I couldn't move, uncertain what do to.

"Aine, let me in."

Mischa had followed me and wanted inside. I wasn't going to open my door to her. Not ever again.

"You can run, but you can't hide." She mocked me. "Come on, Aine. I'm just a little girl. Let me in. It's cold and dark out here. I'm afraid." She sounded exactly like a frightened child.

"Leave me alone."

"I'll huff and I'll puff and I'll blow your door down."

Her giggle sounded so much like a grade-schooler, an innocent child engaged in a foolish prank. Mischa was not innocent and this was no prank. "Go home. Or go back to hell where you came from. I want nothing to do with you."

"You hurt my feelings, Aine. I thought we were friends." There was a brief moment of silence. "No matter. I'm going to leave a present for you."

"No! I don't want anything." The idea of what she might entrust to me was terrifying. "Go away! Leave me alone!" The urge to beg rose up, but I fought it. Pleading would amuse her. She seemed to thrive on the pain of others. "Haven't you done enough?" I thought of Patrick and rage consumed me. I wanted to feel my fingers around her throat. "Just go away!"

Only silence met my response. It seemed that I waited forever. I had to get rid of the wine glasses, but I feared Mischa more than I feared being caught with evidence that might incriminate me.

An eternity later, I moved to the door and threw back the thumb bolt. Inching it open, I peeked out. A frigid breeze hummed through the fir trees, but otherwise the night was silent. There wasn't a trace of Mischa to be found, until I looked at the floor of the porch beside the door. Bright moonlight fell on a doll with auburn hair. She wore a black floor-length dress from the 1800s. The face was a work of art, a bisque replica of a beautiful woman.

I reached out an arm and brought the doll into the cabin. The curled auburn hair was real. I touched it to be certain. And the eyes opened and shut as I picked her up. Her little lips were parted to reveal four perfectly formed teeth—stunning little teeth. Ready to bite.

The doll terrified me. I touched the bisque face, aware that the mint condition of the antique doll meant she was likely quite expensive. What did she symbolize?

Why had Mischa given her to me? Why dolls?

I closed the door and re-latched it. I'd dropped the trash bag on the floor, so I picked it up and pushed it under my bed. Tomorrow

I would get rid of it. I shoved the doll under the bed, too. I had no explanation for her if Joe arrived and asked.

After those things were concealed, I picked up Bonnie's journal and settled in the rocker before the fire. If there was help for me within the pages she'd written, I had to find it. Whether ghost or demon, Mischa had to be banished. She was malevolent. Death followed her. Whoever she touched sickened and died when she was done with them—and she had infiltrated my life. She'd tricked me with her childish image. I'd felt sorry for her, worried about her. She garnered my sympathy and gained access to my life.

All of Granny's machinations, her packing me up and sending me off—all for nothing. In the very woods where I hoped to attain my future, I had found the past. The Cahill past.

And what was Mischa? A dead girl come back for justice? No. Mischa was more. She had power in the corporeal world. She could wield a weapon to beat someone to death and poison wine. And she meant to hurt people. She liked it.

The journal fell open two-thirds of the way through. Several of the pages crumbled along the edges, flakes falling to the floor. The paper was brittle. I'd been careful with it, but it should have been preserved instead of hauled from pillar to post. Mischa had said there were secrets here, and the journal was all I had. Panic that it might disintegrate made me anxious.

It took several moments to calm myself. I was a total emotional wreck. Since the first sighting of a child in the woods, my life had spiraled out of control. Two people were dead. I had to stop it. I'd witnessed the destruction of too many of my relatives: my father lost to drink, my mother dead by her own hand when I was only a little girl; countless cousins victims of violence; or going back generations, the bloodlust of whalers. My line had been doomed since Jonah turned his back on goodness and joined forces with the practitioners of evil. I began to wonder whether Mischa's relationship with my family went back centuries.

A long ago echo sounded in my head and the present faded away, leaving only memory. Aunt Matilde. She stood on the stairs of my home, my real home, where I'd lived with my parents and started school, in Coalgood. Back when Daddy worked at the post office and we'd moved away from the Cahill mountain land and into town.

A fresh start, my mama called that house. Daddy had an education. He'd graduated from high school and passed the civil service test to hire on as a rural route carrier. He was the only one of his brothers to complete the twelfth grade, and he was destined to make good. Everyone said so. He'd escaped the family traditions of addiction and cruelty, but moving away from the Cahill Clan hadn't saved him.

The scene replayed in memory.

Aunt Matilde had my daddy by the arm. She pressed him hard against the landing as he tried to escape her. She was his older sister, and she leaned toward him with such intensity that his back arched over the railing. Watching from the ground floor, I feared he would fall.

"The infant was suffocated," Aunt Matilde said. "She was alone with the child. She talks about another girl, but there was no one there. She goes on and on about her friend that no one sees. She did this, Caleb. Face up to it."

"That's a damn lie, Matilde."

"Rachel told me all about her imaginary friend. About the things the girl tells her to do. Cruel things, Caleb. Rachel's been worried about her. She said you won't listen. That you won't admit the child is sick. Now look. The baby is dead, and you know who's to blame. Your daughter. Rachel is on the verge of losing her mind with grief and guilt."

"Listen to yourself, Matilde. You, of all people, should understand. You have the same blood. This isn't Aine's fault. Rachel can't grasp this. She isn't a Cahill, but you are. You know the burden this family carries. Aine has an ability, and we are fighting it. Rachel doesn't see an imaginary friend, but Aine does." His voice broke. "God help her, she sees it. To her, it's not a monster or a demon, It comes to her like a child, a playmate. We've warned Aine, but—"

"I never took you for a superstitious fool, Caleb. Your son is dead, and it wasn't an imaginary friend who killed him. Your wife is in jeopardy because you won't face the truth. Aine is insane and dangerous."

My father pushed Aunt Matilde so hard she fell against the landing wall with a loud thud. He made a strange sound as he ran up the next flight of stairs to the second floor. Then I heard the door slam and my mother's cry of anguish.

I'd heard the talk—that I'd smothered my infant brother and because of that my mother killed herself. Daddy sold the house and we moved to the old Cahill homestead with Granny Siobhan, and no one talked about me any more. Granny put a stop to it.

Besides, none of it was true. I loved baby William. I would never have harmed him. Never. But I did have a friend. Strange but I couldn't recall her appearance. I only remembered she was about my age and size, and she came to see me when I was in my room alone or walking in the woods. She laughed and skipped around me and told me secrets that shocked the grown-ups.

When we moved to Granny Siobhan's, I left her behind.

Now, the memory surfaced like a fat bubble in a still pond. The truth popped loudly in my head and all external sound disappeared. I was completely alone in silence as memories returned. Mischa had been with me for a long time. With our family even longer, perhaps. Her thumbprint was clear to read in the family history.

The Cahills suffered. Tragic things happened in our family. Hardship moved up and down the family tree. Even relatives who set out to leave the family behind suffered terrible events. Once the word got out, my male cousins had poor luck courting local girls. No one wanted to taste the acrimony of the Cahill legacy. No one wanted to marry into our family. My mother was from Lexington, and even though she was warned, she ignored the Cahill reputation. And she lost her son and her life.

Sins of the father or just a streak of insanity in the family, I didn't know. But addiction, suicide, and loneliness were the trinity of the Cahill Curse. No matter how hard I focused on "the good future" Granny wanted for me, I found myself at the edge of the pit. Education could not rid me of these spirits. Distance could not save me from my dark gift.

Perhaps Bonnie could.

The page the journal opened to was dated Winter 1845.

Henry came to the woods because he wished to live deliberately. He wanted to learn what life had to teach. He feared that lying on his deathbed, he would discover he had not truly lived at all. Noble ambitions for a man who never suffered tragedy until his brother died. My tragedy is that I know he will never know the pain of losing a child or even his parents. He will die young.

I've dreamt his death many times, the filling of his lungs with blood. Consumption. His contamination likely from the pencil factory his family operates. It is indeed bitter when those who love us sow the seeds of our destruction. This has also been the lesson of my life.

I have tried to warn Henry that his health is fragile. He will not listen to me. Over time, he has grown to fear my dreams and portents of death. He sees darkness in me that I cannot erase from his vision. When I visit with the child in the woods, he pretends he cannot see her. Whether he sees her or not, he fears her. How can a man fear something he cannot see? How can he claim to know that she is not the spirit of a dead child? She offers me wise counsel when the Sluagh come pecking at the cabin windows. They wait for Henry, and I will not give him up so readily.

My heart pounded so loudly in my ears, I couldn't think for a moment. I'd never seen this passage. Never. I would have remembered this. My first impulse was to throw the journal in the fire, but I didn't. Mischa had said there were secrets in the journal I was now ready to understand. If I could gain an insight into Mischa and what she intended, perhaps I could stop her. I bent over the journal and continued reading.

I came to Walden Pond for Henry. My love for him has been my greatest joy and my most painful journey. Though it is a contrary thing, I have learned that it is possible to both love and despise the same person. It is one thing to embrace the eccentricities of a man when you are not beholden to him for warmth and food, and it is another matter when the winter wind howls and there is no firewood split for warmth because his thoughts have sent him on another mission.

When I think of leaving him, I know I can't. I fear what she will do if I am not here. Then I despair that she is here because of me, that somehow I have called her to me. God save me if that is the truth, because I have called up a monster.

I closed the journal, unable to read more. From the moment the journal arrived in my hands, I had been Mischa's pawn. How much of this journal was from my aunt, and how much from Mischa? I couldn't tell anymore. But the dread that wedged heavy in my breast belied my fears.

Heavy footsteps and a voice on the porch finally galvanized me to action. I stuffed the journal under the bed and went to open the door for Joe.

35

Flames leaped up the chimney after Joe stoked the fire to the point I feared he might burn the cabin down. He worked not for warmth, but to erase from his mind the cruel death of a young man. I sat on the bed and watched, unable to help him. Unable to help myself. At times, the wind moaned outside the cabin and my heart clutched. She was out there, and I wondered if she might be tormenting me, howling at the windows, wailing under the house. Having her fun at my expense.

I had to find out more about her. If my aunt's journal spoke any truth, the child had wandered these woods for a long time. I'd named her Mischa, and I would call her that because I had no better name for her. But she was older than Mischa. Older than Bonnie. Older than time.

Joe left the fire and came to me. "I'm so sorry," he said. He picked up my hands where they curled uselessly on either side of me on the bed and held them in his large, warm ones. He touched my battered face. "What happened to you?"

"I fell."

"I looked for you at the inn. When I realized you'd gone home in this freezing weather without a jacket, I came after you."

"I couldn't stay at the inn any longer."

He eased down beside me, his arm going around my shoulders to pull me close. "My god, I don't know what Dorothea will do. She feels responsible."

"Why? She had nothing to do with his death."

"He was poisoned. I'm pretty sure of it. Patrick was at the inn all afternoon. He must have been poisoned there. Dorothea told me that she had no idea how he could have eaten anything contaminated, but she believes that's what happened." He turned my face to his with a gentle touch. "What do you think?"

Because I couldn't lie while looking at him, I closed my eyes. "I don't know. It doesn't make any sense. Patrick was just a kid."

Joe's fingers stroked my jaw. His thumb whispered over my bruised and swollen lips. "Patrick made no secret that he . . . enjoyed flirtations with quite a few of the ladies who stayed at the inn. Do you think a jealous husband, or maybe a jealous woman, might have harmed him?"

I didn't answer.

"He meant no harm, and, from what Dorothea said, the ladies enjoyed his attention." Joe sighed. "Chief McKinney will have to question everyone in the inn. And the guests for the Christmas party."

"Let's talk about something else." I couldn't stand it. I wanted to tell the chief and Joe who had poisoned Patrick and also beaten Karla to death, but they wouldn't believe me. No one would believe me. This was the last twist of the knife from Mischa. She couldn't be accused of any crime she committed, because sane people didn't believe she existed.

This time I'd come back to the cabin and foiled her. I'd found the wine and glasses and I would destroy them. Had Joe and I come back together and discovered that open wine and two used glasses, he might have gotten suspicious. Or he might have drunk the wine. He would be dead, too.

Was that her ultimate game? To kill everyone I showed any affection for? I simply couldn't grasp her motivation.

"Hey, you're a million miles away, and from the looks of it, the place you're visiting isn't so nice."

"This is just so incredible. I can't believe Patrick is dead. That he was poisoned."

"We won't know for sure until the autopsy, but I'm willing to bet it's strychnine. Twenty years ago, people used it to kill raccoons and stray dogs. It's a terrible death, and now it's illegal. But there was a time a person could buy it at the drugstore by simply signing a register. It isn't that hard to come by."

I knew that from personal experience, but there was no point in saying so. "Let's go to bed."

"I should go home."

I clutched his shirtsleeve. "No. Please don't!"

A frown crossed his face and then was gone. "Are you afraid, Aine?"

"Yes. Afraid of being alone now. I can't bear it. Please don't go. Spend the night. Please."

His answer was a tender kiss. He slowly unbuttoned the tattered dress I was still wearing and slipped it from my shoulders. My hose were ground into my knees. From the bathroom, he brought a pan of warm water and a cloth. "Lie back," he said.

He soaked the hose out of my wounded knees and removed then, giving my feet attention for their cuts and bruises. He assessed the damage. "It's superficial, and some antibiotic salve will help."

"In the medicine cabinet."

In a moment he returned and smoothed the ointment into my battered flesh. It hurt, but I was strangely distanced from the responses of my own body.

"Are you hurt anywhere else?" he asked as he pulled the covers over me.

"My heart is damaged."

He didn't laugh or mock me, but kissed my forehead. "How about some whiskey?"

"Yes."

He fetched the bottle of good bourbon and two glasses. He gave it to me neat. "Drink up."

I wanted to drink until I forgot everything that had happened. I tossed back the bourbon and felt the burn travel from the back of my throat to my stomach. A momentary churn made me fear I'd vomit, but it settled and I was left with the spreading warmth of the liquor.

Joe eased into bed beside me and we curled together. Before too much time passed, I heard his regular breathing and knew he'd drifted to sleep. The desire to follow him was great, but I couldn't.

No matter that Mischa was not in the cabin. She was in my head, and I had no clue how to exorcise her. Tomorrow, though, I would explore that option. There were plenty of Catholic churches in Concord, and though I'd left the pomp and ritual of the church far behind me, I knew where to find a priest.

I drifted into sleep, and found myself floating in warm brine. Beneath me a huge white body coursed by. The water pulsed with the passing of the mammoth creature. My body got caught in the backwash, and I was pulled deeper out to sea. The creature passed again and again, never touching me, but inexorably dragging me away from land and safety. Struggle as I might, I couldn't break the thrall of the whale.

When no land was visible on the horizon, the whale surfaced. One blurry eye pinned me, and a rush of red blood shot from its blowhole. "You've met your destiny, Aine Cahill." It spoke to me telepathically.

"Do you know the child?" I asked.

A gout of blood blew into the air and fell over both of us. "I do. And so do you."

The whale dove, and I was left alone a thousand miles from land.

When I woke up sweating, I eased away from Joe's body and slipped from the bed. I staggered and nearly fell when I saw the doll sitting on the fireplace hearth. I looked around the dark cabin, but Mischa was gone. She didn't linger when Joe was around.

Beside the doll was Bonnie's journal, open to a page near the end of my aunt's tenure at Walden Pond. Bending forward to hold the journal to the firelight, I read.

Henry has gone into town. He'll lunch with his parents, and I am left here alone, sick and scared. She left me a present today. The doll has a beautiful face, but the four little teeth are somehow disconcerting. The toy of a child should not have teeth. But I know this is not a doll for a child. This is meant for me. I have found the use for my hair she stole. The doll has my hair. She wears a tiny replica of my very own dress. The doll is me. I think she means to take my soul and put it into the doll for her pleasure.

And then I think that I am truly going mad that such terrible thoughts come to me.

At last I knew Mischa's ultimate motive. She had written it in the journal while I slept beside Joe. I feared for my soul.

The journal entry ended. I braced against the stone fireplace, lightheaded with terror. Poor Bonnie. I knew exactly how she felt.

The doll leaned against the hearth, her little hands perfectly formed at her sides. She wore cloth, button-up shoes patterned after the style of the mid-1800s. I touched the hair. My aunt's dark auburn locks had not faded with time. It was still soft and lush. Like my own.

"Bonnie, are you in there?" I whispered.

The doll's blue eyes opened. The tiny teeth pressed into her lip. For a moment I imagined her mouth moved as if she meant to talk, but no words issued from the doll.

"Bonnie?" I whispered as I glanced at Joe. He was still sound asleep, unaware that something dark and cruel had entered his life. "Bonnie?" I shook the doll lightly but stopped when Joe shifted to his back in the bed. He looked so vulnerable asleep.

My impulse was to chuck the doll into the flames. To be rid of it even at the cost of destroying my aunt's image. Yet I couldn't bring myself to burn it. What if Bonnie's soul was trapped inside? Would she burn too?

I held the doll as I sat motionless in the rocker until the peachy glow of sunrise tinted the cabin window. Another day had begun. The night had passed, and I had much to do.

36

The morning sun couldn't penetrate the gray clouds that clotted the sky like huge curds. Snow or rain was imminent. The weather reflected my mood perfectly.

Joe helped me cook breakfast at the inn. He was handy in the kitchen, and he brought in firewood for the dining room fireplaces. A snapping fire helped alleviate the gloom, but the smell of the sausage Joe fried was almost more than I could take. Empty and grieving, I attended the chore that confronted me.

Dorothea tried, but she burst into tears without warning, so I sent her to her quarters. The guests knew about Patrick's death, and several were crying when they showed up in the dining room. The atmosphere was somber. Joe and I did our best, but food was not the solution for what ailed any of us.

By eight-thirty, a half-dozen guests had checked out and the rest were packing. Joe loaded the cars, while I figured bills, ran credit cards, and tried without success to work as efficiently as Dorothea. When the morning rush was over, Joe went to work and I went to talk to my friend and landlady.

She was huddled in her bathrobe staring out her bedroom window at the gray winter morning. Christmas Day. I'd forgotten all about the holiday.

"The kitchen is clean and the guests have gone," I said. "Can I bring you some breakfast?"

"No." She cleared her throat. "Thank you, Aine. I couldn't face people this morning, but I must pull myself together. Patrick's family needs me. It's the least I can do, considering he was poisoned here."

"We don't know that, Dorothea. No one else got sick."

"I have to understand how this happened." She spoke to herself more than me.

Something outside the window caught her attention, and dread made me rigid. "What's out there?"

"Just a child. She's gone now."

I wanted to ask Dorothea to describe what she'd seen but couldn't trust myself not to overreact. "Is there anything else I can do?"

She shook her head and swallowed back a sob. "I hate the idea of an autopsy. He was such a beautiful young man." She struggled to hold back her tears. "But as soon as the autopsy is done, the Leahys will bury him. They don't have a funeral plot. I told them I'd walk through the old cemetery on the hill to find a few suitable spots. They moved here when Patrick was ten, so they have no family buried in the area. I thought it would be nice if he could rest in Sleepy Hollow."

"I can check for you." I didn't mind spending an hour with the likes of Thoreau and Emerson. The old cemetery was quiet, beautiful, and a good place to think. Perhaps I would be inspired to a solution about Mischa. Then again, it might also be the perfect place for Mischa to seek me out. "But maybe you should—"

"Would you?" Dorothea spoke with such relief, I couldn't back out.

"Of course. I'll do it now." The day had warmed, but the overcast skies seeped gloom. At ten o'clock on Christmas Day not many people would be visiting the cemetery. I could do a quick walk-through and scout a few locations for Dorothea. I could also revisit Thoreau's grave.

He was buried with his family, but I wondered where Bonnie's final resting place might be. What had Mischa ultimately done with her corporeal flesh?

The walk into town revealed an isolated community. No childish laughter rang out to celebrate the joy of a new sled or football. The town was quiet. I wondered if it was Patrick's death, or just that folks were inside their homes with a Christmas fire, celebrating as families were wont to do.

In Kentucky, Christmas was a time for outdoor games. A few children would receive ice skates to be used on shallow ponds. I'd never checked for a local rink that offered ice skating, but the notion of children outside seemed to belong to a past century.

Ice skating had always been a fantasy of mine—that I would glide gracefully across the ice on one leg, dressed in a red hat and mittens. I'd bend and pull my extended back leg around and spin, a blur of color. The fantasy made me smile.

The truth was that I'd borrowed my cousin's skates and nearly killed myself. The ease and fluidity I'd imagined remained out of my grasp. My cousin Janelle was like a dancer on the ice. She could spin and swoop, skating backward and even jumping in moves she saw on television.

When she died in a car wreck driving down the mountain, her mother gave me her skates. It didn't matter. I didn't have Janelle's grace or nerve. I'd been so innocent then. Fervent desire centered on simple goals, like ice skating.

The contrast to my current desires elicited a sigh. I wanted to rid myself of a child who was either demon or malevolent spirit who had not only the power but the will to hurt the people around me. And me. If Bonnie's journals were correct, this child had tormented her. How did one escape such a haunting?

The parking lot of St. Benedict's Holy Catholic Church was jammed, so I walked on to the cemetery. Best to get the gravesite chore done. With the clouds wallowing on the horizon, I wanted to get back to the cabin.

I'd come to associate Mischa with darkness and woods. The cemetery was shaded but not close like the path to the cabin or the old shack off Yerby Lane. There were wooded areas, but the paths winding around the graves were open and clearly marked. I would not tarry among the dead. I had enough sadness without reading the heartbreak carved into some of the stones.

Sleepy Hollow was an addition to the original Concord burial ground and had been dedicated by Emerson, who served on the cemetery committee. I had learned this from Dorothea. Her family was buried here, but their plots lay in a western segment.

As I turned off Bedford Road and into the cemetery, a cold chill slipped under my collar. The old lichen-covered graves blended into the landscape, almost like the stones erupted from the soil. From Upland Avenue, I took a northerly direction. There was no one around to ask about empty plots, so I simply searched for unclaimed spaces. I'd investigated the cemetery back in the early fall when the rich yellow leaves of the asters flamed against the deep green firs.

The terrain was hilly, and I paused to admire the bare tree trunks and stone outcroppings. This land could be hard, but equally so the people who settled here.

I was glad the trees were bare. Deep shade would generate anxiety and the expectation of red. The silvery black limbs of the trees reached into the gray sky and I continued on to Author's Ridge where Thoreau, the Alcotts, Emerson, Hawthorne, and their families were buried. For a small town in the mid-1800s, Concord and the surrounding area had produced a surprising outpouring of literary genius. My determination to come here to write was predicated on that. My subconscious hope had been that a spark of genius would ignite in me from near proximity to great minds. Even though they were great minds of the dead.

Leaving the trail behind, I climbed over the ridge and down to Cat's Pond on the far side. Tranquil and quiet, the terrain forced me to acknowledge how deeply I'd grown to care about Walden Pond. So much of Bonnie lingered there, too. To write my dissertation, I needed the feel of the place she'd loved.

Perhaps, though, it was time to pack up and abandon Concord. To head where? A question without an answer. The original idea was to stay at the inn until my dissertation was completed and turned in. I would defend it in April, which was easily doable while living at Dorothea's place. I'd planned for this ever since I'd understood the potential of Bonnie's journal.

"Bonnie never left here, you know."

Mischa had arrived. I should have known I wouldn't escape her. I didn't hurry to look at her.

"Where did Bonnie go after Thoreau left Walden? Do you even know, or is this another little game of yours?" I walked south toward the ridge. If I could get back to the main part of the cemetery, maybe a groundskeeper would make an appearance. Mischa wouldn't ply her torment in front of anyone else. In my experience, her joy depended on my being alone.

"You can't outdistance me."

She had the uncanny ability to read my mind. "Watch and see."

"Aren't you going to thank me for the doll?"

I whirled to confront her. The red hood was back, revealing her sweet face. How could such a countenance cover such wickedness? "How did you steal my aunt's hair?"

"I don't steal. She gave it to me." She laughed and skipped ahead. "She did. I asked for a lock of her hair and she gave it to me."

"The doll's head has more than a lock. You cut her hair while she slept."

She circled me, dancing merrily. "She'd already given me some. I took the rest. She didn't care a whole lot." She personified innocence. "There was nothing she could do about it, anyway. You're curious now, Aine. That's good. Once you explore and understand, you'll view me differently. You're lonely. There's no one who sympathizes with you like I do. I can be such a boon companion. Much better than Patrick. He intended to create trouble for you. Surely you know I'm telling the truth. He was going to get all high school and spill your secrets to Joe and Dorothea. They'd be shocked, wouldn't they?"

Her speech was disconcertingly modern. I grabbed her shoulder and spun her around. "You set me up to take the fall for killing Patrick. You poisoned him with wine, and you left the bottle and glasses where they could be found in my possession. I would have been charged with murder."

A flock of birds burst from bare trees on the lip of the ridge. They flew up into the air and then cut sharply left to aim straight at me. I ducked as they streaked by. The brush of a black wing sliced across my cheek. When I put my hand to it, blood smudged my fingers.

"What did you do with the bottle and glasses?" she asked. "You're clever. Did you bury them? You're too smart to leave them in the cabin where they could be found. Though I doubt Dorothea will feel up to searching your abode any time soon. Guilt is crushing her, poor thing."

"What *are* you?" This time I asked with fear, not anger.

"Just a lost little child. Someone you should pity and protect."

I didn't believe her, but I was too much a coward to contradict her. "What do you want with me?"

She giggled. "Silly! You called me here. What do *you* want?"

The farce she was playing made my fists clench in helpless frustration. "I want you to go away."

She put her hands behind her back and swung her body back and forth. "Not gonna happen. We're sort of like . . . sisters. Don't you see? I could never leave you alone without a friend. We belong together. It's part of the deal. The Cahill deal. You can see me, Aine."

"I don't *want* to see you. I did fine without you."

"Not true." She skipped backward, staying just out of my reach, as if she knew I would gladly choke the life from her.

"You can't kill me, Aine. I'm part of you. We're peas in a pod, two of a kind, made for each other. You know all the clichés."

"If anyone had found the wine with the poison, I would have been arrested and convicted. What fun could you have with me then?"

"Not a chance. I knew you'd find them." She held her arms out, dipping and gyrating. Her blond hair whipped around like a golden skein, and a deeper terror touched me. She could pass for the most adorable child.

When she breathlessly pulled up, she assessed me. The cunning in her blue eyes pierced me. "You're predicable, Aine. I know you inside and out."

"Why bother with me if I'm such a middling example of a human?"

"It's a long story. Do you like stories? I would think you must, since you're studying literature. But do you? Truly?"

As I crested the top of the hill, I struggled to pick up my pace, cutting across the cemetery and angling through the woods. I was headed vaguely toward Author's Ridge where Thoreau and his brethren were buried. Mischa danced beside me.

"Don't you want to hear my story?" she asked.

I didn't answer. Each time I communicated with Mischa, I slid deeper into a frightening world. I jogged. My scraped knees complained, but the pain gave me a focus.

"I'm your burden to carry." Mischa darted in front of me, forcing me to change directions and angle deeper into the woods. "Want to know why?"

"I want you to get the fuck out of my life."

"Am I annoying you, Aine? A lot of annoyances have been eliminated from your life. I wonder how that happens."

I dodged around the trunk of a large black oak. My ankle twisted on the uneven ground and I went down hard. The fall knocked the wind out of me and I couldn't catch my breath. For a moment, I thought I would die there, waiting for Mischa to move in for the kill. I cowered.

Nothing.

I opened my eyes. Above me in the branches of the oak, a large crow peered down at me. Granny Siobhan believed a solitary crow signaled impending death. Whenever we saw one crow, we hunted until we found another. A superstition, but one I remembered with the black eyes of the bird boring into me.

The crow cocked his head. His beak opened, and the sharp tongue flicked in and out, as if he tasted the air.

"Shoo!" I waved my arms and tossed a handful of leaves at him. He didn't move, but his attention shifted to the distance. I followed his line of vision, wondering where Mischa had gone. And why. She could have killed me, but she hadn't. And now she was gone.

I rose to my knees. Mischa was nowhere to be found. The crow clung to his perch not ten feet above my head. He was a big creature, maybe eighteen inches tall. "Shoo!" I stood and fluttered my hands at him.

He jumped to the ground and dared me. His attitude was more human than avian. He seemed to be old. And wise. A descendant of dinosaurs. And a harbinger of death.

I kicked leaves at him. The brown curls fell over his head and he didn't budge.

Striving for calm, I turned to walk away. The bird's lack of fear triggered my panic. I'd gone only a few feet when his beak pulled my pants leg. I pivoted to meet him head-on, and he hopped back to his original place.

"You devil." I spoke in a low tone, and I heard the quiver in my voice. This was a bird. I could kick it to death if need be. I couldn't allow my fear to break me. Surely I could defend myself against a two-pound bird. But at the back of my mind, I knew it was no ordinary crow.

He pecked at the leaf-covered ground, cawed, then pecked more. A grass plug came loose and he tossed it aside and attacked the dirt again. He was after something beneath the grass. The bird was showing me.

I eased forward and knelt. The bird held his position, pecking and looking at me, inviting me closer. I brushed the leaves slowly away and let my fingers rake the grassy earth. When I felt smooth, flat stone, I stopped.

In my peripheral vision, I saw a red blur in the woods some thirty yards away. Mischa in her red coat. But she had company. A young woman with auburn hair piled high on her head. The hem of her dark dress skimmed the ground.

She was there and then gone.

"Bonnie." I whispered her name. I knew it was my aunt. She was in Sleepy Hollow. Anticipation drew me to my feet. "Bonnie?"

The woods were deserted. Even the crow was gone. The mystery of the stone slab remained, though. Easing down on my knees, I pulled at the runners of grass. The soil was dark and pebbled with rocks that tore at my fingertips. I didn't feel the pain. I dug and pulled until the stone was unearthed.

It was a simple pale gray grave marker, long covered by grass, dirt, and leaves. Lichen and mold grew in the granite's cracks, and for a moment, I thought I saw her name. Bonnie Cahill. But it was merely the broken stone and black mold, an illusion.

Bonnie was buried here, though. I knew it. I had no way to prove it, nor would I ever be able to. But I knew. At last, I'd found her. There was no record of her life, because it ended here in Concord when she was a young woman. Her death wasn't recorded; her burial outside sanctified ground.

A mental vision held me captive until it played out. Henry David Thoreau's thin figure labored over a shovel as he dug the grave. The night was dark, a moonless sky, but I recognized the cemetery in my vision—the exact place where I now knelt. The body of my aunt, wrapped in a bloody sheet, rested on the grass beside the grave.

He wept as he fought the unrelenting surface, and I wondered if his tears were for Bonnie or himself. The vision played out like a movie as I watched, helpless, unable to help or hinder Thoreau in his pursuit to bury my aunt's body.

For I knew she was dead. This spot marked Bonnie's grave. Mischa, for whatever purpose, led me to my ancestor's final resting place. She'd told me Bonnie had never left Concord.

She hadn't lied about that, though the journal had led me to believe Bonnie had survived Thoreau. With Mischa, the truth was a twisting snake, but I believed I had finally seen the truth.

How had my aunt died? Had a small child played a role? Mischa was responsible for Karla's death. And Patrick's. Had she murdered Bonnie too? Would I be next?

A sudden wind cut through the woods, rattling the bare limbs until they clacked and clattered like bones. I had to get home. The cemetery was no place to be alone on a gray winter day.

37

I ran down from Author's Ridge to the bottom of the hollow. Tomb-stones, blackened by time, rose up around me. The angel Gabriel, hovering on a stone pedestal, glowered at me with malevolence. I didn't slow. Panic drove me toward the cemetery entrance. At any moment, I anticipated Mischa stepping out from behind a headstone or marble guardian of the dead. She meant to harm me, but first she would torture me. I understood why I was Mischa's choice. She meant to destroy me.

Granny Siobhan's fears of the Cahill Curse were justified—and understated. Granny had tried to save me, but she'd failed.

If Bonnie called this creature to her and, in coming here to inves-tigate Bonnie, I had somehow done the same, I'd sealed my own fate. Bonnie died young while residing at Walden Pond. Her lover, Thoreau, buried her in the town cemetery, but outside the consecrated plots of his family and friends. Even in death she was excluded.

Icy sweat trickled from my temples down beside my ears. The sensation of bugs crawling on my skin made me tear at my face with muddy fingers as I hurried. At last I reached the main entrance of the cemetery, and I forced myself to calm. There were people about. Not many, but a few of the living had come to share Christmas Day with the dead.

Terror coated the back of my throat. I had to get a grip on myself. At a seat made of rough stones, I rested for a moment. I couldn't leave without finding a caretaker and locating possible burial plot sites for the Leahys. I'd promised Dorothea, and there was no escaping this duty. Before I spoke with anyone, though, I needed to rein in my panic.

A middle-aged couple, hand in hand, passed me. They looked with curiosity, then dropped their gazes to the pathway. Shock registered on their faces. I rubbed my cheeks on the shoulders of my coat, trying to dislodge the blood from the bird's wing and the dirt I'd put there clawing at the sweat.

Watching the couple pass, I tried to deduce why they were in a cemetery on Christmas Day. Were they visiting a parent? A child? A sibling? They walked with great dignity, as if this holiday visit to the dead held special significance for them.

My answer came soon enough. They were visiting a dead son. I saw him a hundred yards ahead, a ghostly outline against a towering marble sculpture of a tree trunk. Beside him a faithful dog struck the pose of a pointer.

The tree and dog were incredible works of art, and I knew the boy had been loved, and his family had not lacked for money to erect such a memorial. He watched his parents, but at such a distance I couldn't read his expression.

I could tell he was a young man. No older than eighteen and maybe younger. He wore jeans, hiking boots, and a plaid jacket with the casual grace of a boy who kept fit and busy. I stood, compelled by an impulse I didn't understand. I followed the couple, eager to eavesdrop on their conversation.

The woman spoke softly. "It won't be long until we're with him."

"He has Peanut for company now," the man said, and I knew he referred to the dog at the young man's side.

"Such a waste," she cried. "Some mornings I still can't believe he's dead. I wake up and think, what would Bryson like for breakfast." The woman wept, and the man comforted her by hugging her close.

"It's okay," he said. "He lived exactly as he wanted."

"I can't accept it. It's been ten years, and I still can't accept that he fell down a mountain and that was the end of his life."

For a moment I felt I was losing my mind. It couldn't be, but beneath the disbelief, I knew it was. This was the grave of the boy who'd gotten me pregnant. He'd fallen into a chasm in a skiing accident. Yet perhaps it wasn't an accident after all. Mischa was capable of anything.

The couple regarded the monument in silence for a time. At last the woman put the bouquet of red roses she carried on the grave. "Merry Christmas, son," she said. "Soon. We'll see you soon."

The young man and the dog stood motionless. Sadness surrounded me, and I felt his grief. The couple stood a moment longer, and then turned slowly down the path. When they were gone, I went to the grave and read the headstone. Bryson Cappett, beloved son of Bertrola and Charles Cappett. A smaller headstone contained only one word. Peanut.

I looked around quickly. Mischa had to be nearby. She'd set me up for this. She wouldn't miss watching.

The couple disappeared down a turn in the path, the woman in her dark green coat and heels, the man in a topcoat and fedora. They could have come from 1960 or from down the block. In Sleepy Hollow Cemetery, time didn't hold to the rules of the outside world.

There was no sign of Mischa. She was watching, of that I was sure. But she didn't intend to show herself. It was enough that I now realized the scope of her manipulation. She'd tried to lure me to Concord before, and I'd failed to take the bait. I'd not come to see Bryson buried. There was no other reason for his death than her attempts to bring me to Concord.

The enormity of it froze my muscles. She'd killed my brother, possibly influenced my mother to kill herself, my father, Granny, Bryson, Karla, and now Patrick. She was a monster, just as Bonnie had labeled her.

The central caretaker's office wasn't far away, and I composed myself and headed in that direction. I limped slightly, though I didn't slow. Willpower and determination drove me on.

In the distance, a young man in warm outdoor clothes fired up a gas-powered blower and scattered the fallen leaves from one of the plots.

"Excuse me." I tapped his shoulder because the blower prevented him from hearing my arrival.

"May I help you, miss?" he asked after he'd turned the machine off.

"I need to find the availability of cemetery plots. For a family. The Leahys. Three gravesites." Patrick would not have children. It was safe to assume this Leahy line was fading from the registers of Concord.

"In the newer part of the cemetery there are family plots available. And single, too. But most people want a place for their loved ones to be near. You need to speak to Mr. Tagget, the director. He's off today." He kicked at the leaves. "I'm just here for the last details so it looks good for the folks who'll come by after church. Folks visit their relatives on Christmas."

"I hate to interrupt your work, but could you show me a few possibilities?" I didn't want to venture into the back sections of the cemetery, but with this young man at my side I felt safe from Mischa's mischief.

He put the blower down and wiped his hands on a handkerchief. "Right this way." He fell into step beside me. "Christmas Day is a sad time to be looking for a burial place. You related to the Leahy kid who died at the inn last night?"

"Yes," I said, unwilling to satisfy his curiosity further. "Please show me."

"Remember, you have to complete the deal with the boss. I don't handle the money."

"It's fine. I just want to have an idea of the location. His parents will finalize matters."

He pointed up the hill. "There's some space there. Still, it's not right to bury a boy so young." He set off up the incline. "Was he really murdered?"

"Yes," I answered. "He was."

38

The small Catholic church was somber, the pews plain and uncushioned, but sunlight sheered through the leaded glass windows, giving off jewel tones and a sense of holy peace. The gathering of Concordians spilled out of the church and into the yard. There wasn't enough room for all who had come to pay their final respects to Patrick Leahy, murder victim.

I'd taken a seat in the back of St. Benedict's and saved a place next to me for Joe. Chief McKinney had drafted Joe as a "consultant" with the investigation into Patrick's murder. As a park ranger, Joe had training in law enforcement and the best tracking and woodland skills of anyone in the area. No one said it, but it was obvious to me that McKinney had moved to show his support for Joe and to stop malicious rumors before they sprang up.

Dorothea had spent the last two nights in the hospital—her blood pressure off the charts. She left the hospital against doctor's orders to attend the funeral and sat up front with the family. I worried she might collapse before the service even began.

The hum of voices rose around me. Though the words were indistinct, the mood was palpable. Concord was upside-down with speculation and fear. I was now the inn's only guest and had taken over Dorothea's duties, though they mostly consisted of taking cancellations and unlocking doors for police detectives.

Joe spent every night with me, but we were both locked in private cells of silence. He refused to discuss the case, and I couldn't bear to hear it. We went to bed and made savage, passionate love. But we didn't talk. Not really. I had too many secrets.

Mischa hid from me. No fleeting sightings filtered through the trees as I ferried back and forth to the inn twenty times a day. She was there, though. I sensed her. And she left presents for me. A dead bluejay, crushed by a cruel hand. The tail of a squirrel, stump still seeping blood. A decapitated Barbie doll, her perfect body twisted and contorted into unnatural positions.

I spent hours at the inn, doing everything I could for Dorothea. I avoided the cabin, and I couldn't bring myself to open Bonnie's journal. The thing I'd viewed as my salvation now seemed a force of darkness. Mischa was attached to the journal. She was a co-author, if not the sole writer. I'd come to believe she sent it to me. By design.

She'd stolen my brother, then my mother. She'd driven my father to an early grave with alcohol. Even Granny Siobhan. I'd assumed she'd died of a heart attack. Natural causes. She'd been sitting at the kitchen table writing a letter to me. To me.

Her death came shortly after the arrival of the journal. It had been left in the English Department of Brandeis. The secretary said she'd missed the delivery man, but there was no return address. My assumption was that Granny had sent it, a surprise to push me toward the Ph.D. she so desperately wanted me to have.

I'd learned differently when I wrote home—the mountains were no place for land lines or cell phones, so I'd dashed off a letter filled with thanks and my plans for my doctoral work.

Granny's response had shocked me. She'd begged me to destroy the journal. She'd urged me to mail it to her so she could read through it.

229

But I hadn't. I'd kept it. Thrilled by the potential it offered.

A week later, Granny was dead. The letter she'd begun to me had begged me to burn the journal and come home. And now I had to wonder whether Mischa had prompted her heart attack. Had she taken my grandmother because she attempted to thwart her scheme?

By reading the journal, had I called Mischa to me? Since I'd divorced myself from it, she'd disappeared. Perhaps all I had to do was steer clear of the journal and she'd stay away from me. And the people who crossed my path.

What would happen to Mischa if I burned the account of my aunt's life? I'd considered this possibility before, but as I sat in the church listening to the final words spoken for Patrick Leahy, I now knew I had to destroy the journal somehow.

In the recent past, I'd been stopped by the possibility that somewhere in the journal was a way to destroy Mischa. My aunt Bonnie had powers. She'd seen and communicated with the dead. My own powers were developing apace. I'd seen Bryson and his dog in the cemetery. Sitting in the church, I caught the ethereal silhouette of a multitude of the dead hovering near the pulpit. Unlike Mischa, they had no desire to harm me. They ignored me, drifting about the place they viewed as a safe haven; but with practice, I might be able to get help from the other side.

The journal might unlock secrets to the world of the dead. I needed to read it one more time to find any help that I could before I disposed of it. I'd come to view the journal as a multi-leveled work. It captured the voice and emotions of who I had supposed was a dead relative who felt closer to me than anyone alive. Now, I believed the journal was a game designed by Mischa. The journal changed as she wished it, but I still believed there were answers written into the pages.

My kinship with Bonnie had been clear from the first paragraph. In a tragic way, I was reliving her life. The parallels were undeniable. And upsetting. I knew where both Bonnie and Thoreau were buried. I didn't want to die in Concord as a young woman. If Bonnie's journal could help me, I had to bring myself to read it again.

"All rise."

Father Declan O'Rourk's voice cut through my thoughts. He was a young man, not ashamed to show he was touched by the sadness of Patrick's death. The service began, and the familiar vocal patterns, lifting and falling, comforted me.

Joe had not appeared, and I began to doubt he'd arrive before it was over. Chief McKinney was in the back of the sanctuary, his gaze drifting over the mourners. Hoping, perhaps, the killer was in attendance.

That wasn't true. Mischa had killed Patrick, and she wouldn't come here. I wondered if she could cross the church's threshold, or if she'd wail in anguish from the power of good. Even if she entered and sat right down, no one would see her but me. Patrick's murder, like Karla's brutal death and Mischa's disappearance, was destined to be another unsolved crime in Concord. Unless I could figure out a way to expose her.

I didn't listen to Father O'Rourk's words. His tone was soothing, but I knew the drill by heart. I'd been at too many funerals. The priest's job was to profess his belief that Patrick was in a better place, a happier place, where he would be joined by those who loved him in the not-too-distant future.

The service ended with a hymn I didn't know. I filed outside into the late December sunshine.

"Aine!" Joe called. He was there after all! "Are you going to the Leahys' home?" he asked.

I shook my head. More than anything, I wanted solitude. I needed to think. Action was required. Immediate action. I'd drifted for the past three days, but now I had to develop a rational, decisive plan.

"I've been called to a state rangers' meeting in Boston, but I'm reluctant to leave you alone." He didn't touch me. Not in public.

"I'm fine," I told him. I backed it up with a tight smile. "Really, I'll keep an eye on Dorothea."

"Are you sure?"

"Go on. Has Chief McKinney discovered any clues about how this happened?"

He squinted against the glare of the day as he searched the crowd. "He said he was hoping for a break, but he didn't give me any details. There's nothing I can tell you."

A short murmur swept over the congregants standing outside the church. The crowd seemed to part. A man in a gray suit stood at the edge of the crowd, clenching and unclenching his hands. He stared at Joe with anguish and hatred.

"Who is he?" I asked.

"DeWitt Lobrano."

"Shit," I whispered. "Let's go." I grabbed Joe's arm to pull him along the sidewalk, but he balked.

"I won't run. I didn't hurt his daughter. I won't skulk off like I'm guilty."

"Please, Joe." I tugged and begged. A scene between Joe and the father of a dead child was the last thing anyone needed after Patrick's funeral. "Let's go to your truck. You can take me back to the inn. I'm not well." I tried to reason with him even as he dragged me toward Lobrano.

"Joe!" My sharp tone was like a bomb. Everyone hushed and gave us their full attention. DeWitt Lobrano remained on the edge of the church grass. Before Joe could move, I doubled over and vomited.

A murmur swirled through the spectators, and Joe put an arm around me for support. "I'll take you home," he said.

When I looked up, Mr. Lobrano was gone. At the edge of the churchyard, standing among the hedges, was a blond girl in a red jacket. I closed my eyes and began to weep. The reprieve was over. She was back.

39

I awoke, too hot, in my bed in the cabin. Joe must have stoked the fire to the maximum, because sweat trickled down my neck and ribs. Pushing back the heavy quilts gave immediate relief. The cabin was dark and there was no evidence of Joe. He might have driven to town for food or medicine. Or perhaps he'd gone on to his meeting.

Uneasiness swept over me at the realization that I was alone. Night had fallen. Without Joe, there was nothing between me and whatever waited outside. No locked door had ever stopped Mischa. It wouldn't now. If she wanted in, she would be standing beside my bed.

The thought went through me like electricity, and I threw the covers all the way off and sat on the side of the bed. Sudden awareness of another presence in the cabin made me wish for a weapon. The canister of pepper spray Dorothea had given me was still in my coat pocket, if I could get to it. Turning slowly, I saw Patrick. Or perhaps it was Mischa in Patrick's form. Either way, it was a cruel vision.

He stood on the other side of the bed and slowly began to unbutton his shirt. In the dim light of the cabin, I couldn't see him clearly, but

I knew the outline of his body, the lean torso, the round tautness of his buttocks in the tight jeans. He was so young and beautiful.

And so dead.

"Aine, have you missed me?" he asked. "I've missed you. I watched for Joe to leave so I could come to you."

"If you are truly Patrick, you'll leave. You're scaring me."

He only smiled and eased the shirttail from his jeans.

"Why are you here?" My body tensed, ready to move quickly.

"I love you," he said. "You know I do."

I shook my head. "That's not possible, Patrick. It can't be."

"I'm here for you." His shirt dropped to the floor, and his muscled chest was a study in light and shadows. "Remember the first time? It will be like that forever." He unbuckled his belt and the snap of his jeans.

"This can't be." I kept my voice steady. I could not afford to faint. Mischa had corporeal powers. For all I knew, Patrick did too. If I fainted, I would be easy prey. The idea of such a thing made me gasp.

"Let me touch you," he whispered, stepping out of his pants. "I'm so cold. Let me lie beside you in the bed."

"Go away!" I jumped up and moved across the room.

"I'm here for you, Aine." He crawled across the bed and stood on the side I'd just vacated. He sat down, the firelight catching the contours of arms and back. He patted the quilt. "Come here, Aine. It won't be scary once you let me kiss you."

"Patrick, you're dead."

He tipped his head like a mischievous child. "I know that. But it doesn't matter. You can cross between the living and the dead. It's your talent, Aine."

"No. That's not true. I can see you, but I can't cross over. I can't touch you. You aren't real. You're a phantom."

"Let me kiss you and you'll see. In your heart, you know the truth. You know what happened to your aunt. You've always known. You simply didn't care to believe it." He reached for my hand and the brush of his fingers was cold. I could indeed feel his touch. "You've always walked with one foot among the living and one with the dead. I've learned so much since I died."

"What happened to Bonnie?" Though the dead are not to be trusted, it was worth asking. It was possible he knew the truth. Bonnie had died young. I found her grave. Thoreau had buried her as close to his final resting place as he could without claiming her as family. He should have married her. She gave him everything and yet she still wasn't good enough to be his wife.

"You think you know, don't you?" Patrick tugged at my hand, trying to pull me off balance and into the bed with him.

I snatched my hand away.

"I do know," I said. "She killed herself. That's why she isn't buried in the cemetery proper. Suicides can't be buried in church ground. Bonnie couldn't take that little bitch Mischa, or whatever her name is. She shadowed Bonnie, she eroded her confidence and harmed the people Bonnie loved, just as she's dogging me. I'll figure a way to kill her."

"Do you *really* believe that?" Patrick asked.

The longer he sat on my bed, the grayer his flesh became. I'd never noticed that about Mischa. She seemed able to manifest without consequence. She was stronger than Patrick. Perhaps because of her age. She was hundreds of years old. Maybe thousands, a concept that offered me no comfort.

"Bonnie didn't kill herself." He was matter-of-fact. "She isn't excluded from the cemetery for that reason."

I had to stop talking with him. The more I spoke, the more power he drew from me. I was his link to life, to all he'd once known. "Bullshit." I picked up my jeans and slid into them. If he wouldn't leave the cabin, I would.

"You saw her burial. You lived it. The cold night. The desperation of her lover. The blood seeping through her shroud."

"That was a dream. A vision. A might-have-been. It wasn't the truth. Mischa makes me see things that aren't real."

"It was real and you know it. You can see the dead, and you can see the past. I wonder if you can see the future or if you're too afraid to look."

His words horrified me, but I couldn't block them. I had to get away. I'd witnessed Thoreau digging her grave, the shrouded body lying on the ground, the splotch of blood staining her front. I'd seen it all. My gift. What a terrible joke. This wasn't a gift, it was a sentence to hell.

"Think! The blood, Aine. Why was she bleeding?"

"Shut up!"

Patrick laughed his old carefree laugh. "You can't hide from the truth." He teased me like a grade-schooler, and a chill of recognition passed through me.

"Mischa?" I whispered her name.

Patrick only laughed again. "We're really working on you, aren't we?"

I had been right to suspect her, damn her to hell. My jacket hung on a peg by the door and I eased sideways to grab it and slip it on. My boots were on the floor beside the fireplace. I stepped into them without tying the laces.

"Going somewhere?" Patrick asked.

"I won't stay here with you."

"Now that I'm dead, I'm not so easy to avoid. You hurt me, Aine. When you dumped me. You treated me like I was nothing." There was a new element in his voice. Anger.

"Go away, Patrick. Leave me be."

"Why did you hurt me?" He demanded an answer. Patrick was suddenly on his feet.

"Who are you?" This was Patrick, yet it wasn't.

"I know things you should hear." He advanced.

My back pressed against the door as my hand found the knob and gripped it. I could make a break for outside. I didn't have a vehicle. I would have to run through the woods to the inn. The keys were in my pocket. I could get inside, maybe. But so could he, just as he'd gotten in here.

"Don't be in such a hurry to run. I have information you'll want, Aine. It might change your dissertation a little, but you'll want to hear it."

"Patrick, please, stop. Just go away. You're scaring me."

"You should be afraid, but not of me. It's your blood that should scare you. If you'll admit the truth, perhaps you can save yourself."

"What truth?" My fingers clutched the doorknob, but inertia held me, trapped. As terrible as Patrick was, what waited outside the door could be worse.

"Your aunt was murdered, Aine."

His words destroyed all thoughts of fleeing. "What are you talking about?"

"She called up things that shouldn't have been brought to the light."

I couldn't listen. He was a liar. The dead lie. All of them. Granny Siobhan tried to prepare me. The day after my infant brother died, Granny warned me against talking with him or any of the dead. Not even my mother, who followed my brother to the grave. I could hear Granny's voice, feel her bony fingers pressing my upper arms. "The dead lie, Aine. When they come to you in memory with promises, don't listen. When they bring guilt or accusations, turn them away. These are not the spirits of anyone you knew. It's your imagination. Clever imitations. Resist everything they tell you. They never rest and they never stop lying. Don't traffic with them. Don't trust anything. Cut them out of your life."

"You don't want to acknowledge what really happened, do you, Aine?"

"You're a liar." I put my hands over my ears.

"Bonnie was murdered. She didn't kill herself."

"Shut up!"

"Thoreau killed her. He found her at his table with the dead she'd called forth, a regular little tea party of decaying corpses. Among them was his beloved older brother John. He sought her out for her talents, but he wasn't prepared for the full extent of raising the dead."

"Shut up!" I banged the back of my head against the door to knock his voice out. "Shut up!"

"John was at the table, flesh falling off his bones. He was something of a mess. When David Henry saw the full horror of what Bonnie had done, he stabbed her with the kitchen knife. He thought killing her would end what she'd begun. We both know that isn't true."

I could hear him clearly, though my hands covered my ears. I slid down the door until I sat with my knees up to my chin. I closed my eyes and tried to call forth something pleasant from my past. Granny sitting on the front porch of her mountain home with the laurels in bloom all around. I could see her in her cotton dress and apron, shelling crowder peas into a pan on her lap. The peas pinged into the bottom of the pan as her thumb slid down the crease and she turned the hull inside out to release what would be our supper.

But then she looked at me, and she spoke words I didn't remember. This wasn't a real memory. This was something Mischa conjured and put in my head. I fought against it, but Granny's voice came through.

"If you see them in the woods, Aine, don't speak to them. They can't harm you unless you converse with them. If you engage them, they'll get their claws into you and use you to come here to a place meant only for the living." Granny shelled the peas, her fingers flying, but her gaze rested on me.

"But I see Mama. She wants to tell me things."

"It isn't your mother. It's something else. Leave it be, Aine. I want you to grow up strong. Education will dampen their whispers. You'll learn to ignore them. Remember that. Ignorance breeds trouble. Get an education and shut your ears to their whispers and promises."

"Mama says I should listen."

Granny put the pan of peas on the porch floor and rose to her feet. She was a tall, angular woman in a dark dress. Her fingers dug into my arms and she shook me, hard. "You have to fight, Aine. Go to your room and finish the paper you're writing. If you get into boarding school, you'll stand a chance."

She released me, but I felt the pressure of her fingers as I ran to my room and found my paper and pen.

"You've gone visiting in the past, haven't you, Aine?" Patrick drew closer. "You see it more clearly now. They tried to trick you. To stop you from reaching your full potential. Old Granny Siobhan didn't want you to accept the gift of your blood. She and your father deceived you into believing that the things you see are dangerous and bad. But it's your gift. The Cahill gift."

His eyes mesmerized me and I lost the will to escape. He was so beautiful, young and vibrant. No longer dead but alive. His hand brushed across my face like a web of fire.

The lights of a vehicle came through the cabin window and struck the wall beside my bed. In the swath of light, Patrick faded. A few seconds later, Joe pushed against the door, trying to enter. My body blocked him, and I shifted so he could enter.

"Aine!" He sounded terrified when he saw me. "What have you done?"

I touched my cheek. Blood was seeping down my face where Patrick's hand had claimed me.

40

Joe poured coffee for himself and pulled up my desk chair beside the fireplace where I sat, draped in a quilt in the rocker.

"We need to talk about what happened last night." Joe stared into the fire. I'd been so upset the night before, I'd taken a sleeping pill and dove into oblivion.

"I had a bad dream and somehow scratched my own face. That's all. I've been upset, and it got to my subconscious."

A moment of silence passed. "Aine, you hurt yourself."

My fingers lightly traced the four claw marks on my cheek. "It isn't serious."

"I'm worried. This has been a lot for all of us to handle. Karla, Patrick. It's too much. Can I call your family?"

"There's no one to call." No one I wanted near me. "I've been on my own since I went to boarding school. My father and grandmother, the people who raised me, are dead. My mother died when I was a child." I'd dodged Joe's prior efforts to talk about my family. Whaling, bloodlust, moonshining, drugs—there wasn't a single aspect of my family I wanted to share.

"There's no one?" He held his mug in both hands, his elbows on his knees and his shoulders slumped.

"I'm not your responsibility. Don't worry." Bitterness crept into my tone.

His sigh was long. "I haven't wanted to tell you this. The chief thinks someone at the inn poisoned Patrick. He's been questioning the guests who were here at Christmas. McKinney won't say it, but Patrick was poisoned on the inn grounds. It couldn't have happened any other way. He didn't ask, but I'm backing out of the investigation."

There it was. Not an accusation, but a hint of suspicion. Had Joe found the wine with the poison, I'd be in a cell by now. "He *suspects* it was someone at the inn, or he *knows* it? Who would do such a thing?"

"I heard Patrick flirted with the female guests."

I pulled the quilt more tightly around me. "So what? Patrick was a free spirit. He never harmed a soul. Those ladies enjoyed his attention, and none of it was serious."

"Jealousy can make a person do strange things."

I wondered if he was thinking of Karla and the way she'd attacked me. I'd never done anything to her, but I was with Joe, the man she'd set her cap for. Jealousy had driven her to extremes.

That wasn't the case with Patrick. Still, I was tempted to let Joe think that a spurned lover was at the root of the murder. Those suspicions would lead to naught. Sipping my coffee, I chose silence.

"Aine, were you involved with Patrick?"

Even though I'd anticipated the question for some time, I choked on a swallow of coffee. Joe waited for me to finish coughing. I threw back the quilt, but he stopped me with a softly spoken query.

"Were you?"

"Why would you ask such a thing?"

"Patrick told Dorothea he was in love with you."

A strange echoey silence crashed in my ears. "He had a crush on me." I pushed out of the rocker. "Are you accusing me of something?" Heat had rushed to my cheeks.

"No, I'm asking a question. It's the same one McKinney will ask, so you'd better be ready to answer."

"You think I poisoned Patrick because I was jealous of the inn guests he flirted with?" The idea was insane. "Do I strike you as a desperate woman?"

"No, you don't. But that's not an answer to my question," he said quietly. "Patrick said he loved you and that you were sleeping with him. If that's true, I need to know."

"I don't believe this."

He put his cup on the kitchen counter. "I'm trying to help you."

"No, you're accusing me. I'm just not sure of what. Sleeping with Patrick?" Anger hardened my tone. "Or are you accusing me of poisoning him? Am I a suspect?"

"Only someone with access to the wine at the inn could have done it. I was in the PD yesterday and overheard some deputies talking. The autopsy showed strychnine. Wine was the delivery method. Someone poisoned the wine, gave it to Patrick, and then removed the remainder of the wine. It had to be someone with unlimited access."

Joe was very close to the truth. Only he'd never believe that Mischa poisoned Patrick. Not me. Never me. The genius of Mischa's setup unfolded in my head. I was trapped. If I told the truth, I'd appear completely crazy.

"Does Dorothea believe I'd kill Patrick?"

"No." He abandoned the fire and came to me in the tiny kitchen. "And I don't either. But it doesn't look good. Were you sleeping with him?"

The truth curled like a snake, ready to strike. "Yes. I slept with him. Once. It was a casual fling. I thought better of it and broke it off."

"Then he was in love with you? He told Dorothea the truth."

If Joe felt anything at my admission, he didn't show it. "Patrick loved the idea of being in love. He wasn't serious about me. The seduction was a game. It made him feel like a man. It was sex on a cold afternoon. It was exciting, forbidden. But it *wasn't* love. To think it would be motive for murder is ridiculous."

"Aine, call your family."

My first impulse was to beg him to listen to me, but it wouldn't do any good. "I didn't betray you, Joe."

"You didn't? What would you call it?" The flash of his temper gave me hope.

"Once I started seeing you, I broke it off with Patrick."

"He was in the cabin all the time."

"He brought firewood and meals. What was I supposed to do, keep him outside in the cold? He knew I had feelings for you. Maybe he didn't like it, but he accepted it. It only happened once. You and I hadn't gotten serious."

"He was a teenager, Aine. Surely you see how wrong your behavior was."

"Patrick wasn't an innocent. He pursued me. I resisted, but he pursued." I flushed as I spoke, but I held my head high. "I didn't seduce him, it was the other way around. Yes, I think it was wrong. I was lonely. And scared. He kept my fears at bay for an hour or two. Was I using him? In that sense, yes. The truth is, we didn't harm each other."

"And he fell in love with you."

"No!"

"Did he threaten to tell me about the affair?"

"Don't be ridiculous. He was a teenager, not a blackmailer. If you think so little of me, if you suspect me of murdering him, why did you even come here? Maybe *you're* the one who uses *me* for a convenience fuck."

"Who clawed your face?" He grabbed my shoulders. "What are you playing at, Aine?"

"Turn me loose." I tried to twist free of him but he held me. "Let go, you bastard!" I kicked at him, but he pushed me backwards onto the bed. He fell with me, covering my body with his.

"Tell me the truth." He pressed me hard into the mattress.

I bucked, but he was much stronger. The more I fought, the heavier he became until I couldn't catch my breath. "You're hurting me."

"Tell me the truth!"

I wished I could. More than anything, I wanted to tell him about Mischa—the things I knew and the things I suspected. But he'd think me insane. His anger tempered my tongue. Instead of fighting, I felt myself slipping from the present into the past. I had a clear and distinct vision of Bonnie.

She is sitting at the small table in the cabin she shared with Thoreau. Around the table are the dead. She questions them about crossing the distance between the dead and the living. Their answers ring with hollowness. Her eagerness to learn is evident in her posture and expression.

The door bursts open and Thoreau steps in, disgust on his features. "What is this?" He asks, but he knows the answer, has long suspected that Bonnie has been calling up the dead.

"What are you doing? You know this is wrong!" he cries.

The departed vanish, and Bonnie attempts to calm him, to explain. But his disgust is too great. The kitchen knife is lying beside the basin and he grasps it, plunging the blade into Bonnie's heart.

The most terrible smile touches her lips as she slumps to the ground.

"Aine!" Joe slapped me lightly on the side of my face.

It was true. Call it a dream or vision or a gift to see the past, I had no doubt it was true. Thoreau murdered my aunt. He killed her in disgust and terror for her actions, for raising the dead. Joe would do the same to me.

Fury shot through me. Self-preservation. If I told Joe about Mischa, about the things she'd done, he would never believe me. And if he did, he would blame me for opening the door. I'd unwittingly brought Mischa into his life, and she'd impacted him in only negative ways. He'd never understand, so I had to get away from him.

"Aine! What is this?" He straddled me, holding me pinned to the bed as he reached into his pocket and brought out the scrimshaw tooth. "Where did you get this?"

How had he found the tooth? It had been securely hidden in a cubbyhole in the wall behind my desk. I couldn't answer because I had no idea what to say.

"Aine, where did this come from? The writing here. The inscription means 'The dead never rest.' Where did you get this? The little girl on the ship—where did it come from?" He shook me, digging into my arms and shoulders. The pain was almost a relief. "You'll tell me the truth or you'll regret it."

"Get off me!" I pushed hard, and this time he climbed off, towering over me, ready to snare me if I made a break for it.

"Where did this come from?"

"I told you. My forebears were sailors. One of them must have made it. My granny gave it to me when I was a little girl. My essay about *Moby Dick* won a scholarship to Amberton boarding school. I used my family's history for the paper." I tried to snatch the tooth, but he pulled it back.

"'The dead never rest.' What does that mean?"

"How should I know? The tooth is two hundred years old, Joe. Someone on my distant grandfather's ship carved it. Where did you find it?"

"You left it in my pocket, Aine. You meant me to find it." He looked at me as if he didn't know me. "You see things. Or you pretend to. I watch you, and it frightens me."

Mischa, the little bitch, had planted the whale's tooth in Joe's pocket. She was setting me up. If he ever learned the tooth had been stolen from a New Bedford museum, he wouldn't believe another word I said.

"Watch me all you want. I haven't killed anyone." I pushed his chest hard, and he drew back so I could sit up.

"You see something in the woods. What is it?" His left eye twitched.

"The wind." No way I could tell him anything different. He would think me insane, and he already suspected I could murder. "Would you leave now? I need to work on my dissertation."

"You're a liar, Aine."

"The dead are liars." The words slipped from me before I realized what I was saying.

Had I slapped him, the change could not have been more profound. His gaze narrowed and he backed away from me. In a few seconds, he was out the door and gone.

41

For an hour, I lingered before the fire and did nothing. I knew what I had to do, but I feared the consequences. Bonnie's journal was my only hope for answers. But if I opened it, I might give Mischa and her minions more corporeal power. I had begun to believe there was a direct correlation between reading the book and the strength of Mischa's abilities. The more I read, the stronger she seemed to become. And now Patrick had manifested. As well as a brief glimpse of what I took to be Bonnie.

Or perhaps my gift to *see* the dead had grown and strengthened with each session with the journal. Bonnie could be transferring her gift to me as my comprehension broadened and I sensed the darker meaning behind her writing.

I needed to examine the journal, front to back, with my new understanding that Mischa was adding clues, rewriting history. Somewhere in the words there was an answer. But in reading the journal, how much energy would I give Mischa and her ilk? Limbo held me in a deadly grip.

Fear finally jolted me from the rocker to the stash beneath my bed where I kept the journal hidden. It was then that I discovered that the wine bottle and glasses, such incriminating evidence, were missing. I hadn't forgotten them, but inertia and fear had prevented me from disposing of them. Now it was too late. They were gone, and Mischa would make certain they reappeared in the worst possible place. This was a game to her. She played it out, baiting the trap, setting the snare, and waiting.

I searched beneath the bed again, but my grasping fingers clutched only the leather-bound journal. The pages flaked as I pulled it toward me. In the last week, the journal had grown more delicate. The fear that it would disintegrate before I could glean its knowledge took hold of me once again.

Settling into the rocker, I held the journal in my lap, acutely aware of the brittle and worn leather cover. The image of a crow was burned into the leather like a brand. I'd never appreciated the significance, but now my finger traced the outline of the large bird.

I opened to a passage about Thoreau near the beginning. He and Bonnie had been formally introduced on the street and then later at a salon. Then she met him in the woods near Walden Pond while searching for herbs. Her interest was piqued.

The most interesting man has entered my life. I've met him several times in the woods while I was gathering herbs, seemingly by accident. He talks of nature. He is a shy man, and I find that refreshing. We have spent several hours together, walking about the woods at Walden Pond. He explains how all things in the natural world are connected. His deliberate movements, and the tiny silences that punctuate his speech, give me to think he is a man careful of word and deed. I want to know more of him.

This was as I remembered, but now I saw that I had no idea what Bonnie was doing in the Walden woods except the one statement she made about hunting herbs. She had been a governess, not a cook or medicine woman.

I skipped ahead and began to read again. A sharp clack at the window startled me. The hair on my neck stood straight up, and I feared to turn around. The noise came again. Clack. Someone was demanding admittance.

My hands trembled as I turned the page. The brittle paper buckled and half a sheet drifted to the floor. My aunt's spidery handwriting—black ink across the yellowed page—stared up at me.

The Sluagh haunt the woods of Walden. Since the trees have all been cut in Concord proper, the birds have no home but the woods. The young man, Henry, is building a cabin in the midst of the stand of trees. Near the pond. He tells me he intends to live here for two years, two months, and two days. He wants to learn the value of solitude. I fear he will learn something else, something dangerous.

There is a child in the woods who watches him. Perhaps she longs for a father, or a brother. Yet when my blood pounds harshly in my veins, I think it is something else she wants. She knows I see her, and she has no fear of me. I am not a threat to her ambitions.

This had never been part of the original journal. Glass shattered. I turned slowly to see the windowpane beside the front door had been broken. Pieces scattered the cabin floor. Perched on a jagged edge of glass was a crow. He stood tall, cocking his head from side to side as if assessing me.

"Shoo!" I waved a hand at him, but he ignored me. Any moment, he'd enter the cabin. The idea galvanized me to action, and I dropped the journal and ran at the bird. He held his ground until the last minute, when he lazily fluttered to the edge of the porch. He confronted me, head tilting to the left. His eyes, so black and shiny that they reminded me of stones, reflected my own image back to me.

Desperate to keep the bird out of the cabin, I jammed a piece of cardboard in the place of the broken glass. I would call a glazier to repair the damage when I went to the inn.

When I returned to the rocker and the book, I couldn't bring myself to lift it. The pages might contain wisdom, but the price for it would be dear.

It was becoming hard to ignore the parallel between Bonnie and Henry and me and Joe. A cabin in the woods near Concord. And a little girl with ulterior motives. My aunt had ended up murdered by her lover, if Patrick and my visions could be believed. The dead were liars, and I didn't know how trustworthy my visions were. Still, as I'd seen this morning, Joe's attitude toward me had changed greatly. No longer was he the tender lover. He'd become cold and accusing.

Much as Thoreau had done to Bonnie, according to Patrick. In Patrick's version of history, my aunt had ended up stabbed and buried on a rocky hillside.

I doubted Joe would stab me, but he would pin a murder on me if he thought me guilty. No matter how absurd the accusation, he would believe I was guilty if evidence was found. To that end, I had to find the wine bottle and glasses. Had I been thinking clearly, I would have washed the glasses and bottle and simply put them away in the cabin. Now Mischa had them. They could reappear at any time.

I couldn't afford for that to happen.

I found a plastic bag I'd tucked under the sink and put it in my pocket. The day outside was bright and sunny, a winter day with no sharp wind. It would be a good day for walking, and I knew exactly where to go. Walden Pond. If Mischa was up to planting evidence, that would be the place.

42

The roadblock into Walden Pond was up—today was an official holiday. Since I was on foot, it was easy to duck under it. I did so and followed the main road in. There was no snow, and I checked behind me to be sure my footprints were not distinctive. The hard ground barely registered my passing.

At the cabin, I stopped long enough to pick up a shovel from the little tool shed. I knew the combination to the lock. Joe had shown me once, and I had a good mind for numbers. I meant to be prepared if I happened upon the missing evidence.

I followed the trails to the place where Karla had been murdered. The yellow crime-scene tape fluttered in the wind. No one had taken it down. It remained strung between the beautiful oaks, catching the wind with a gentle flapping sound.

At first I didn't see anything, but when I shifted, the sunlight glinted off the glasses. They'd been left on a fallen tree as if someone had set up a picnic—the two glasses, the bottle, and a small bouquet of leaves.

Before I approached, I searched for her. This was too easy.

If she was near, I couldn't see her or sense her, and I set to work. The place I chose to bury the bottle and the glasses was near a small shrub. There were no stones there, and I dug swiftly, down two feet. I put the two glasses and the empty bottle in and filled the hole. Gathering debris and leaves, I covered all traces of my work.

I scattered a few more leaves, checking to be sure I left no trace of my visit. Picking up the shovel, I turned. Mischa stood some thirty yards away, watching. Her smile was superior.

"Stay away from me," I said. I couldn't let her spook me into a hasty mistake.

"Up to no good, are we, Aine?" She came forward, her hood low over her eyes, revealing only the curve of her cheek and her smile.

"You set me up, but I figured it out."

"Poor Patrick. He does like to talk, doesn't he?"

The urge to kill her was overwhelming. "He was a harmless young man. You didn't have to poison him."

"He talked too much, and he had things he meant to tell Joe. I explained this to you. I acted to protect you."

"The same reason you killed Karla. To protect me."

"You aren't as dumb as you look," she said, swishing back and forth like a child.

"Don't do that. You're not a little girl." I started back to the tool shed to replace the shovel.

"Better wipe off your prints."

I froze. I'd taken my gloves off to scatter the leaves and then picked up the shovel. She was right. I dredged my gloves from a pocket and put them on. Using the bottom of my coat, I wiped down the handle.

"You have questions. Go ahead and ask. Maybe I'll answer them."

"Why Bonnie? Why Thoreau? Why me?"

"You know the answer to that, silly." We hiked in tandem. "It's the Cahill Curse." She burst ahead of me and twirled around before she faced me, walking backward. "*I'm* the Cahill Curse."

"That doesn't make any sense."

"Think about it, and it will." She giggled. "Shall I give you a hint? I'll give you a hint." She galloped ahead, spun and stopped, a finger to her lips as if to shush me. "I'm your Moby Dick."

Before I could ask her what she meant, she ran off through the woods. Her red coat flashed through the bare black and gray trunks, and then she was gone.

A deep exhaustion bored into my bones as soon as I entered my cabin. My actions had cost me Joe, and there was no undoing it. I'd come to rely on him, on his presence during the dark nights, the weight of his body a wall against fear and danger.

Depression fell upon me like a suffocating blanket. Sleep, the joy of escape, beckoned me, but I was afraid. Patrick haunted my dreams, and I didn't know if my heart could take a second go-round with him.

I picked up the crumbling journal and stowed it under the bed. Just in case Joe came back, though I knew he wouldn't. Why I wanted to hide the journal from him, I couldn't say. I'd hoped, what seemed like a million years ago, to build a life on my aunt's writing. I'd viewed the journal as solid gold, a key to the kingdom of academia. Such thoughts were laughable. Now I couldn't think about my future. I doubted I had one.

My sense of duty said I should go to the front desk of the inn and make sure the messages on the answering machine were returned and business attended to. But I couldn't. My muscles had no strength.

I opened a new bottle of wine, topped off a glass, and drank it too fast. I poured another glass and went to the medicine cabinet in the tiny bathroom. The prescription sleeping pills were there and I shook two into my palm. If I slept deeply enough, I could avoid Patrick. I sought unconsciousness. I hoped to embrace near-coma, not dreams.

Even though it was only mid-afternoon, I took the medicine, finished the second glass of wine, and crawled into my bed. The sleeping pills tugged at me almost instantly, but when I yielded to sleep, it was Morpheus who courted me, and the lid to the Devil's toolbox opened.

I found myself reliving memories of the time when my mother was alive and my father delivered the mail at Coalgood.

My mother wore red lipstick, and she moved with quick, sure energy. She was like a butterfly, here and there, so beautiful in the mountain sunlight. She'd planned to be a nurse, but she'd married Daddy and gotten pregnant with me and then my brother. She said having us was better than wearing white stockings and ugly shoes and wiping peoples' bums. She said that I made her life complete, but several times I found her thumbing through catalogues for nursing school.

I remembered the house in Coalgood. Every memory was filled with sunshine. My room was purple and white, and my bedspread had Tinker Bell on it. We picked berries and wild plums and swam in the cold creek not too far from town.

I saw my mother standing in the yard in her cut-off jeans and a red T-shirt that matched her lipstick. Her dark hair curled down her neck and she laughed at me, beckoning me to follow her to the creek. More than anything I wanted to walk beside her, to feel her hand on my shoulder or stroking my hair.

She carried a bucket for the dewberries we would pick for jam and pies. I loved for her to bake. She sprinkled scraps of piecrust with sugar and cinnamon and baked them like cookies for me. And when the pies were cooling, she'd make homemade ice cream to melt on top of the cobblers.

"Let's pick berries," she said.

I ran after her into the woods, needing nothing more than to be in her presence.

As soon as I entered the shadow of the trees, she disappeared. So did the sunlight. The green of the forest faded to black and gray. I was alone. In the distance I heard a low roar. A waterfall? Whitewater? I realized I was lost. Not a single landmark told me anything about my surroundings.

"Aine!" My mother called to me, but I couldn't see her anywhere. "Run, Aine. Don't stay there. Run! She's coming!"

Fear propelled me forward, and I was no longer a child. I was grown, my tennis shoes grabbing the rocks and roots of the trail as I hurried downhill, toward the dull roar.

"Mama!" I called to her, but there was no answer. So I ran harder. The trees thinned and the water sound grew louder. It came in waves, a loud crash with a shushing whisper. I broke from the trees into acres of wild rose bushes. There was no help for it. I had to go through them.

Thorns tore at my clothes and skin. Blood drops rose along the path where the stickers pierced me. Tiny drops of blood covered my arms and legs with thin whip lines. But I could see the water, and I wasn't far from the strip of sand that marked the edge of the ocean. Somehow, I'd made my way to the place where life began.

At last I gained the sand and a pier that reached far into the ocean. My sneakers slapped the boards as I sprinted down the endless pier. At the end, I stopped, heaving for breath. The small wooden platform was miles from shore. The waves rose around me, mountains that crested and fell in all directions, but none swamped the tiny platform where I stood.

"Come home, Aine."

I heard the voice from the depth of the water. "I'm not of the sea," I replied. "I'm a mountain girl. The land."

A giant eye blinked at me beneath the blue water. Terror filled me, but I didn't retreat. "Who are you?"

The eye rose to the surface and I saw that it was part of a huge whale. A white whale. "I'm your past and future," the whale said.

"Moby Dick."

The whale's laugh was merry. "No such creature ever existed."

"I never harmed you," I pointed out.

"It's in your blood." The whale was pensive now.

"No." I shook my head. "I never harmed you at all. I wouldn't. That was a long time ago."

"Blood stains your hands."

"No."

R. B. CHESTERTON

"I could swallow you." The whale opened its mouth and the sun and sky were obliterated. There was nothing but the darkness of its maw.

I knew then that darkness was my destiny. Sucked into the belly of a whale. Like Jonah.

"Out of the darkness ye shall rise," the whale said as it slowly sank back into the ocean. "Remember, the dead never rest."

43

A hard knocking at my door woke me from the dream. For a moment I felt as if I were being held underwater. When I broke the surface, I called out and the knocking ceased. I'd gone to bed in my clothes, so I straightened them as best I could and went to answer the door.

Chief McKinney stood on the small porch, his hat in his hand. "Miss Cahill," he said. "May I come in?"

I checked behind me to be sure the journal was put away and then stepped back. "I was asleep."

"Sorry to disturb you." He followed close behind me and I imagined his breath on my neck.

I considered asking him if Joe was too afraid to come for my arrest, but I didn't. I pointed to the desk chair and the rocker before the dead fireplace. Without Patrick or Joe to bring in the wood and keep the fire stoked, I'd let it go out. "I should get some wood," I said. Dusk had fallen and the tiny warmth the sun gave had disappeared. It would be freezing cold in another hour.

"Not on my account," the chief said. "I won't be long."

I couldn't read intention in his expression, but his next words made my heart thud.

"We're worried about you, Aine. Joe's expressed his concern, and Dorothea, even distracted as she is, thinks you're under too much stress. Since the night I found you in the snow, you've been . . . peculiar."

"How so?" I folded my hands in my lap to still their trembling. The cabin was cold, and I shivered. My quilt had fallen to the floor earlier, and I picked it up and spread it over my lap.

"Since you've come to town, we've experienced two murders—"

I didn't let him finish. "And you think I'm responsible for Karla's and Patrick's deaths?" My voice rose. "You think I'm a killer?"

"No, Aine," he said patiently. "You're a young woman whose past doesn't check out. That's what I'm here about. I need some straight answers."

"My family is my business. I shouldn't have to drag their reputation behind me."

"I called the school. Brandeis doesn't have you registered as a doctoral student. They said you dropped out of the program last year when you had an altercation with a professor."

"So? When I finish my dissertation, I'll sign up for the final classes. Why should I have to pay them while I'm writing?" I resented his implications. He was calling me a liar.

"You told Dorothea you would present your dissertation in the spring. You can't defend unless you're enrolled in the doctoral program."

"I'm a student. Classes don't begin until the middle of January. I have to go in and sign up. That's all. I planned to do it the sixteenth."

"I need a contact for your relatives."

"My granny is dead and so is my father. My mother died when I was a child."

The litany of losses brought no sympathy from the chief. "Who is a contact for you?"

"My uncles, aunts, and cousins are engaged in criminal endeavors. I haven't spoken to any of them since my grandmother's funeral.

The Cahills. Look them up and call them if you want. They won't remember me. And I sure don't want to remember them."

His shoulders relaxed a little, and so did I. It was only normal for the law to question the stranger in town. It was a part of great literature.

"Have you seen anything strange around town?" he asked.

"What do you mean?" Was it possible the chief had seen something unusual?

"A stranger in the woods around Walden Pond."

"Like who?" I couldn't risk too much.

"The night you were caught in the blizzard, you said something about a young girl. You were nearly frozen to death and incoherent, so I didn't put any credence in it. I've changed my thinking. Aine, is there someone in the woods?"

I couldn't be certain if he meant to trick me or not. I couldn't risk it. Mischa was my cross to bear. "It must have been the fever talking. I don't know what you mean."

He sighed. "Very strange things are happening in Concord. A woman was beaten to death and now a young man is poisoned. Both are connected to you. Both are connected to Joe."

I couldn't disagree with his assessment, so I said nothing.

"When was the last time you saw Patrick?" he asked.

Here it was. I had to be careful. "The day he died. He came to the cabin while I was putting on my makeup for the Christmas Eve party. He brought some logs for the fire and banked it so I would have warmth when the party was over. He did that every day."

"Was he upset?"

No way was I going to explain about his crush. "About what?"

"About you." He was like the crow, smart, alert, and I knew Joe had told him about my fling with Patrick.

"No, he wasn't upset with me in the least. I failed to make Joe understand that Patrick enjoyed flirting with all the women staying at the inn. Including me. Dorothea pretends she doesn't know, but that's a social convention. Patrick was funny and fun. He was popular with the ladies, but it didn't mean a thing. Our affair, if you can call it that, was casual. It was a fling." I flipped my fingers. "It was a momentary thrill for both of us. I'm sorry if that offends your sense of morality, but that's what it was. We were both consenting adults."

"Morality isn't my business. Murder is." He sat forward. "You're keeping things back, Aine. I don't know what, but I sense it. I promise you, I'll find out. It would be best for you to tell me now."

"I don't know what you're talking about." I kept my expression calm even though my heart thundered like pounding horse hooves.

"You have information about both these deaths. I'm not accusing you, but I know you're not completely innocent."

"If I knew anything, I'd tell you. I'd tell Joe. I'm in love with him." The words surprised me as much as McKinney.

"I'm not sure that's good news, Aine." He stood up. "Don't leave Concord."

"I have to go to Brandeis to register for my classes."

"Check in with me before you go. I mean it, Aine. I won't be happy if you drive out of Concord without clearing it with me."

"Am I a suspect in Patrick's death?"

"You're a person of interest." He opened the door and closed it firmly behind him, but not before I'd seen night slipping toward the cabin. Soon darkness would swallow me, and I would be all alone. Except for the child in the woods, the creature who wanted to lay claim to my soul.

44

New Year's Eve blew into town indistinguishable from the preceding week. Cold, alone, swaddled in blankets, I tried to sleep but couldn't. So I counted the minutes until the end of one year and the beginning of the next. There was no knock at my door, no Auld Lang Syne. No call from Joe. Not even Dorothea came to wish me a happy new year. The sentiment of my friends came through loud and clear. I was suspect.

Mischa, too, left me alone. She was sly, letting me twist in my loneliness. She could have come inside any time she chose, but she lurked about the forest instead. I sensed her there, watching for any sign of weakness from me.

But I could be sly, too. By refusing to look out the window or door, I refused to acknowledge she was near. I had no doubt she had plans for me, but I wouldn't play into her hands. The cabin didn't protect me, but it worked as cover. At least for the moment.

I wondered how long it would be before Chief McKinney returned to arrest me for crimes I hadn't committed. Each breath I took felt constricted. Things were closing down around me.

When the small bedside clock showed midnight, I pulled Bonnie's journal out from under the bed. I turned on the lamp at my desk and sat down. This time I wouldn't be stopped. I would find the truth.

I flipped to the back of the journal. The last page was new, the beautiful script clean and undamaged, as if it had just been written.

There is great mischief afoot in the woods at Walden Pond. The child I've worked so hard to befriend is not a child. She is something old and evil. The Sluagh do her bidding, and they have been spying on me. Even the friendly warbler who sings so sweetly each morning takes his orders from the child. The woods are bleak and dark, and things I fear roam about freely.

Tonight I will call forth the old spirits, the women of Salem, the crones of the Iroquois, the women of Bedford who watched their men sail away with no hope of return. I will bring their spirits to me in the woods and seek a remedy for this evil child that slips through the trees laying traps and plotting against me.

In the past week, she has killed an elderly woman, Mary Shoats, on the outskirts of Concord. A woman I was known to visit. A woman already under suspicion because she knew the healing herbs, and also those that can make a woman slip a child. Mary was a good woman who knew that sometimes there was no food for another mouth. One child unborn or five already living who might starve. Mary was kind in the way of nature, the way a mother cat will kill a malformed kitten. But she'd drawn attention to herself, and there was talk against her.

She was found dead Monday, her head bashed in where she sat at her kitchen table. The bloody rock was discovered in my basket behind the livery stables in a pile of old hay. My basket was stolen the week before, but there are those who don't believe me. They think I killed old Mary.

My vision blurred and I covered my eyes for a moment. My aunt Bonnie had been framed for a murder, just as I had.

My pointer finger traced the crisp writing and I read on.

This tragedy has called attention to my living arrangement with Henry. I have become quite scandalous, I fear. Funny how the mark of shame rests only on me. Henry is not accused, because it is believed that I somehow cast a spell over him and dragged him, unwilling, into sin. I am his Eve.

He is unhappy, and I know that his family is disappointed in him, because he's chosen to live outside the bonds of marriage. While they are saddened by him, they find me to be the harlot. Henry is an innocent victim of my conniving ways. I have corrupted him, at least in their view of it.

He spends more and more time alone in the woods, and now I have begun to fear the child will harm him. She will do anything to spite me. I am not certain why, but I sincerely believe she hates me.

So I will call up the spirits of those wise, dead women to help me. I will find a way to banish the child from the woods. To rid my life of her. I have determined to do whatever is necessary to end her.

A crash against the window made me jump and scream. It had to be a bird. One of her spies, watching me. She knew every move I made.

There were only a few more pages to read. Bonnie's words—these new words that had never been in the journal before—showed me a bleak future. Whatever help she'd obtained from the sage crones of the past, it wasn't enough to fight Mischa. The child was older and wiser than the combined knowledge Bonnie consulted. In the end, Bonnie died. Whether by her own hand, murdered by Thoreau, or killed by the very child she'd once befriended. What chance did I stand against the darkness inside Mischa?

I clutched the journal to me. If I packed up and left Concord today, would it save Joe? Would Mischa chase me around the globe, murdering those who dared come close to me? My aunt had been haunted by this creature nearly two hundred years before. Had the cunning Mischa merely waited for another Cahill to fall into her web? Was it my bloodline that stirred her from her sulphuric slumber? Without the answers to those questions, I wasn't certain my departure would stop her here in Concord.

And there was the little matter of Chief McKinney ordering me to stay in town. If I chose to go home to Kentucky, though, he would never find me. There were hollers in the mountains only my relatives knew how to find. Thus their success as moonshiners.

A sudden homesickness for the mountains sent me to my feet, still holding the journal. The night was still and dark, but in my imagination I went to the rocky ground and sunshine of May in the Kentucky mountains. The wild phlox and wood poppies flowering blue and yellow. The electric green of the new leaves on the trees. A land of sun and warm breezes, nothing like the bone-rattling cold of January in Massachusetts.

I had not cried for the mountains. Not ever. I left for boarding school as a child, rushed away from gossip and a father who drank to deaden himself. Granny Siobhan was the only person who ever believed in me, and she was a stout oak to shelter behind in a gale. After she died, there was no yearning for home. Nothing to miss.

In boarding school, I was the butt of jokes and pranks. The other girls mocked my accent, but the teachers were encouraging and found my interpretation of the novels and stories we read to be unique. I wonder now how much they knew of my background, if they were aware that I could likely never go home again. What had Granny told them about my circumstances? Too late to ask now.

Water under the bridge, as Granny would say.

This night, though, I missed the mountains. There were places where waterfalls covered secret caves. I'd explored them and found the carcasses of small animals. Skulls with sharp incisors that might be a cat or fox, or something else. Creatures lurked in the mountains, older than the rocks themselves.

My hands and arms ached from the intensity of my grip on the journal. And I was freezing. I needed firewood, but I was afraid to brave the woodshed. The cabin couldn't keep Mischa out, but it felt safer nonetheless. Outside, she could come from any direction. But it was chance Mischa or freeze. My feet were numb, and I worried that frostbite would take my fingers or toes. Or my nose, like my poor cousin.

That grotesque image sent me shuffling into my boots and coat. The woodpile was behind the toolshed in back of the cabin. The trail to it was obscured with bushes that Dorothea always intended to ask Patrick to cut back. Now that would never happen. I found my heaviest gloves and opened the door.

The night was silvered in moonlight. If the moon wasn't full, it was close. It cast long shadows painting the tree trunks black and silver. My breath frosted as I eased down the steps and hurried along the path. I needed at least two armloads, but I would make do with one for the remainder of the night. Tomorrow I would stack the split logs to the porch rafters for easy access.

I was only halfway to the woodpile when I heard the giggle. I couldn't determine which direction it came from, but there was no doubt who it was.

"Mischa." I spoke her name with authority. Servility would have no impact on my destiny. If she meant to kill me, she would.

The musical laugh came again. On a whispery breeze, I heard her voice. "She'll come to us."

I kept moving. If she wanted to confront me, she'd have to abandon the woods and show herself. I aimed to grab the firewood and rush back inside.

But it wasn't Mischa looming in the center of the trail. It was a woman in a long black dress. She wore her hair in a bun, but she reached up and loosened the pins to let it fall down her back, a deep auburn cascade. She was beautiful in a severe way. And I knew her.

"Bonnie." I was afraid to approach her. "Help me, please."

"She has need of you," she said, and she floated toward me without walking.

I stumbled from the surge of fear. "No." I backed up several steps before I gathered my courage and held my ground.

"She has need of us both. We offer a path. She fears us."

She was close enough to reveal pale skin and dead eyes. Though her dress was black, the front was soaked in blood.

"I'm nobody's path." I couldn't let her convince me otherwise. "What happened to you?"

She chuckled, a dark and smoky sound. "My destiny. Just as yours will happen to you. We're cursed. The lot of us. Cahill blood has damned us. But you and I carry the darkest curse. We can see her, and that's the thing she covets most. The thing she fears the most."

"Why do you serve her, Bonnie?"

She looked confused. "There's no escape for me. She tricked me, and now I'm hers. As you will be, too."

I wouldn't believe that. I couldn't. "Tell me how to fight her. I'll save you."

She floated closer. "You can't win. I tried. She's cunning. She made me trick you with the journal. She knew the lure would be irresistible. She's planned this from the day you were born."

"Why?"

"You see her, and with that sight you can defeat her."

"How?" I tried to grasp her arm, but I captured only air. "You have to tell me."

"I tried to tell you. In the journal. She made me write it, but I put things in it, for you. To help you." She heard something and flickered, as if she might fade away. Fear shifted across her face. "She's coming."

"Did Thoreau kill you, or did you kill yourself?"

"It's a fiction, Aine. You read what *she* writes. And you see what she projects. Find the difference and save yourself if you can. I tried to fight her, but I didn't succeed. For all these years, she's held me here. Waiting for you."

I couldn't let her manipulate me. *She* might not be real. It could be another of Mischa's tricks, using my aunt to control me. "I won't be wandering these woods for centuries."

"You won't have a choice. Unless you walk between the worlds. Let go of life a little. Reach for the twilight."

She flickered like a bad connection, and then she was gone. The path was clear. I hurried to the woodpile, loaded my arms, and rushed back to the cabin just as Joe's truck bumped down the driveway.

45

I raced toward the truck with everything I had in me, dropping the wood as I went. I ran as if my life depended on getting to him, because it did. His accusations were forgiven. He'd seen the error of his ways and returned to me.

Everything seemed to be slow motion. It took an hour to gain the hundred yards. More than anything in the world I wanted to be in Joe's arms. To feel his body against me, sheltering me. Protecting me. He was solid and real against the phantasms in the woods.

He opened the truck door and slid out. I hurled myself at him with a cry that sounded like a savage, wounded animal.

"Aine!" He held me tight. "What's wrong? What are you doing out in the cold?"

"I went for firewood." I pressed against him but couldn't resist looking over my shoulder. The two of them, Bonnie and Mischa, stood side-by-side behind the first row of trees. Bonnie's hands hung limply. Mischa's black eyes watched me, and a cruel smile curled. "There's someone in the woods and they mean to hurt me. Please don't let them."

"Who?" Joe looked in the same direction, but confusion touched his features. "Who's out there?"

He couldn't see them, and they knew it. That's why Mischa was so smug. But I had to tell him now, to make him understand the danger I faced, that we both faced. I knew what I wanted then. I wanted Joe. I wanted to leave Walden Pond. To go somewhere new and start again, with Joe.

"Who do you think is out there?" he asked.

"It's Mischa." The instant I said the name, I realized my mistake.

Joe's pushed me away. "I can't do this." He slid behind the steering wheel of the truck.

"You don't understand." I tried to hold on to his arm, but it was useless. I blocked the door before he could close it. "She's not really a child. She's evil."

"Stop it, Aine. I don't know what you think you're doing, but stop. I don't know why you feel the need to hurt me, but I've had enough."

I couldn't help myself. I'd held the secret for so long, been helpless to prevent her from harming and toying with everyone around me. She'd done terrible things, and she meant to hurt Joe. "She killed Karla and Patrick. She may have killed my aunt Bonnie. She's very old, Joe. So old. She looks like a child, but she's ancient. An ancient evil."

He started the truck. "You need help. You're hysterical." He snatched the door from my grip and slammed it.

Dead calm stole over my bones. I drew my shoulders back and met his gaze. I'd frightened him. He wasn't afraid *of* me, he was afraid *for* me. He thought I'd lost my mind. I stilled completely and his hand stalled on the gearshift. "Come inside and I'll explain."

"I can't take more of this. I should leave. I shouldn't have come here."

"Why did you?"

"I care about you, Aine. I'm afraid for you."

"It's fine." I dipped my chin twice. "I'm fine. Just come inside. Please."

He removed the key from the ignition, eased out, and slammed the door. He was hesitant to enter the cabin with me. "What did you see? Just tell me. I looked but there was no one there. Aine, I don't know what's going on with you. *Who* killed Karla and Patrick?"

He wasn't ready to hear the complete truth. But I could try a bite at a time. "I'll tell you once we're inside. It's cold out here."

"You go in. I'll get the firewood."

"I'll help." No way was I going to leave him alone in the woods for Mischa to club in the head with a fire log and pin the blame on me.

The woods sighed and crackled as we went to the woodpile. A breeze had sprung up and the bare limbs above us chattered like skeletons. Joe gathered an armload of small logs, and I picked up the wood I'd dropped, or as much of it as I could make out in the moonlight. While I worked, I listened for the crunch of leaves or a giggle. Mischa watched me. So did Bonnie. They watched my every move.

I had to determine if Bonnie had thrown in with the little bitch or if Mischa had trapped my aunt's soul. Could I save Bonnie? Did she want to be saved? She'd sounded so plaintive and trapped. But Mischa was a master manipulator. When Bonnie advised me to let go of life and seek the twilight, was it a trick to put me in a place where Mischa could harvest my soul?

"Aine?" Joe's voice sounded hollow, empty.

"Yes." I swung around to find him frozen, staring into the woods. "What is it?"

"There's someone out there. In the woods. I don't see them, but I sense them. Who is it?"

If he could believe me, a future together was possible. Whatever future we chose to build. But we couldn't remain so exposed. "To the cabin. Hurry."

"Who poisoned Patrick? You know, don't you?" He demanded more than asked.

"Come on, Joe." I ran.

He had no choice but to follow. Would Mischa let us gain the interior, or would she do something terrible, something cruel?

At the steps of the porch, I slowed. Joe almost bumped into me. "What is it?"

I couldn't move forward. The doll with my aunt's hair was leaning against the front door. A nail was driven into her heart. A dark substance that looked like blood spread down the front of the doll and onto the wooden porch.

Mischa meant to make my aunt pay, and dearly, for our conversation.

"Son of a bitch," Joe muttered. His breath warmed the back of my ear. "Who did that?"

We stood on the steps, an easy target. I chunked the fuel on the porch and grabbed Joe's coat sleeve. With a mighty tug I hauled him after me. I pushed the front door open, jumping over the doll and goo as I urged Joe to follow. When he was inside, I slammed the door and slid the thumb bolt home.

"What in the hell is going on, Aine?"

"Sit down." I fought to remain calm. If I became emotional, erratic, he'd never believe me. He'd think I was insane.

"Let me light a fire, then we need to talk."

As he laid the wood I retrieved the lighter and kindling and gave them to him. In under two minutes flames jumped high, then settled down as the logs caught. I huddled near the fireplace. Near Joe.

After he'd warmed a bit, he went to the kitchen and poured two glasses of red wine and brought one to me. I took it and basked in the warmth of the flames, wondering how I would ever make him understand the things that had happened.

"Tell me, Aine."

"You won't believe me."

"Try." He hesitated. "I want to believe you."

I glanced at him. His expression held no softness, and a pulse jumped in his throat. I would try with a little part of the story and see his reaction. "It's a longish explanation."

He went to the bed and gathered the pillows, fixing a pallet on the floor beside the hearth. We sat cross-legged, profile to the flames, as the cabin gradually warmed.

"What are you involved in, Aine?"

I reached out to touch him but dropped my hand to my lap. "I didn't hurt anyone, but I'm being framed."

"By who? Why?"

I put a hand on his knee. "Give me a chance to tell you. Promise me you'll let me finish. Before you label me crazy, you have to hear the whole thing. I deserve that much."

"Go ahead."

I told him about my family. I told him all of it, how Jonah Cahill let the starvation of his family in Ireland turn him into a hard man who turned his back on goodness, how he took whatever he could, to hell with the consequences. About the family's moonshining and Oxy dealing. About my brother's murder, the way my mother killed herself, and my father's drinking. About the Cahill Curse, and the way it showed itself in me.

"You truly see spirits, dead people?" There was no inflection in his voice and I couldn't be sure if he believed me or not.

"I do. Granny taught me how to hold them back, and she sent me away to school, hoping education would shut off that part of me. Granny thought she could protect me from the gift if she sent me away from the mountains and my relatives. And it worked for a long time."

"But you see them anyway."

Here was my moment. Joe was more receptive to my abilities than I'd ever dared hope. "I do see the dead." I let that sink in. "There is one in particular. A child. I call her Mischa, because that's who I thought she was, at first. I assumed she was the spirit of the young girl who went missing a decade ago."

The color drained from Joe's skin. Not even the flickering fire could hide his pallor. "Aine, this is wrong. There's no proof Mischa is dead."

"Let me finish. You promised to let me finish."

"Why are you doing this, bringing up the past? I never hurt her. I wouldn't do such a thing."

I was almost relieved I'd finally met resistance. His willingness had seemed too easy.

"Please, Joe. Just listen." When he indicated he would, I continued. "I saw a child in the woods. When I realized she wasn't a living child, I made an assumption, but I was wrong." He started to interrupt me but I didn't let him. "This isn't the spirit of a dead child. She isn't Mischa Lobrano. She is something much older and very evil. I don't know who or what she is, but she intends to harm me."

"Harm you? How?"

"She killed Karla and Patrick, and she means to blame it all on me. She did the same thing to my great-great-great-great aunt Bonnie. She used Bonnie, gained her confidence, and then she murdered Bonnie and tried to frame Thoreau." My words tumbled over each other as I tried to talk fast. Joe was beginning to balk. I could see the stubborn disbelief in the jut of his jaw. If he'd tried to sell this story to me, I would have felt the same skepticism.

"What are you talking about? Your great-aunt was murdered? But how was Thoreau involved?"

I'd failed to tell Joe or anyone the implications of my source for my dissertation. He had no clue how I intended to rewrite literary history. There was so much to catch him up on, and I was losing him. "My great-aunt was Thoreau's lover. Her name was Bonnie Cahill, and she lived with him at Walden Pond. I told you about her. That she'd left a diary of sorts. But it's more than just her musings. It records the time she lived with Thoreau. She—"

"No more!" His hands captured mine and he squeezed.

I tried to yank free, but he held me tightly, which only made me tug harder. When he refused to let me go, I panicked and began to twist and turn. The tighter he held me, the harder I fought against him. He said my name over and over, but I ignored him.

"Be still and I'll turn you loose." His words finally penetrated the black fog that had settled over me. Though my impulse was to struggle, I went limp. He dropped my hands. "Aine, Thoreau lived alone at Walden Pond. It's a well-known fact. He didn't have a woman with him. He was a bachelor. A virgin. He died when he was still a relatively young man, unmarried and never bedded."

"That's a fallacy." I spoke clearly and without any emotion. I wanted to stomp my foot and throw a fit, as I had done as a child, but it wouldn't do any good and I knew it. Only reason would win Joe, and I felt it slipping outside my reach. "That's bullshit, a convenient belief that suits the tourist industry you've built up around Thoreau and his mooning about solitude."

Joe's expression registered nothing. He'd shut himself away from me. "If Thoreau had a woman at the cabin, everyone in Concord would have known. Emerson. The Alcotts. No one would have gone along with such a deliberate falsehood."

"They knew. They all knew. But they let Bonnie be his secret."

He only shook his head.

"I have proof." I'd wanted to share Bonnie's journal with him for a long time. I'd never shown anyone. It had been a bond between me and my aunt, the sustenance that fed my secret ambition. Now I no longer cared about dissertations or degrees. I wanted to save myself and Joe.

"The journal. Written in hand, no doubt."

I ignored the skepticism. "Let me get it. I'll show you. Bonnie said there was a way to defeat Mi—the girl."

I left him beside the fire holding his wine and mine while I went to my bed. I reached under, my fingers groping for the familiar leather-bound journal. But there was nothing there.

Flattening myself on the floor so I had a longer reach, I tried again. My nails clicked on the bare floor and I found something mealy and crumbled scattered under the bed. When I lifted the bed skirt and looked, I had to accept there was nothing there—except bread crumbs. I picked up several and examined them. Mischa had crumbled a piece of toast under my bed.

It took a moment for the full reality of what she'd done to set in. While I'd been out at the woodshed, she'd sneaked in and taken the journal and left crusty old food. She'd stolen my most valued possession and left the doll made with Bonnie's hair at my front door. A doll with a nail driven through her heart. Bonnie would really suffer for trying to help me.

"What's wrong, Aine?"

I sat up. "It's gone."

He wasn't surprised or worried. "Really. How convenient."

He'd never believed me about the journal. A part of me understood his reaction. It was normal, the doubt anyone would have when confronted with visitations of spirits, dead girls, ancient evil, family curses, and desecrated dolls.

But I needed better than doubt from the man I'd fallen in love with. He must have read my need on my face because he put the wine glasses on the mantle and wrapped his strong arms around me. But I didn't feel safe. He didn't believe me. Not about the journal and not about Mischa. His protection was a sham, because he believed I needed safeguarding from myself.

"It's okay. Don't worry now," he whispered as he stroked my back.

When he thought I'd collected myself, he led me to the rocking chair and assisted me into it as if I were a child. A docile child. I didn't move, but my brain wasn't obedient.

He knelt in front of me. "Aine, can I look at your dissertation?"

"No." He didn't believe anything I told him. Why should I let him read the paper?

"You've been using Bonnie's journal, you said. Maybe I can learn something from the passages."

He was right. I'd quoted sections from the journal. Maybe the dissertation could help him understand. "It's on the desk. Please hand it to me."

He stacked books and papers, checking over the desk twice before he paused. "There's nothing here."

The little bitch had taken my printed pages, along with the journal. I rose and went to the desk. When I turned the computer on, I opened the file marked Dissertation. "See, you gave me the title in the coffee shop. *A Conspiracy of Silence.*" I opened the file.

The jumbled words on the page looked as if a child had been at play. They were nonsensical, the unhinged gibbering of a fool.

Joe's hand captured my wrist, as if he expected me to flee. The opposite was true. I sank to my knees at the desk. She'd erased my file. She'd destroyed the months of hard work. And she'd taken the journal, my only hope of fighting her, of saving myself and Joe and maybe Bonnie.

"She destroyed it all." She'd taken everything. Every single thing that mattered. Even Joe. By painting me as crazy, she'd taken him, too.

Joe stared at me with pity.

"You won't believe me when I tell you she stole it. Mischa, or whatever you want to call her. She took all of it. She set me up." I thought of Bryson Cappett, who lay buried in the Concord cemetery. "She's been working me for years."

Joe knelt beside me. "That doesn't make any sense, Aine."

"Then why did she murder Patrick and Karla? Answer that? Why did she kill two people and try to frame me?"

"I don't want to upset you, but you're sounding . . . paranoid." He grasped the arms of the rocker. "Tell the truth, Aine. You haven't written a word since you've been here. Before he died, Patrick told Dorothea you weren't doing anything. He said you hadn't written a paragraph, not even an outline. He was worried about you."

I opened my mouth to speak, but whatever I said wouldn't change Joe's opinions. I was too hardheaded to quit without a fight, though. "Patrick saw the printed pages stacked right there on my desk."

"And they're suddenly gone."

My life was like a loop. Every action I'd taken in the past ten years led straight back to Mischa. Even before that. She'd destroyed my family, my chance at happiness, my mother who refused to see the darkness in the Cahill blood. She'd played me like a finely tuned fiddle. "I'm fine, Joe. Really. It's okay that you don't believe me." I closed the laptop.

"I'll help you find a good doctor, Aine. I've already checked into it. Dr. Hitchens has the best reputation in Massachusetts."

So it had come to this. If I escaped murder charges, I'd spend the rest of my life in a mental institution. How long would I last before I found a way to kill myself? This was Mischa's ultimate goal. To harvest my soul for her own use.

"Thoreau didn't kill Bonnie." How clearly I saw it. The vision Mischa had sent to me was a sham. Bonnie had killed herself. This was what Mischa wanted from me. She wanted me to take my own life.

"Thoreau didn't kill anyone, Aine. There never was a Bonnie. At least not one living at Walden Pond," Joe insisted.

The truth of his words should have cut me, but I was beyond that. Or maybe I'd begun to suspect before he said it. Even back in the 1850s there should have been some documentation of Bonnie's life in Concord. If she'd had a permanent residence, a record should have existed. Had she even been a governess for the Emerson family? I didn't know. Like the branch of the traveling Cahills, she might have stayed for only a brief few months and moved on. My entire world had been constructed of Mischa's lies.

"I've been such a fool. Bonnie told me the truth. She said it was all a fiction. Now I understand." It was the ultimate con. And I'd bought it without even a questioning glance. The journal had arrived and I'd hoarded it, building dream upon dream upon ambition. The demon knew exactly how to set the hook with a bombshell journal that would turn the reading of Thoreau on its ear. She'd appealed to my ego, my desire to be a stand-out academician. And now I realized that Bonnie had probably never lived with Thoreau. The journal had been created at Mischa's direction, a way to lure me here. To bring me into her clutches.

She'd had me at every corner. Let me dream what she wanted me to imagine, showed me lamp-lit shacks and pretty blond children who skipped and sang. She'd used my own naïveté and ambition as the cruelest of weapons. And if she couldn't win me over, then she'd made certain I would be locked away in prison or a mental ward. Tremors passed through me.

"Aine, you need to rest. You look exhausted."

"Go home." I rose and put the computer on the table. "Just leave."

"I can't." He seemed dismayed.

"You can and you will."

He shook his head. "No, Aine. I can't leave you. I'm afraid you may harm yourself."

"Don't be absurd."

"I'm not going anywhere, and neither are you. I'll stay with you tonight, and tomorrow we'll visit Dr. Hitchens. Hear what he has to say."

The way he charted out my future—my disposal—terrified me. If he took me to a mental institution and said I was delusional, no one would ever believe me. "Joe, I'm not crazy. I've been naïve and foolish, but I'm perfectly sane."

"You've been here months, Aine, and done nothing. All the talk about your degree . . . you aren't even in the doctoral program at Brandeis." His voice broke. "Sure, last year you were enrolled, but not now. The chief told me all of this, and he told me your answers. But when I look for this big paper you're supposed to be writing, I can't find a page. You've done nothing toward your dissertation. Everything you've told me about why you're here in Concord is a lie."

"There is a journal. I've read it many times. I no longer believe it's the story of my aunt and Thoreau, but once you read it, it will prove to you that everything I'm saying is true."

"It isn't me you should worry about convincing. It's the chief. You were at Walden Pond the night it snowed so hard. You were close to the place Karla was killed. And you were in the kitchen at the inn for several days before Patrick was poisoned. You had access to the wine. You had opportunity and motive to kill them both."

"I know."

"I can't leave you alone."

"For fear I'll harm myself? Don't give it another thought. I'm not suicidal. That's exactly what Mischa wants. Then I'll be hers."

He stood by the fireplace where the flames leaped and crackled. "I have to ask you. I'm sorry, but I need to hear you say it. Did you kill them?"

"Tell me, Joe. Did *you* kill them? And Mischa, a little girl who maybe knew too much about you. What really happened to her?" That hit home and he blanched. "It doesn't feel so good to be accused, does it?"

He turned abruptly and went out the door, closing it softly behind him.

I was alone in the cabin.

46

Mischa had taken everything. She'd robbed my life of meaning. And worse, she'd set me up for two murders.

To fight her, I had to recover the journal. I didn't think Mischa would destroy it. It was her weapon to torment me. She'd leave it, page by page, around the area. A scrap here and there to force me to play her game. I understood her last, clever little message. Bread crumbs. Hansel and Gretel. The way home. She'd left me bread crumbs to follow. Taunting me. Tricking me. Pushing me to whatever evil purpose she intended.

The last thing I'd read from Bonnie, the message she'd written in the book and left for me, involved her attempts to locate help. She'd gone to Salem, to those who she'd heard were practitioners of the dark arts. I understood her decision to seek witchcraft to fight Mischa. I'd been shocked at first that Bonnie would consider such a thing, but now what other option was there? Granny Siobhan had warned me against speaking with the spirits. She'd told me there were tricksters among the dead, those pretending to be one thing when they were evil. She'd tried to safeguard me from the thing that could destroy me, but she'd handicapped me. I didn't know how to use my gift.

Bonnie had turned to Salem, a community, back in the 1850s when travel was arduous, a fair distance from Concord. She'd consulted an herbalist, a gentler name for the crones who knew the art of conjure. What path was open to me? Since I knew of no practicing magicians or conjure women who used native plants, I had only one recourse. A priest. I'd meant to visit one, but Patrick's death had derailed my plans. Now I had no choice. Time was running out. McKinney would be at my door soon enough to snap the cuffs on and charge me.

Father Declan O'Rourk at St. Benedict's Holy Catholic Church had conducted Patrick's funeral. That was a place to start. As soon as it would be decent to rouse the priest, I would go there. As soon as dawn struck the darkness from the sky. My nerve was not strong enough to take on Mischa lacking sunlight.

I spent the rest of the night sitting in the rocker before the fire, searching the Internet for possible help. At times I nodded off, but I was always half alert. Each strange noise brought me wide awake, fear choking the breath from me. Like it or not, I was afraid of her.

Several times, the Sluagh pecked at my window during the hours that Nyx ruled. I refused to look at them, but I heard their sharp beaks tap, tapping. Then there would be the flutter of wings and a raucous caw. Silence for an hour or more. Then again, the tapping. They didn't really desire entrance; they meant to torment me.

At times I jumped from my rocker when I thought of a place she might have hidden the journal. I had to locate it. In my heart, I knew she'd taken it, but I couldn't stop myself from searching.

Dawn broke the eastern sky, and I yanked on my boots and heavy coat and gloves and raced out of the cabin. The inn was shuttered when I passed. Only a week ago, Dorothea would have been in the kitchen, hot biscuits coming out of the oven and coffee brewing. So much had changed.

I knew I should stop at the inn and check on Dorothea, but instead I raced by. St. Benedict's was all I could think about. The priest had a picturesque cottage behind the church. He would be there. Where else would a priest be at dawn on a freezing January morning?

By the time I reached Concord, the early risers in the town were retrieving morning papers, heading to coffee shops, warming their cars for the commute to work. The bustle of normality reassured me, and I slowed my pace, allowing my lungs to catch up.

I didn't want to arrive at the priest's at the crack of day panting and wild-eyed. There were those who already thought me insane. I needed the priest to believe me, not to think I was mental. To that end, I needed to plan what I would tell him. Only there seemed no way to broach the subject of Mischa without sounding crazy. That was her trump card.

The nearer I got to the church, the slower my speed. When I gained the stone steps to the chapel, I sought a cohesive plan. Still undecided how to proceed, I entered the church and sat down. A moment of reflection was called for.

I knelt and said a prayer from childhood. The remembered words sent me back to the past, back to Coalgood, when we had our home on the edge of town, Mama, Daddy, and me.

I went to mass twice a week with Mother. I remembered the hard wooden church pew, Mama's stomach blocking my view of the priest as he came down the aisle, swinging the incense and singing a prayer. My pregnant mother found it peaceful. I thought it was funny to see a man in a dress singing. Did my mother see something in me even then that she felt a need to haul a four-year-old to church twice a week?

After she died, she tried to come to me. I would catch glimpses of her outside my window at Granny Siobhan's. She looked so sad. Sometimes she held my little brother. Sometimes her wrists leaked blood. At Granny's urging, I had turned away from her. Now, I wondered if I'd done the right thing. Maybe she hadn't come to haunt me but to help me. I had no doubt that she loved me.

I remembered my blue Sunday dress, the one I wore only to Mass. Gauzy and light, like wearing air. We went to early Sunday service, because it was Daddy's only day off. After mass, Mother and I would change our clothes. We sometimes went for a picnic beside the river. My parents were happy. My father didn't drink then. He went to work and came home to a hot meal on the table and time with his family. I was happy too.

When Mother became pregnant, she joked that she was big as a whale. She would lie in the sunshine on the picnic cloth, her stomach a huge mound, and she would laugh when my father dribbled cold river water on her.

I put my head on her stomach, listening. But the things I heard were not happy sounds. There was the swell and fall of the ocean, the turning of the fetus in the womb, like a whale calf just born. My baby brother was doomed before he drew his first breath, for he too was a Cahill.

The whisper of a prayer spoken by a woman who knelt at the altar brought me out of my reverie.

Strangely enough, the Concord church smelled exactly like the one in Coalgood. The scent of hot wax and old wood. This church, though, had stained-glass windows and beautifully carved Stations of the Cross. The altar was gold and intricately designed, and a huge arrangement of lilies centered the front where congregants knelt to take the wafer and the wine.

I was mildly surprised when a woman came out of the confessional. My watch showed only 6:30. As she hurried past me, wiping at her face, I recognized Mrs. Leahy, Patrick's mother. She did a double-take when she saw me, but instead of stopping to speak, she rushed by. Whatever burden she carried, Father O'Rourk had been willing to hear her confession at an early hour.

He exited the confessional, a tall man with a perpetual five o'clock shadow. I wondered idly if he fit the phrase black Irish. His green gaze found me, and he came forward.

"Miss Cahill, I haven't seen you in the congregation before." I must have appeared startled because he smiled. "We're a small church. I know all the parishioners. With a name like Cahill, I figured you were Catholic, but non-practicing."

"You have it right."

"And yet you're here." He waited.

"Yes, to see you." I spoke slowly, thoughtfully. He was used to grieving and hysterical women. I doubted he was prepared for one asking for an exorcism.

He carried the weight of his parishioner's secrets with grace. What would it be like to know the sins of a multitude of people? I could barely manage my own.

"Have you come to confess?" he asked.

"In a manner of speaking." I'd not intended to use the confessional, but it occurred to me that anything I divulged would be protected if I did. "Yes, a confession."

His robes rustled as he allowed me to precede him to the booth. Once inside the polished confines with the grate separating us, I lost my confidence. Father O'Rourk went through the prayers. I half-listened, trying to find a way to launch into what I needed to say.

When the silence grew between us, I finally spoke. "There's evil in the woods, Father. An ancient evil. I'm haunted, and I need an exorcism."

Father O'Rourk cleared his throat, a ploy to gain time before he responded. "What form does this evil take, Aine Cahill?" he asked.

It was the perfect question. The one I could answer clearly and begin the story of my relationship with the demon I called Mischa.

By the time I finished, it was 7:30. Father O'Rourk gave me a penance to do and told me he would take my request for an exorcism to his superiors. He met me outside the confessional, an older man than he'd been an hour before.

"Aine, have you talked with anyone else about this?"

"Joe Sinclair. I've tried to tell him, but he won't listen. Not really." I tried to smile but produced only a twitch. "He thinks I'm mad. "

"I see." He touched my shoulder, a gesture of compassion. "Will you be safe to go home?"

"You'll take it to the higher church authorities? And quickly?"

"I promise."

"What are my chances?"

His expression showed concern. "I don't know. This is new to me. Not to the church," he hastened to add. "But to me. I've never petitioned for an exorcism. And I'm not clear. Do you honestly feel that you're possessed?"

I'd been rather vague on that point, because I wasn't certain. "I'm the only one who sees her. She seems attached to me, as she was to my aunt Bonnie. Does that make me possessed? I don't know. But if it is me, I want her gone."

"Is there any evidence she killed Joe's former girlfriend and Patrick?"

"Yes." The wine glass with the poison. The glasses also implicated me, but if the priest believed me, and they were necessary to gain an exorcism, then I would tell.

"What evidence?"

I had to be certain of the exorcism before I told him. "When the Holy See agrees to exorcise me, I'll tell you."

"You can't bargain with God." He tried to be stern, but he was clearly worried.

"I'm not. I'm bargaining with you and the Church."

"Be careful, Aine. I wish you'd let me call a relative. You shouldn't be alone now."

"They're the last people who could help me. The church believes in evil. You preach that the sins of the father visit the son. Believe me, my family doesn't need to be here."

"I have your cell phone number. I'll put in a call to Rome and let you know the minute I hear."

"Thank you, Father."

I left the church and emerged into a bright day. The town was bustling, and I decided on a coffee at the Honey Bea. Before another hour got away from me, though, I had to find Bonnie's journal and haul my computer to an expert. If he could resurrect my dissertation, I would find bits and pieces of the journal in the text. My aspirations for a doctorate were destroyed, but if I could prove there had been a journal, maybe Joe would believe me about Mischa. My work had to be on the hard drive somewhere. I wouldn't give up without a fight.

But first I had to go to Walden Pond.

47

I knew Mischa would hide pages of the journal at Walden. It made perfect sense. It was where I first saw her, and where it would all end. The path home. If the church granted an exorcism, I would have it here beside the pond where Bonnie's life ended. Where Karla was murdered. Where I met Joe.

Birdsong trilled at Walden, though spring was still a long distance away. I settled onto a fallen log on the edge of the woods. The sun warmed my face, and I basked in pleasure. I was toasty even when the wind kicked up and blew across the pond.

Back in the 1800s, the 61-acre lake had provided ice for Southern cities as well as the Caribbean, Europe, and India. Frederic Tudor, Boston's Ice King, cut ice from the lake and shipped it in huge blocks to the warmer climates, but that was before electricity put a Frigidaire in every home.

Thoreau had written about the ice harvesters. I'd read it somewhere. Funny, but so much of the information I'd reaped had begun to jumble in my head. For an English doctoral student, I was becoming careless of my sources. But what did it matter. I could no longer remember why I'd wanted a Ph.D. Now, I wanted to save myself. And Bonnie. I wanted to confront Mischa and send her back to the hell Jonah Cahill had pulled her from.

I had to find the journal. I'd delayed enough. The confrontation with Mischa was something I dreaded. I knew her tactics, and I wondered if she was aware of my visit to the priest. She spied on me all the time. She probably knew. But was she worried? It might be leverage to get the journal back.

I didn't know where Bonnie had died, but I did know where Karla's body had been found in a shallow depression. I'd find the first page there. Bread crumbs. Mischa had used the journal to manipulate my ego. She wanted me at the pond, and she knew me well. She'd been one step ahead of me since I was born. Unless I figured out a way to destroy her, she'd take my soul.

Passing the model of the cabin where Thoreau lived, I peeped in at the wood-burning stove and the narrow bed. There was hardly room to turn around. "Intimate" didn't begin to describe the arrangement. I could have lived like that with Joe. It would have been joyful. Still, Dorothea's cabin was much more spacious, perfect for the two of us—if Mischa hadn't interfered.

I hiked down the trail wondering if she *could* be killed. If she could be exorcised or banned or sent back to hell where she belonged, would I be free of her?

I chose the trail into the deep woods. Behind me, I heard the crackle of a dry stick. Mischa. Or Bonnie. I prayed my aunt would come to help me. I doubted she was able to do so.

I continued. Behind me branches swished and snapped, and in front of me the birds fell silent. Out of the corner of my eye I saw a splinter of red floating through the trees about fifty yards to my left. When I looked full on, I saw nothing except the black trunks. She was following me, shadowing each action I took.

The sun slid behind a thick gray cloud, and unease settled over me. Mischa had almost killed me the day she'd lured me to Yerby Lane on a false journey. If her intention was to kill me now, she might succeed if I wasn't smarter and more cunning than she was.

When I came to the small glade beside the two oaks, I stopped. Turning slowly in a circle, I looked for the journal page. This was the place. It was logical. Mischa was a very practical girl.

But all I saw were woods and leaves and tree trunks and the tatter of crime-scene tape that remained tied around the trunk of one of the oaks. The impression where Karla had been discovered was between two oaks. Stones and tree roots made digging next to impossible. I knew that from burying the wine glasses.

When no journal pages were in evidence, I wondered what Mischa had in store for me. My inclination to come to Walden was correct, I just knew it. She wanted me here, but not, it seemed, for the reason I assumed.

She was here. Watching me. Hiding in the woods and darting out. A game. Everything was a game with her. If I called her, she would giggle and come to me, as docile as a lamb. But she was no innocent.

I entered the trees' shadows. "Come out, you murdering bitch. I'm not afraid of you."

She sped through the trees, a blur here and there, childish laughter trailing behind as she ran. This was fun for her.

I took the pepper spray but left my bulky purse in the clearing and gave chase, knowing she was preternaturally fast. I'd never catch her, but the fantasy of my hands choking her slender throat was satisfying. I pursued her. And she ran me in a circle. Ten minutes later, I ended up where I'd begun. She was gone.

The wind kicked up, and a page from the journal blew against my leg. The wind crumbled it to dust before I could save it.

Another page tangled in a dead tree limb as it broke into bits and disintegrated. I ran to snatch it and caught a fragment of the crumbling old page. *She hides in the edge of the trees* was written in fading brown ink.

I slid it into the pocket of my jacket. I could show McKinney this. It was evidence, if not a lot.

I saw her ten feet from the edge of the trees. She held the journal in both hands. She set free another page that fluttered among the branches of an elm and then burst into shreds.

"Your aunt and Thoreau. You'd be laughable if you weren't so pathetic. How you wanted to believe. A true believer, Aine. So desperate in your need to be somebody. Even when you couldn't find proof that Bonnie existed, let alone shared years with a famous man, you still clung to the belief."

None of it had been real. For the past four years, my life had been Bonnie's journal. It had dictated all of my decisions, my sacrifices, my dreams. I felt empty of all emotion or hope. All of it had been Mischa. With her powers she'd created the one fantasy she knew I couldn't resist. I was no match for her.

"Now you understand. You're here, exactly where I want you. Just as Bonnie came here. She almost escaped me. She almost figured it out and broke the curse. But in the end, she couldn't. Her gift, her ability to see the dead, owned her. And then she was mine. Like you, Aine, she couldn't shoulder the burden."

Mischa tossed the journal down, and it exploded in a cloud of dust.

When I looked for her, she was gone. But someone was in the woods. Not Mischa or Bonnie. She came slowly forward.

"Aine, it's me, your mother." She stood at the edge of the woods. She wore denim shorts and a red-checked shirt. Her tennis shoes had once been white, but now they were covered with bloody gore and a multitude of flies. They buzzed and swarmed about her feet.

She held up her hands and blood dripped off her elbows. "Look what you made me do, Aine. You were so bad. So naughty. I couldn't live with the things you did. You sentenced me to eternal hell."

I put my hands over my ears. Mischa meant to punish me. This was not my mother. This was not the woman who'd held me against her pregnant belly while we lay on a checked picnic cloth in the Kentucky sunshine.

"There's a devil in you, Aine." Mother was closer. Her dark hair curled around her face and her red lips moved, but I blocked her cruel words. I couldn't listen.

"Your baby brother, Aine. Little William. He laughed when you tickled him. Your innocent little brother. You suffocated him. Do you remember? I left you alone with him for five minutes, and you put a pillow over his face and smothered him. It was my fault. I knew you were bad. I knew you were filled with evil. But you were my child and I loved you. I thought my love could heal you, but I was wrong."

She was close enough to touch. Blood soaked the ground around her and the buzzing of the flies was a deep whisper.

"You're a liar. You aren't my mother. The dead lie." I didn't run. Couldn't. I was mesmerized by the sight of her. I hadn't seen my mother in twenty years, but this apparition looked exactly as I remembered her.

"You belong to her, Aine. You always did. I tried to block it. But you were bartered to her the day Jonah Cahill turned to serve the darkness."

"No." It was a trick. I knew it, but her words still hammered me. "That was hundreds of years ago. It had nothing to do with me."

"Bryson Cappett. Dead these ten years, moldering in a grave. Because of you."

"No." Bryson had fallen during a hike. He'd been supremely athletic. "No." I repeated the word because I knew now for sure that Mischa had pushed him. "I'm not to blame for what she does."

"Your father, dead from drink. He knew what you were and he couldn't live with it. He's waiting for you, too."

She battered me with the past. "I was a child. I couldn't help him."

"You destroyed him. And your granny, too. Caleb couldn't look at you without knowing what you were. And Granny Siobhan, once she knew you had the journal, she realized you were lost. Doomed. She tried to tell you, but the truth stopped her heart. It always goes back to you, doesn't it?"

"I don't believe you." But I did. I did believe her. The things she said were all true. While I hadn't raised a hand to do any of the acts she recounted, they happened because of me. "I was a child."

"I should have slit your throat the minute I knew what you were."

"Mama. . . ." I only wanted her love. "I didn't mean to be bad."

"Stop it here and now. Stop it before more innocent people are harmed. It's the only way, Aine. Bonnie realized this. She did what had to be done."

"What should I do?"

She stepped closer. "Come to me. I'll take care of you."

I wanted nothing more than to rush to her, to bury my face in her stomach the way I'd done as a child. Behind her, I saw my father, a glimmer of substance in the trees. There were others. Some I knew, some I didn't. They waited for me. If I stepped beyond the veil, I could leave behind all the worry and fear.

"That's right, Aine. The pain will end."

Sunlight glinted from an old tree stump not thirty feet away. I walked toward it and saw the knife. It hadn't been there a moment before. I picked it up and felt the blade, so sharp; it would slice cleanly. Pushing up the sleeves of my coat, I looked at the thin skin covering the pale veins. I wouldn't have to cut deep.

My mother held out her arms, as if to welcome me.

"Will Joe be safe?" I needed one assurance.

"He has his own destiny." My mother's fingers beckoned. "Hurry, Aine. Hurry. We're waiting for you."

I placed the blade against my skin. One swift cut. There would be some pain as the blood left, but it would be over quickly.

"I'm coming, Mama." I looked up to smile at her. Something in the darkness of her eyes stopped me.

The dead are liars.

Granny Siobhan had repeatedly warned me. I could hear her voice.

"Aine, hurry. I can't wait much longer."

Her smile stopped me cold. "Mischa?"

"Hurry, darling. I'm waiting?"

But it wasn't my mother who waited, it was the demon. She'd used the oldest trick in the world. Bait and switch. I recognized it. A raw sound tore from my throat as I lunged at her, knife slashing. She wouldn't push me into taking my own life. That's what she wanted. That was her goal. Then she'd truly own me.

My mother disappeared. The wraiths dissipated with her. Not even Mischa was left. I was alone in the place where Karla had been beaten to death, and the afternoon had fled.

The sun poised on the treetops in preparation of disappearing. I'd been tranced by the dead, and soon night would cover Concord like a bell jar. I would be alone in the woods.

I caught the flash of red just beyond clear vision. Mischa. She'd failed, but she was expert at clinging to the shadows. She wasn't banished, just momentarily defeated.

A childish laugh echoed from her location. "I almost had you then. Almost. Play with me, Aine. It's your destiny. You're mine, you know. You're cursed and I'll have you before it's over. I have all the time in the world."

For the first time in weeks, I felt in complete control. She'd done her worst and failed. Now that I understood, I would be vigilant. I traced my way back through the woods. I had to find my purse and get out of Walden Pond. Mischa had played me for a fool, and she'd used my own dead mother to try to trick me. But I'd survived.

I understood there was no journal. Gone, turned to dust. I had no evidence to prove my innocence, but there would be a way. I only had to find it.

I broke into the clearing and picked up my bag. When I started toward the path, I saw the wine glasses, clotted with dirt and debris, sitting on an old, fallen tree trunk. They'd been dug up. I dropped to my knees and used my hands to dig the hole deeper. I had to rebury them, return them to the earth. Such things should stay buried.

I'd just placed them in the ground when I heard a dog barking and scrabbling through the underbrush. Men shouted behind the dog. They'd come at last to arrest me for Patrick's murder. I bent to the task of covering the evidence. Mischa would win, but I wouldn't make it easy.

When I looked up, Chief McKinney stood twenty yards away. Behind him were two officers. One of them held a bloodhound on a stout leash.

"Stand up, Aine," the chief said. "Move away from whatever you're trying to bury."

I was a rabbit, caught too far from my warren, paralyzed by the hound and the hunter.

"Stand up." He spoke sharply.

I rose slowly, my hands covered in dirt. I tried to hide them behind me, but it was too late. He'd seen. I side-stepped away from the glasses, hoping to distract him.

He grasped my elbow, pulling me away from the spot.

"Liam, see what's there," McKinney said. "She was digging in the ground with her bare hands."

The policeman without the dog came forward and within moments had both wine glasses.

"Why would you bury glasses?" McKinney asked. "I think I know the answer."

Nothing I said would make a difference. Mischa had ensnared me on this plane, but she would not have my spirit. I would go to prison for a murder I didn't commit. And she would be waiting. She would reappear in my life. A warden, a correction officer, a priest—the irony evoked a smile. I would be on the lookout.

"What are you doing here?" McKinney asked.

"Waiting for Father O'Rourk." It wasn't an out-and-out lie.

"The priest at St. Benedict's?"

At least I'd startled him. He hadn't expected that answer. "Yes."

"Why would he be here?"

"I asked him to meet me here. To perform an exorcism."

McKinney's hand tightened on my elbow as if he expected the forces of evil to take hold and send me flying through the woods. "Aine, you're not well."

"No, I'm not." I tried to snatch free, but he held on. "I'm possessed. I've brought this to Concord, or I've awakened it. I have to stop it before anyone else is hurt."

McKinney signaled an officer. Now they would bring the cuffs. I would be taken to jail, charged, and there I would remain for the months it took to bring the case to court.

"Aine, I put in some calls to your family members in Kentucky."

A flock of crows broke from the wild grass, cawing as they flew overhead. The Sluagh. "They were surprised, no doubt, to hear I was alive and in Massachusetts. I told you everyone close to me is dead. What would the rest of them care about me?"

"Your aunt Matilde was glad to hear you were okay." McKinney waited for me to respond. I was smarter than that. I had no idea what my relatives knew of me, much less said about me. Matilde suspected me of murdering my brother, and I wondered if she'd been only too glad to heap that gossip on the chief.

McKinney eased me toward the car. One of the cops bagged the wine glasses. They would go to forensics for testing. The poison would be detected and I would be straight-lined on Patrick's murder. It was too beautiful. Even I had to admit the pure genius of the plan and its execution. Give it to Mischa. She was brilliant when it came to ruining people's lives.

I started toward the front seat, but he opened the back door and assisted me in. Still, I wasn't cuffed. When McKinney was behind the wheel, I put my hands on the grill. "Am I under arrest?"

"For what?" he asked, genuinely surprised.

"What are you doing with me?"

"It's growing dark, Aine. And colder. You don't need to be out in the woods."

It wasn't an answer, but it also wasn't an accusation. "So where are you taking me? To my cabin?"

He drove until we were out of Walden Pond without answering. "I spoke with Dorothea. She's taking care of your things, Aine."

"Why?" I couldn't grasp what he was getting at. He wasn't acting like he thought I was a murderer. But he also wasn't treating me like I was innocent. "My things are perfectly fine." What had been valuable was already lost. There was nothing for Dorothea to worry about.

"There's someone I want you to speak with."

"Joe?"

He slowed the cruiser and pulled to the shoulder. "Joe's in jail."

"What?"

"He's charged with the murders of Karla Steele, Patrick Leahy, and Mischa Lobrano. We found the child's remains this afternoon."

He was trying to trick me. He thought I'd jump to confess if Joe was in danger. "Joe didn't kill anyone." I could defend Joe without sacrificing myself.

"I know you were hiding the wine glasses to protect him, Aine. I know all about it."

"What? There's nothing to know. Joe didn't hurt anyone."

"It's hard to accept, I realize you have feelings for him, but Joe isn't the man we thought he was. I've defended him for a decade. Even though all the evidence pointed at Joe as Mischa's killer, I couldn't accept it. What we had was circumstantial. Not strong enough to send a man to prison. And now I have two more dead people."

"Joe didn't kill anyone."

"It's in your nature to defend him, Aine. But the evidence is too clear."

"I'm not lying. He's innocent." I grasped the grill that kept me from climbing into the front seat. "He didn't do any of this." Instead of pinning the murders on me, Mischa loaded the blame on Joe. It was genius.

And completely evil.

Everything that pointed to me as the killer also pointed at Joe. And he had more motive than I to get rid of Karla and Patrick. The climax, the best, though, was Mischa's body. I wasn't even around when Mischa, the real Mischa, disappeared, so I couldn't be a suspect. All along, Joe had been her intended target for the fall. Her plan was so much more complicated than I'd ever thought. She'd send Joe to jail to punish me, to break me, to push me to the action I had to take. Ultimately, she would destroy everyone I loved until I could stand it no longer and I took my own life.

The patrol car eased into a parking spot behind the jail. My heart fluttered like the Sluagh battering my windows.

McKinney opened the back door and gently helped me out.

"Are you arresting me?"

"Of course not."

I balked. "I don't want to go here." Then I thought of Joe. "Is Joe inside?"

"He is. He's asked to see you."

I lurched forward. My limbs weren't completely in my control. My brain ordered "walk" and my body pitched forward in staggers. Like I'd had a stroke.

Sympathy passed over McKinney's face, and it angered me. "Take me to Joe."

"We need to ask a few questions first."

So that was the game. If I answered their questions, I could see Joe. If I didn't, they'd keep me from him. "I have questions too." I had to figure out how Mischa had unearthed the child's body. The child whose name and image she'd stolen so she could trick me into being her foil.

"Where did you find the little girl's body?" I wasn't saying anything until he answered.

"In the Walden woods. Not too far from the entrance." McKinney spoke cautiously.

"How did you find her?" I asked.

"Anonymous tip."

"Someone came forward after a decade?" I didn't bother to cover my incredulous tone.

He nodded.

I pressed. "And this anonymous person knew exactly where the body was buried?" McKinney was a trained lawman. Didn't he see the caller was likely the killer and that Joe was just being set up?

"Exactly." He hesitated. "The caller was a woman."

"Really. A young woman?"

"Yes." There was pity in the way he looked at me.

"And she knew where the body was. The exact location? How would she know?"

McKinney sat on the edge of his desk where he was within arm's reach. "We figure Joe told her. Maybe confessed about killing the child."

"Why would he, assuming he murdered the child? He was home free. Why would he tell anyone?"

McKinney's voice lowered. "Pillow talk. Lots of criminals can't resist telling a girlfriend. Some want absolution. Others brag. Joe is the absolution kind of man."

"You think this woman was his girlfriend?" Jealousy was a wasp sting. "Who is she?"

McKinney looked at me. "The call came from your cell phone, Aine. Not an hour ago. You called and told us, and we found the body, all in fifteen minutes. He'd limed the body and covered it in plastic, which is why the cadaver dogs missed her, back when she first disappeared."

I couldn't quite process what he was saying. "My phone?"

"I expected you to deny it. But there's no doubt." He reached into his back pocket and brought forth my telephone. "I took this out of your purse when we picked you up." He flipped to recent calls and showed me the number to the police department. "You did your best to disguise your voice."

"I didn't call you." This was insane. "You punched in that number yourself, and now you're trying to make it seem like I implicated Joe in the murders."

"He doesn't have to know, Aine. I won't ever tell him. You did the right thing. I can sympathize with how hard it was. Even in all the confusion, you knew right from wrong. I think with professional help, you'll be able to get through this."

He signaled to a slender woman standing in the hall. She came forward. She held a clipboard and pushed her glasses up her nose.

"Aine, this is Dr. Marshall. She's a psychiatrist. She's going to help you."

The enormity of Mischa's calculations unfolded like a tsunami, wiping out all of my hopes and plans. Joe was accused of murder—by Mischa pretending to be me—and I was headed for a long tenure in a mental institution. If Mischa couldn't have me, I'd be locked up. She'd found my phone in my purse when I'd dropped it to chase after her. She'd seen the opportunity and seized it. She'd framed me as the person who sent Joe to prison.

"I didn't call you," I insisted. He wouldn't believe me, but I had to try. "It was Mischa." That got their attention.

"A dead child can't use the phone. You know that, Aine." Dr. Marshall came at me as she spoke. "We're going to work to help you reconnect with the real world. Dead children don't make phone calls."

"Not Mischa; the ghost child. The other one. I don't know her real name. She uses the image of Mischa. She's a demon. Ask Father O'Rourk. I told him about her today."

"I spoke with the priest," McKinney said softly.

"He can't do that! It's forbidden. It's sacred what I say to a priest. Only between us." Every single person I'd trusted had betrayed me. This was exactly how Joe must feel. I had to tell him I hadn't done this. I couldn't have. He'd never told me where the child was buried because he didn't kill her.

"Father O'Rourk didn't violate the confessional." McKinney put a calming hand on my back. "He would only say you were greatly troubled. It was Mrs. Leahy who told me. She saw you in the church and went back. She overheard what you said to the priest."

"She eavesdropped on a confession?"

His gaze shifted to the psychiatrist.

"I have to talk to Joe. I'm not saying another word until I do."

McKinney glanced at the shrink. She shook her head slightly.

I gave them no warning. I went for her. She had no right to determine my fate, to decide I couldn't see the man I loved. My fingers laced in her dark brown hair and I jerked savagely. She shrieked in fright and pain.

McKinney's arms wrapped around me, restraints I struggled against but couldn't break. He didn't say a word, just let me wear myself out. The doctor scooted to the closed door and backed up against it.

"She should be sedated," she said. "She's a danger to herself and others."

"Aine," McKinney whispered in my ear. "You're making it so much worse on yourself."

"Let me see Joe." I grew perfectly still and limp. "I promise I'll do whatever you say if you let me see him. Just for a few minutes."

"He's asking for you," the chief said.

"I tried to tell him last night. I tried to warn him about Mischa. He wouldn't listen." I had to make Joe hear me. I'd figure out a way to prove his innocence. If it took me the rest of my life, I would. But I couldn't be locked up. "Chief, give me five minutes. I can prove I'm not insane and that Joe didn't kill anyone. I know it sounds crazy, but there is something, some*one*, out there who killed the little girl, Karla, and Patrick. This same entity killed my aunt Bonnie and meant to pin the blame on Thoreau."

I shouldn't have said the last part. Before I brought up the town celebrity, the chief was at least listening. "Dorothea told me about your obsession with Thoreau. He was to be your dissertation topic, I believe."

"I don't care about that. Please, let me talk to Joe."

McKinney's palm centered my back. "I'll take you to the cabin to gather a few of your things. We have a lot of decisions to make. I want to help you, Aine. Your aunt said she wasn't in a place to offer assistance. She said you were on your own."

I heard everything he said, but I didn't care. I'd never counted on the Cahills to save me. Quite the opposite. But I had to find a way to prove Joe's innocence.

Under the chief's guidance, I preceded him out the door and to the cruiser. I slid in the front seat before he could protest. Without argument, he drove to the inn.

"Who'll help Dorothea?" I asked him. "Patrick's gone. Joe's gone. Now I'll be gone."

"I'll check on her. I think she may sell the inn. She has family in Florida. A better climate for her. Patrick's death is too much for her. I hate to see it happen, but she should go."

"Can I tell her good-bye?"

"She doesn't want to see you, Aine. She said she'd box up the rest of your things and send them to your family."

"Where will I go?"

"Boston University Medical Center, for an evaluation. From there, probably the Massachusetts Bayside Institution. It's a top-notch facility. Dr. Marshall has evaluated your medical record. She's talked with Dorothea and your adviser at Brandeis. He said you were a student with a lot of potential. Anyway, we'll see how your treatment goes."

"And Joe?"

"Dr. Marshall said I shouldn't lie to you. That the plain truth is the best thing. Joe's in for a tough time. He'd likely be remanded and stay in jail until his trial. Massachusetts doesn't have a death penalty. Life without parole." His tone was carefully neutral.

We drove past the inn and through the woods until we came to the cabin and pulled to a stop. The sun was gone, but light still lingered in the sky. Granny Siobhan had called this time the gloaming. She'd said it was when spirits woke from their slumbers to prepare for the night's work.

"Aine." McKinney tapped my shoulder. "You don't have a lot of personal things here. I'll box up your computer and books. They won't let you have that for the first few weeks. You pack your clothes and personal things."

"I know you think you're helping me, but you aren't." I tried to sound reasonable, but he ignored me. I noticed the cabin door ajar. It would be freezing inside. Colder than out here. And darker.

"Wait here and let me check inside," McKinney said. "I don't think Dorothea would leave the door open." He got out of the car and left me sitting.

His boots echoed on the small front porch. Gun drawn, he entered the cabin. I opened the car door and eased my feet to the ground.

McKinney reappeared in the doorway and motioned me inside. "Get some things and let's go back to the jail. I'll let you talk to Joe."

There was no point arguing. I did as he told me. On the porch, I paused for a moment. "I'm not lying," I told him. I reached into my pocket for the scrap of paper, but it was only dust and lint. It was gone, evaporated like the rest of Mischa's lies.

"The lab tested the glasses you were burying. Since we knew we were looking for strychnine, it was a simple procedure. There was evidence of the poison in one glass. Joe's fingerprints were on both of them."

"My prints were on the glasses too. Joe was always at my cabin and we often drank wine. So I'm not the best housekeeper. He didn't kill anyone, chief."

"I wish I could believe you," he said. "Joe is like a son to me. It's hard for me to accept what he's done—and that he's fooled half the town for ten years."

"Maybe it was me," I said.

"If I didn't believe Joe guilty, I'd never have locked him up." He pointed to the car. "Let's go, Aine. Dorothea said to leave your keys on the doormat." He went down the porch, loaded with boxes he began to stack in the trunk.

I pulled the cabin and inn keys from my pocket and dropped them in the center of the O in WELCOME. A roughened edge of paper caught my eye and I pulled it from beneath the mat. The handwriting was fluid and clean. I recognized it. Bonnie's.

The dead are liars, Aine. Never listen to them.

I tucked the page in my jeans pocket.

Back in the car, McKinney circled and headed slowly through the woods.

A flash of red followed us on my side, deep within the dusky shadows of the trees. Mischa. She easily kept apace of the patrol car.

This wasn't over. I wasn't beaten. Whatever happened to me, I wasn't dead. I didn't belong to her.

Not yet.

Acknowledgments

Writing is a strange, solitary job. Writing scary stories is a journey not for the faint of heart. There are too many times when my dogs bark at something outside the darkened window or a bottle brush limb scratches across a screen that I become frightened. Runaway imagination. But I love stories with a little chill. I love the sense of something behind me, half-hidden in the shadows. Watching. Delicious.

This book takes place at Walden Pond, but not the real Walden Pond of 2014. My Walden lingers in the past and in my imagination. It is a place haunted by many things. One autumn I went to visit a writer friend of mine, Kristine Rolofson, in Rhode Island. It was the perfect fall weekend that we never see in the Deep South—leaves in burnished red and gold, blue sky, crisp air. Kristine is a generous tour guide and took me all around her neck of the woods.

We went to Walden Pond and the Alcott house and the whaling villages. It was fascinating to learn about a way of life as alien to me as living on the moon. Never in a million years did I dream I'd be visited by a story in this setting. And yet, here it is.

Understand that I've taken great liberties with Thoreau and the area. The story demands certain things, and the past isn't around to defend itself. So I used it to my advantage.

Aside from thanking Kristen and husband Glen, who shared their love of their home area with me, I want to thank Suzann Ledbetter for her skillful eye on story. Dean James, sometimes you are struck with genius in helping me untangle the snarl. This was one of those times. Jennifer Haines Williamson, you have a good eye for story. Also thanks to John Kwiatkowski and my generous pre-readers who gave me good feedback. Several northern readers were very helpful with climate and geography.

It is a joy to work with Pegasus Books. Maia Larson is an editor that any author would kill to work with. Claiborne Hancock makes each writer feel like a valuable part of the team. The book cover and interior design—this is what the printed book is all about. Thank you Michael Fusco and Maria Fernandez.

I can't imagine the long, long journey of writing and selling a book without agent Marian Young on my side. Of all the doubts a writer can have in this crazy business, her integrity and classiness are never in question.

And I want to thank my family and friends. Some of them don't like to be scared, and they read the book anyway. They whined a good bit, but they read it, and I was deeply gratified that I disturbed them. Thank you all.